P9-AFV-015

Wheeler, Andrew, 1976-
Another castle.
Grimoire /
2017.
bk   08/15/17

WITHDRAWN

ANOTHER CASTLE

GRIMOIRE

ONI PRESS

AN ONI PRESS PUBLICATION

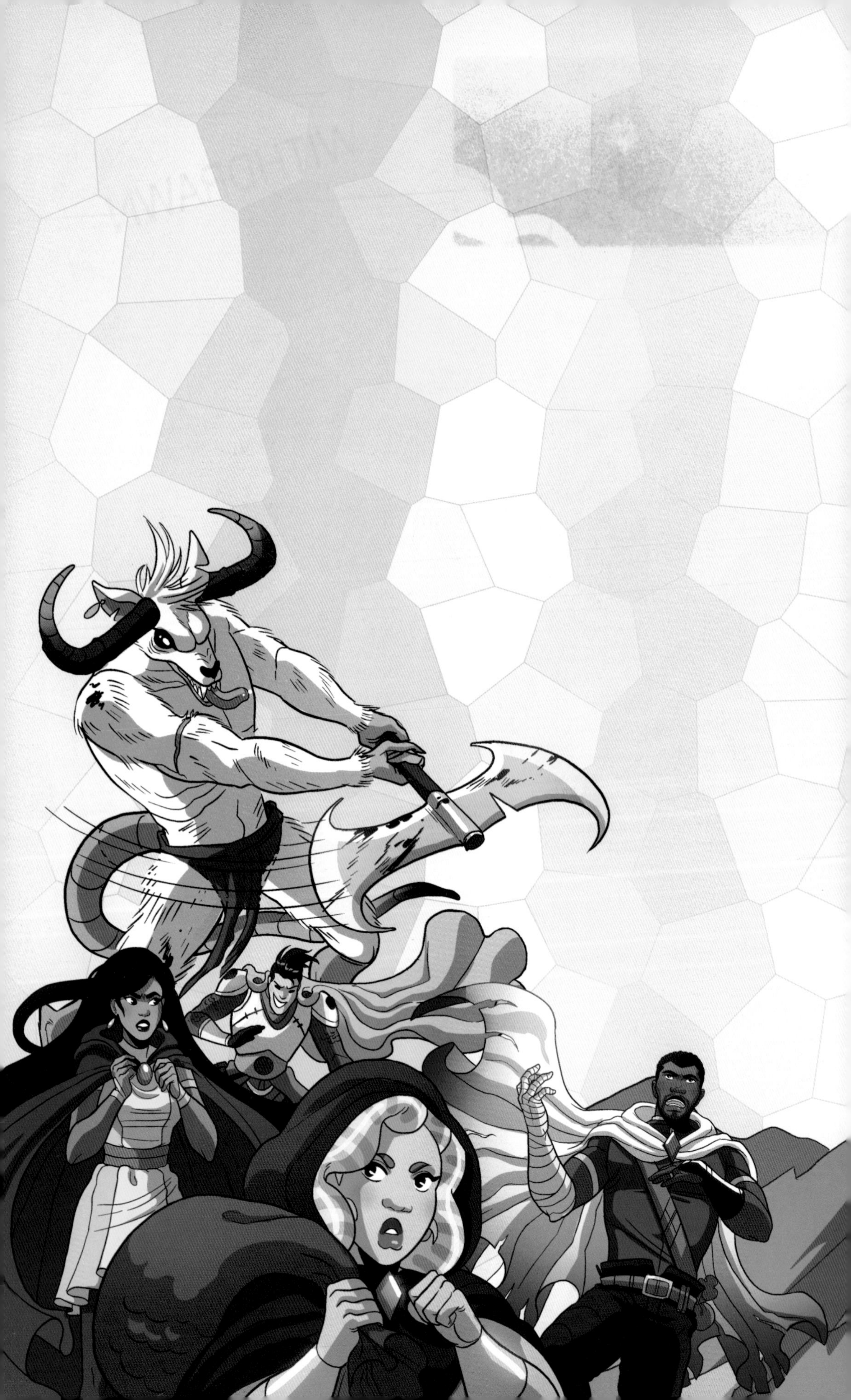

ANOTHER CASTLE

GRIMOIRE

WRITTEN BY **Andrew Wheeler**

ILLUSTRATED AND COLORED BY **Paulina Ganucheau**

LETTERED BY **Jenny Vy Tran**

DESIGNED BY **Hilary Thompson**

EDITED BY **Ari Yarwood**

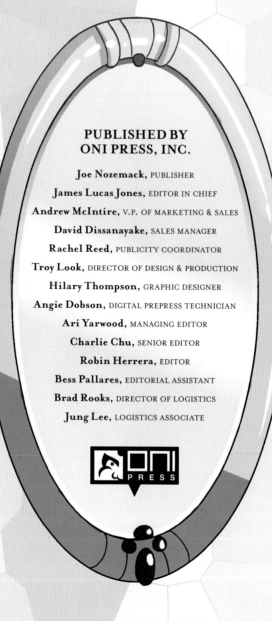

PUBLISHED BY
ONI PRESS, INC.

Joe Nozemack, PUBLISHER

James Lucas Jones, EDITOR IN CHIEF

Andrew McIntire, V.P. OF MARKETING & SALES

David Dissanayake, SALES MANAGER

Rachel Reed, PUBLICITY COORDINATOR

Troy Look, DIRECTOR OF DESIGN & PRODUCTION

Hilary Thompson, GRAPHIC DESIGNER

Angie Dobson, DIGITAL PREPRESS TECHNICIAN

Ari Yarwood, MANAGING EDITOR

Charlie Chu, SENIOR EDITOR

Robin Herrera, EDITOR

Bess Pallares, EDITORIAL ASSISTANT

Brad Rooks, DIRECTOR OF LOGISTICS

Jung Lee, LOGISTICS ASSOCIATE

ONI PRESS

ORIGINALLY PUBLISHED AS ISSUES 1–5
OF THE ONI PRESS COMIC SERIES *ANOTHER CASTLE*.

onipress.com • facebook.com/onipress • twitter.com/onipress
onipress.tumblr.com • instagram.com/onipress

@wheeler • andrewwheeler.co.uk
@plinaganucheau • paulinaganucheau.tumblr.com
@jenvyjams • jenvyjams.com

FIRST EDITION: FEBRUARY 2017 • ISBN 978-1-62010-311-1 • EISBN 978-1-62010-312-8

1 3 5 7 9 10 8 6 4 2

LIBRARY OF CONGRESS CONTROL NUMBER: 2016950325

PRINTED IN SINGAPORE.

ANOTHER CASTLE: GRIMOIRE, February 2017. Published by Oni Press, Inc. 1305 SE Martin Luther King, Jr. Blvd., Suite A, Portland, OR 97214. ANOTHER CASTLE: GRIMOIRE is ™ & © 2017 Andrew Wheeler & Paulina Ganucheau. All rights reserved. Oni Press logo and icon ™ & © 2017 Oni Press, Inc. Oni Press logo and icon artwork created by Keith A. Wood. The events, institutions, and characters presented in this book are fictional. Any resemblance to actual persons, living or dead, is purely coincidental. No portion of this publication may be reproduced, by any means, without the express written permission of the copyright holders.

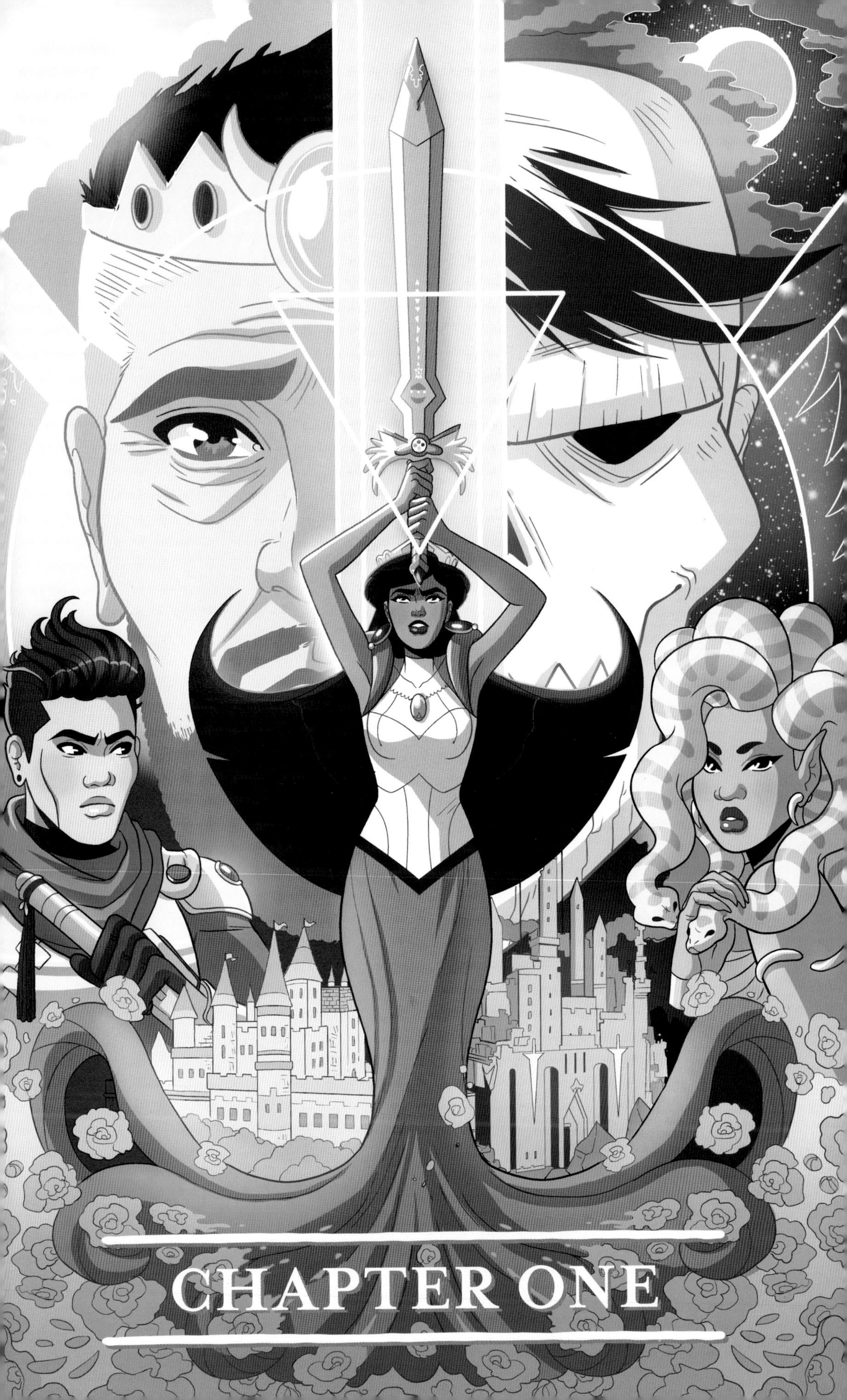
CHAPTER ONE

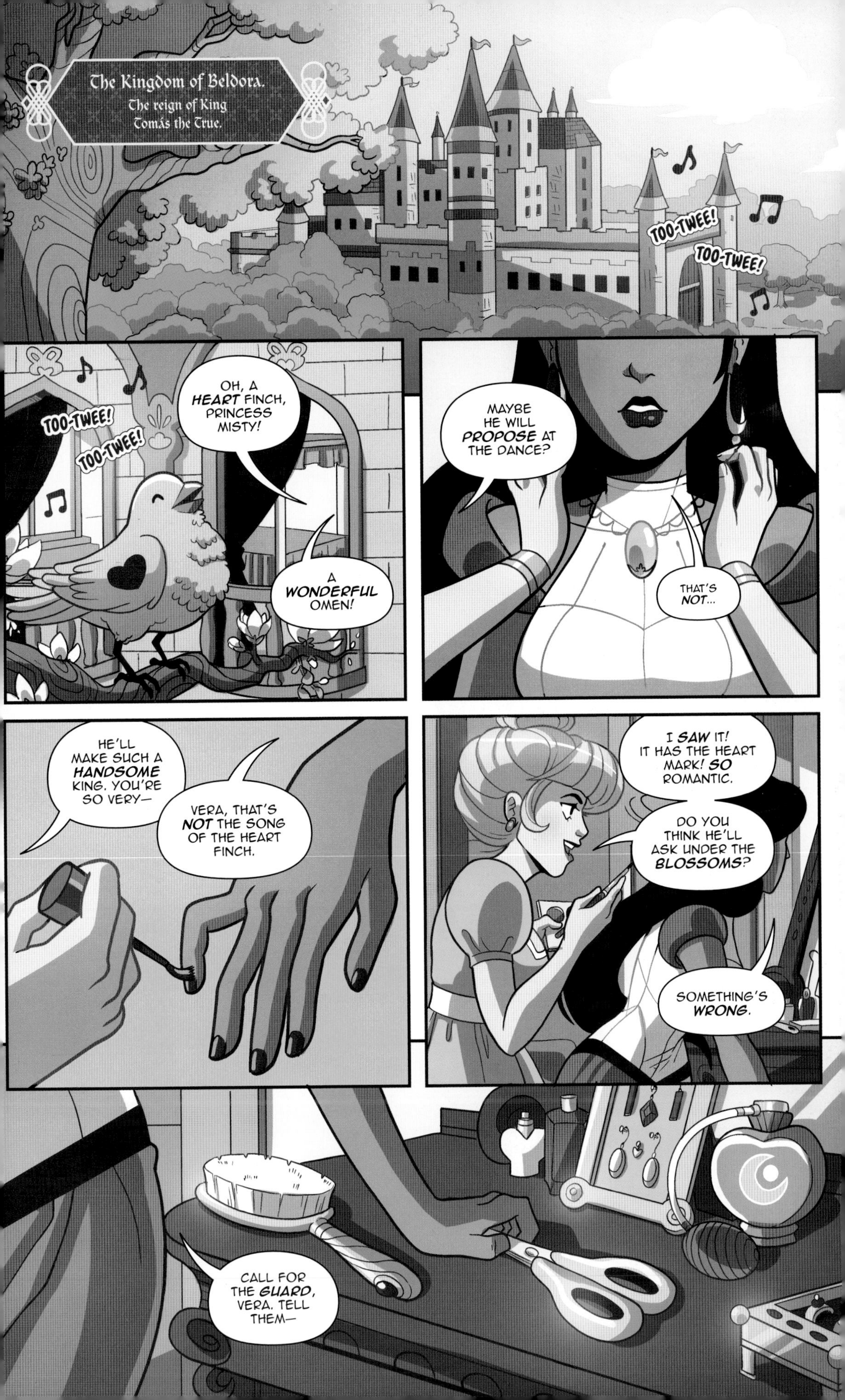
The Kingdom of Beldora.
The reign of King Tomás the True.
TOO-TWEE!
TOO-TWEE!
TOO-TWEE!
TOO-TWEE!
OH, A HEART FINCH, PRINCESS MISTY!
A WONDERFUL OMEN!
MAYBE HE WILL PROPOSE AT THE DANCE?
THAT'S NOT...
HE'LL MAKE SUCH A HANDSOME KING. YOU'RE SO VERY—
VERA, THAT'S NOT THE SONG OF THE HEART FINCH.
I SAW IT! IT HAS THE HEART MARK! SO ROMANTIC.
DO YOU THINK HE'LL ASK UNDER THE BLOSSOMS?
SOMETHING'S WRONG.
CALL FOR THE GUARD, VERA. TELL THEM—

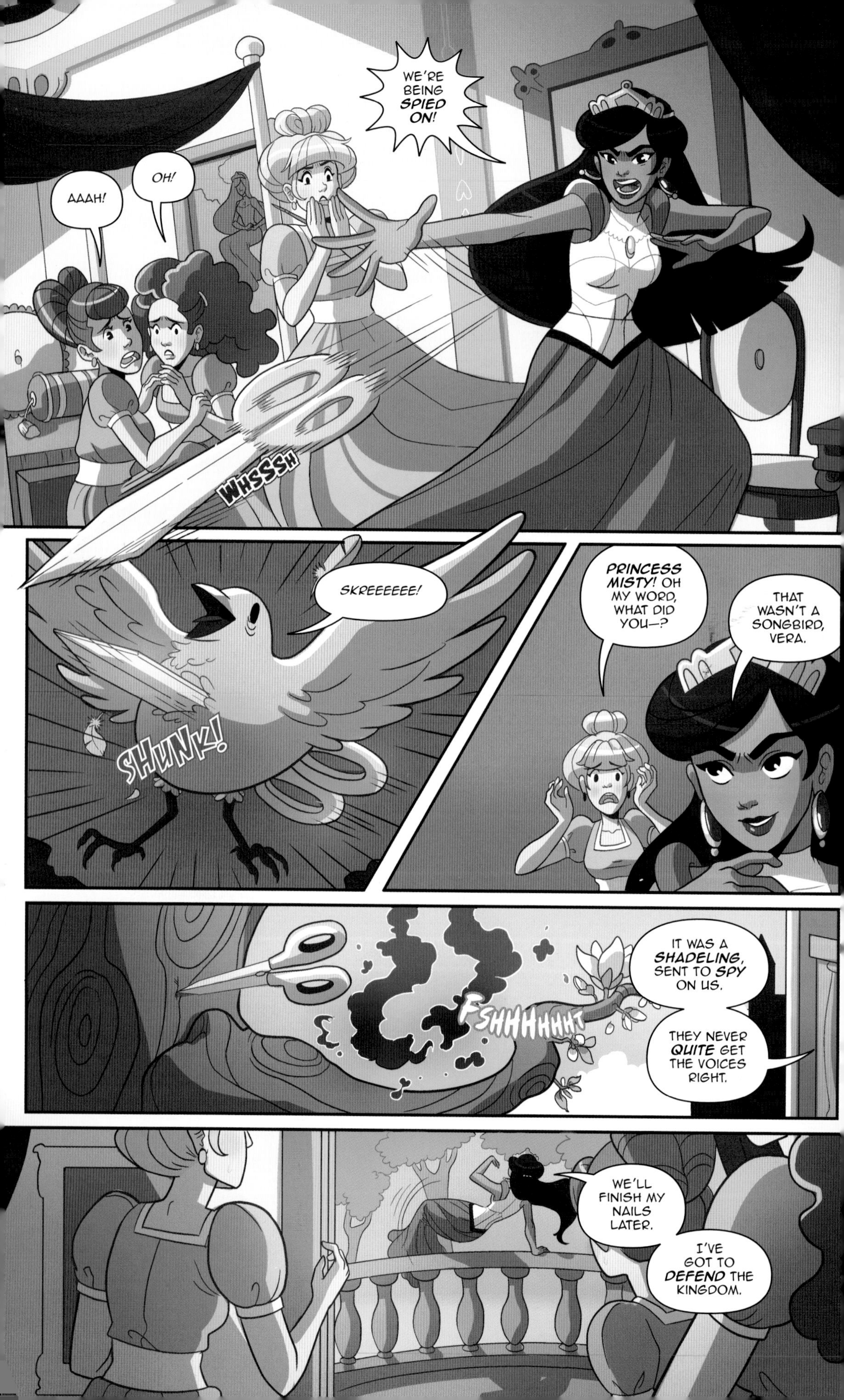
WE'RE BEING SPIED ON!
AAAH!
OH!
WHSSSH
SKREEEEEEE!
SHUNK!
PRINCESS MISTY! OH MY WORD, WHAT DID YOU—?
THAT WASN'T A SONGBIRD, VERA.
IT WAS A SHADELING, SENT TO SPY ON US.
THEY NEVER QUITE GET THE VOICES RIGHT.
FSHHHHHHT
WE'LL FINISH MY NAILS LATER.
I'VE GOT TO DEFEND THE KINGDOM.

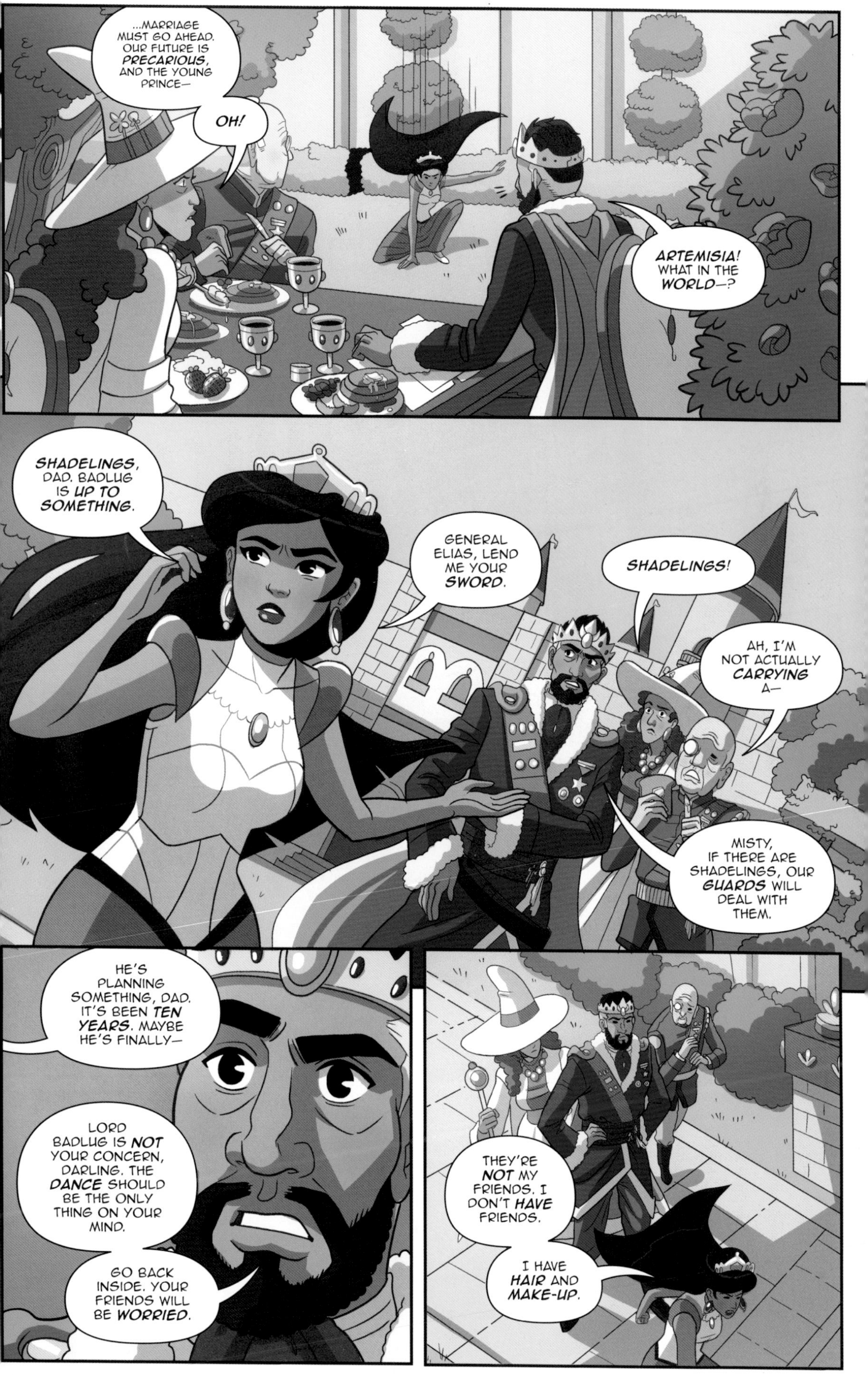
...MARRIAGE MUST GO AHEAD. OUR FUTURE IS PRECARIOUS, AND THE YOUNG PRINCE—
OH!
ARTEMISIA! WHAT IN THE WORLD—?
SHADELINGS, DAD. BADLUG IS UP TO SOMETHING.
GENERAL ELIAS, LEND ME YOUR SWORD.
SHADELINGS!
AH, I'M NOT ACTUALLY CARRYING A—
MISTY, IF THERE ARE SHADELINGS, OUR GUARDS WILL DEAL WITH THEM.
HE'S PLANNING SOMETHING, DAD. IT'S BEEN TEN YEARS. MAYBE HE'S FINALLY—
LORD BADLUG IS NOT YOUR CONCERN, DARLING. THE DANCE SHOULD BE THE ONLY THING ON YOUR MIND.
GO BACK INSIDE. YOUR FRIENDS WILL BE WORRIED.
THEY'RE NOT MY FRIENDS. I DON'T HAVE FRIENDS.
I HAVE HAIR AND MAKE-UP.

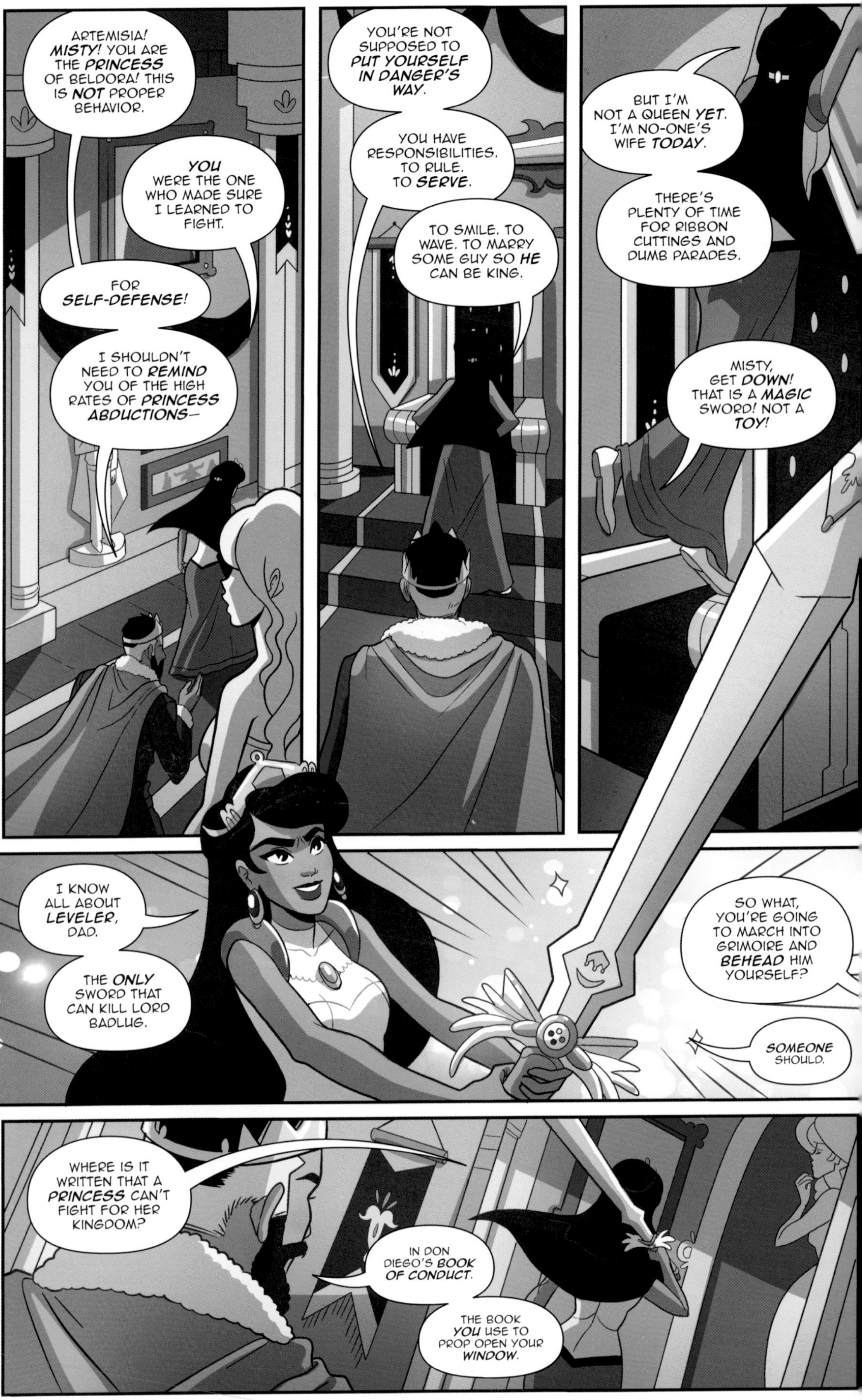

ARTEMISIA! MISTY! YOU ARE THE PRINCESS OF BELDORA! THIS IS NOT PROPER BEHAVIOR.
YOU WERE THE ONE WHO MADE SURE I LEARNED TO FIGHT.
FOR SELF-DEFENSE!
I SHOULDN'T NEED TO REMIND YOU OF THE HIGH RATES OF PRINCESS ABDUCTIONS—
YOU'RE NOT SUPPOSED TO PUT YOURSELF IN DANGER'S WAY.
YOU HAVE RESPONSIBILITIES. TO RULE. TO SERVE.
TO SMILE. TO WAVE. TO MARRY SOME GUY SO HE CAN BE KING.
BUT I'M NOT A QUEEN YET. I'M NO-ONE'S WIFE TODAY.
THERE'S PLENTY OF TIME FOR RIBBON CUTTINGS AND DUMB PARADES.
MISTY, GET DOWN! THAT IS A MAGIC SWORD! NOT A TOY!
I KNOW ALL ABOUT LEVELER, DAD.
THE ONLY SWORD THAT CAN KILL LORD BADLUG.
SO WHAT, YOU'RE GOING TO MARCH INTO GRIMOIRE AND BEHEAD HIM YOURSELF?
SOMEONE SHOULD.
WHERE IS IT WRITTEN THAT A PRINCESS CAN'T FIGHT FOR HER KINGDOM?
IN DON DIEGO'S BOOK OF CONDUCT.
THE BOOK YOU USE TO PROP OPEN YOUR WINDOW.

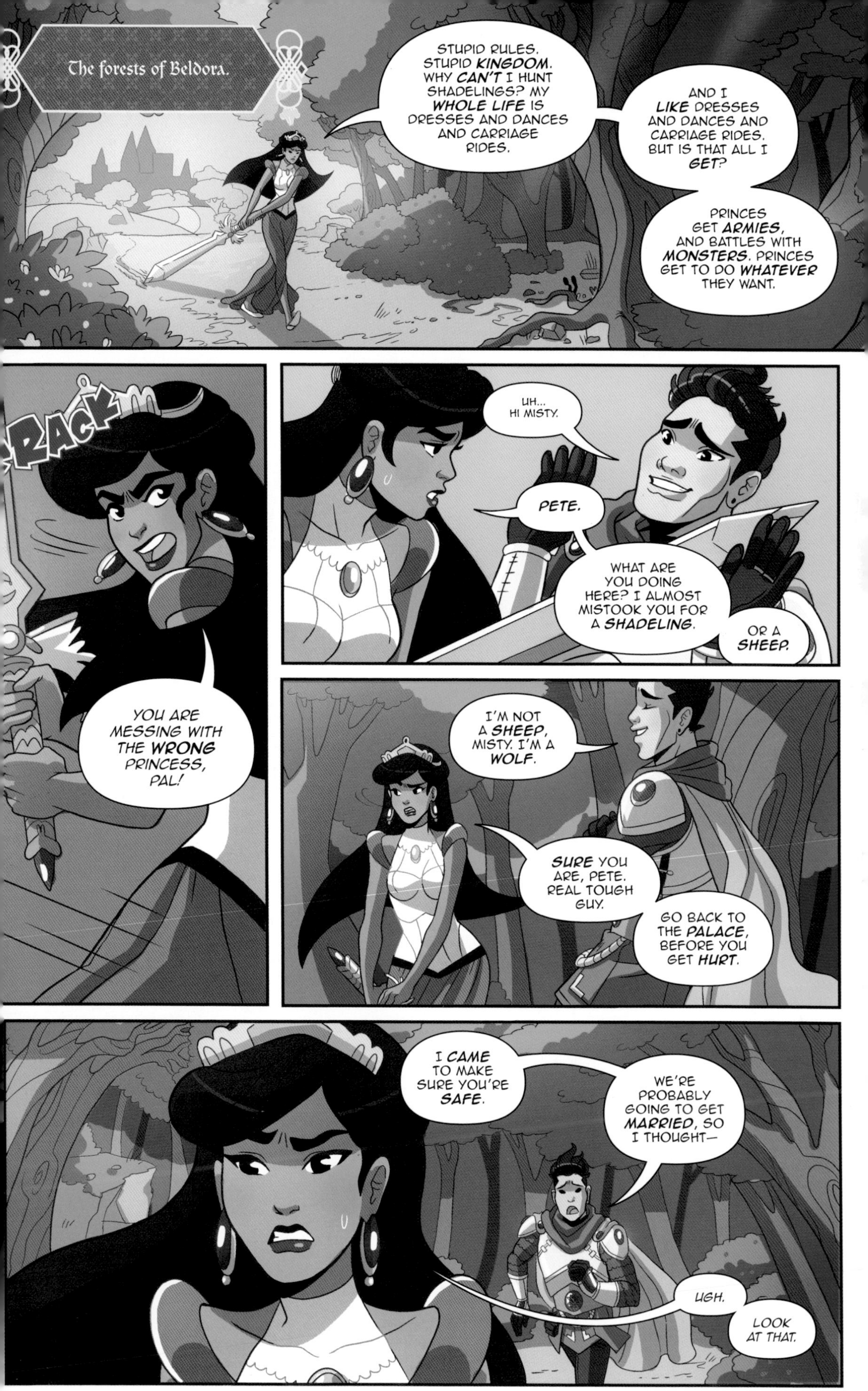
The forests of Beldora.
STUPID RULES. STUPID KINGDOM. WHY CAN'T I HUNT SHADELINGS? MY WHOLE LIFE IS DRESSES AND DANCES AND CARRIAGE RIDES.
AND I LIKE DRESSES AND DANCES AND CARRIAGE RIDES. BUT IS THAT ALL I GET?
PRINCES GET ARMIES, AND BATTLES WITH MONSTERS. PRINCES GET TO DO WHATEVER THEY WANT.
CRACK
YOU ARE MESSING WITH THE WRONG PRINCESS, PAL!
UH... HI MISTY.
PETE.
WHAT ARE YOU DOING HERE? I ALMOST MISTOOK YOU FOR A SHADELING.
OR A SHEEP.
I'M NOT A SHEEP, MISTY. I'M A WOLF.
SURE YOU ARE, PETE. REAL TOUGH GUY.
GO BACK TO THE PALACE, BEFORE YOU GET HURT.
I CAME TO MAKE SURE YOU'RE SAFE.
WE'RE PROBABLY GOING TO GET MARRIED, SO I THOUGHT—
UGH.
LOOK AT THAT.

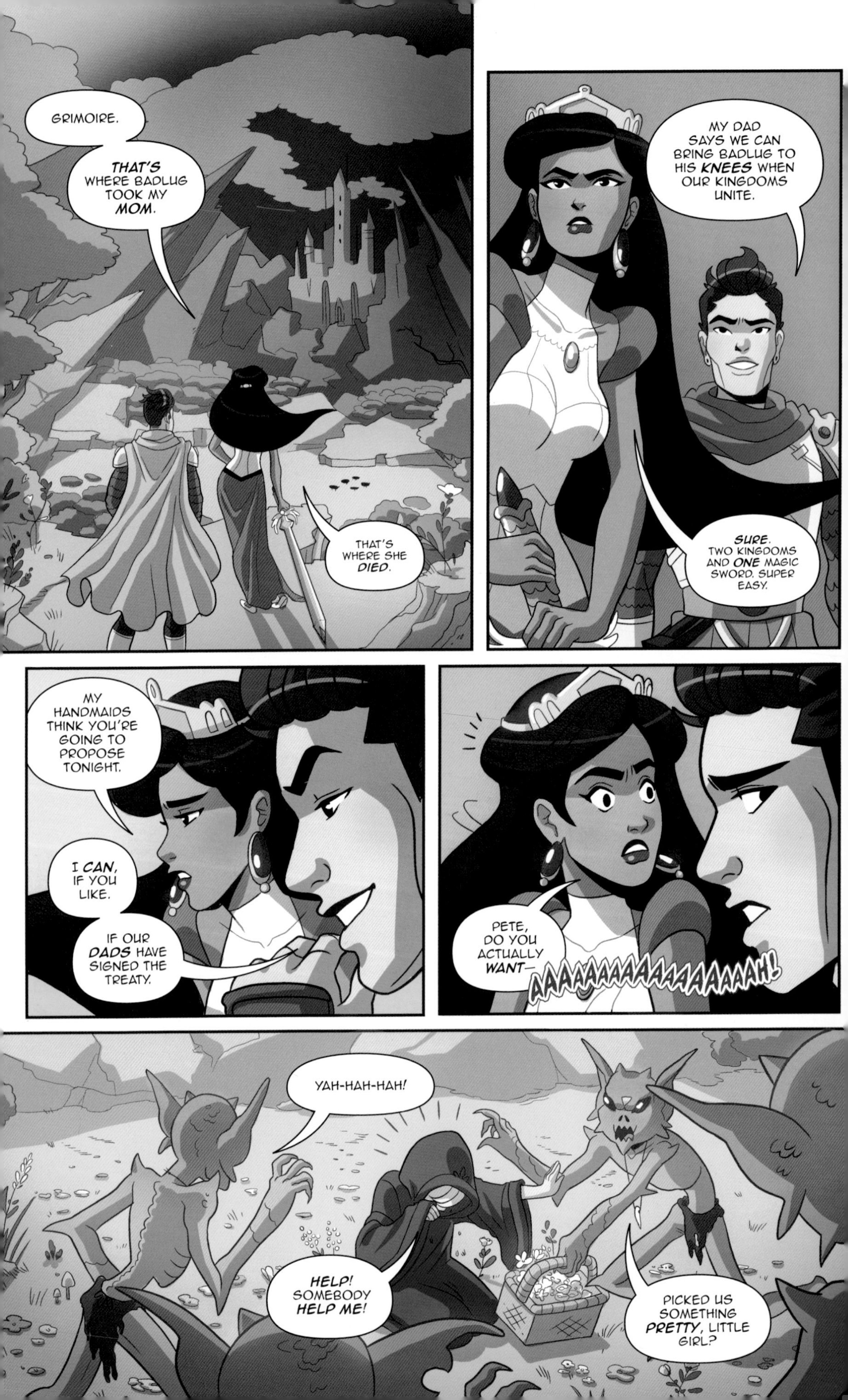
GRIMOIRE.
THAT'S WHERE BADLUG TOOK MY MOM.
THAT'S WHERE SHE DIED.
MY DAD SAYS WE CAN BRING BADLUG TO HIS KNEES WHEN OUR KINGDOMS UNITE.
SURE. TWO KINGDOMS AND ONE MAGIC SWORD. SUPER EASY.
MY HANDMAIDS THINK YOU'RE GOING TO PROPOSE TONIGHT.
I CAN, IF YOU LIKE.
IF OUR DADS HAVE SIGNED THE TREATY.
PETE, DO YOU ACTUALLY WANT—
AAAAAAAAAAAAAAAAAH!
YAH-HAH-HAH!
HELP! SOMEBODY HELP ME!
PICKED US SOMETHING PRETTY, LITTLE GIRL?

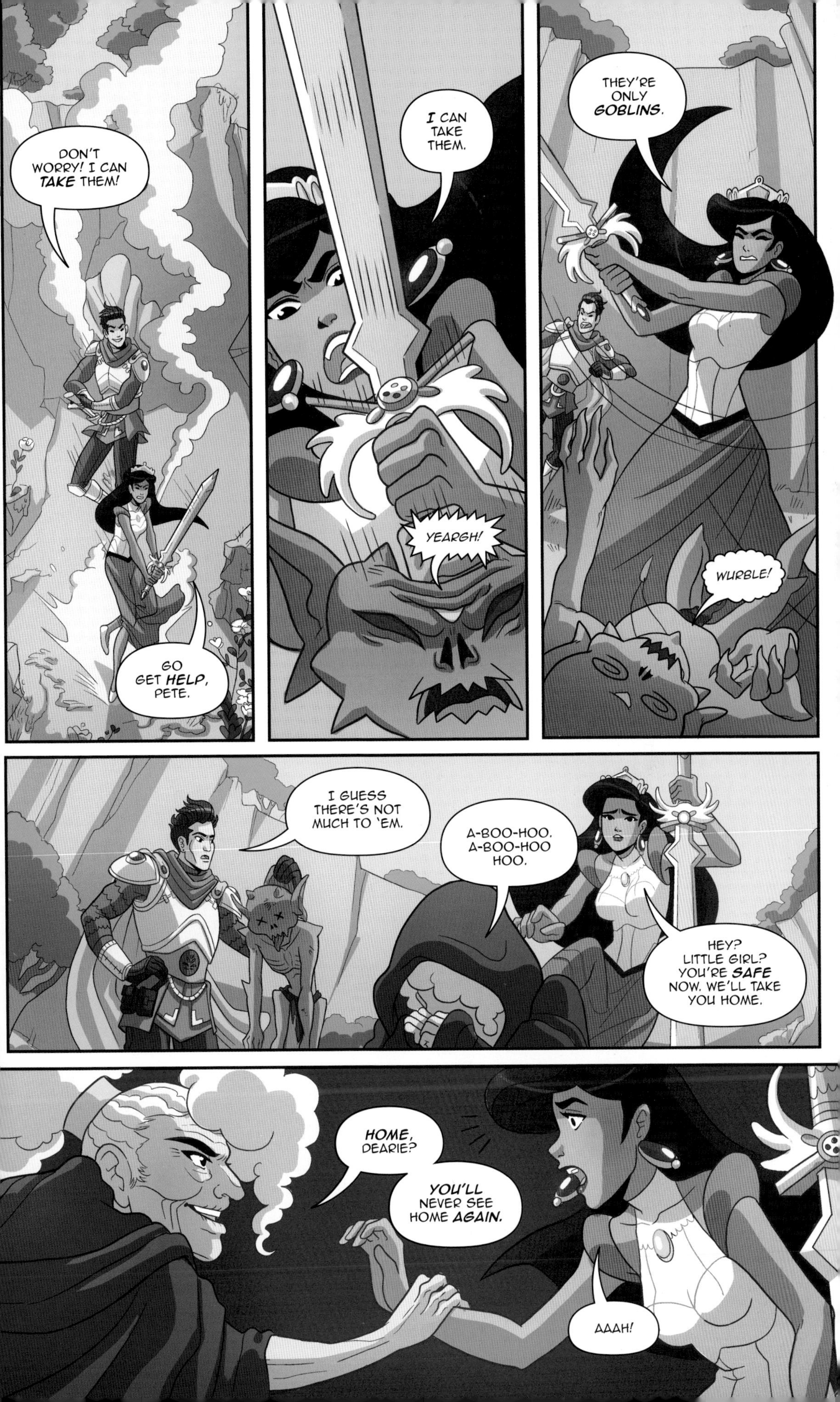
DON'T WORRY! I CAN TAKE THEM!
GO GET HELP, PETE.
I CAN TAKE THEM.
YEARGH!
THEY'RE ONLY GOBLINS.
WURBLE!
I GUESS THERE'S NOT MUCH TO 'EM.
A-BOO-HOO. A-BOO-HOO HOO.
HEY? LITTLE GIRL? YOU'RE SAFE NOW. WE'LL TAKE YOU HOME.
HOME, DEARIE?
YOU'LL NEVER SEE HOME AGAIN.
AAAH!

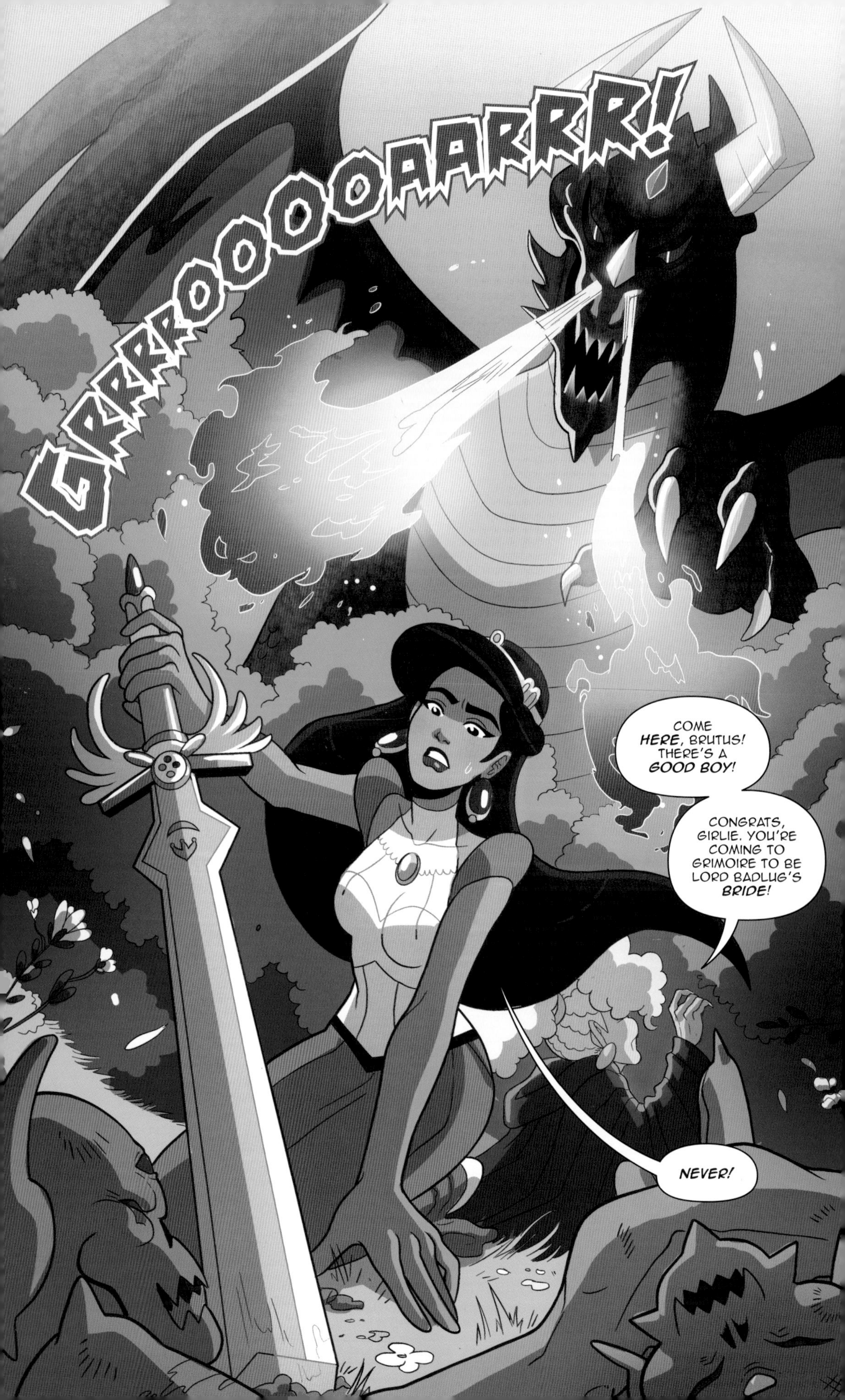
GRRROOOOOAARRR!
COME HERE, BRUTUS! THERE'S A GOOD BOY!
CONGRATS, GIRLIE. YOU'RE COMING TO GRIMOIRE TO BE LORD BADLUG'S BRIDE!
NEVER!

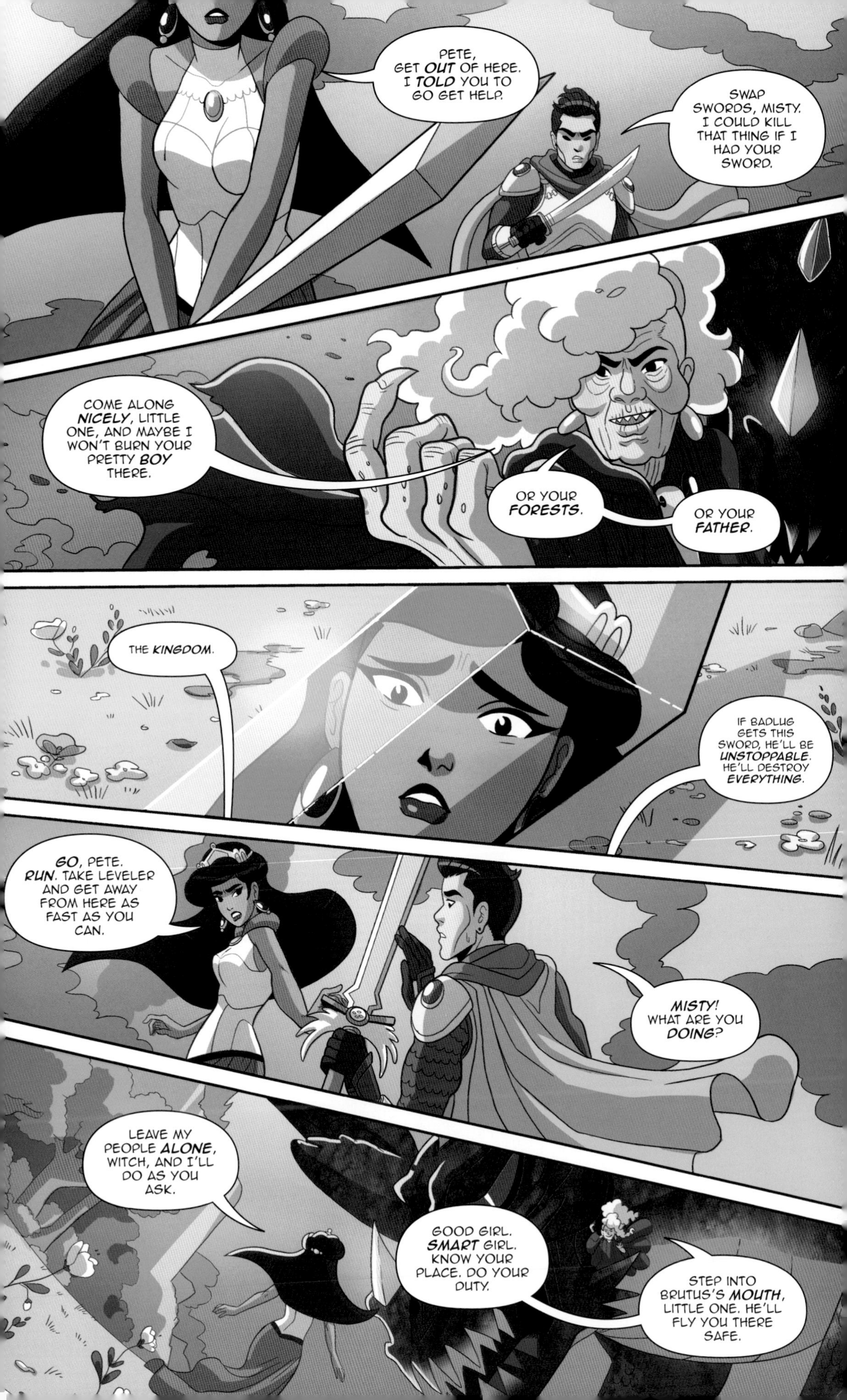
PETE, GET OUT OF HERE. I TOLD YOU TO GO GET HELP.
SWAP SWORDS, MISTY. I COULD KILL THAT THING IF I HAD YOUR SWORD.
COME ALONG NICELY, LITTLE ONE, AND MAYBE I WON'T BURN YOUR PRETTY BOY THERE.
OR YOUR FORESTS.
OR YOUR FATHER.
THE KINGDOM.
IF BADLUG GETS THIS SWORD, HE'LL BE UNSTOPPABLE. HE'LL DESTROY EVERYTHING.
GO, PETE. RUN. TAKE LEVELER AND GET AWAY FROM HERE AS FAST AS YOU CAN.
MISTY! WHAT ARE YOU DOING?
LEAVE MY PEOPLE ALONE, WITCH, AND I'LL DO AS YOU ASK.
GOOD GIRL. SMART GIRL. KNOW YOUR PLACE. DO YOUR DUTY.
STEP INTO BRUTUS'S MOUTH, LITTLE ONE. HE'LL FLY YOU THERE SAFE.

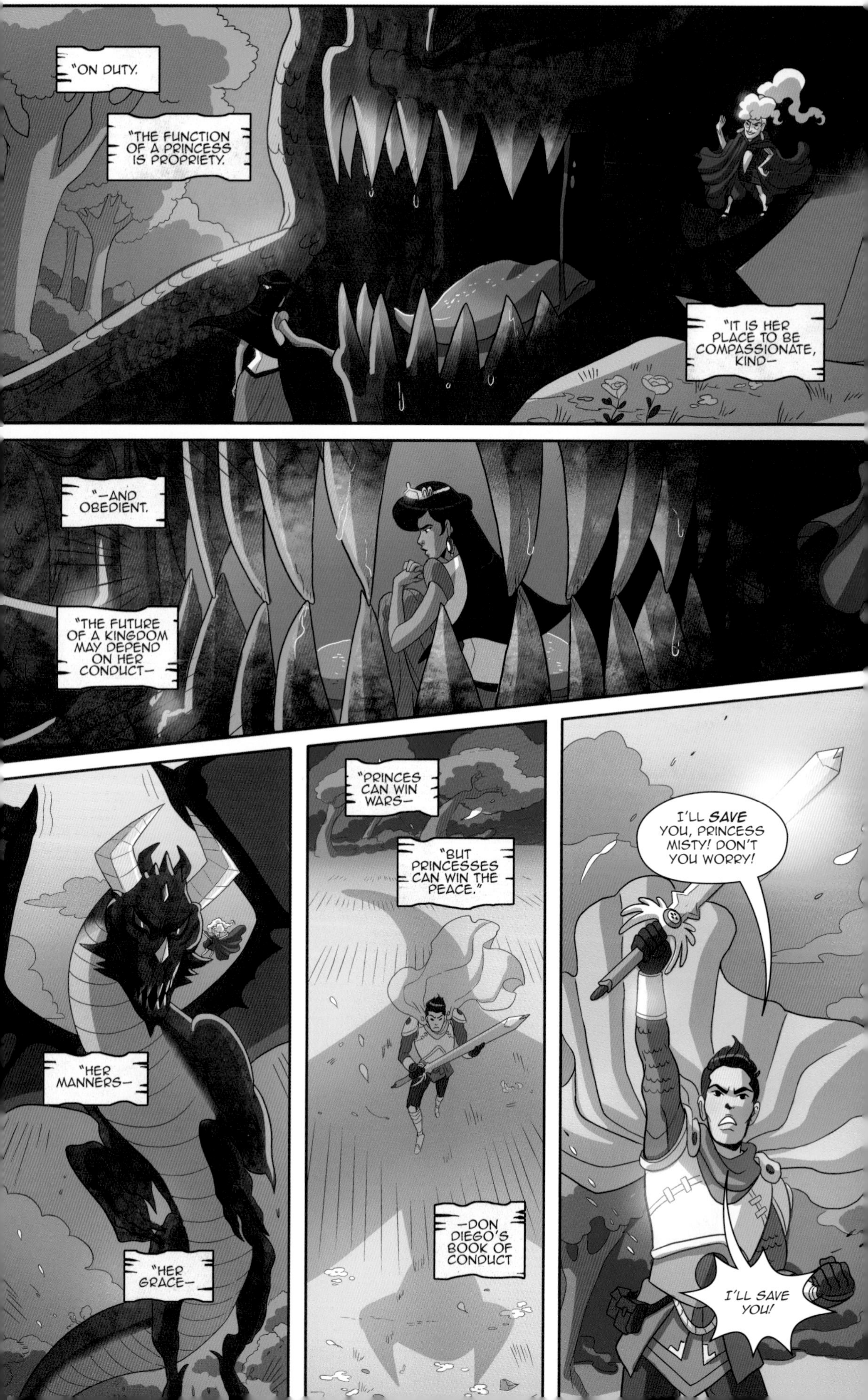
"ON DUTY.
"THE FUNCTION OF A PRINCESS IS PROPRIETY.
"IT IS HER PLACE TO BE COMPASSIONATE, KIND—
"—AND OBEDIENT.
"THE FUTURE OF A KINGDOM MAY DEPEND ON HER CONDUCT—
"HER MANNERS—
"HER GRACE—
"PRINCES CAN WIN WARS—
"BUT PRINCESSES CAN WIN THE PEACE."
—DON DIEGO'S BOOK OF CONDUCT
I'LL **SAVE** YOU, PRINCESS MISTY! DON'T YOU WORRY!
I'LL SAVE YOU!

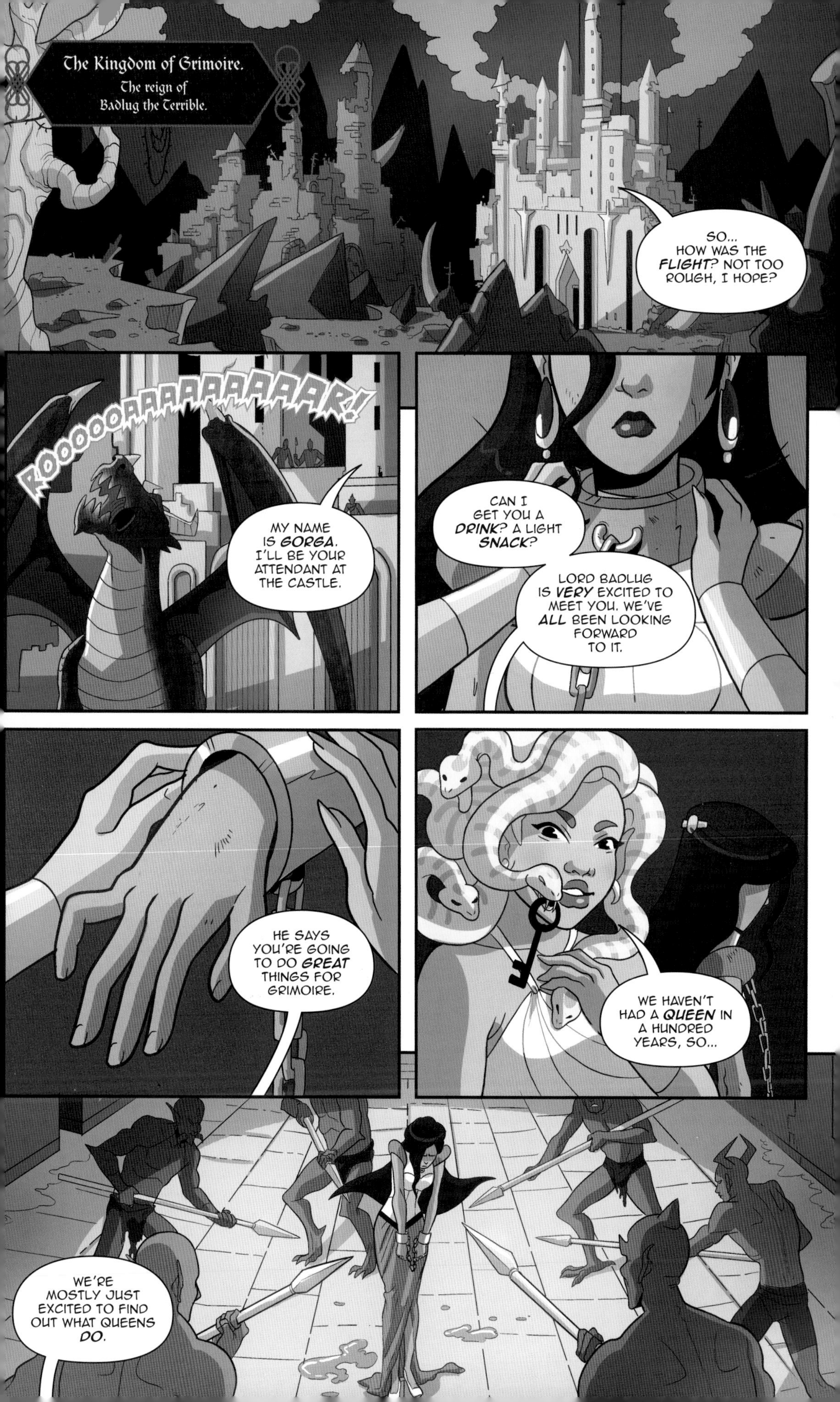
The Kingdom of Grimoire.
The reign of Badlug the Terrible.
SO... HOW WAS THE FLIGHT? NOT TOO ROUGH, I HOPE?
ROOOOOAAAAAAAAAAR!
MY NAME IS GORGA. I'LL BE YOUR ATTENDANT AT THE CASTLE.
CAN I GET YOU A DRINK? A LIGHT SNACK?
LORD BADLUG IS VERY EXCITED TO MEET YOU. WE'VE ALL BEEN LOOKING FORWARD TO IT.
HE SAYS YOU'RE GOING TO DO GREAT THINGS FOR GRIMOIRE.
WE HAVEN'T HAD A QUEEN IN A HUNDRED YEARS, SO...
WE'RE MOSTLY JUST EXCITED TO FIND OUT WHAT QUEENS DO.

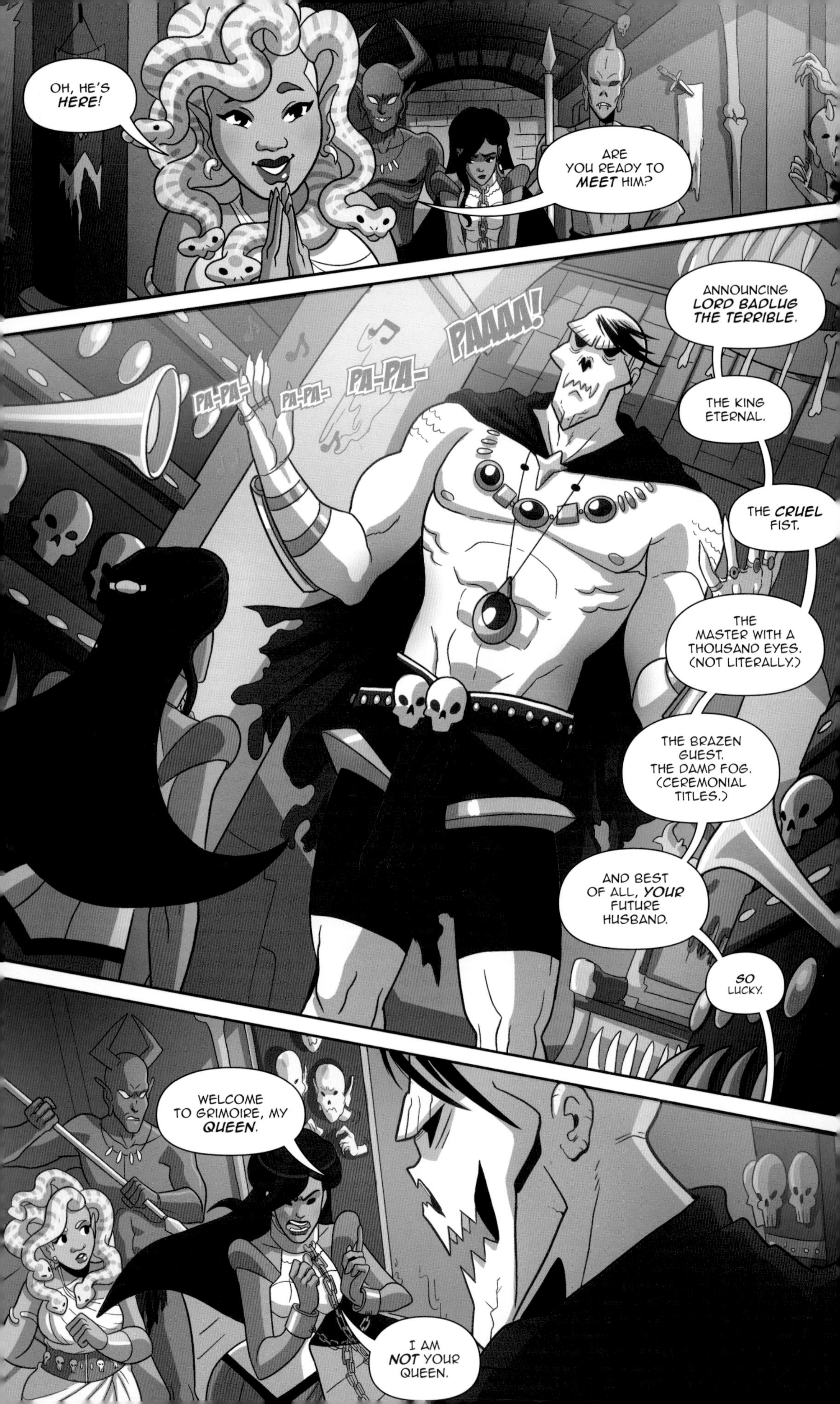

OH, HE'S *HERE*!
ARE YOU READY TO *MEET* HIM?
ANNOUNCING *LORD BADLUG THE TERRIBLE*.
PA-PA- PA-PA- PA-PA- PAAAA!
THE KING ETERNAL.
THE *CRUEL* FIST.
THE MASTER WITH A THOUSAND EYES. (NOT LITERALLY.)
THE BRAZEN GUEST. THE DAMP FOG. (CEREMONIAL TITLES.)
AND BEST OF ALL, *YOUR* FUTURE HUSBAND.
SO LUCKY.
WELCOME TO GRIMOIRE, MY *QUEEN*.
I AM *NOT* YOUR QUEEN.

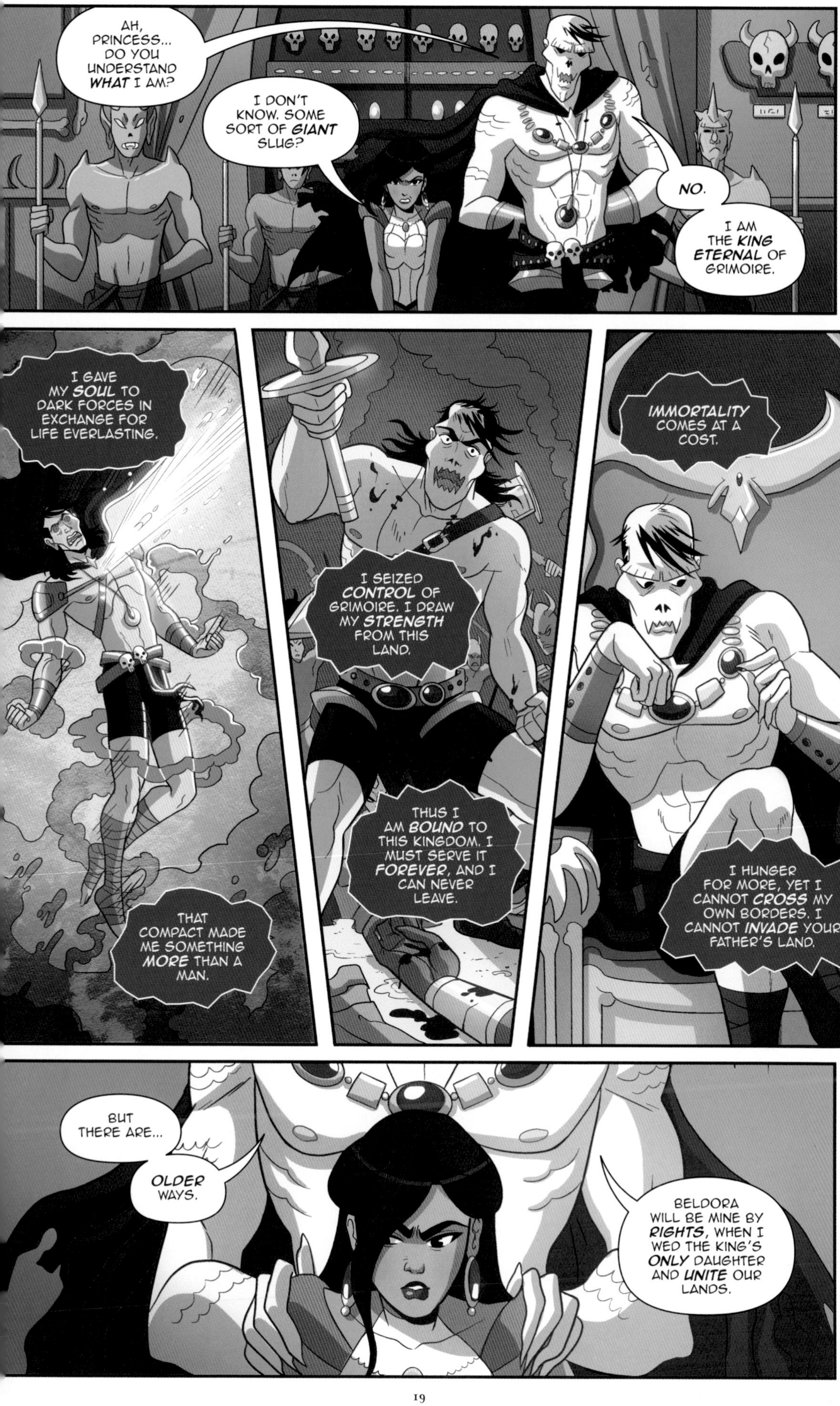
AH, PRINCESS... DO YOU UNDERSTAND WHAT I AM?
I DON'T KNOW. SOME SORT OF GIANT SLUG?
NO.
I AM THE KING ETERNAL OF GRIMOIRE.
I GAVE MY SOUL TO DARK FORCES IN EXCHANGE FOR LIFE EVERLASTING.
THAT COMPACT MADE ME SOMETHING MORE THAN A MAN.
I SEIZED CONTROL OF GRIMOIRE. I DRAW MY STRENGTH FROM THIS LAND.
THUS I AM BOUND TO THIS KINGDOM. I MUST SERVE IT FOREVER, AND I CAN NEVER LEAVE.
IMMORTALITY COMES AT A COST.
I HUNGER FOR MORE, YET I CANNOT CROSS MY OWN BORDERS. I CANNOT INVADE YOUR FATHER'S LAND.
BUT THERE ARE...
OLDER WAYS.
BELDORA WILL BE MINE BY RIGHTS, WHEN I WED THE KING'S ONLY DAUGHTER AND UNITE OUR LANDS.

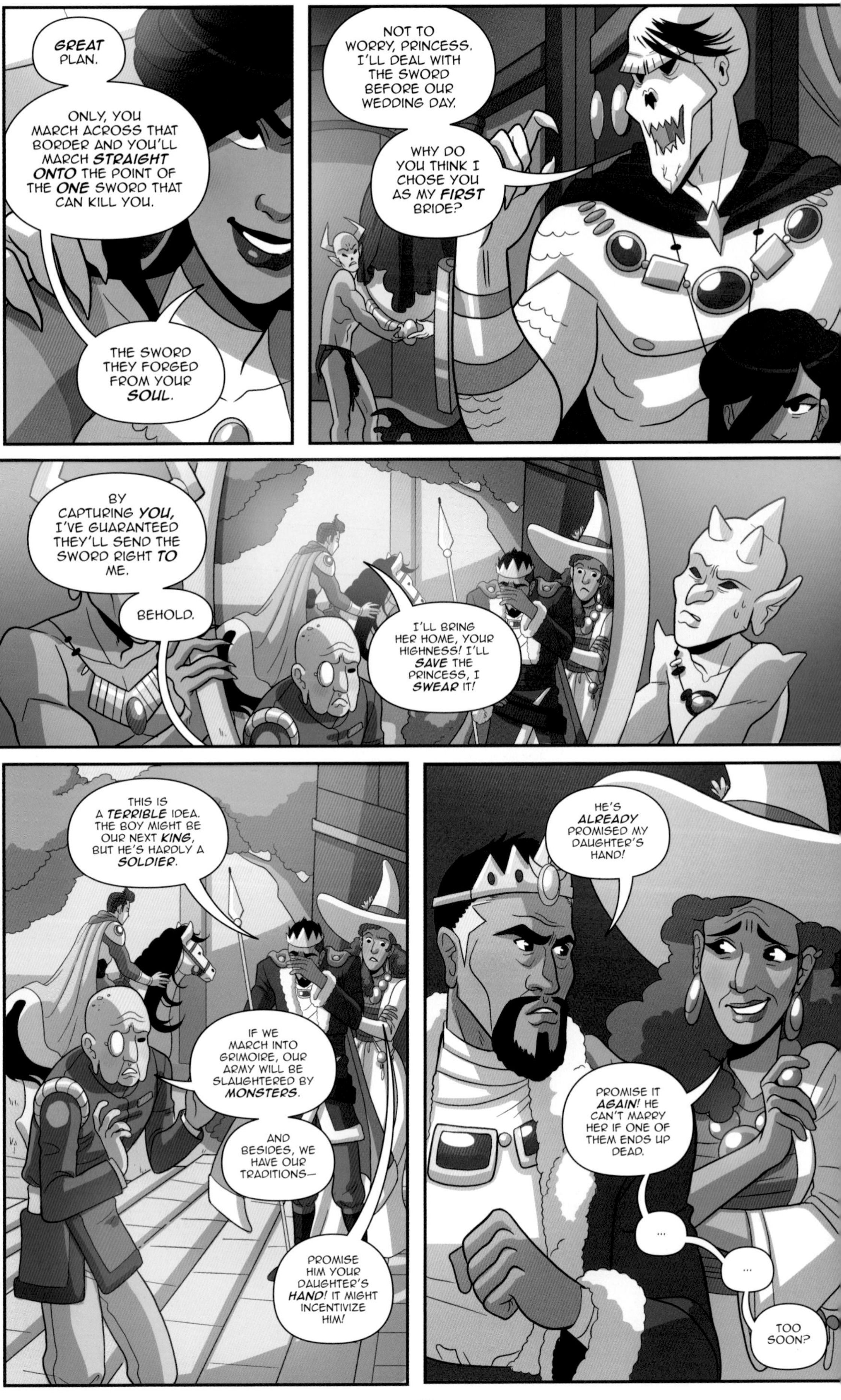

GREAT PLAN.
ONLY, YOU MARCH ACROSS THAT BORDER AND YOU'LL MARCH STRAIGHT ONTO THE POINT OF THE ONE SWORD THAT CAN KILL YOU.
THE SWORD THEY FORGED FROM YOUR SOUL.
NOT TO WORRY, PRINCESS. I'LL DEAL WITH THE SWORD BEFORE OUR WEDDING DAY.
WHY DO YOU THINK I CHOSE YOU AS MY FIRST BRIDE?
BY CAPTURING YOU, I'VE GUARANTEED THEY'LL SEND THE SWORD RIGHT TO ME.
BEHOLD.
I'LL BRING HER HOME, YOUR HIGHNESS! I'LL SAVE THE PRINCESS, I SWEAR IT!
THIS IS A TERRIBLE IDEA. THE BOY MIGHT BE OUR NEXT KING, BUT HE'S HARDLY A SOLDIER.
IF WE MARCH INTO GRIMOIRE, OUR ARMY WILL BE SLAUGHTERED BY MONSTERS.
AND BESIDES, WE HAVE OUR TRADITIONS—
PROMISE HIM YOUR DAUGHTER'S HAND! IT MIGHT INCENTIVIZE HIM!
HE'S ALREADY PROMISED MY DAUGHTER'S HAND!
PROMISE IT AGAIN! HE CAN'T MARRY HER IF ONE OF THEM ENDS UP DEAD.
...
...
TOO SOON?

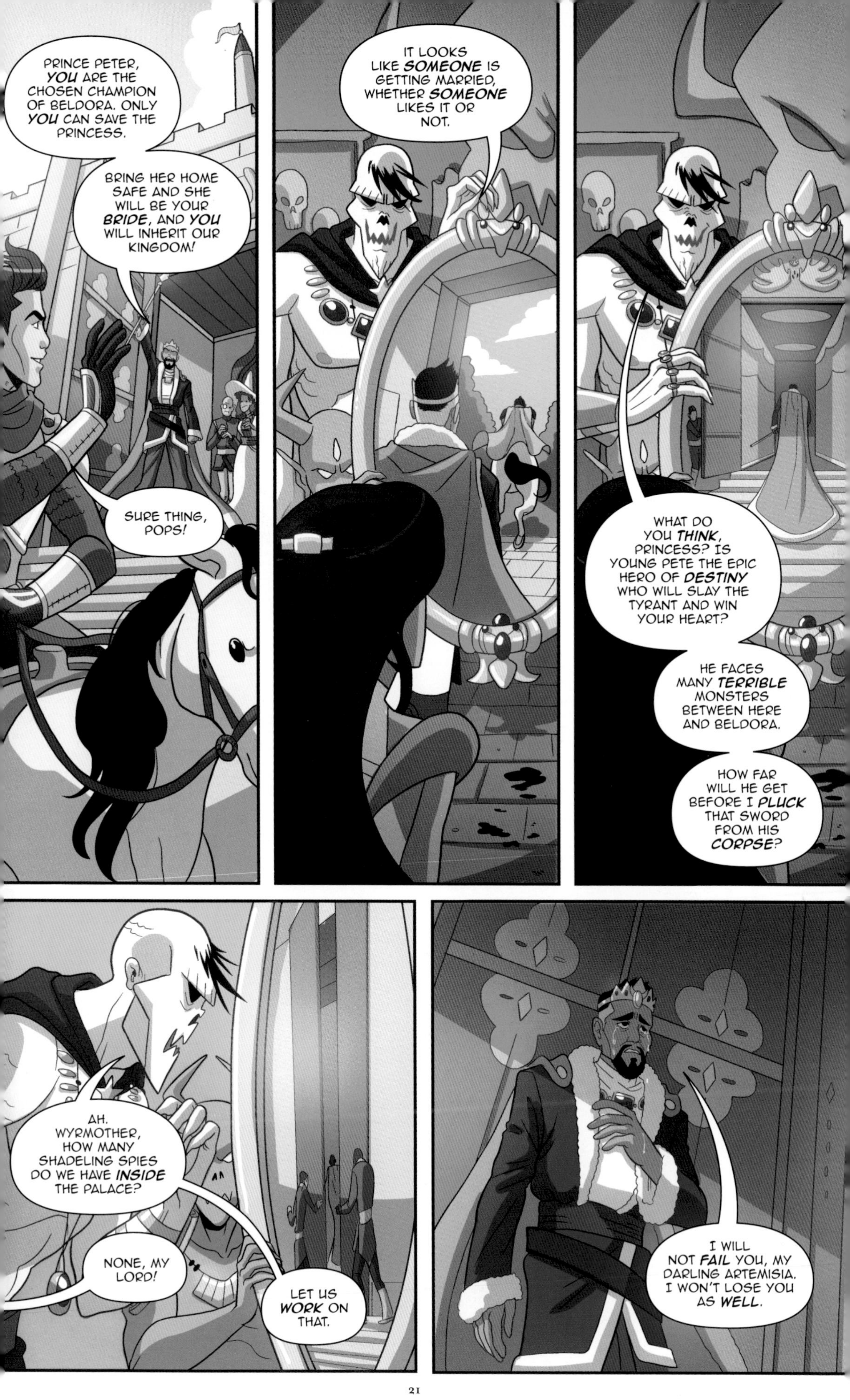
PRINCE PETER, YOU ARE THE CHOSEN CHAMPION OF BELDORA. ONLY YOU CAN SAVE THE PRINCESS.
BRING HER HOME SAFE AND SHE WILL BE YOUR BRIDE, AND YOU WILL INHERIT OUR KINGDOM!
SURE THING, POPS!
IT LOOKS LIKE SOMEONE IS GETTING MARRIED, WHETHER SOMEONE LIKES IT OR NOT.
WHAT DO YOU THINK, PRINCESS? IS YOUNG PETE THE EPIC HERO OF DESTINY WHO WILL SLAY THE TYRANT AND WIN YOUR HEART?
HE FACES MANY TERRIBLE MONSTERS BETWEEN HERE AND BELDORA.
HOW FAR WILL HE GET BEFORE I PLUCK THAT SWORD FROM HIS CORPSE?
AH. WYRMOTHER, HOW MANY SHADELING SPIES DO WE HAVE INSIDE THE PALACE?
NONE, MY LORD!
LET US WORK ON THAT.
I WILL NOT FAIL YOU, MY DARLING ARTEMISIA. I WON'T LOSE YOU AS WELL.

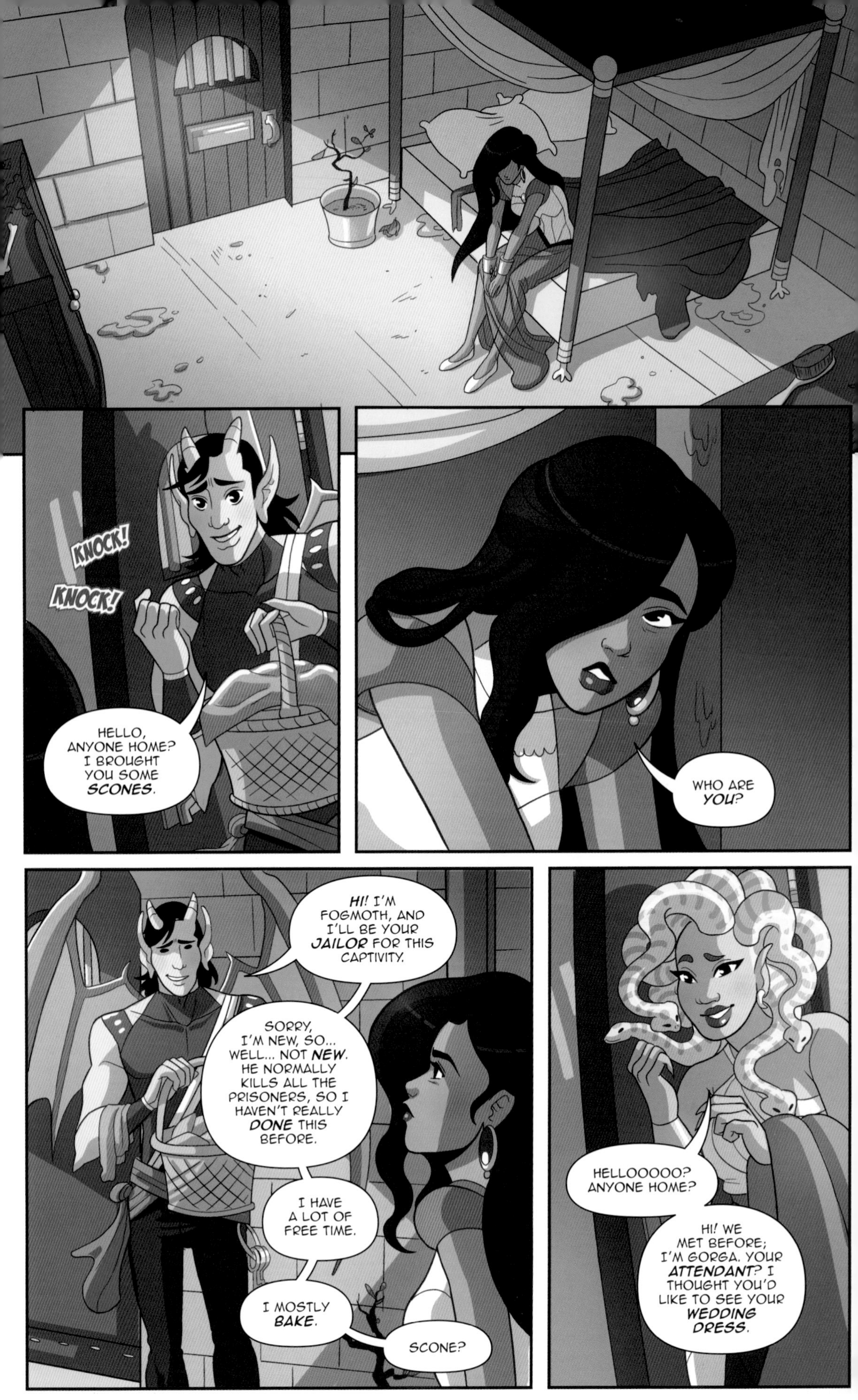
KNOCK!
KNOCK!
HELLO, ANYONE HOME? I BROUGHT YOU SOME SCONES.
WHO ARE YOU?
HI! I'M FOGMOTH, AND I'LL BE YOUR JAILOR FOR THIS CAPTIVITY.
SORRY, I'M NEW, SO... WELL... NOT NEW. HE NORMALLY KILLS ALL THE PRISONERS, SO I HAVEN'T REALLY DONE THIS BEFORE.
I HAVE A LOT OF FREE TIME.
I MOSTLY BAKE.
SCONE?
HELLOOOOO? ANYONE HOME?
HI! WE MET BEFORE; I'M GORGA, YOUR ATTENDANT? I THOUGHT YOU'D LIKE TO SEE YOUR WEDDING DRESS.

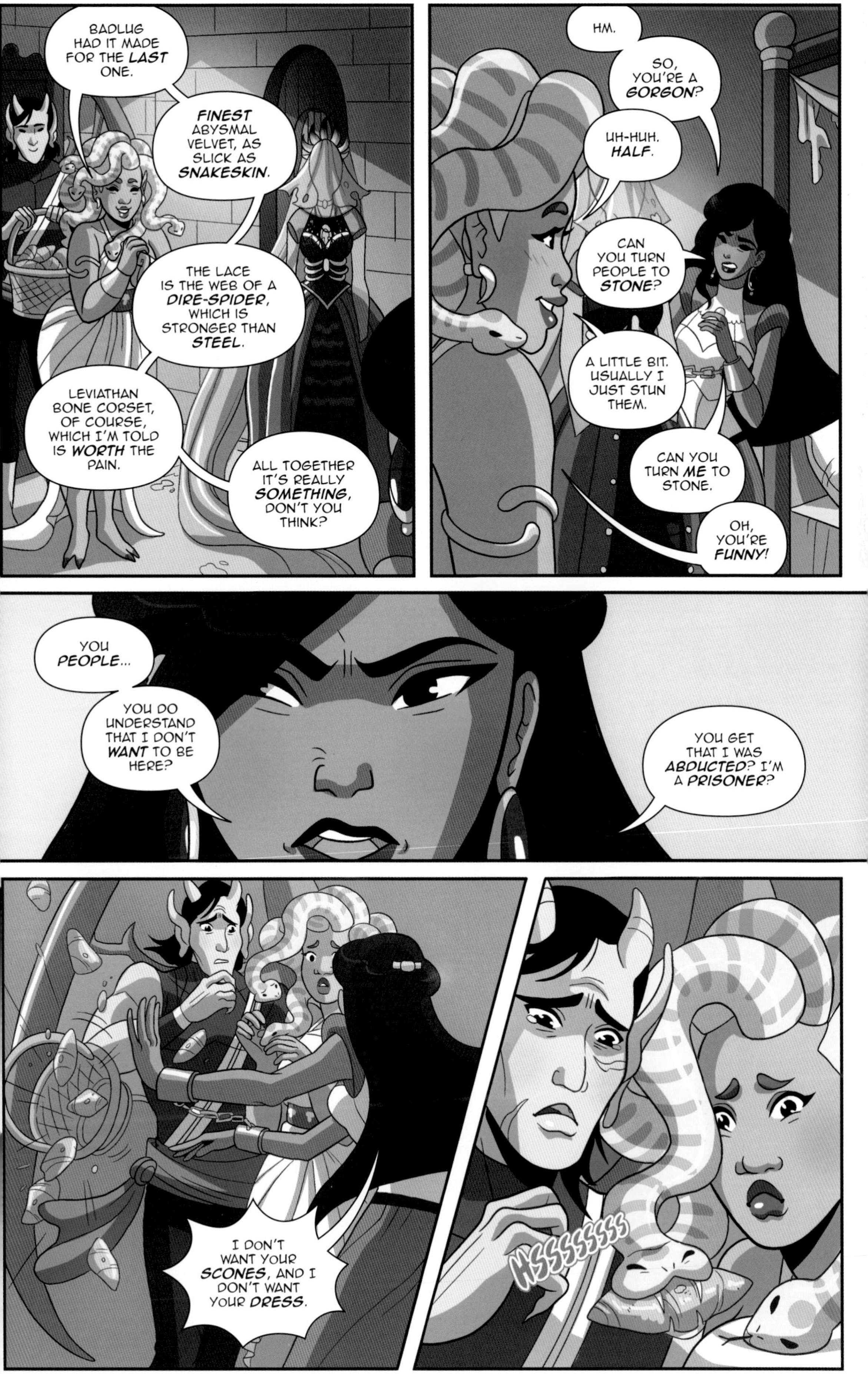
BADLUG HAD IT MADE FOR THE LAST ONE.
FINEST ABYSMAL VELVET, AS SLICK AS SNAKESKIN.
THE LACE IS THE WEB OF A DIRE-SPIDER, WHICH IS STRONGER THAN STEEL.
LEVIATHAN BONE CORSET, OF COURSE, WHICH I'M TOLD IS WORTH THE PAIN.
ALL TOGETHER IT'S REALLY SOMETHING, DON'T YOU THINK?
HM.
SO, YOU'RE A GORGON?
UH-HUH. HALF.
CAN YOU TURN PEOPLE TO STONE?
A LITTLE BIT. USUALLY I JUST STUN THEM.
CAN YOU TURN ME TO STONE.
OH, YOU'RE FUNNY!
YOU PEOPLE...
YOU DO UNDERSTAND THAT I DON'T WANT TO BE HERE?
YOU GET THAT I WAS ABDUCTED? I'M A PRISONER?
I DON'T WANT YOUR SCONES, AND I DON'T WANT YOUR DRESS.
HSSSSSSSS

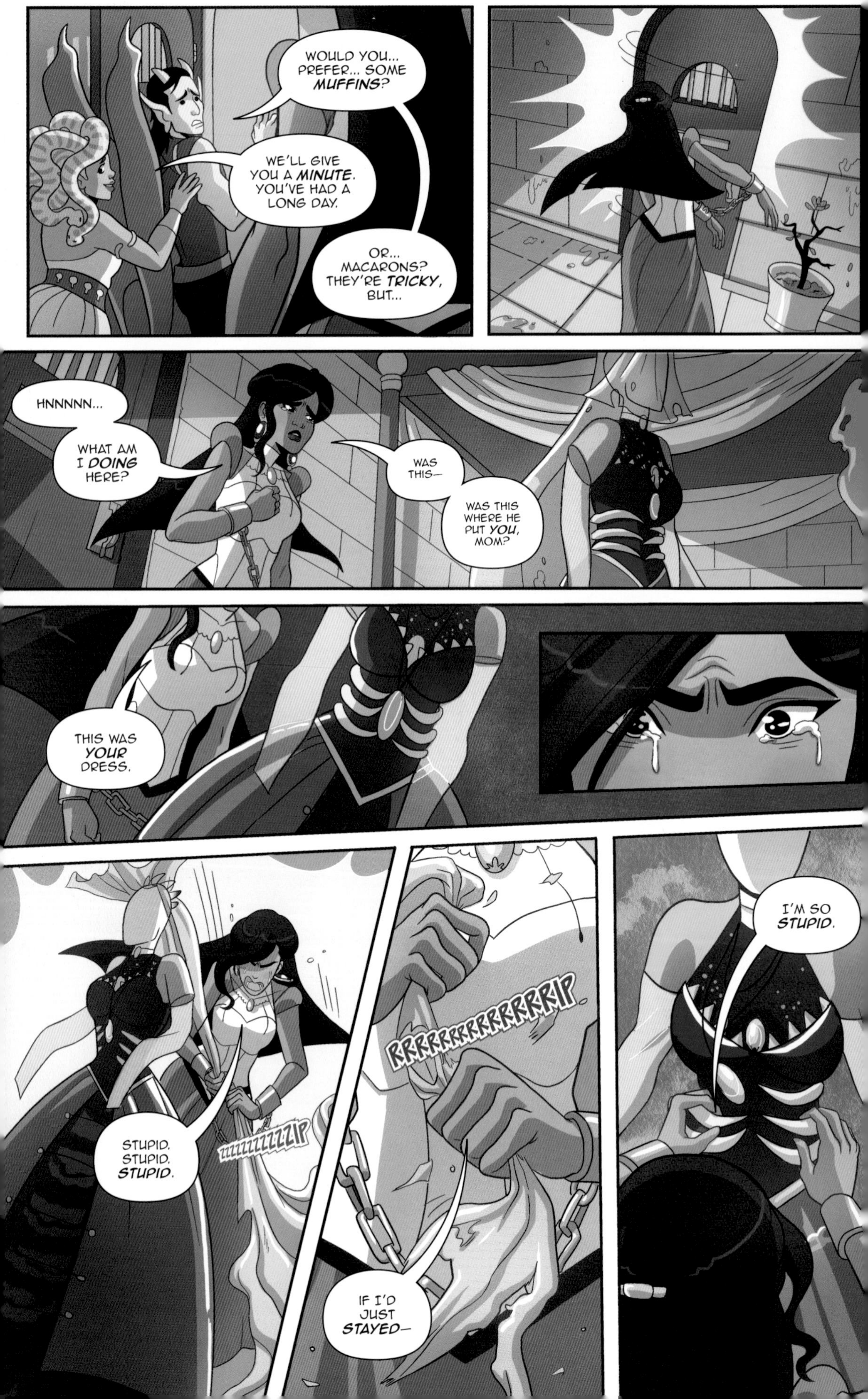
WOULD YOU... PREFER... SOME MUFFINS?
WE'LL GIVE YOU A MINUTE. YOU'VE HAD A LONG DAY.
OR... MACARONS? THEY'RE TRICKY, BUT...
HNNNNN...
WHAT AM I DOING HERE?
WAS THIS—
WAS THIS WHERE HE PUT YOU, MOM?
THIS WAS YOUR DRESS.
STUPID. STUPID. STUPID.
ZZZZZZZZZZZIP
RRRRRRRRRRRRRRIP
IF I'D JUST STAYED—
I'M SO STUPID.

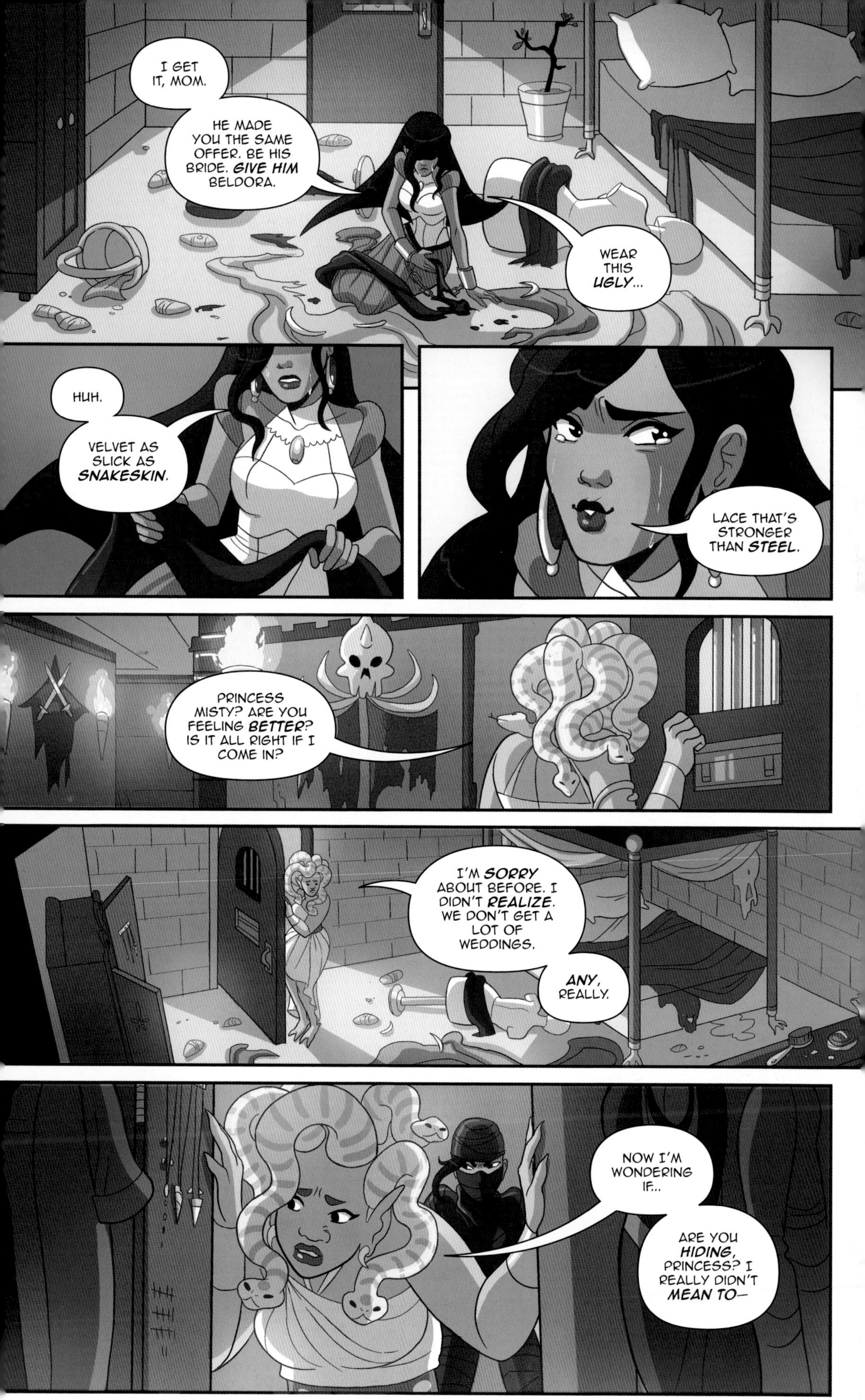
I GET IT, MOM.
HE MADE YOU THE SAME OFFER. BE HIS BRIDE. GIVE HIM BELDORA.
WEAR THIS UGLY...
HUH.
VELVET AS SLICK AS SNAKESKIN.
LACE THAT'S STRONGER THAN STEEL.
PRINCESS MISTY? ARE YOU FEELING BETTER? IS IT ALL RIGHT IF I COME IN?
I'M SORRY ABOUT BEFORE. I DIDN'T REALIZE. WE DON'T GET A LOT OF WEDDINGS.
ANY, REALLY.
NOW I'M WONDERING IF...
ARE YOU HIDING, PRINCESS? I REALLY DIDN'T MEAN TO—

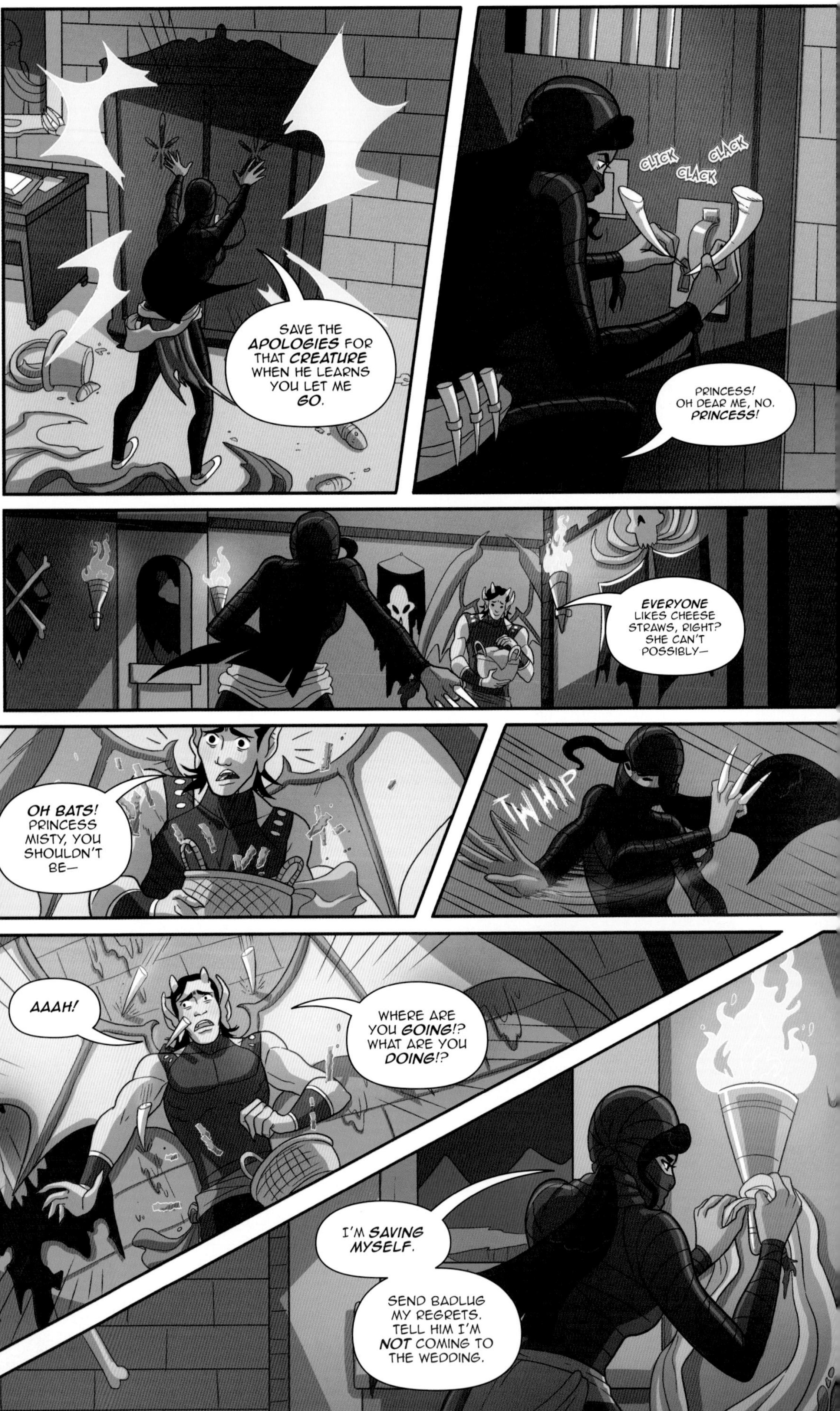
SAVE THE APOLOGIES FOR THAT CREATURE WHEN HE LEARNS YOU LET ME GO.
CLICK CLACK CLACK
PRINCESS! OH DEAR ME, NO. PRINCESS!
EVERYONE LIKES CHEESE STRAWS, RIGHT? SHE CAN'T POSSIBLY—
OH BATS! PRINCESS MISTY, YOU SHOULDN'T BE—
TWHIP
AAAH!
WHERE ARE YOU GOING!? WHAT ARE YOU DOING!?
I'M SAVING MYSELF.
SEND BADLUG MY REGRETS. TELL HIM I'M NOT COMING TO THE WEDDING.

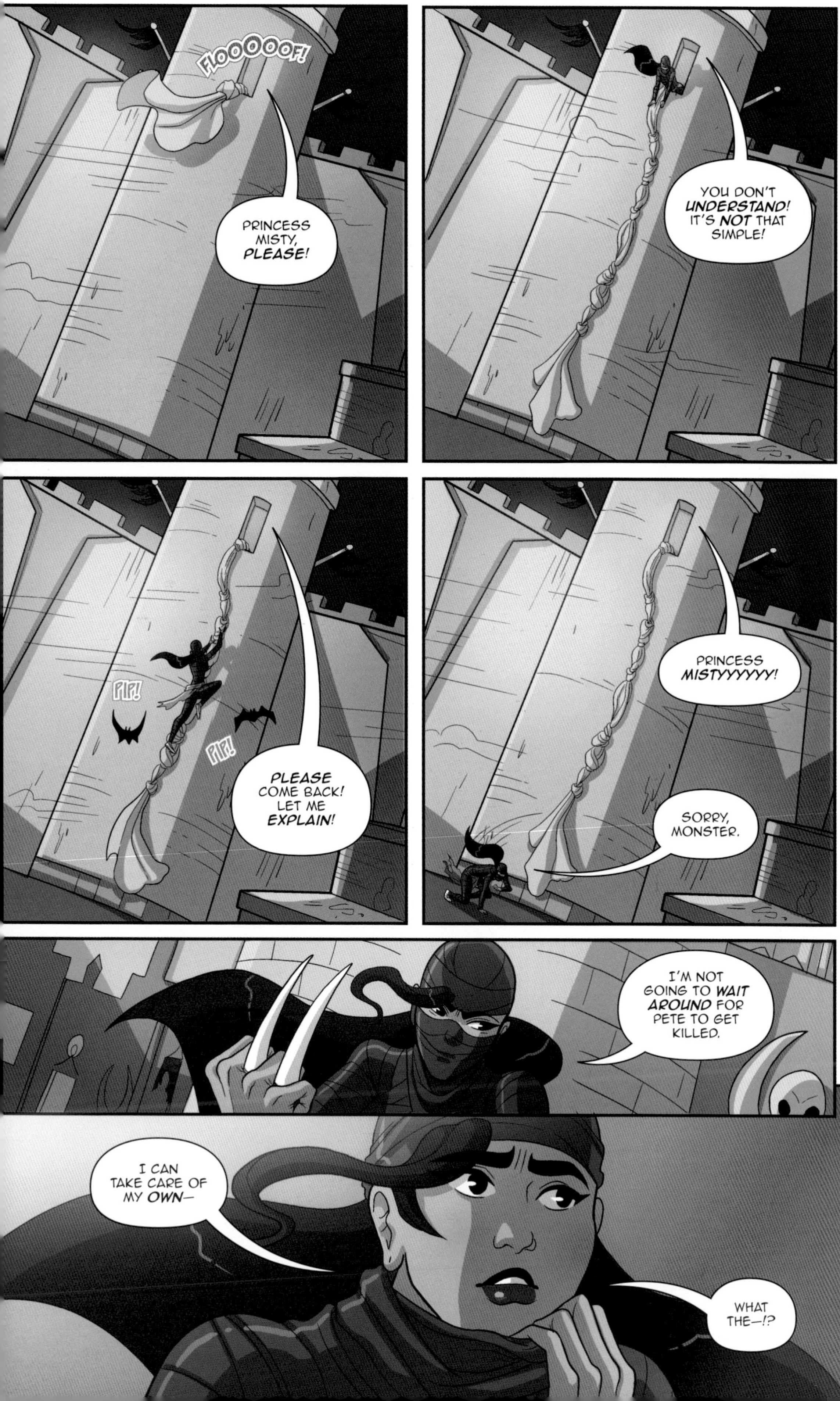
FLOOOOOF!
PRINCESS MISTY, PLEASE!
YOU DON'T UNDERSTAND! IT'S NOT THAT SIMPLE!
PIP!
PIP!
PLEASE COME BACK! LET ME EXPLAIN!
PRINCESS MISTYYYYYY!
SORRY, MONSTER.
I'M NOT GOING TO WAIT AROUND FOR PETE TO GET KILLED.
I CAN TAKE CARE OF MY OWN—
WHAT THE—!?

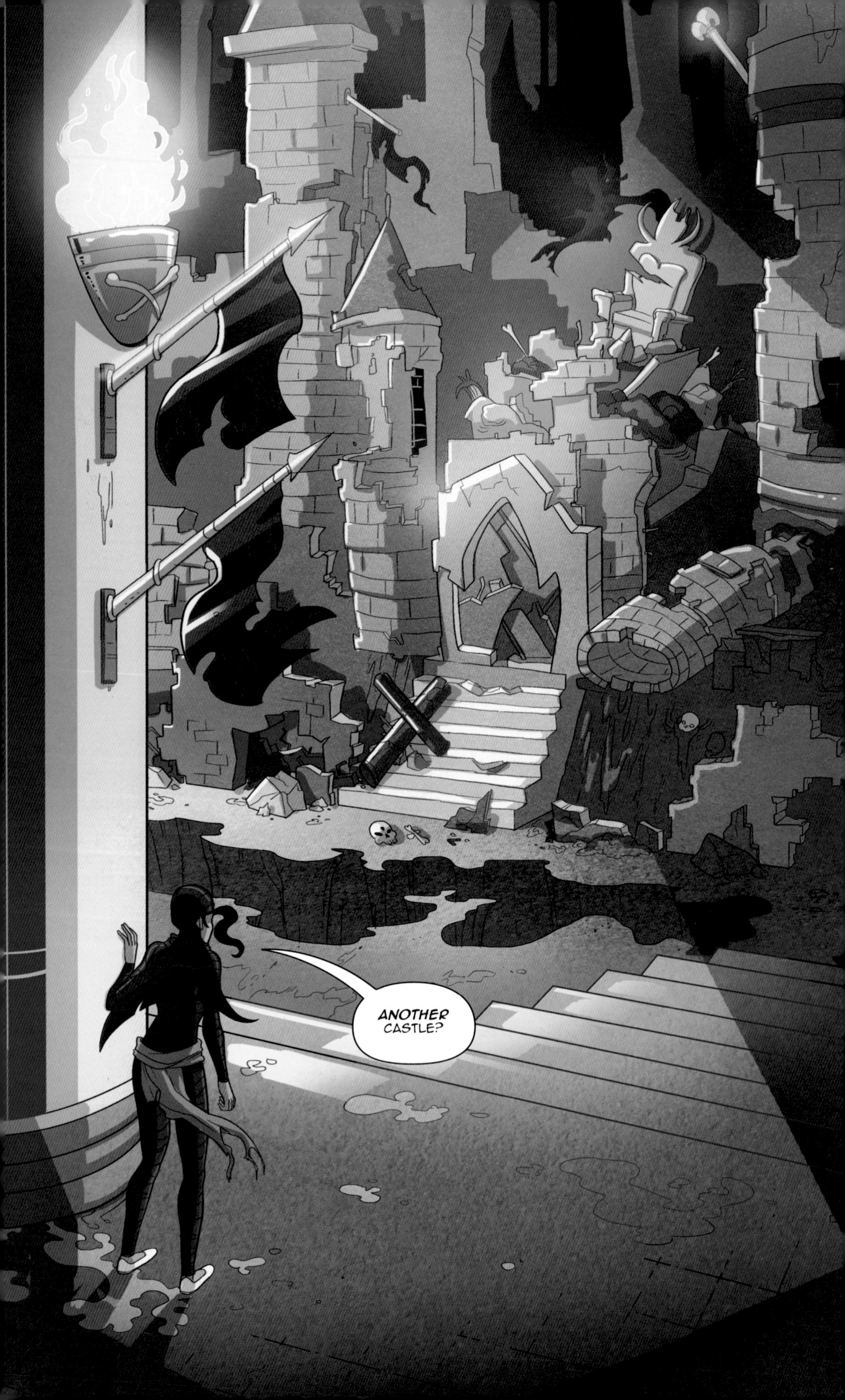
ANOTHER CASTLE?

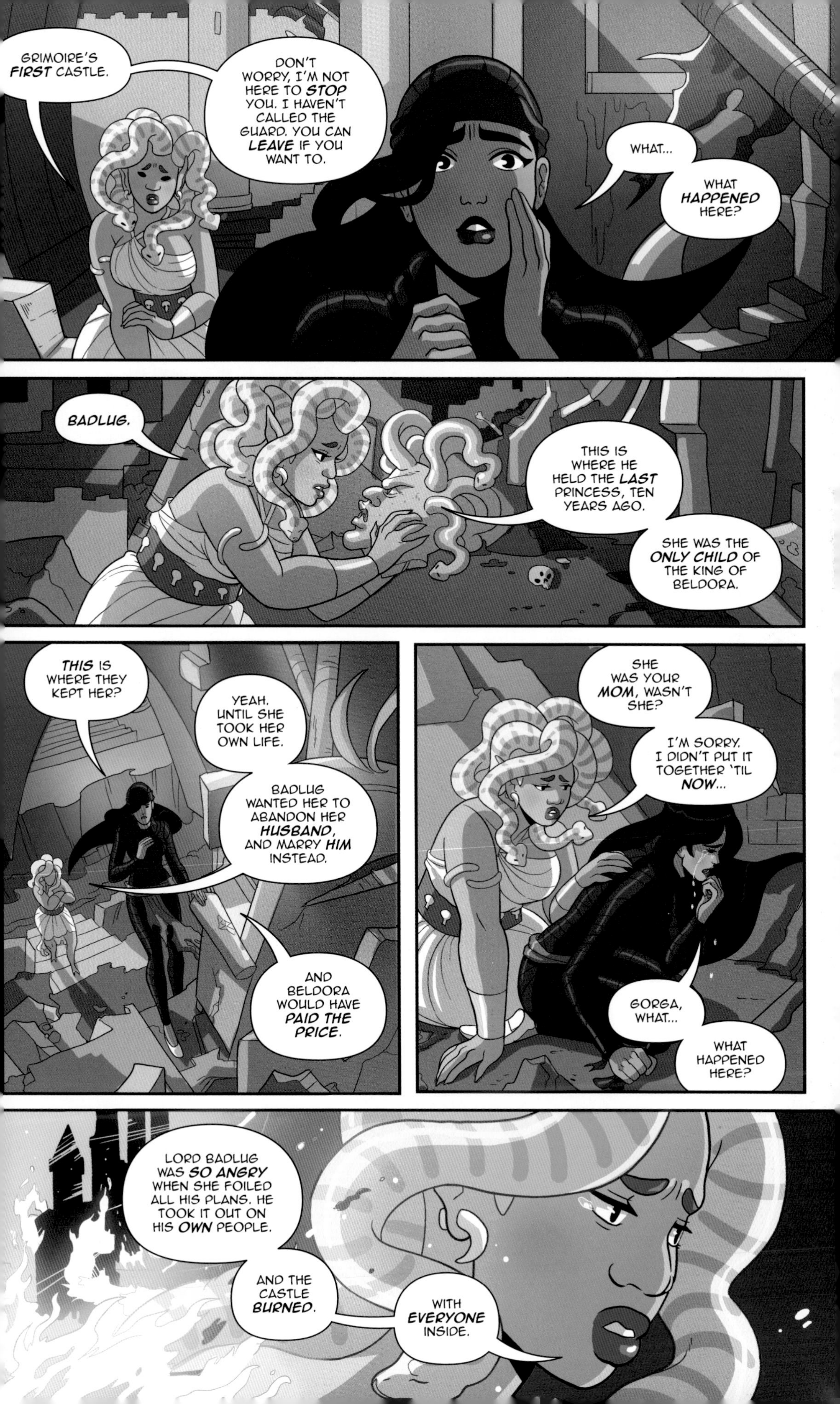
GRIMOIRE'S FIRST CASTLE.
DON'T WORRY, I'M NOT HERE TO STOP YOU. I HAVEN'T CALLED THE GUARD. YOU CAN LEAVE IF YOU WANT TO.
WHAT...
WHAT HAPPENED HERE?
BADLUG.
THIS IS WHERE HE HELD THE LAST PRINCESS, TEN YEARS AGO.
SHE WAS THE ONLY CHILD OF THE KING OF BELDORA.
THIS IS WHERE THEY KEPT HER?
YEAH. UNTIL SHE TOOK HER OWN LIFE.
BADLUG WANTED HER TO ABANDON HER HUSBAND, AND MARRY HIM INSTEAD.
AND BELDORA WOULD HAVE PAID THE PRICE.
SHE WAS YOUR MOM, WASN'T SHE?
I'M SORRY. I DIDN'T PUT IT TOGETHER 'TIL NOW...
GORGA, WHAT...
WHAT HAPPENED HERE?
LORD BADLUG WAS SO ANGRY WHEN SHE FOILED ALL HIS PLANS. HE TOOK IT OUT ON HIS OWN PEOPLE.
AND THE CASTLE BURNED.
WITH EVERYONE INSIDE.

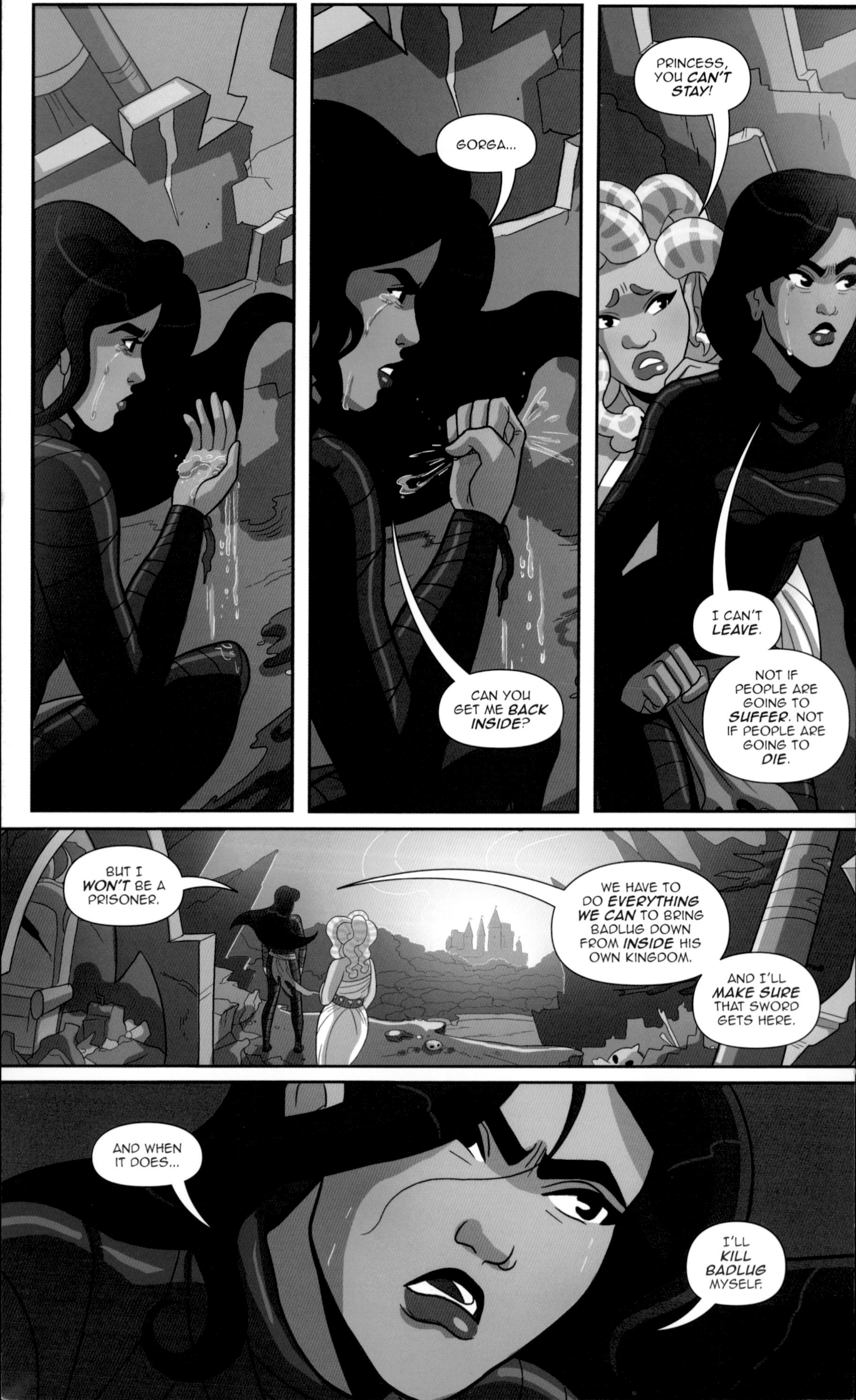
GORGA...
CAN YOU GET ME BACK INSIDE?
PRINCESS, YOU CAN'T STAY!
I CAN'T LEAVE.
NOT IF PEOPLE ARE GOING TO SUFFER. NOT IF PEOPLE ARE GOING TO DIE.
BUT I WON'T BE A PRISONER.
WE HAVE TO DO EVERYTHING WE CAN TO BRING BADLUG DOWN FROM INSIDE HIS OWN KINGDOM.
AND I'LL MAKE SURE THAT SWORD GETS HERE.
AND WHEN IT DOES...
I'LL KILL BADLUG MYSELF.

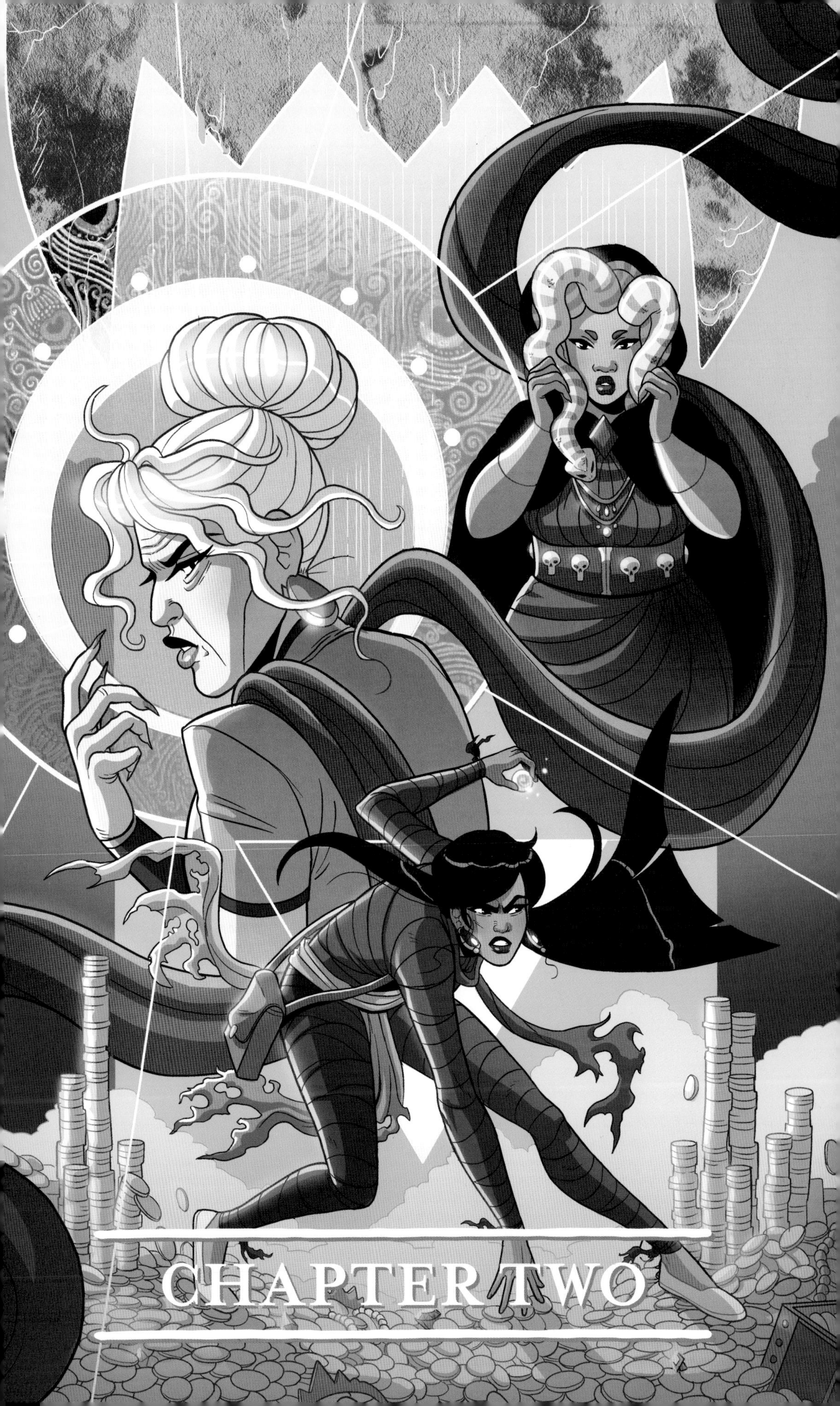

CHAPTER TWO

The Vale of Rattro.
The lair of the Verminotaur.

DON'T YOU GET IT? *I'M* THE *HERO!*

FFFFSSSSS!

I'LL *SLAY* THE VILLAIN, *SAVE* THE KINGDOM, *RESCUE* THE PRINCESS.

SWSHHH!

YOU DON'T STAND A *CHANCE!*

NOT AGAINST PETE THE *DASHING*, PRINCE OF AVENTURA, SECOND-IN-LINE TO THE—

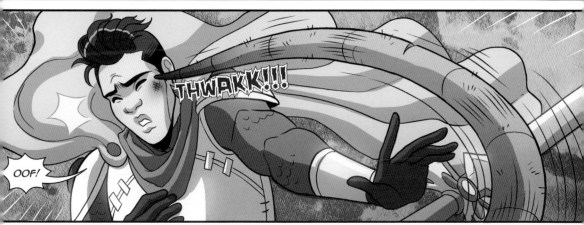

THWAKK!!!

OOF!

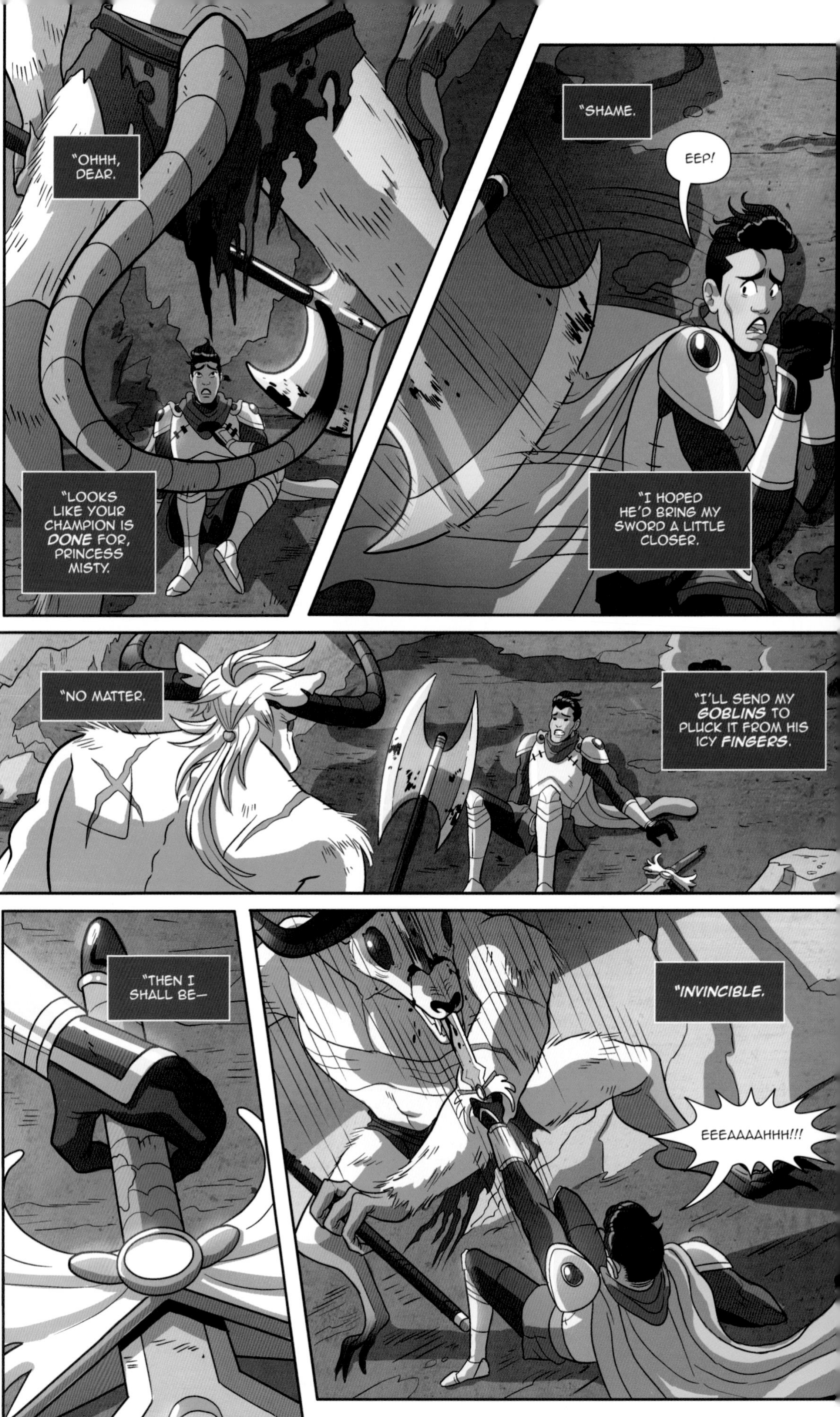

"OHHH, DEAR.
"LOOKS LIKE YOUR CHAMPION IS *DONE* FOR, PRINCESS MISTY.
"SHAME.
EEP!
"I HOPED HE'D BRING MY SWORD A LITTLE CLOSER.
"NO MATTER.
"I'LL SEND MY *GOBLINS* TO PLUCK IT FROM HIS ICY *FINGERS*.
"THEN I SHALL BE—
"*INVINCIBLE*.
EEEAAAAHHH!!!

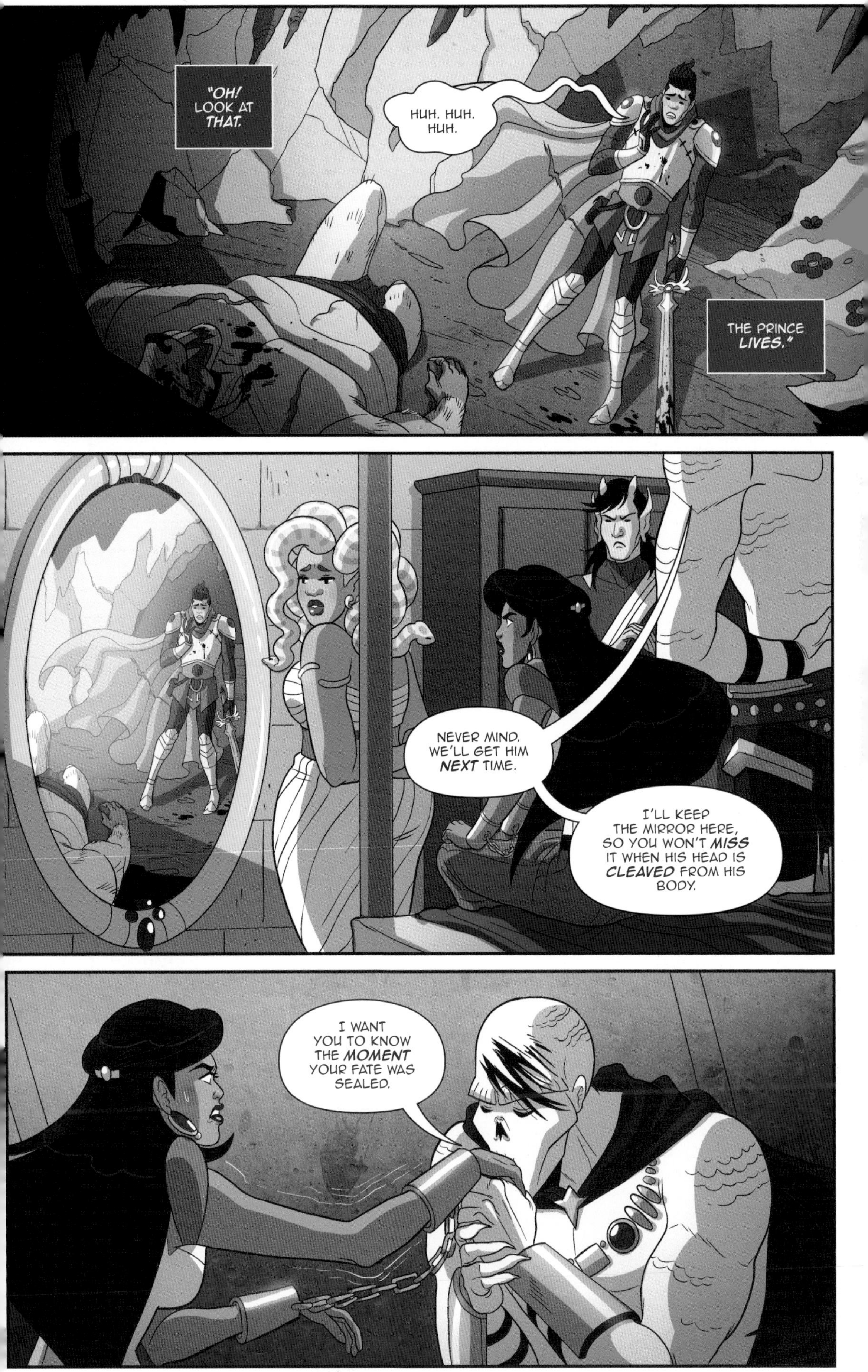
"OH!
LOOK AT
THAT.
HUH. HUH.
HUH.
THE PRINCE
LIVES."
NEVER MIND.
WE'LL GET HIM
NEXT TIME.
I'LL KEEP
THE MIRROR HERE,
SO YOU WON'T MISS
IT WHEN HIS HEAD IS
CLEAVED FROM HIS
BODY.
I WANT
YOU TO KNOW
THE MOMENT
YOUR FATE WAS
SEALED.

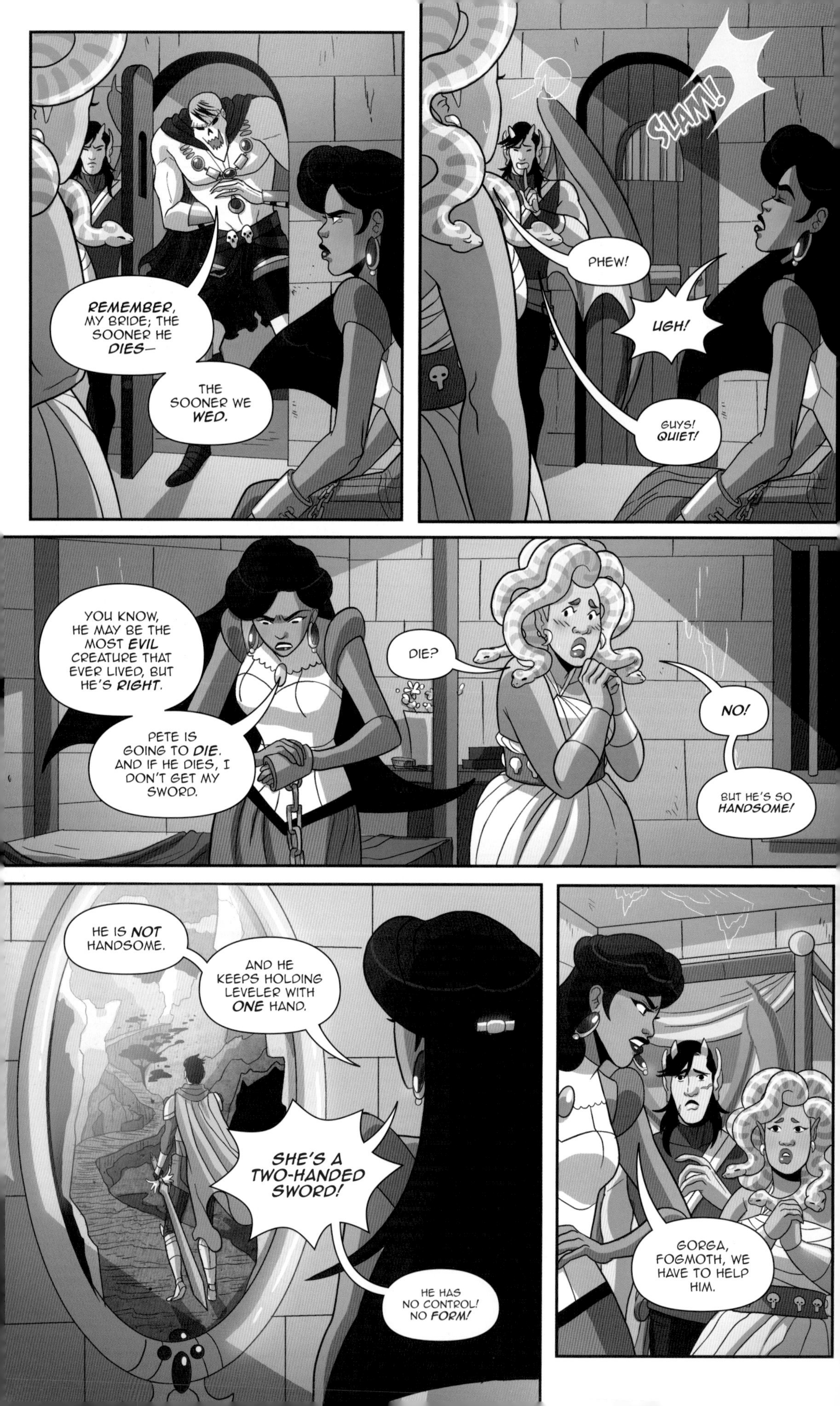
REMEMBER, MY BRIDE; THE SOONER HE DIES—
THE SOONER WE WED.
SLAM!
PHEW!
UGH!
GUYS! QUIET!
YOU KNOW, HE MAY BE THE MOST EVIL CREATURE THAT EVER LIVED, BUT HE'S RIGHT.
PETE IS GOING TO DIE. AND IF HE DIES, I DON'T GET MY SWORD.
DIE?
NO!
BUT HE'S SO HANDSOME!
HE IS NOT HANDSOME.
AND HE KEEPS HOLDING LEVELER WITH ONE HAND.
SHE'S A TWO-HANDED SWORD!
HE HAS NO CONTROL! NO FORM!
GORGA, FOGMOTH, WE HAVE TO HELP HIM.

HOW MANY MONSTERS DOES PETE HAVE TO *FIGHT* TO GET TO GRIMOIRE? CAN WE GO OUT AND *KILL* A FEW OF THEM?

WHAT? YOU CAN'T JUST—

HERE. I BROUGHT YOU SOMETHING.

THESE ARE ALL THE MONSTERS HE HAS TO DEFEAT. THEY'RE IN ORDER OF *TERROR*, SO THE VERMINOTAUR WAS ONE OF THE *EASY* ONES.

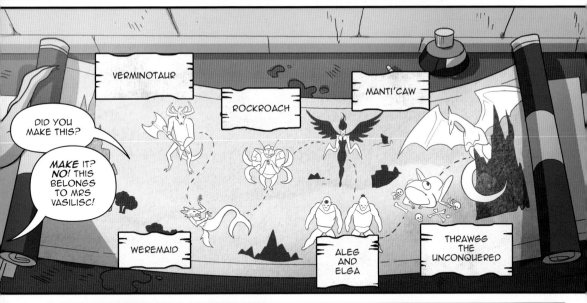

VERMINOTAUR

ROCKROACH

MANTI'CAW

DID YOU MAKE THIS?

MAKE IT? *NO!* THIS BELONGS TO MRS VASILISC!

WEREMAID

ALEG AND ELGA

THRAWGG THE UNCONQUERED

MRS VASILISC WON THE CONTRACT FOR THE MONSTERS ON THE BELDORA ROAD. THIS WAS PART OF HER PITCH.

CONTRACT?

THE MONSTERS HAVE A *BOSS?*

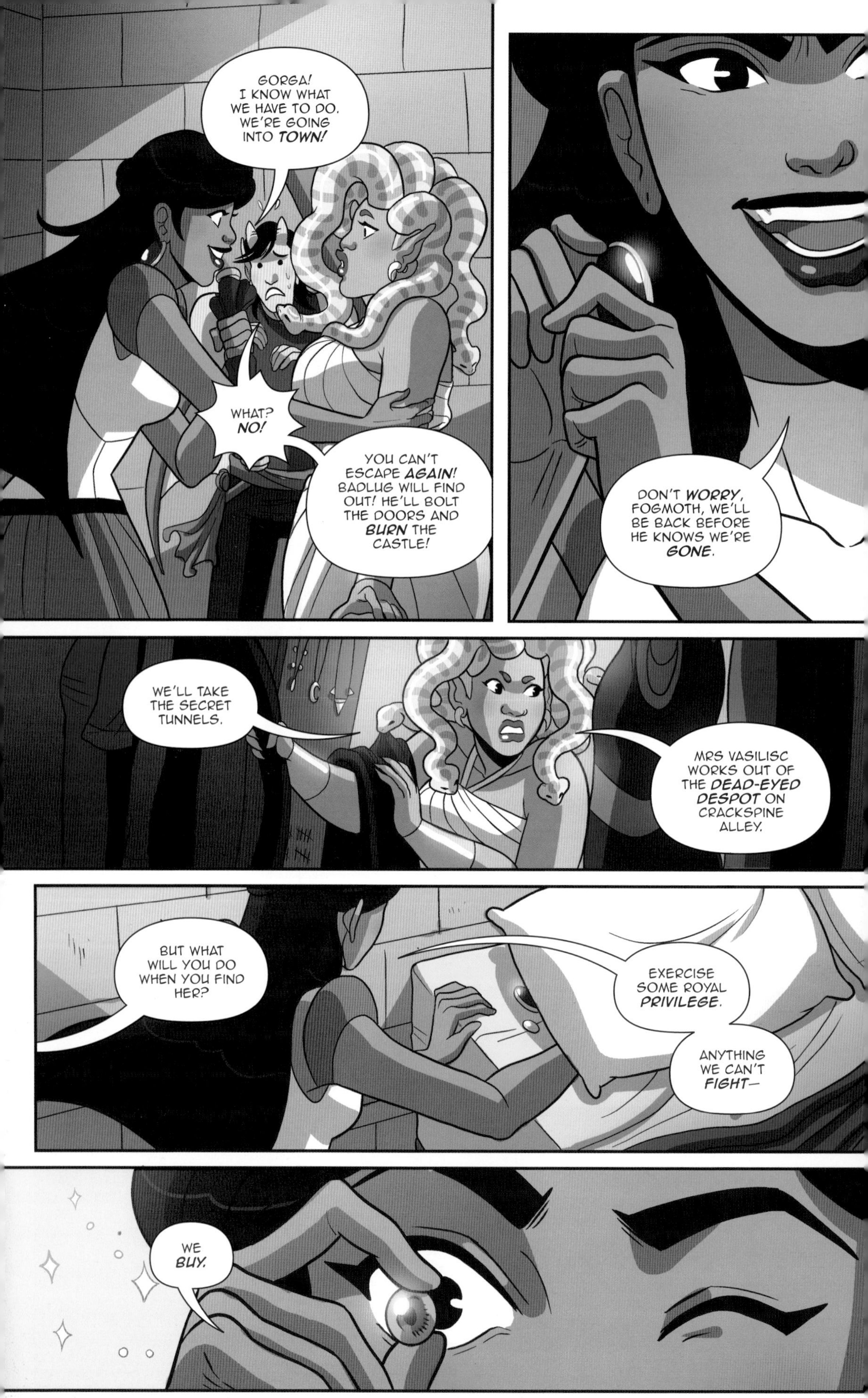
GORGA! I KNOW WHAT WE HAVE TO DO. WE'RE GOING INTO TOWN!
WHAT? NO!
YOU CAN'T ESCAPE AGAIN! BADLUG WILL FIND OUT! HE'LL BOLT THE DOORS AND BURN THE CASTLE!
DON'T WORRY, FOGMOTH, WE'LL BE BACK BEFORE HE KNOWS WE'RE GONE.
WE'LL TAKE THE SECRET TUNNELS.
MRS VASILISC WORKS OUT OF THE DEAD-EYED DESPOT ON CRACKSPINE ALLEY.
BUT WHAT WILL YOU DO WHEN YOU FIND HER?
EXERCISE SOME ROYAL PRIVILEGE.
ANYTHING WE CAN'T FIGHT—
WE BUY.

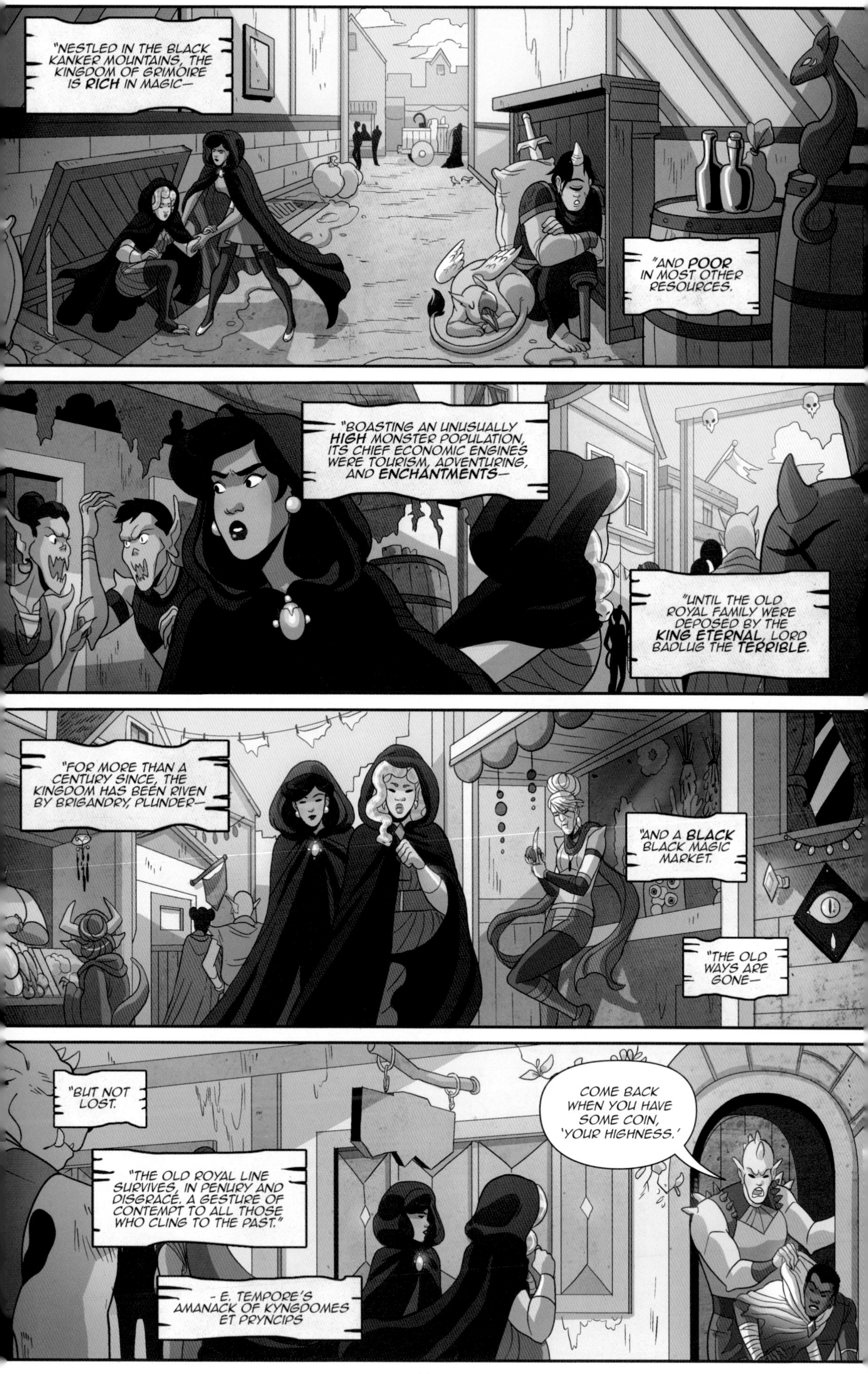
"NESTLED IN THE BLACK KANKER MOUNTAINS, THE KINGDOM OF GRIMOIRE IS RICH IN MAGIC—
"AND POOR IN MOST OTHER RESOURCES.
"BOASTING AN UNUSUALLY HIGH MONSTER POPULATION, ITS CHIEF ECONOMIC ENGINES WERE TOURISM, ADVENTURING, AND ENCHANTMENTS—
"UNTIL THE OLD ROYAL FAMILY WERE DEPOSED BY THE KING ETERNAL, LORD BADLUG THE TERRIBLE.
"FOR MORE THAN A CENTURY SINCE, THE KINGDOM HAS BEEN RIVEN BY BRIGANDRY, PLUNDER—
"AND A BLACK BLACK MAGIC MARKET.
"THE OLD WAYS ARE GONE—
"BUT NOT LOST.
"THE OLD ROYAL LINE SURVIVES, IN PENURY AND DISGRACE. A GESTURE OF CONTEMPT TO ALL THOSE WHO CLING TO THE PAST."
- E. TEMPORE'S AMANACK OF KYNGDOMES ET PRYNCIPS
COME BACK WHEN YOU HAVE SOME COIN, 'YOUR HIGHNESS.'

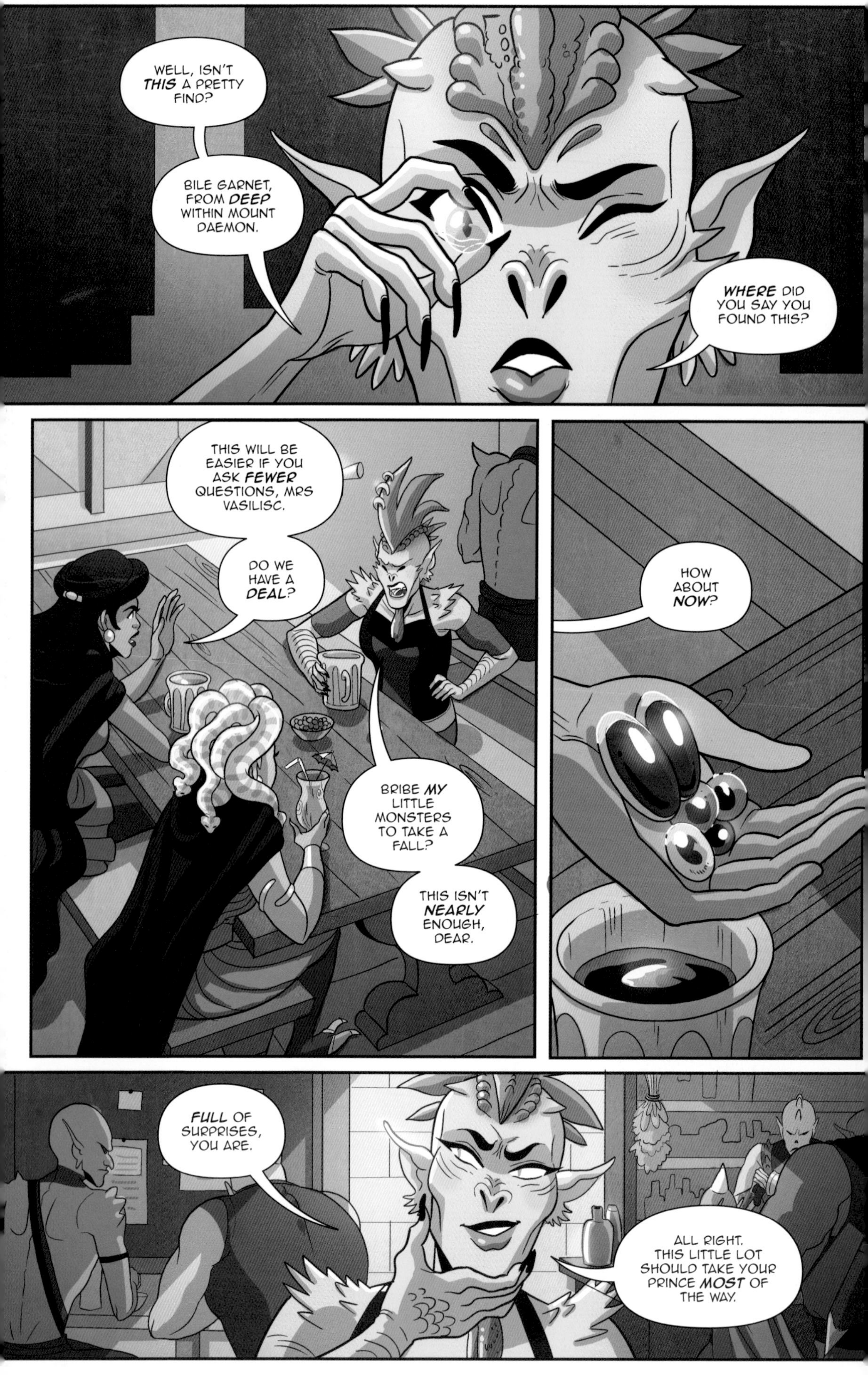
WELL, ISN'T THIS A PRETTY FIND?
BILE GARNET, FROM DEEP WITHIN MOUNT DAEMON.
WHERE DID YOU SAY YOU FOUND THIS?
THIS WILL BE EASIER IF YOU ASK FEWER QUESTIONS, MRS VASILISC.
DO WE HAVE A DEAL?
BRIBE MY LITTLE MONSTERS TO TAKE A FALL?
THIS ISN'T NEARLY ENOUGH, DEAR.
HOW ABOUT NOW?
FULL OF SURPRISES, YOU ARE.
ALL RIGHT. THIS LITTLE LOT SHOULD TAKE YOUR PRINCE MOST OF THE WAY.

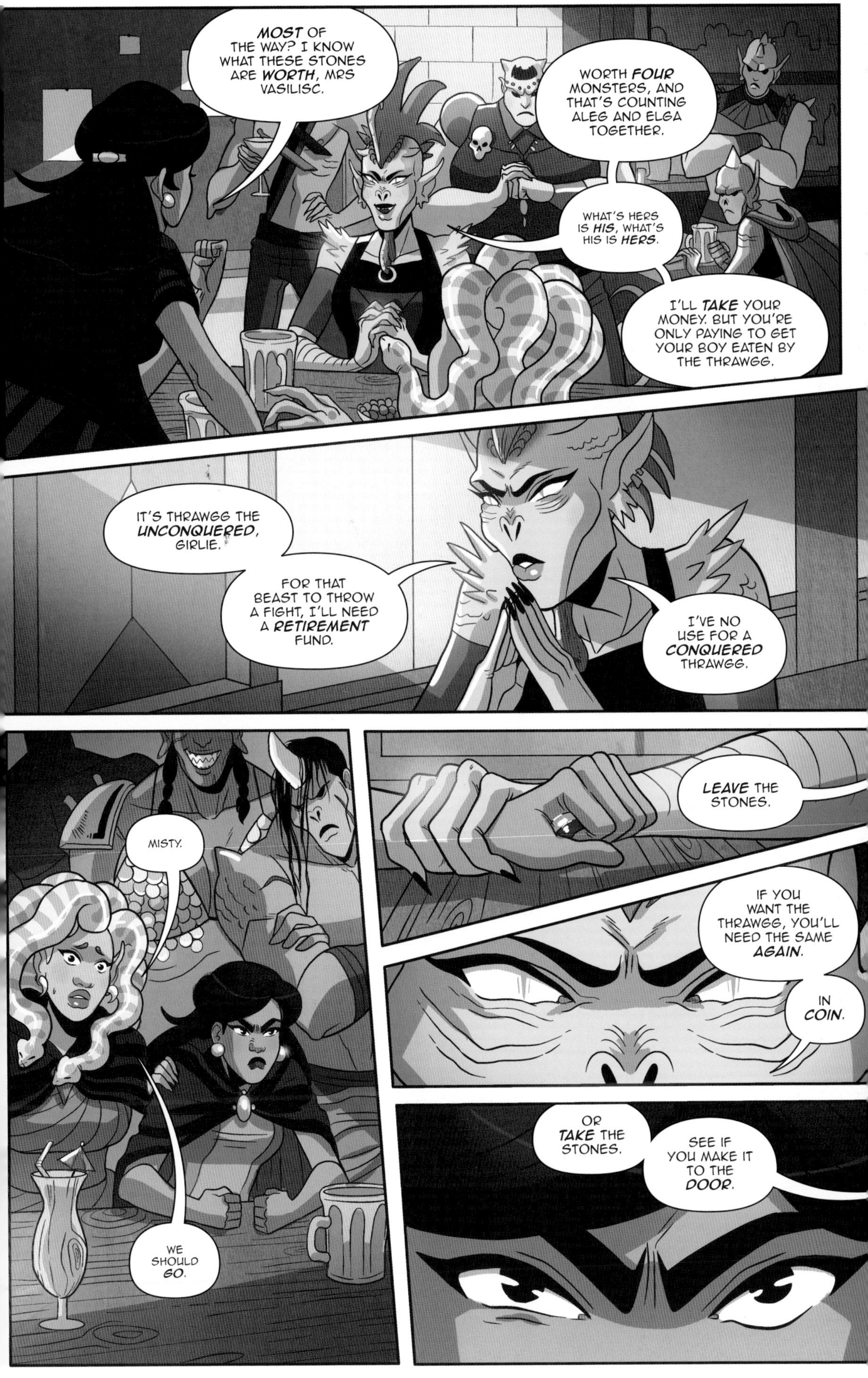

MOST OF THE WAY? I KNOW WHAT THESE STONES ARE WORTH, MRS VASILISC.
WORTH FOUR MONSTERS, AND THAT'S COUNTING ALEG AND ELGA TOGETHER.
WHAT'S HERS IS HIS, WHAT'S HIS IS HERS.
I'LL TAKE YOUR MONEY. BUT YOU'RE ONLY PAYING TO GET YOUR BOY EATEN BY THE THRAWGG.
IT'S THRAWGG THE UNCONQUERED, GIRLIE.
FOR THAT BEAST TO THROW A FIGHT, I'LL NEED A RETIREMENT FUND.
I'VE NO USE FOR A CONQUERED THRAWGG.
MISTY.
WE SHOULD GO.
LEAVE THE STONES.
IF YOU WANT THE THRAWGG, YOU'LL NEED THE SAME AGAIN.
IN COIN.
OR TAKE THE STONES.
SEE IF YOU MAKE IT TO THE DOOR.

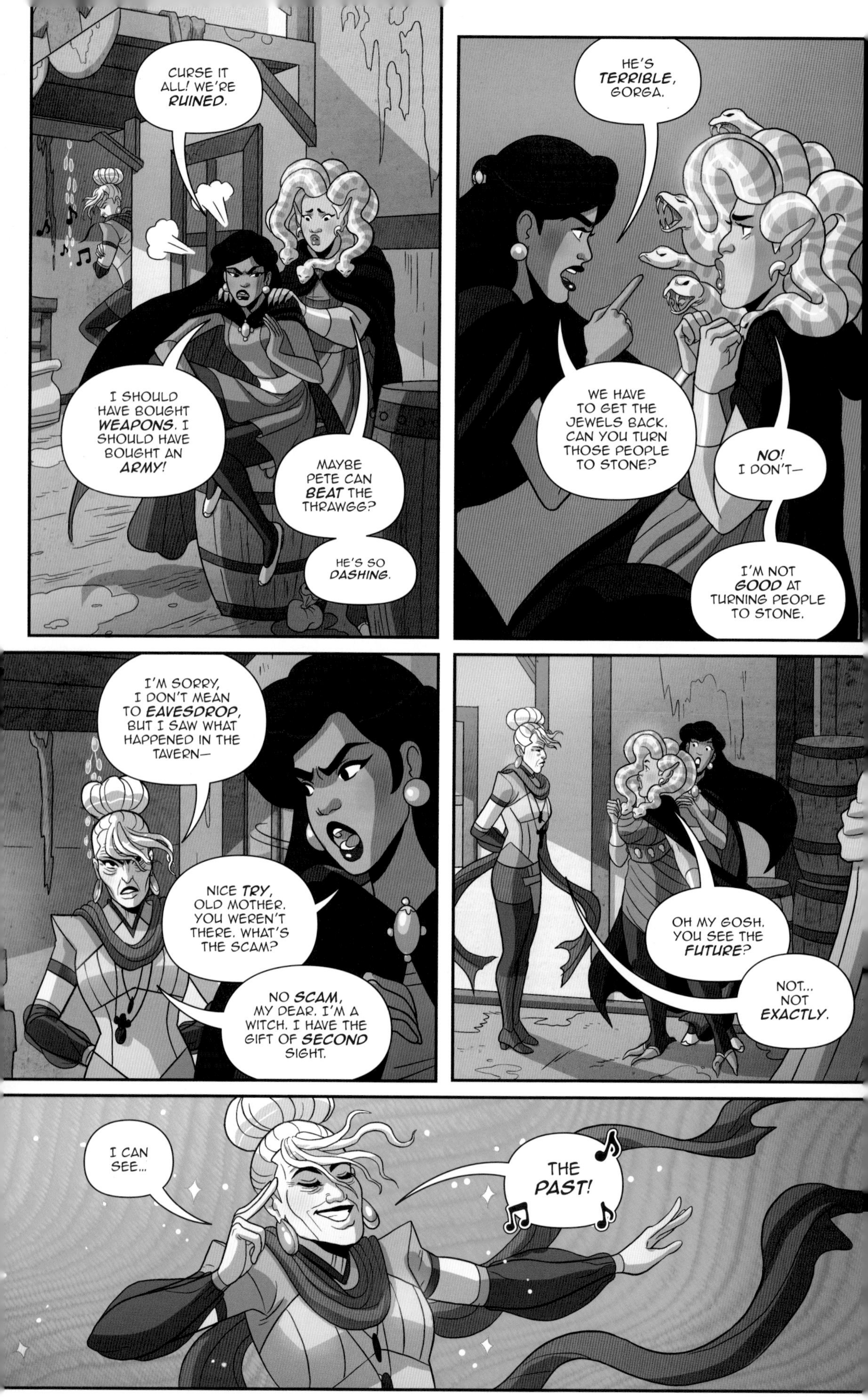

CURSE IT ALL! WE'RE RUINED.
I SHOULD HAVE BOUGHT WEAPONS. I SHOULD HAVE BOUGHT AN ARMY!
MAYBE PETE CAN BEAT THE THRAWGG?
HE'S SO DASHING.
HE'S TERRIBLE, GORGA.
WE HAVE TO GET THE JEWELS BACK. CAN YOU TURN THOSE PEOPLE TO STONE?
NO! I DON'T—
I'M NOT GOOD AT TURNING PEOPLE TO STONE.
I'M SORRY, I DON'T MEAN TO EAVESDROP, BUT I SAW WHAT HAPPENED IN THE TAVERN—
NICE TRY, OLD MOTHER. YOU WEREN'T THERE. WHAT'S THE SCAM?
NO SCAM, MY DEAR. I'M A WITCH. I HAVE THE GIFT OF SECOND SIGHT.
OH MY GOSH, YOU SEE THE FUTURE?
NOT... NOT EXACTLY.
I CAN SEE...
THE PAST!

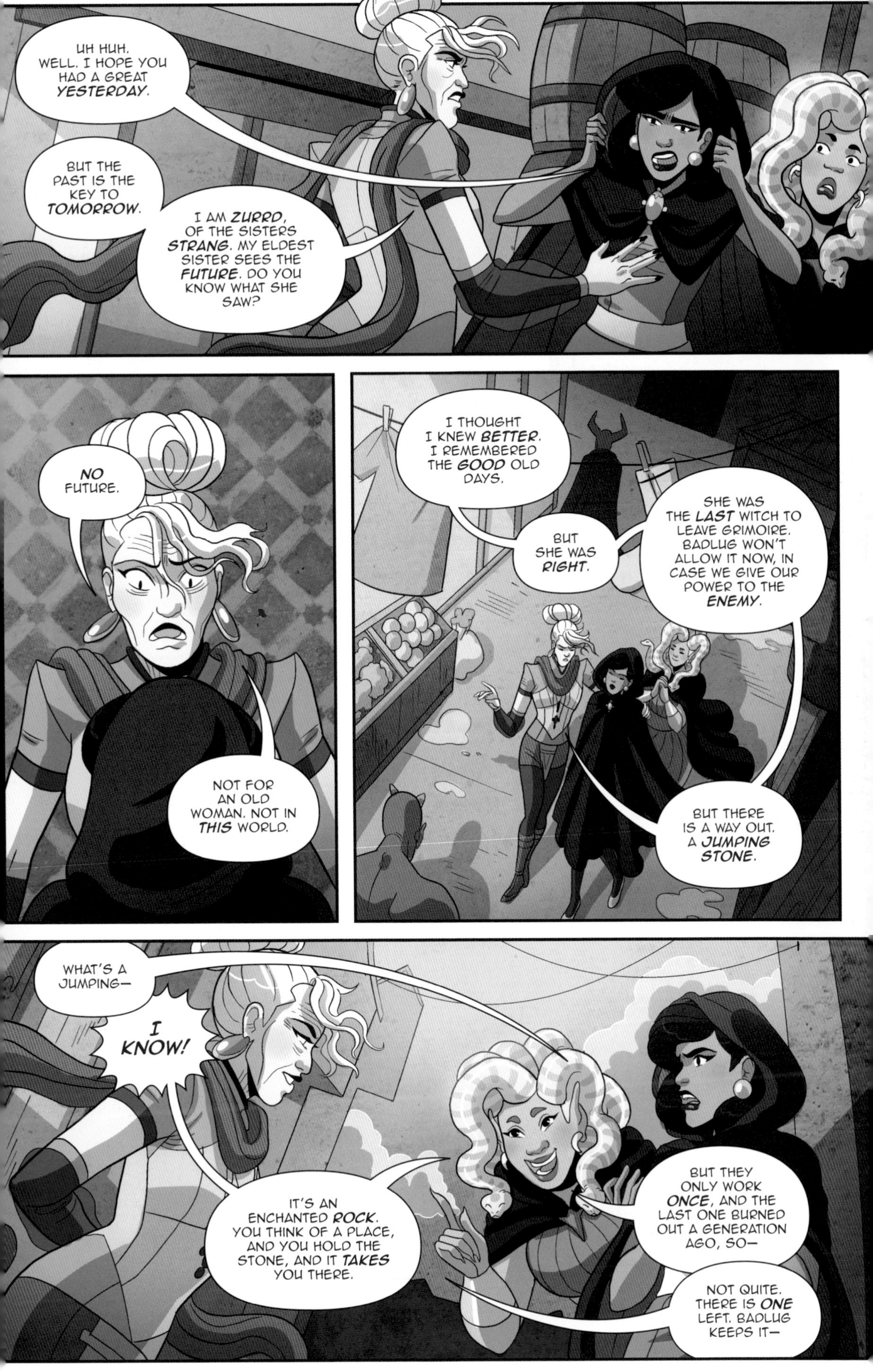
UH HUH. WELL. I HOPE YOU HAD A GREAT YESTERDAY.
BUT THE PAST IS THE KEY TO TOMORROW.
I AM ZURRD, OF THE SISTERS STRANG. MY ELDEST SISTER SEES THE FUTURE. DO YOU KNOW WHAT SHE SAW?
NO FUTURE.
NOT FOR AN OLD WOMAN. NOT IN THIS WORLD.
I THOUGHT I KNEW BETTER. I REMEMBERED THE GOOD OLD DAYS.
BUT SHE WAS RIGHT.
SHE WAS THE LAST WITCH TO LEAVE GRIMOIRE. BADLUG WON'T ALLOW IT NOW, IN CASE WE GIVE OUR POWER TO THE ENEMY.
BUT THERE IS A WAY OUT. A JUMPING STONE.
WHAT'S A JUMPING—
I KNOW!
IT'S AN ENCHANTED ROCK. YOU THINK OF A PLACE, AND YOU HOLD THE STONE, AND IT TAKES YOU THERE.
BUT THEY ONLY WORK ONCE, AND THE LAST ONE BURNED OUT A GENERATION AGO, SO—
NOT QUITE. THERE IS ONE LEFT. BADLUG KEEPS IT—

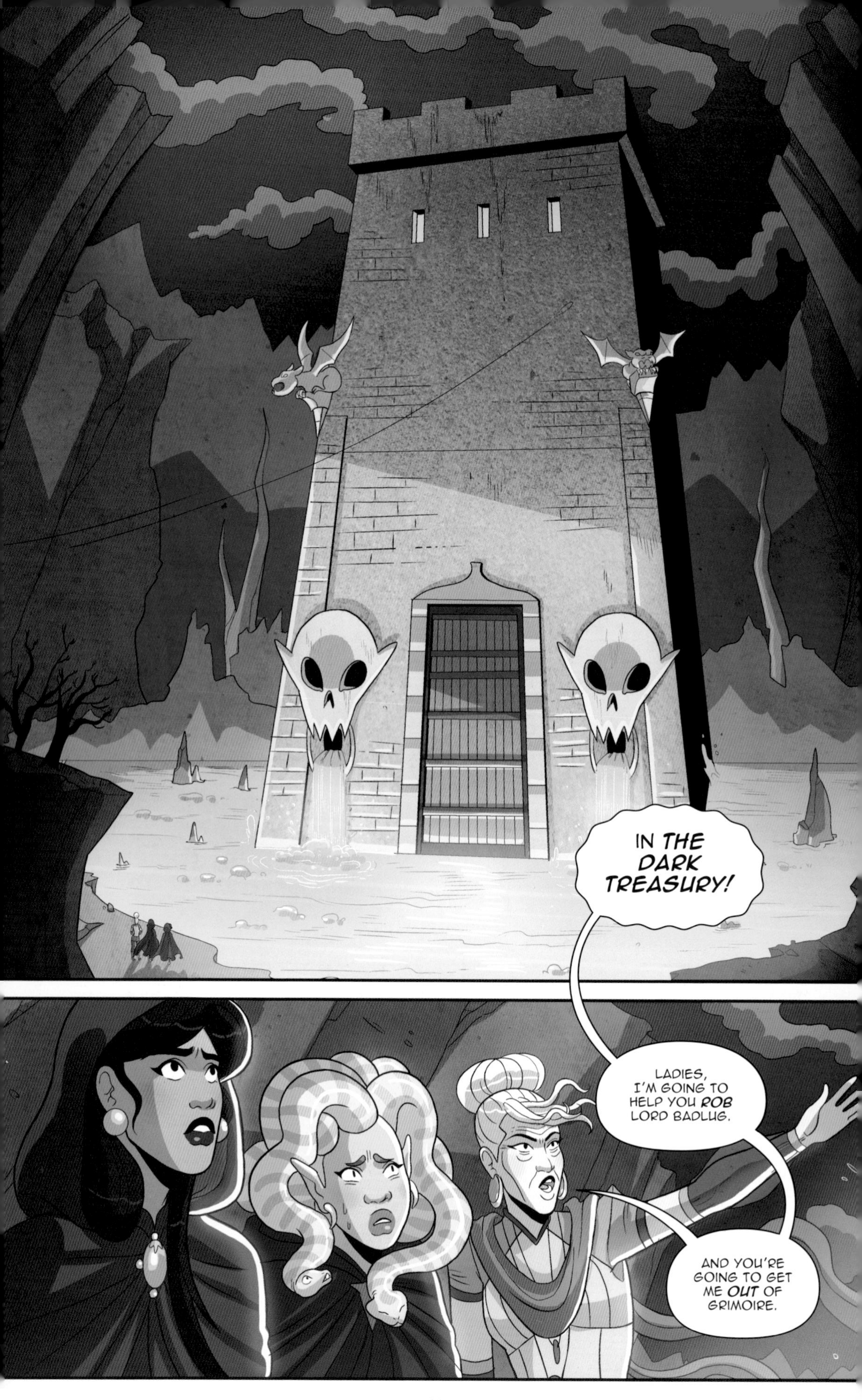
IN THE DARK TREASURY!
LADIES, I'M GOING TO HELP YOU ROB LORD BADLUG.
AND YOU'RE GOING TO GET ME OUT OF GRIMOIRE.

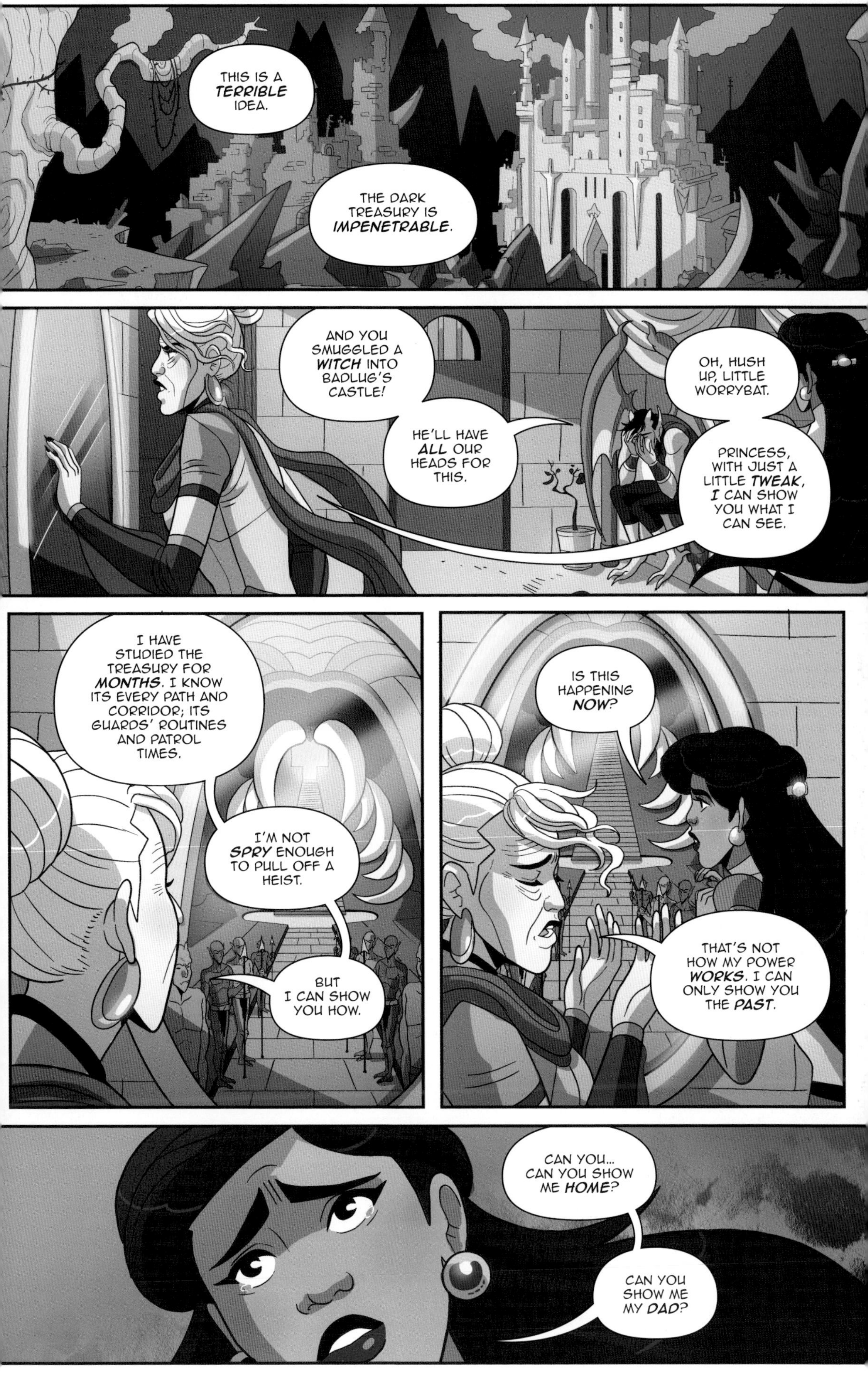
THIS IS A TERRIBLE IDEA.
THE DARK TREASURY IS IMPENETRABLE.
AND YOU SMUGGLED A WITCH INTO BADLUG'S CASTLE!
HE'LL HAVE ALL OUR HEADS FOR THIS.
OH, HUSH UP, LITTLE WORRYBAT.
PRINCESS, WITH JUST A LITTLE TWEAK, I CAN SHOW YOU WHAT I CAN SEE.
I HAVE STUDIED THE TREASURY FOR MONTHS. I KNOW ITS EVERY PATH AND CORRIDOR; ITS GUARDS' ROUTINES AND PATROL TIMES.
I'M NOT SPRY ENOUGH TO PULL OFF A HEIST.
BUT I CAN SHOW YOU HOW.
IS THIS HAPPENING NOW?
THAT'S NOT HOW MY POWER WORKS. I CAN ONLY SHOW YOU THE PAST.
CAN YOU... CAN YOU SHOW ME HOME?
CAN YOU SHOW ME MY DAD?

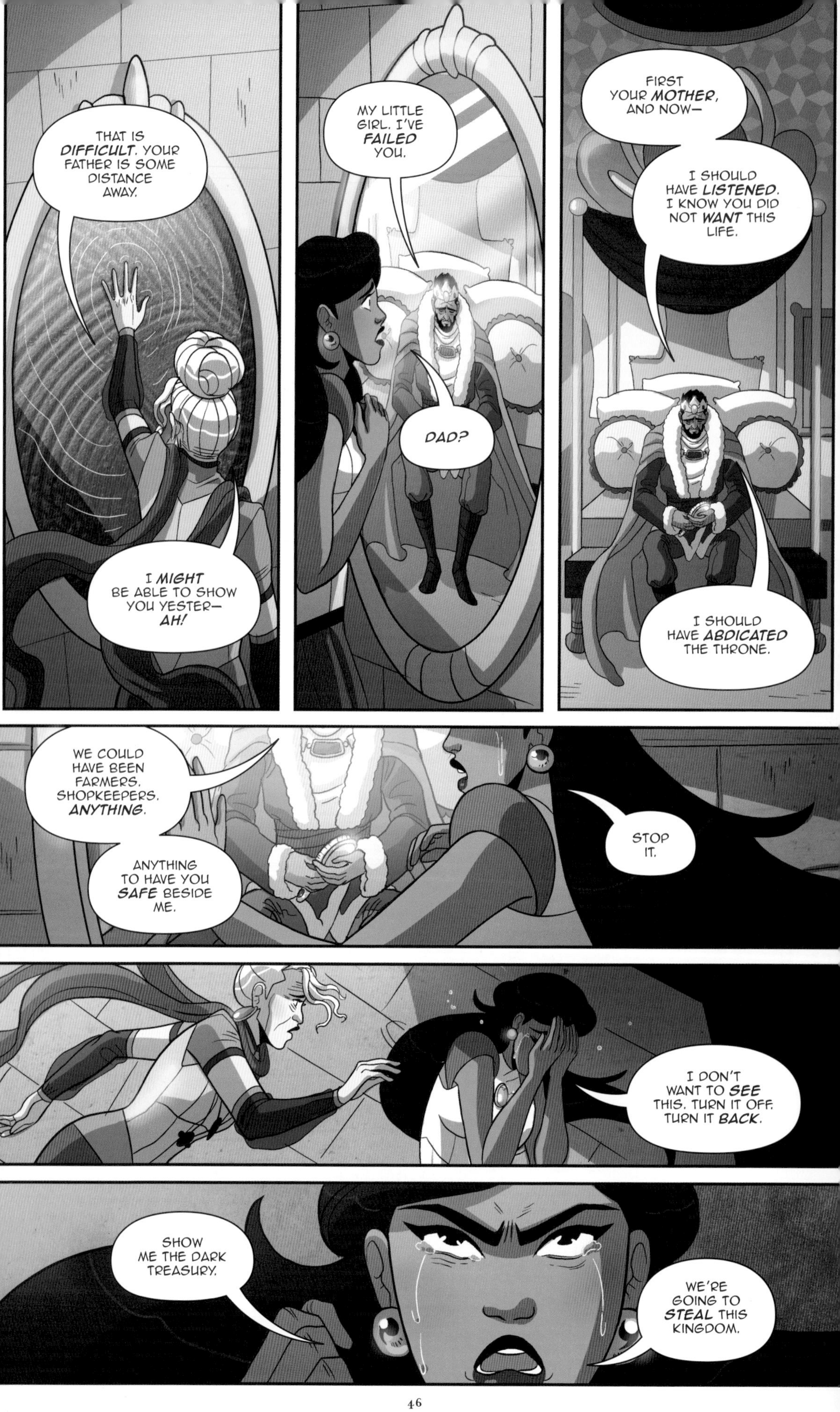
THAT IS DIFFICULT. YOUR FATHER IS SOME DISTANCE AWAY.
I MIGHT BE ABLE TO SHOW YOU YESTER— AH!
MY LITTLE GIRL. I'VE FAILED YOU.
DAD?
FIRST YOUR MOTHER, AND NOW—
I SHOULD HAVE LISTENED. I KNOW YOU DID NOT WANT THIS LIFE.
I SHOULD HAVE ABDICATED THE THRONE.
WE COULD HAVE BEEN FARMERS. SHOPKEEPERS. ANYTHING.
ANYTHING TO HAVE YOU SAFE BESIDE ME.
STOP IT.
I DON'T WANT TO SEE THIS. TURN IT OFF. TURN IT BACK.
SHOW ME THE DARK TREASURY.
WE'RE GOING TO STEAL THIS KINGDOM.

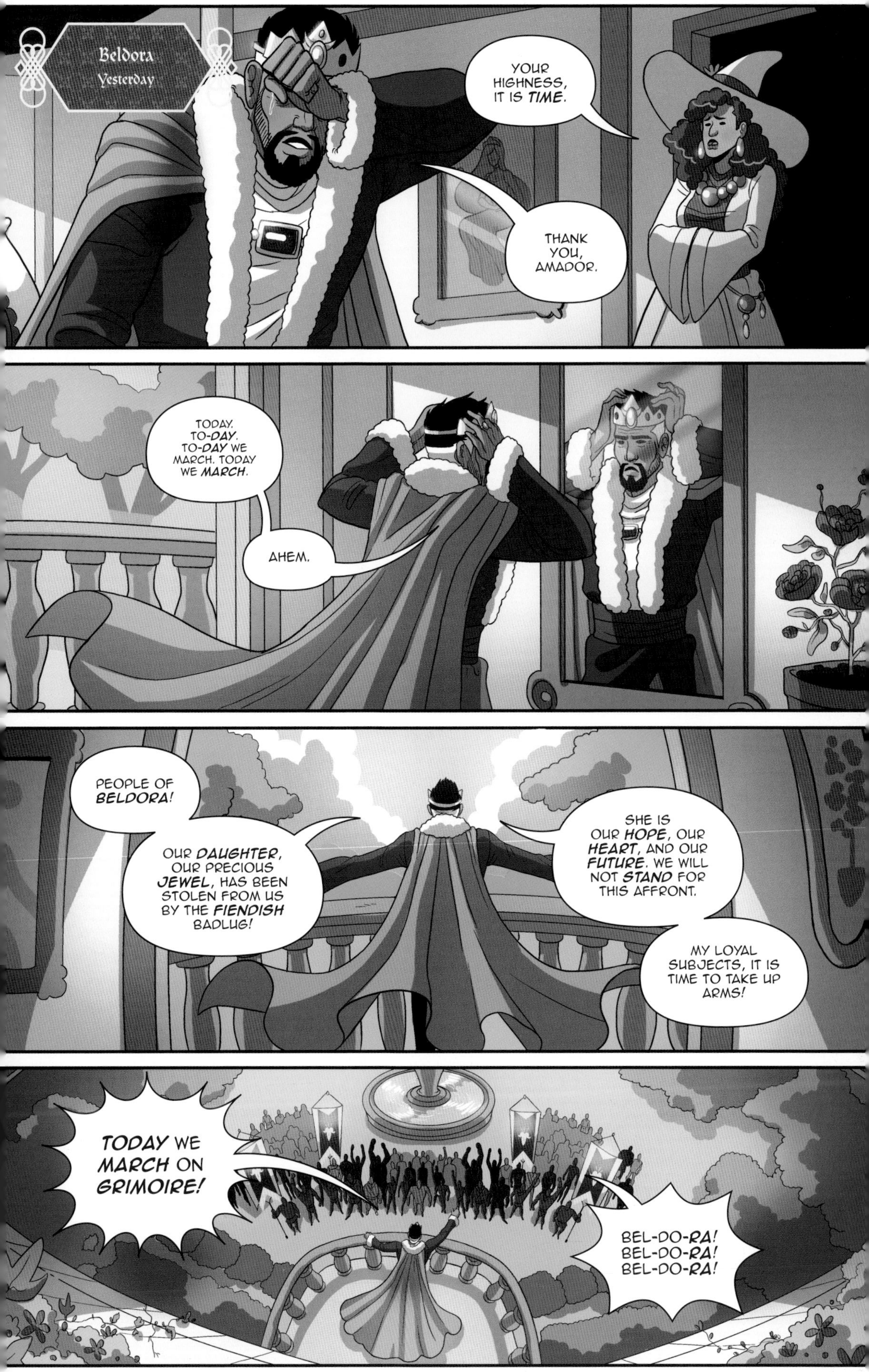
Beldora
Yesterday
YOUR HIGHNESS, IT IS TIME.
THANK YOU, AMADOR.
TODAY. TO-DAY. TO-DAY WE MARCH. TODAY WE MARCH.
AHEM.
PEOPLE OF BELDORA!
OUR DAUGHTER, OUR PRECIOUS JEWEL, HAS BEEN STOLEN FROM US BY THE FIENDISH BADLUG!
SHE IS OUR HOPE, OUR HEART, AND OUR FUTURE. WE WILL NOT STAND FOR THIS AFFRONT.
MY LOYAL SUBJECTS, IT IS TIME TO TAKE UP ARMS!
TODAY WE MARCH ON GRIMOIRE!
BEL-DO-RA! BEL-DO-RA! BEL-DO-RA!

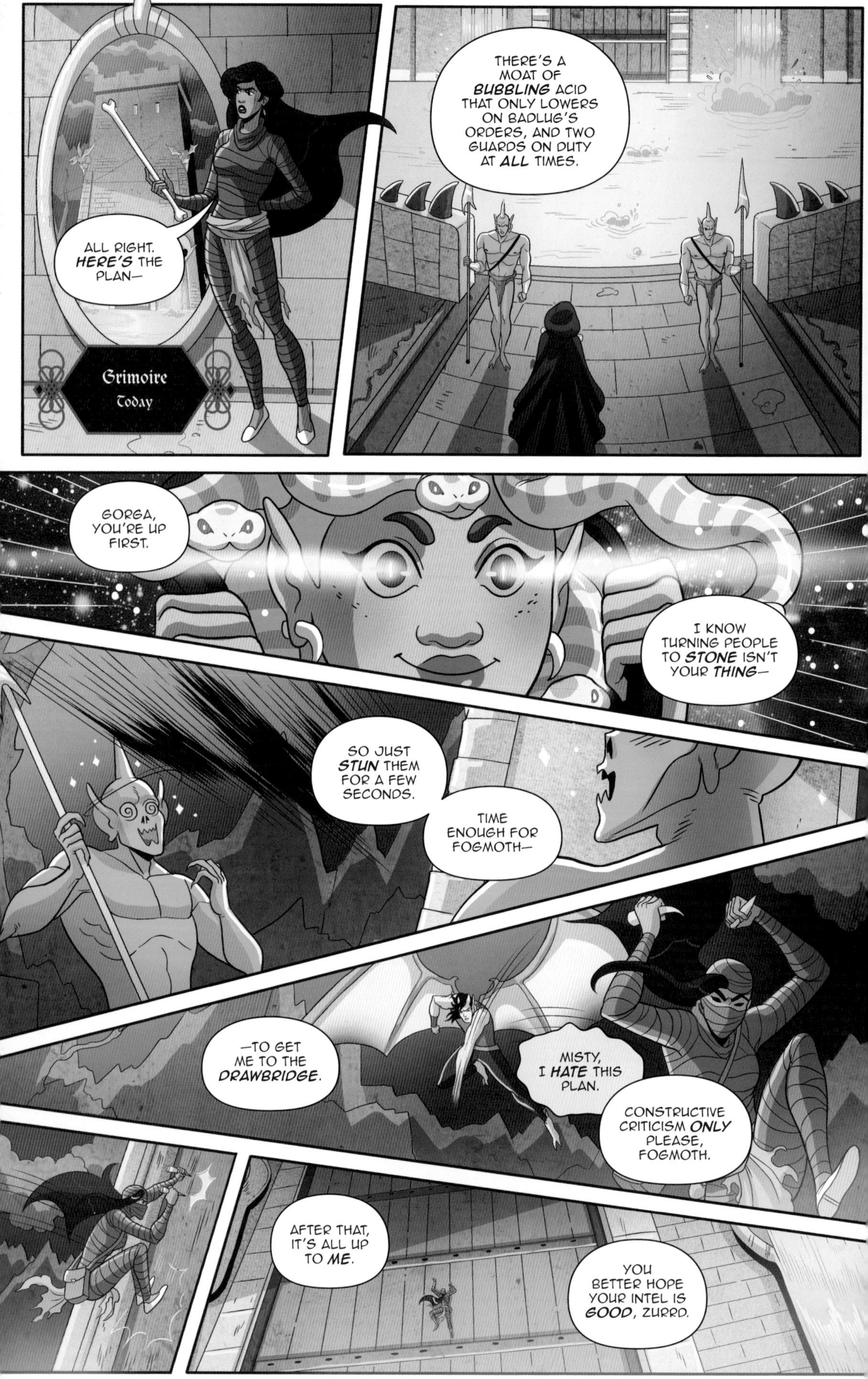
Grimoire
Today
ALL RIGHT. HERE'S THE PLAN—
THERE'S A MOAT OF BUBBLING ACID THAT ONLY LOWERS ON BADLUG'S ORDERS, AND TWO GUARDS ON DUTY AT ALL TIMES.
GORGA, YOU'RE UP FIRST.
I KNOW TURNING PEOPLE TO STONE ISN'T YOUR THING—
SO JUST STUN THEM FOR A FEW SECONDS.
TIME ENOUGH FOR FOGMOTH—
—TO GET ME TO THE DRAWBRIDGE.
MISTY, I HATE THIS PLAN.
CONSTRUCTIVE CRITICISM ONLY PLEASE, FOGMOTH.
AFTER THAT, IT'S ALL UP TO ME.
YOU BETTER HOPE YOUR INTEL IS GOOD, ZURRD.

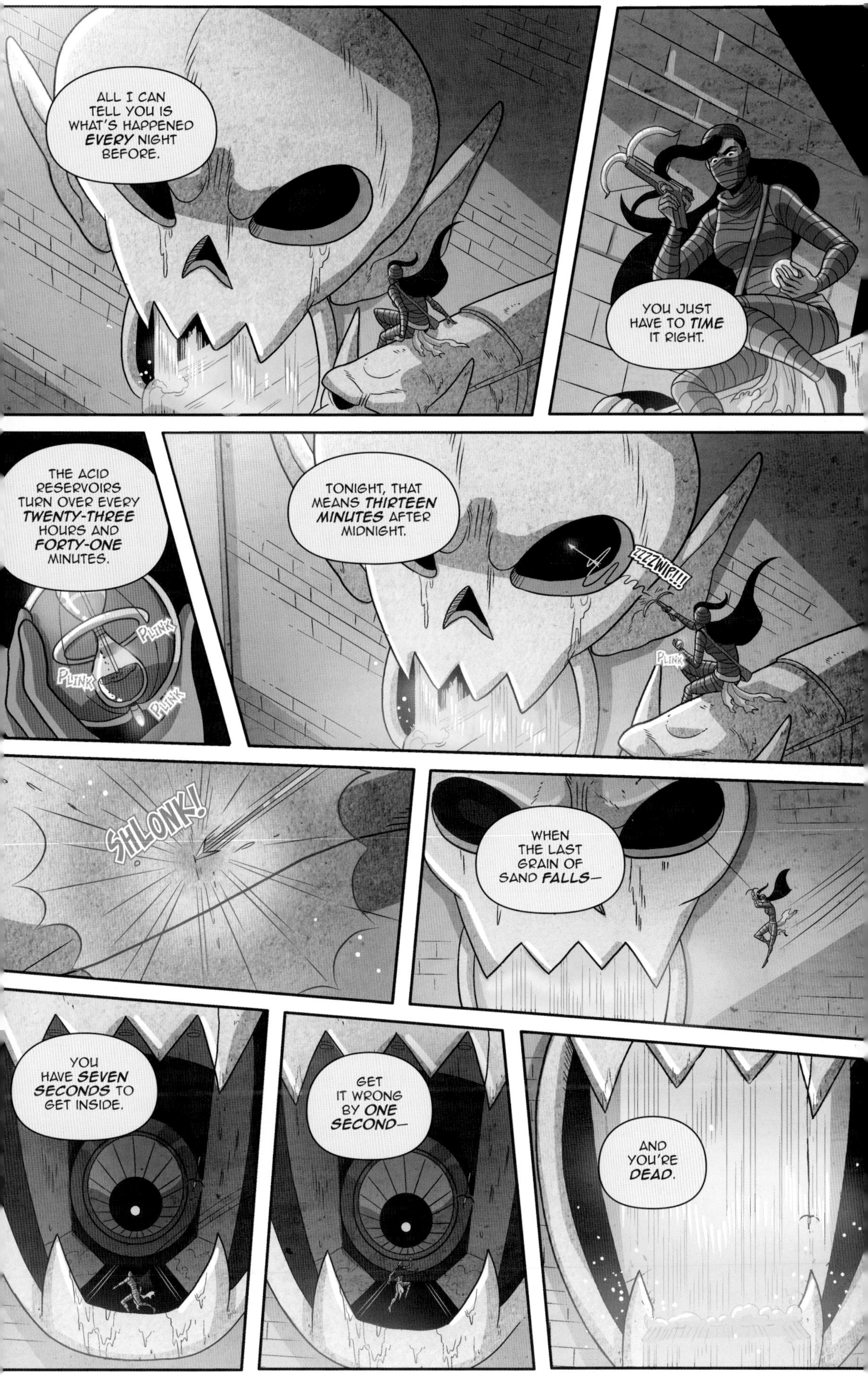
ALL I CAN TELL YOU IS WHAT'S HAPPENED EVERY NIGHT BEFORE.
YOU JUST HAVE TO TIME IT RIGHT.
THE ACID RESERVOIRS TURN OVER EVERY TWENTY-THREE HOURS AND FORTY-ONE MINUTES.
PLINK
PLINK
PLINK
TONIGHT, THAT MEANS THIRTEEN MINUTES AFTER MIDNIGHT.
ZZZZWIP!!!
PLINK
SHLONK!
WHEN THE LAST GRAIN OF SAND FALLS—
YOU HAVE SEVEN SECONDS TO GET INSIDE.
GET IT WRONG BY ONE SECOND—
AND YOU'RE DEAD.

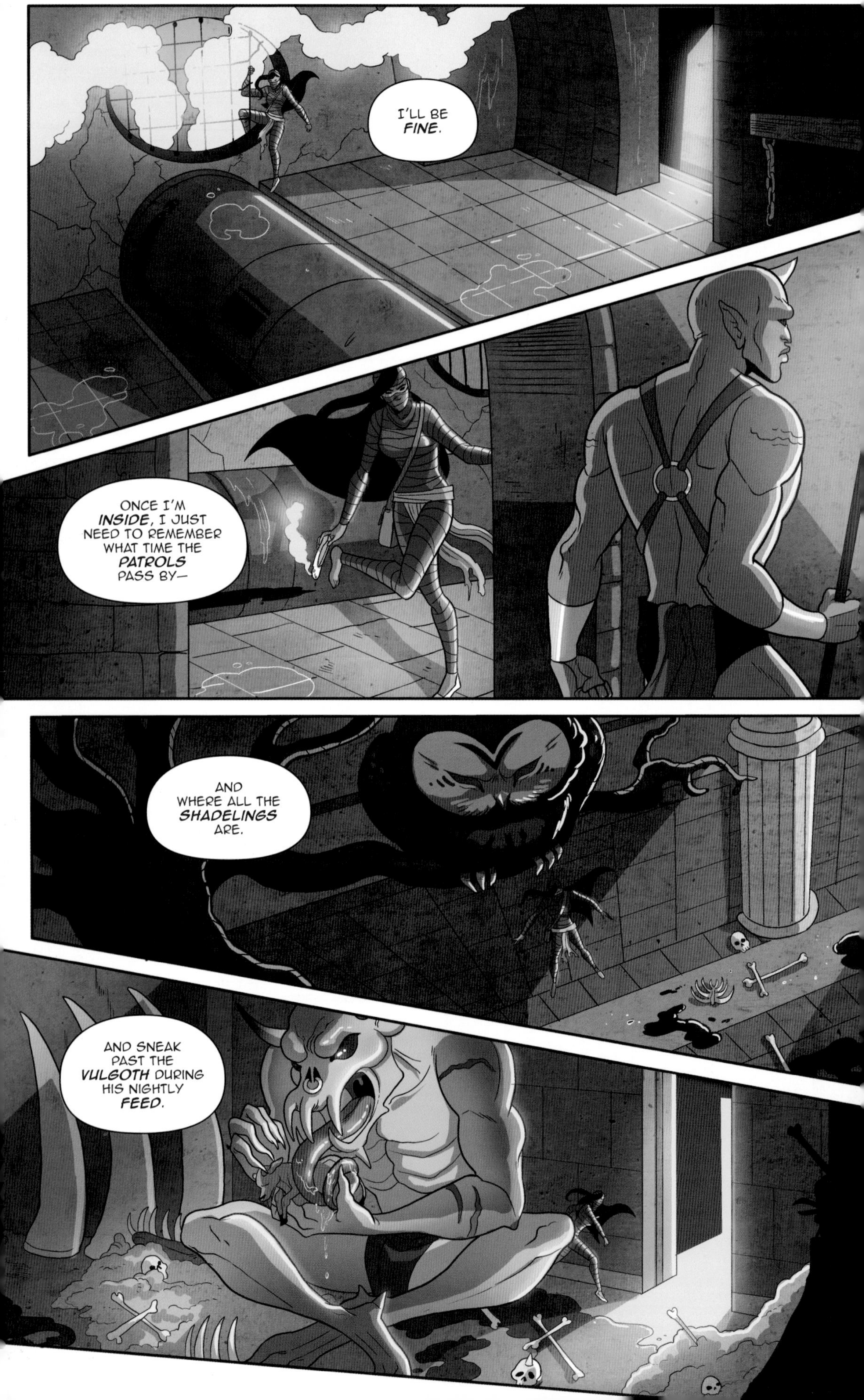
I'LL BE FINE.
ONCE I'M INSIDE, I JUST NEED TO REMEMBER WHAT TIME THE PATROLS PASS BY—
AND WHERE ALL THE SHADELINGS ARE.
AND SNEAK PAST THE VULGOTH DURING HIS NIGHTLY FEED.

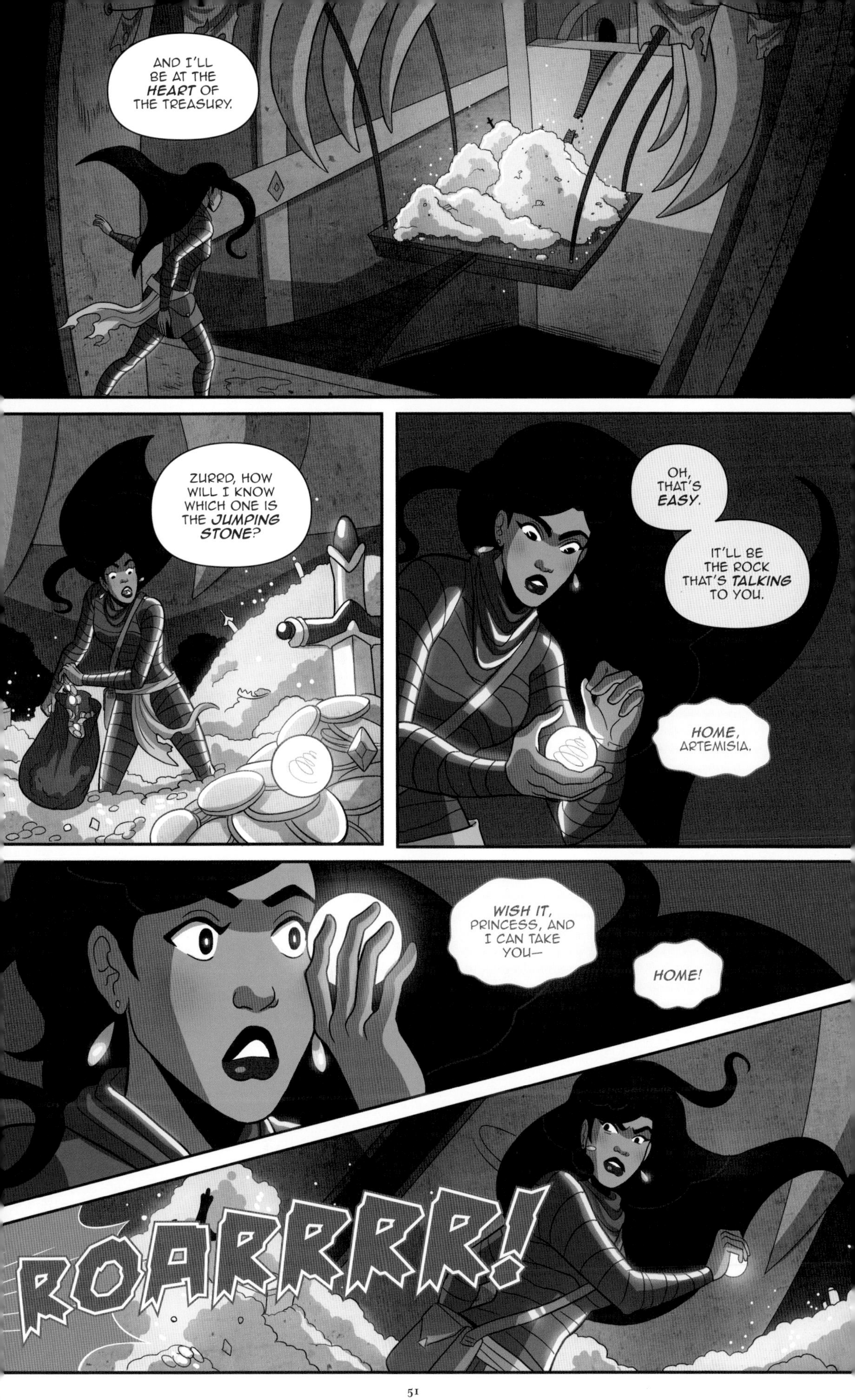
AND I'LL BE AT THE HEART OF THE TREASURY.
ZURRD, HOW WILL I KNOW WHICH ONE IS THE JUMPING STONE?
OH, THAT'S EASY.
IT'LL BE THE ROCK THAT'S TALKING TO YOU.
HOME, ARTEMISIA.
WISH IT, PRINCESS, AND I CAN TAKE YOU—
HOME!
ROARRRR!

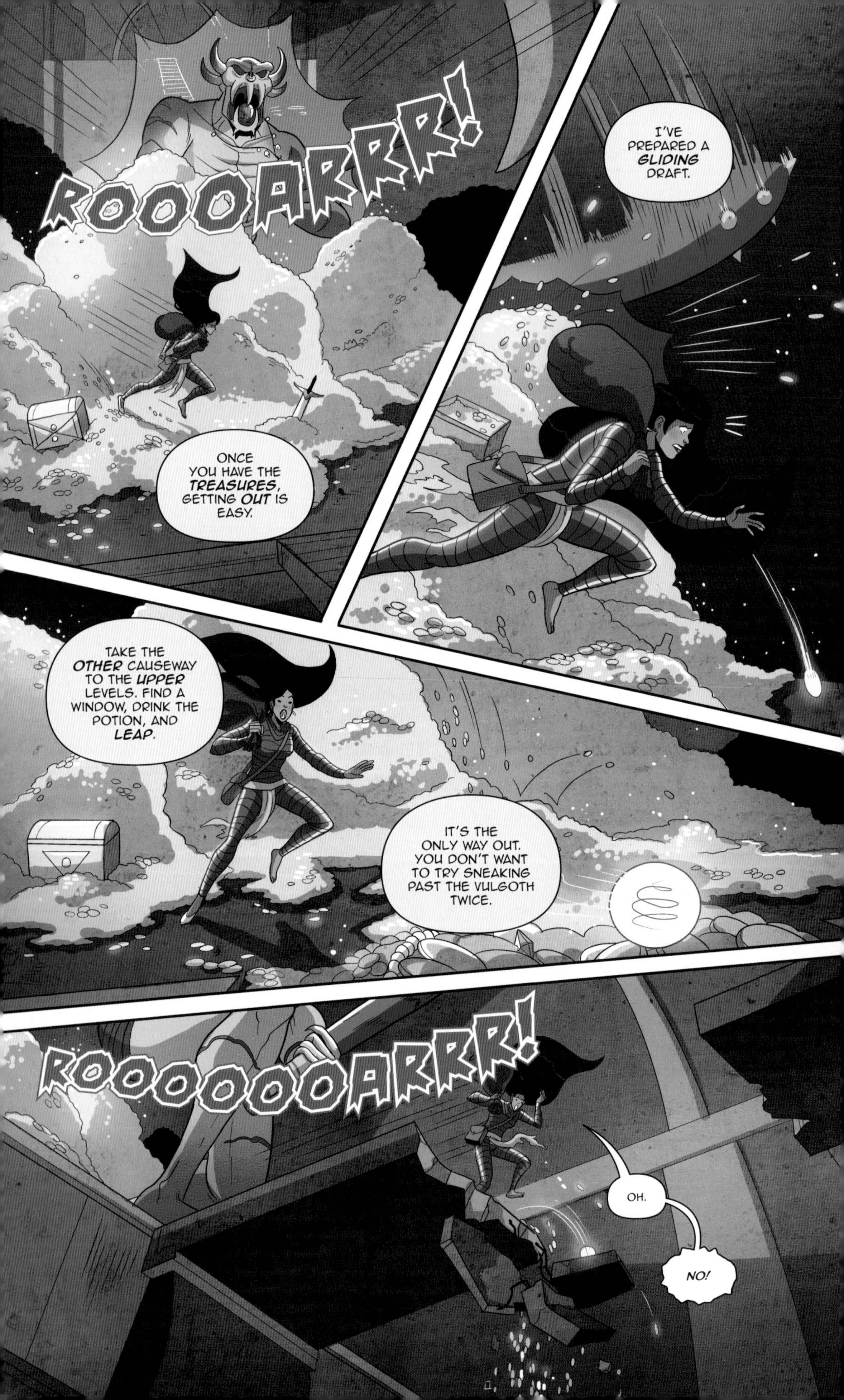
ROOOARRR!
ONCE YOU HAVE THE TREASURES, GETTING OUT IS EASY.
I'VE PREPARED A GLIDING DRAFT.
TAKE THE OTHER CAUSEWAY TO THE UPPER LEVELS. FIND A WINDOW, DRINK THE POTION, AND LEAP.
IT'S THE ONLY WAY OUT. YOU DON'T WANT TO TRY SNEAKING PAST THE VULGOTH TWICE.
ROOOOOOOARRR!
OH.
NO!

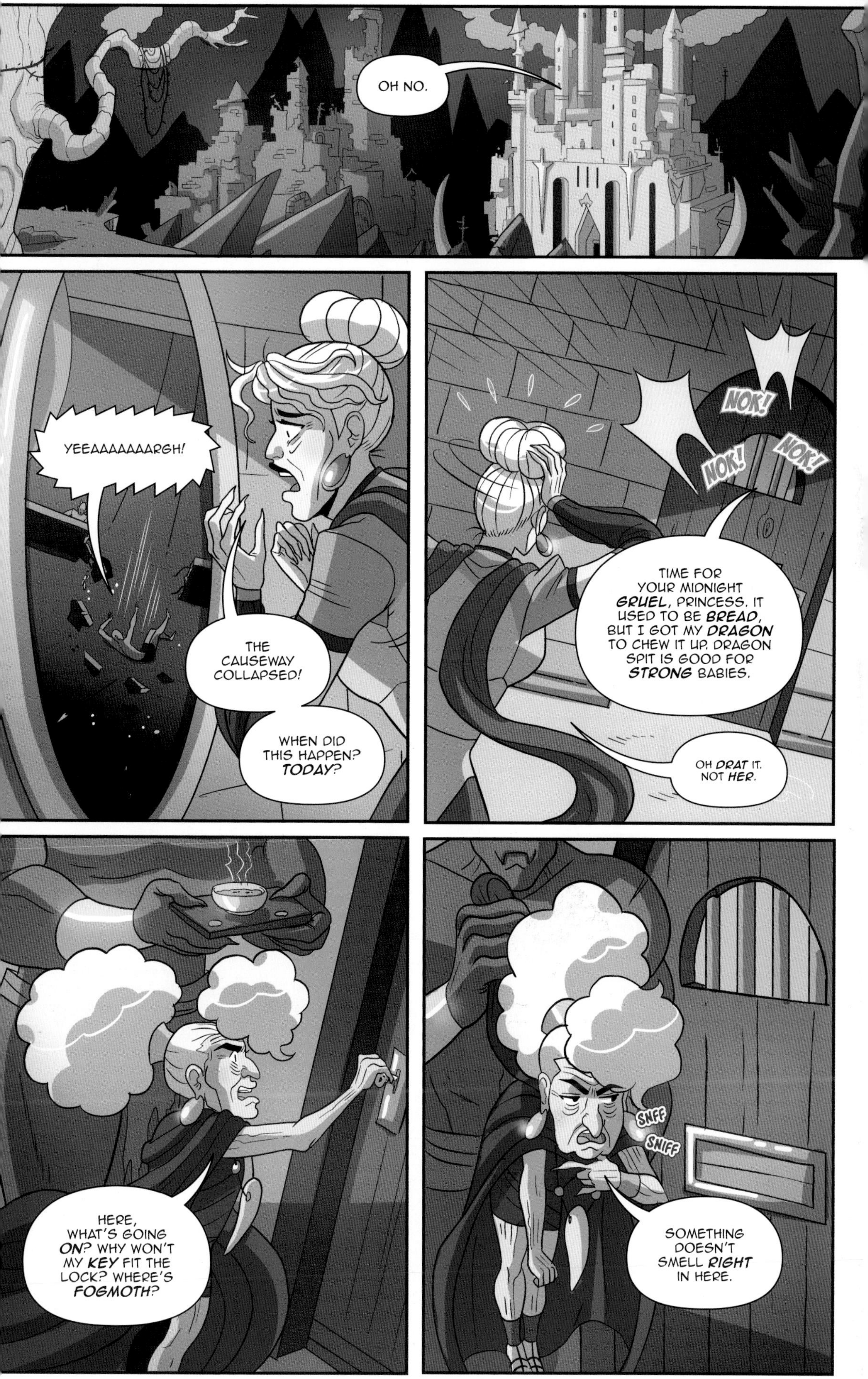
OH NO.
YEEAAAAAAARGH!
THE CAUSEWAY COLLAPSED!
WHEN DID THIS HAPPEN? TODAY?
NOK!
NOK!
NOK!
TIME FOR YOUR MIDNIGHT GRUEL, PRINCESS. IT USED TO BE BREAD, BUT I GOT MY DRAGON TO CHEW IT UP. DRAGON SPIT IS GOOD FOR STRONG BABIES.
OH DRAT IT. NOT HER.
HERE, WHAT'S GOING ON? WHY WON'T MY KEY FIT THE LOCK? WHERE'S FOGMOTH?
SNFF
SNIFF
SOMETHING DOESN'T SMELL RIGHT IN HERE.

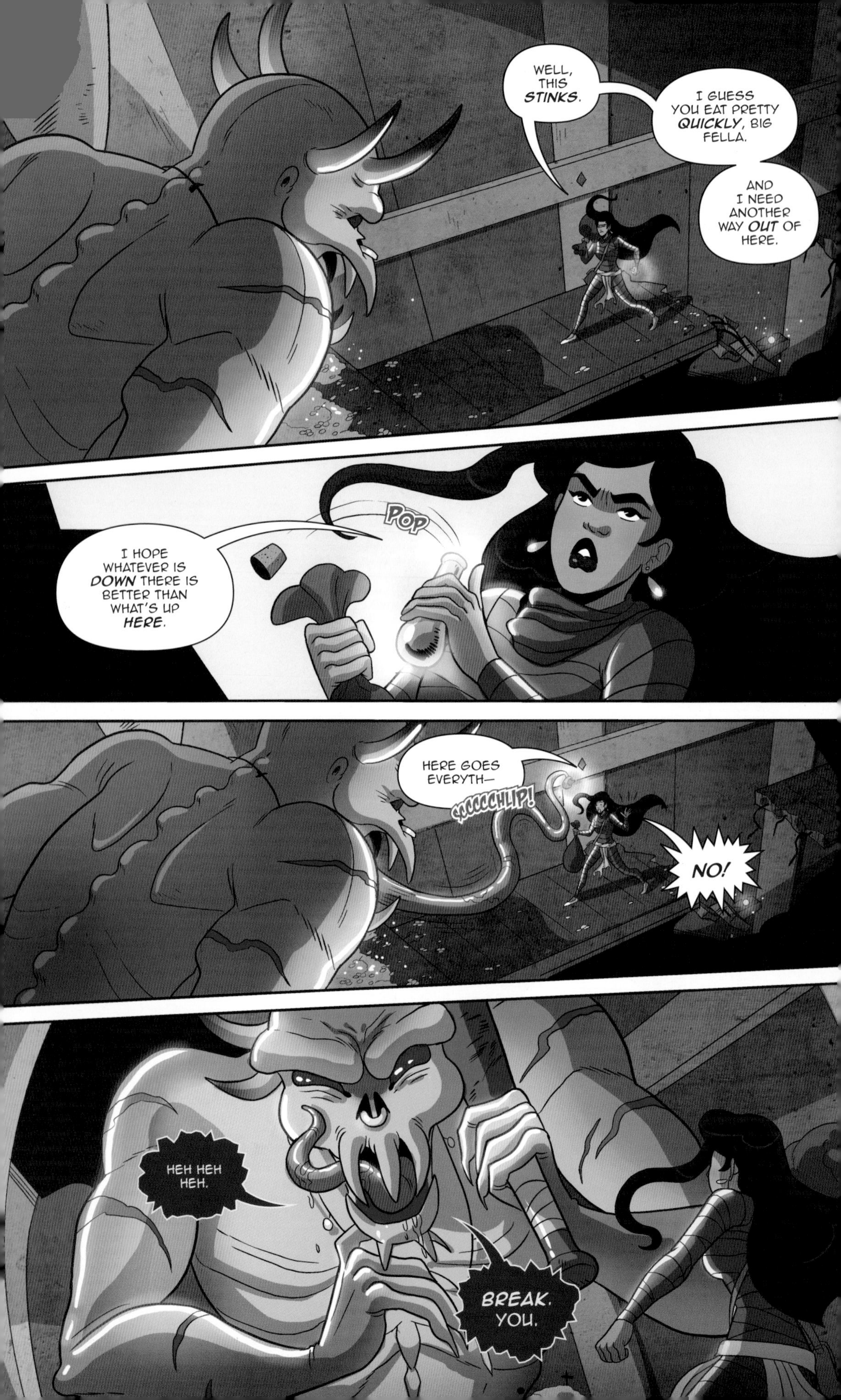

WELL, THIS STINKS.
I GUESS YOU EAT PRETTY QUICKLY, BIG FELLA.
AND I NEED ANOTHER WAY OUT OF HERE.
POP
I HOPE WHATEVER IS DOWN THERE IS BETTER THAN WHAT'S UP HERE.
HERE GOES EVERYTH—
SCCCCCHLIP!
NO!
HEH HEH HEH.
BREAK. YOU.

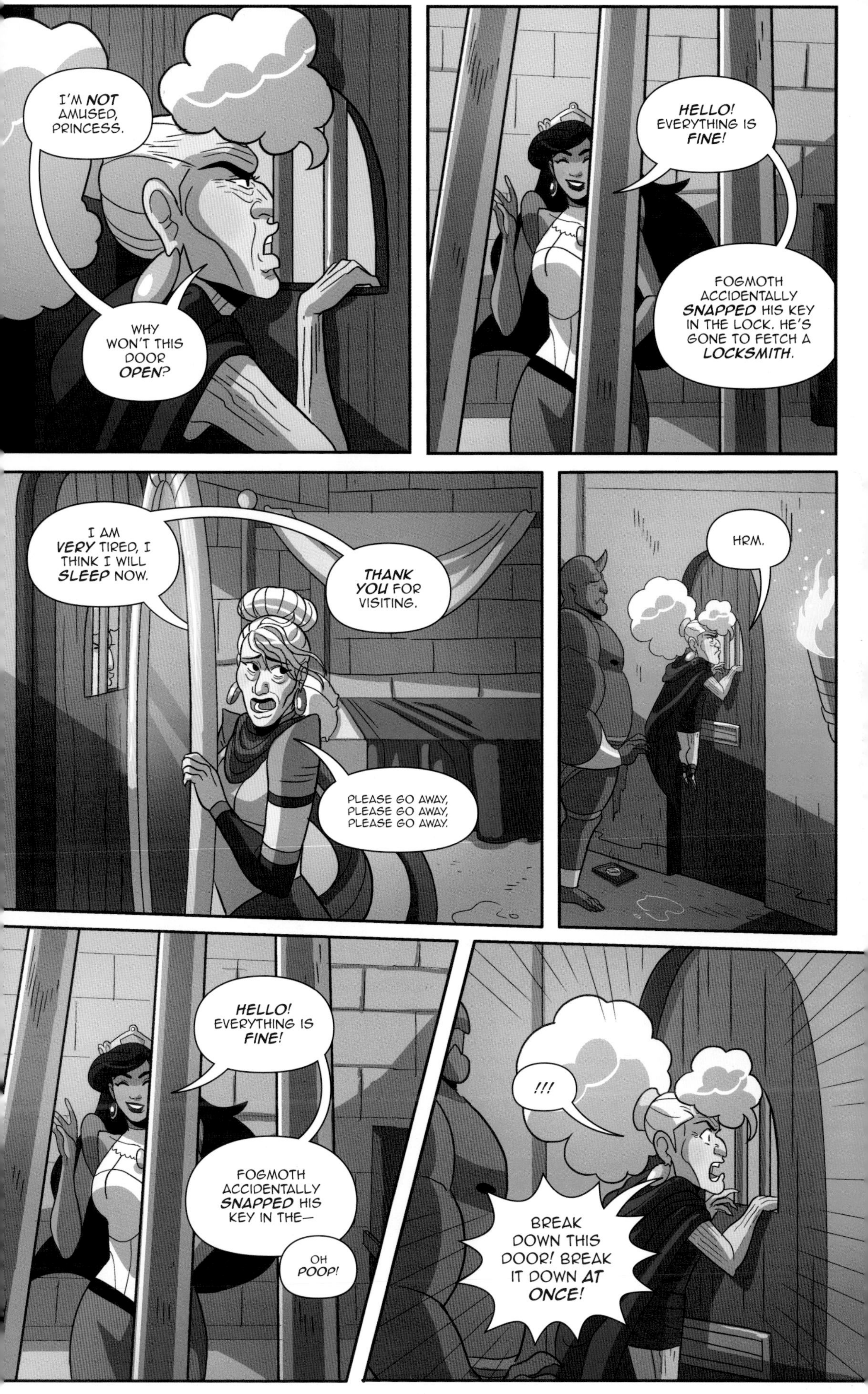

I'M **NOT** AMUSED, PRINCESS.
WHY WON'T THIS DOOR **OPEN**?
HELLO! EVERYTHING IS **FINE!**
FOGMOTH ACCIDENTALLY **SNAPPED** HIS KEY IN THE LOCK. HE'S GONE TO FETCH A **LOCKSMITH**.
I AM **VERY** TIRED, I THINK I WILL **SLEEP** NOW.
THANK YOU FOR VISITING.
PLEASE GO AWAY, PLEASE GO AWAY, PLEASE GO AWAY.
HRM.
HELLO! EVERYTHING IS **FINE!**
FOGMOTH ACCIDENTALLY **SNAPPED** HIS KEY IN THE—
OH **POOP!**
!!!
BREAK DOWN THIS DOOR! BREAK IT DOWN **AT ONCE!**

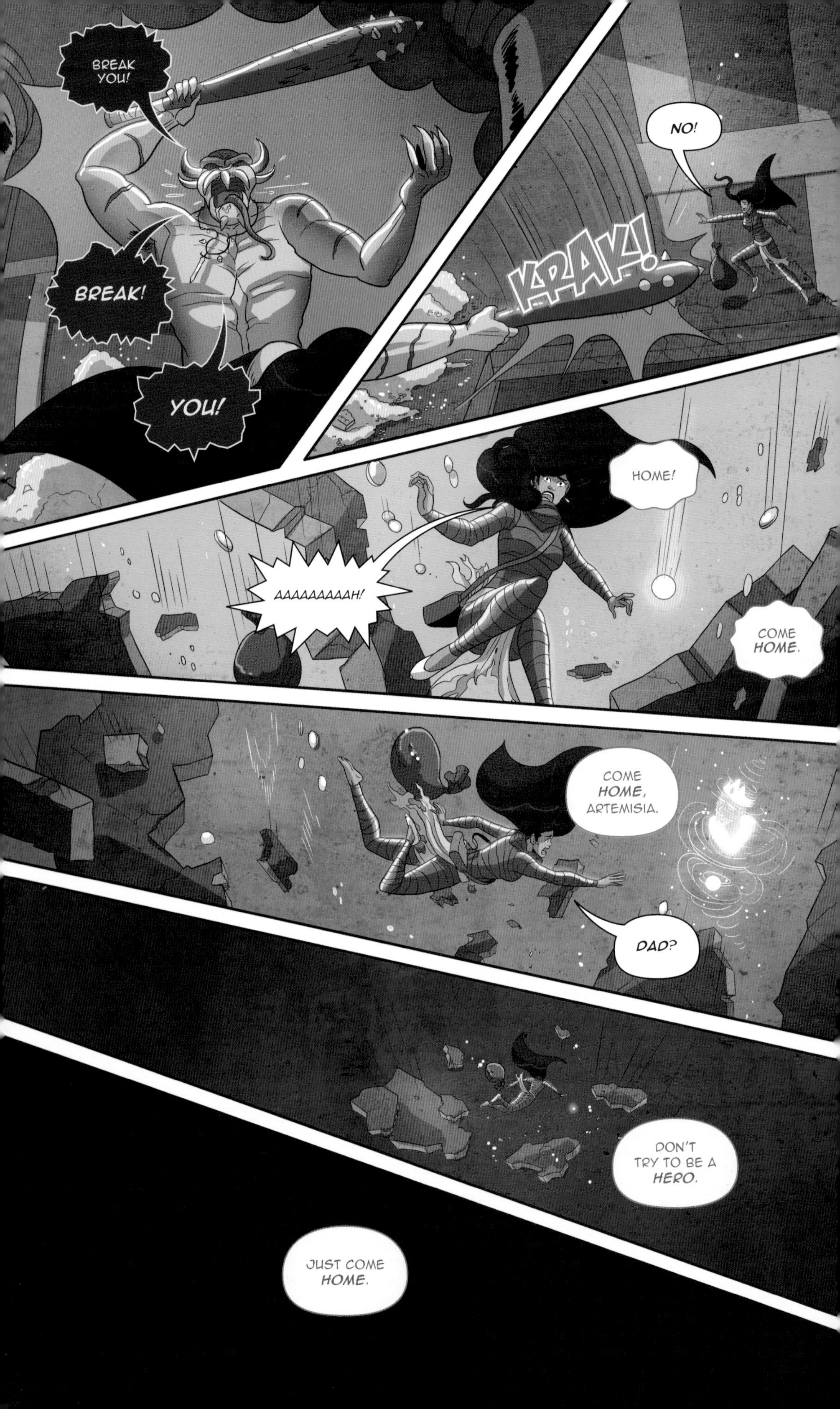
BREAK YOU!
BREAK!
YOU!
NO!
KRAK!
HOME!
AAAAAAAAAAH!
COME HOME.
COME HOME, ARTEMISIA.
DAD?
DON'T TRY TO BE A HERO.
JUST COME HOME.

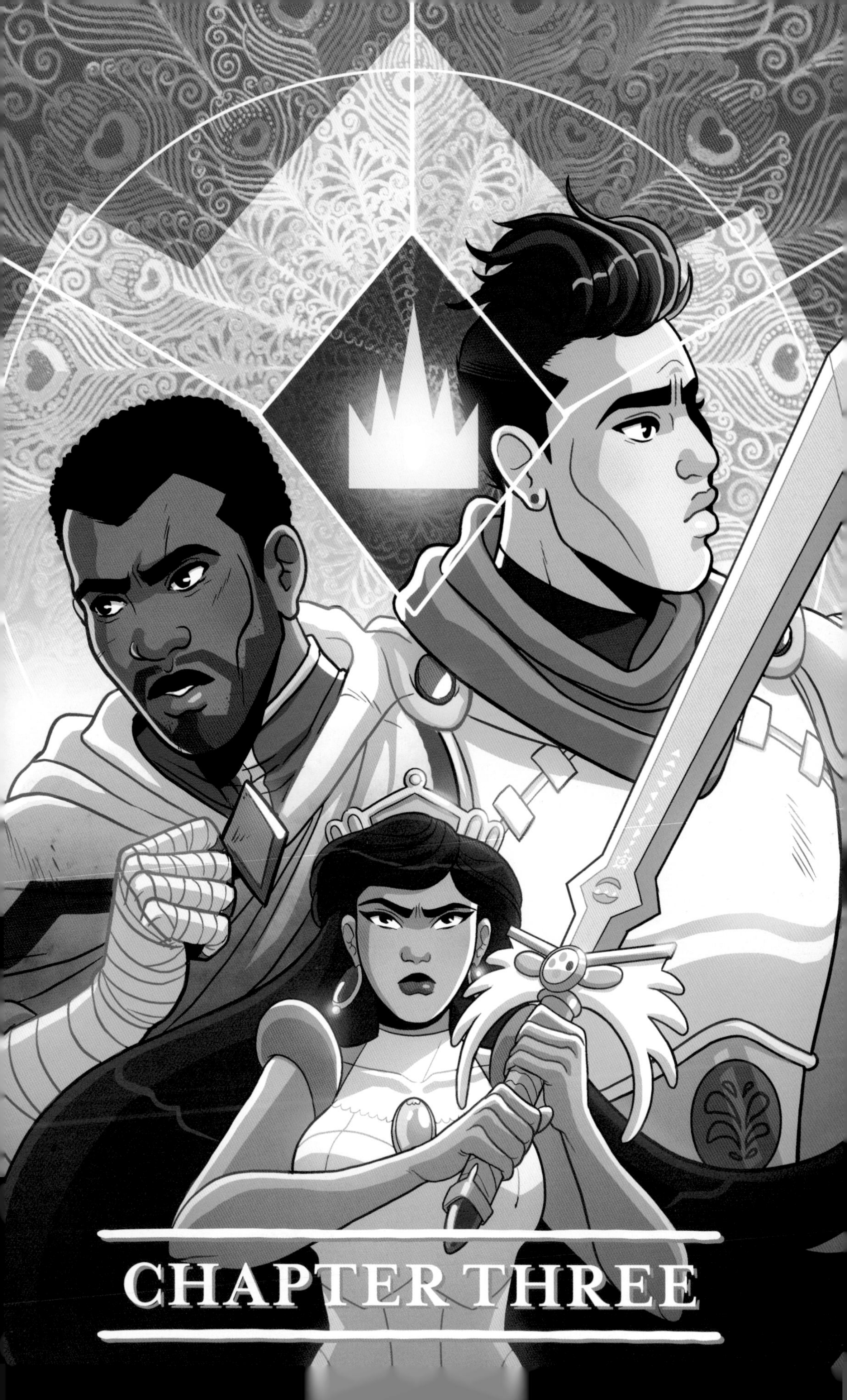

CHAPTER THREE

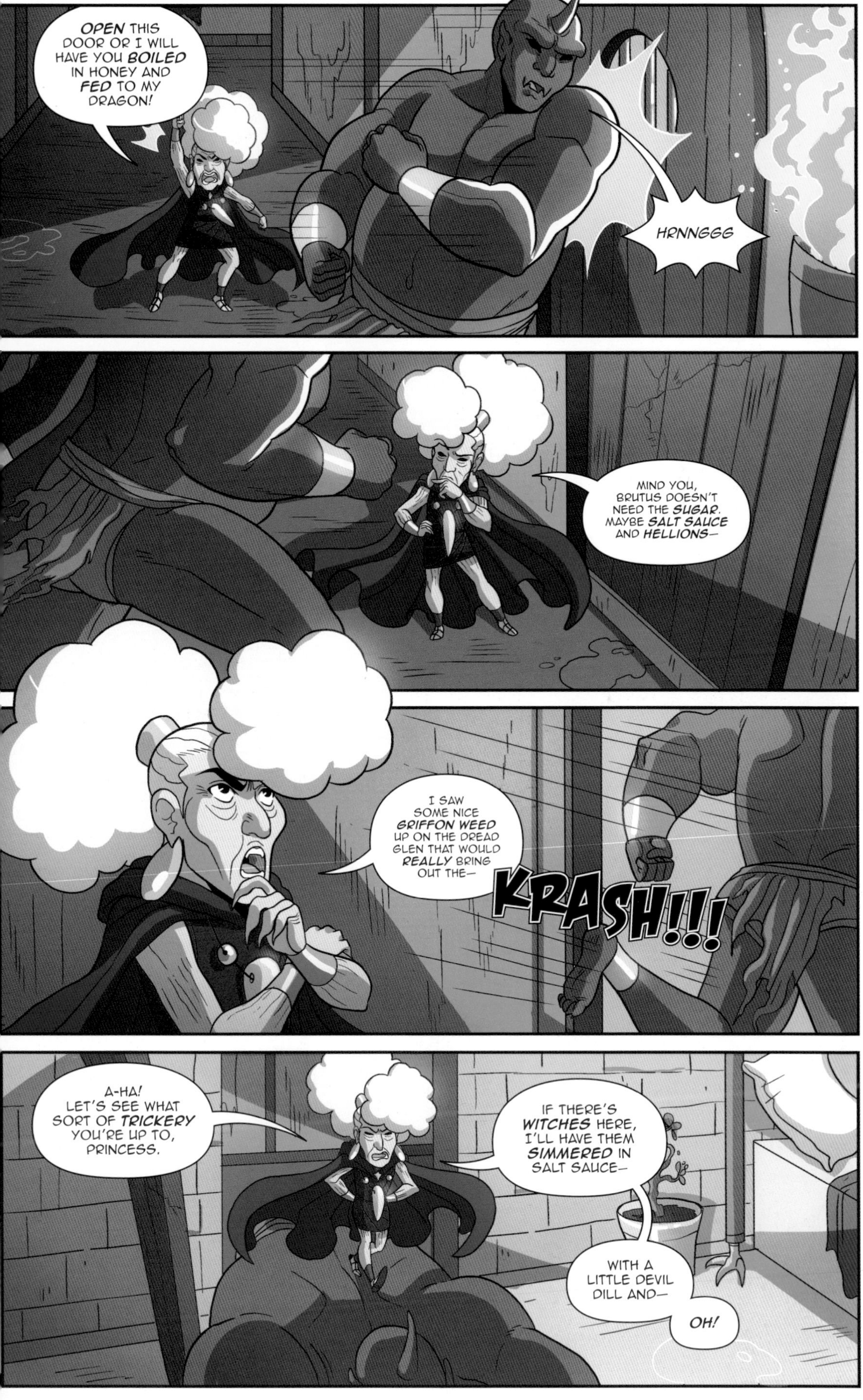

OPEN THIS DOOR OR I WILL HAVE YOU BOILED IN HONEY AND FED TO MY DRAGON!
HRNNGGG
MIND YOU, BRUTUS DOESN'T NEED THE SUGAR. MAYBE SALT SAUCE AND HELLIONS—
I SAW SOME NICE GRIFFON WEED UP ON THE DREAD GLEN THAT WOULD REALLY BRING OUT THE—
KRASH!!!
A-HA! LET'S SEE WHAT SORT OF TRICKERY YOU'RE UP TO, PRINCESS.
IF THERE'S WITCHES HERE, I'LL HAVE THEM SIMMERED IN SALT SAUCE—
WITH A LITTLE DEVIL DILL AND—
OH!

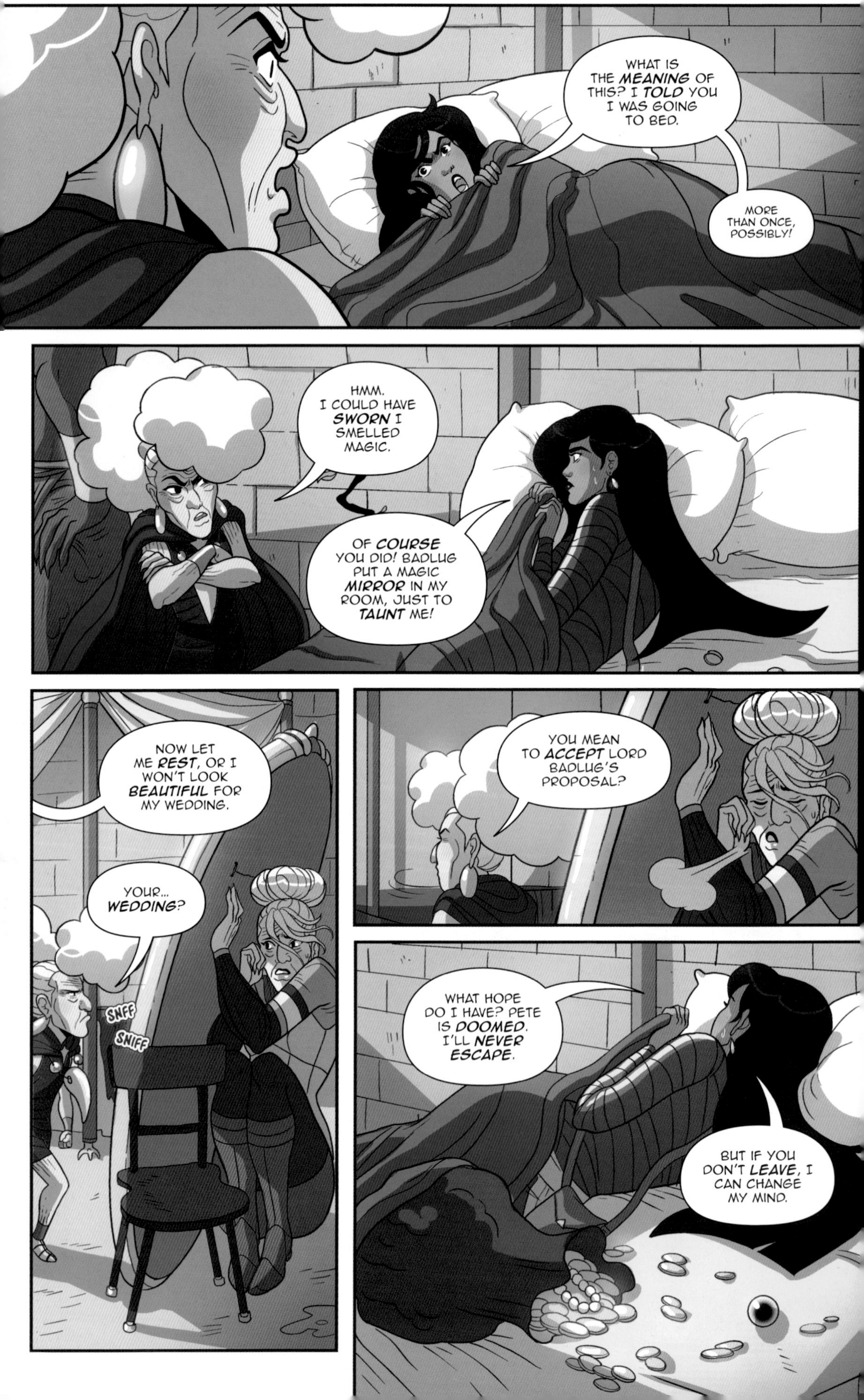
WHAT IS THE MEANING OF THIS? I TOLD YOU I WAS GOING TO BED.
MORE THAN ONCE, POSSIBLY!
HMM. I COULD HAVE SWORN I SMELLED MAGIC.
OF COURSE YOU DID! BADLUG PUT A MAGIC MIRROR IN MY ROOM, JUST TO TAUNT ME!
NOW LET ME REST, OR I WON'T LOOK BEAUTIFUL FOR MY WEDDING.
YOUR... WEDDING?
SNFF
SNIFF
YOU MEAN TO ACCEPT LORD BADLUG'S PROPOSAL?
WHAT HOPE DO I HAVE? PETE IS DOOMED. I'LL NEVER ESCAPE.
BUT IF YOU DON'T LEAVE, I CAN CHANGE MY MIND.

ALL RIGHT. VERY WELL.

I HAVE TO WRITE DOWN A RECIPE ANYHOW.

BUT MY *EYES* ARE EVERYWHERE. ANY *MISCHIEF* AND I'LL CATCH YOU.

DARK DREAMS, MY DEAR. *DARK* DREAMS.

SLAM!

PHEW.

THAT WAS *HUMILIATING.*

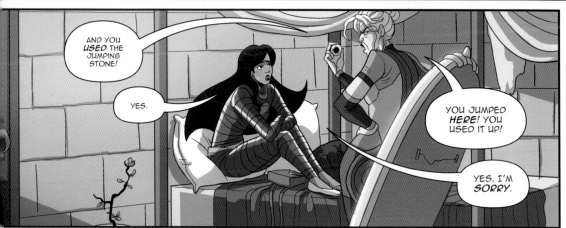

AND YOU *USED* THE JUMPING STONE!

YES.

YOU JUMPED *HERE!* YOU USED IT UP!

YES. I'M *SORRY.*

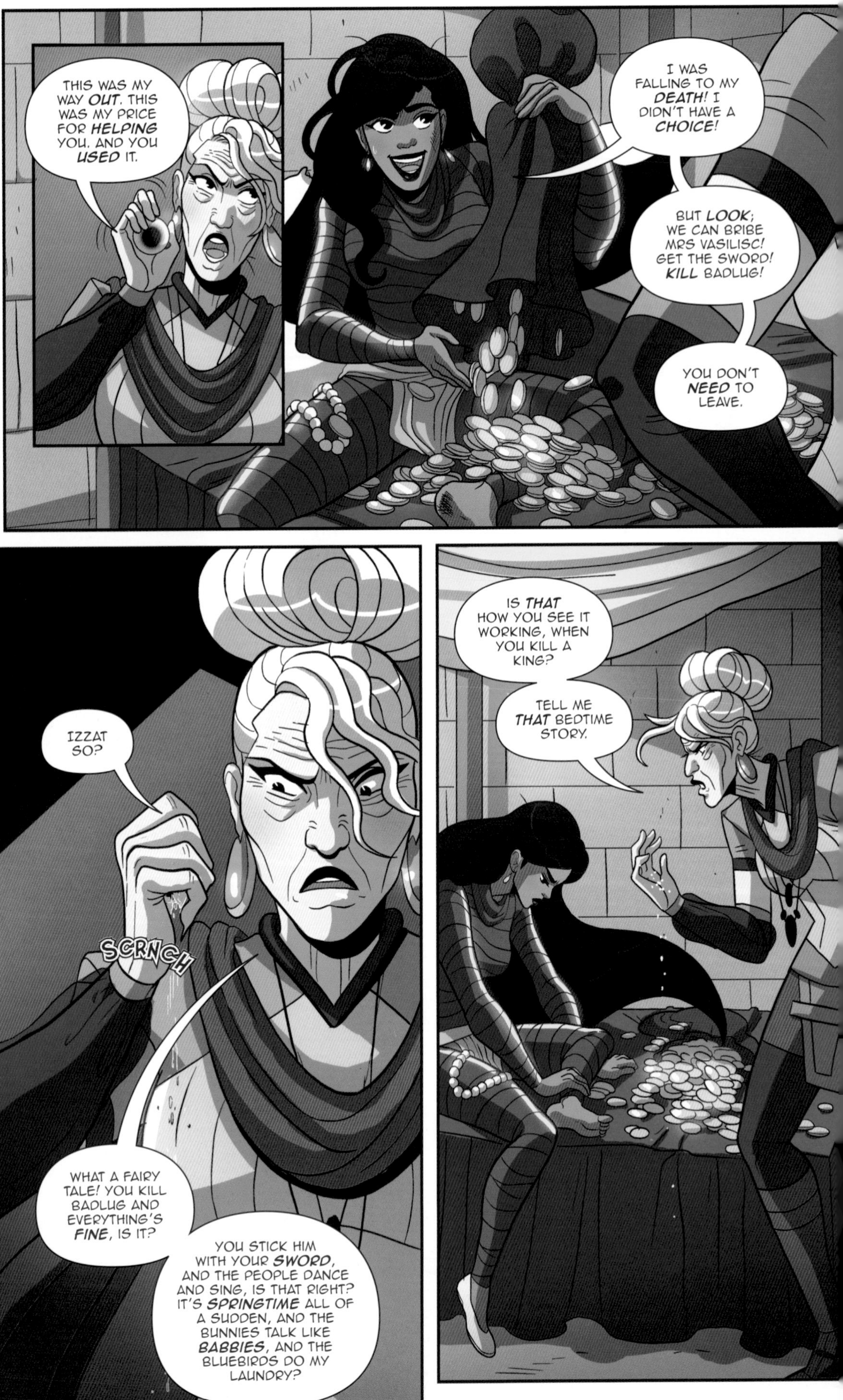
THIS WAS MY WAY **OUT**. THIS WAS MY PRICE FOR **HELPING** YOU. AND YOU **USED** IT.
I WAS FALLING TO MY **DEATH**! I DIDN'T HAVE A **CHOICE**!
BUT **LOOK**; WE CAN BRIBE MRS VASILISC! GET THE SWORD! **KILL** BADLUG!
YOU DON'T **NEED** TO LEAVE.
IZZAT SO?
SCRNCH
WHAT A FAIRY TALE! YOU KILL BADLUG AND EVERYTHING'S **FINE**, IS IT?
YOU STICK HIM WITH YOUR **SWORD**, AND THE PEOPLE DANCE AND SING, IS THAT RIGHT? IT'S **SPRINGTIME** ALL OF A SUDDEN, AND THE BUNNIES TALK LIKE **BABBIES**, AND THE BLUEBIRDS DO MY LAUNDRY?
IS **THAT** HOW YOU SEE IT WORKING, WHEN YOU KILL A KING?
TELL ME **THAT** BEDTIME STORY.

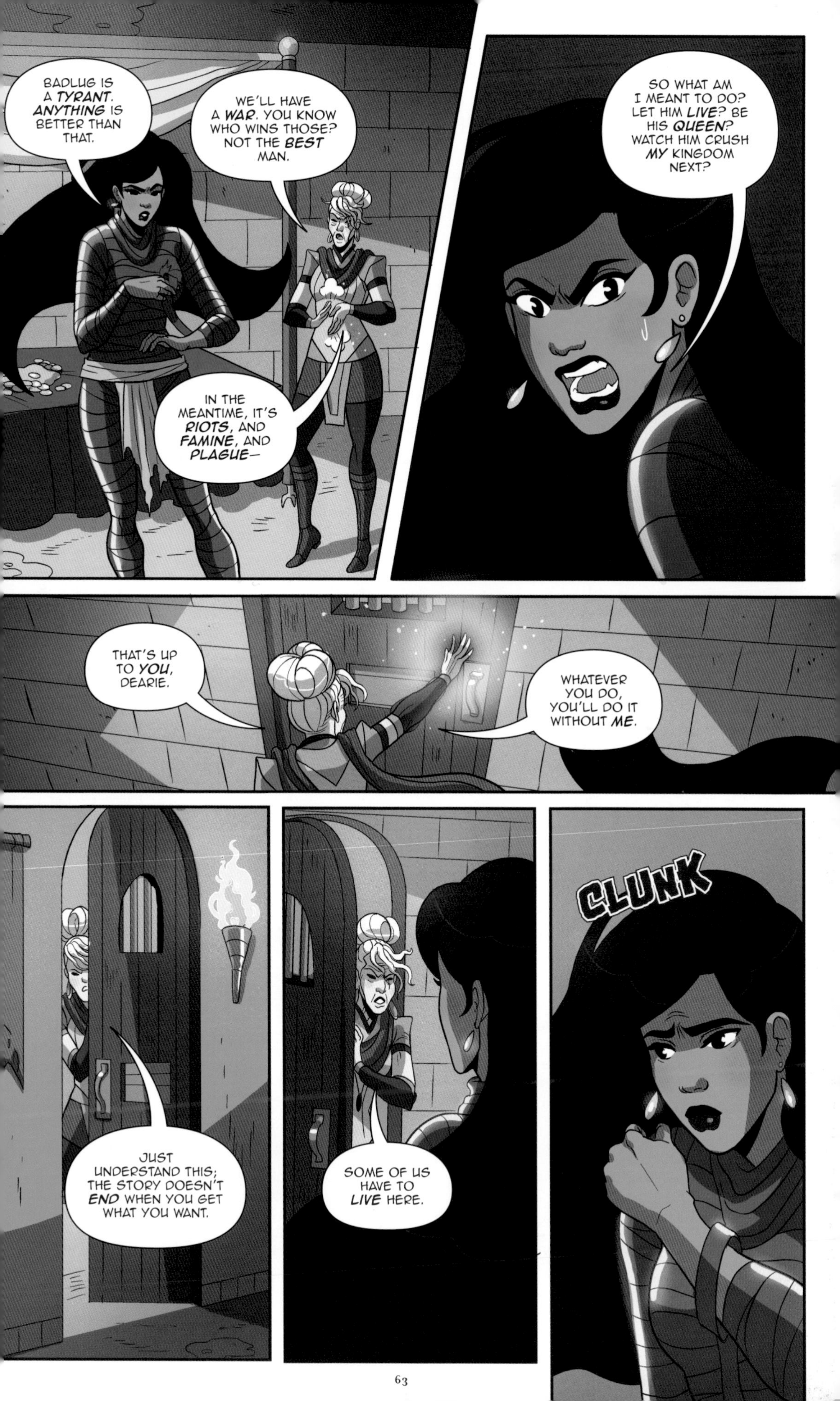
BADLUG IS A *TYRANT*. *ANYTHING* IS BETTER THAN THAT.
WE'LL HAVE A *WAR*. YOU KNOW WHO WINS THOSE? NOT THE *BEST* MAN.
IN THE MEANTIME, IT'S *RIOTS*, AND *FAMINE*, AND *PLAGUE*—
SO WHAT AM I MEANT TO DO? LET HIM *LIVE*? BE HIS *QUEEN*? WATCH HIM CRUSH *MY* KINGDOM NEXT?
THAT'S UP TO *YOU*, DEARIE.
WHATEVER YOU DO, YOU'LL DO IT WITHOUT *ME*.
JUST UNDERSTAND THIS; THE STORY DOESN'T *END* WHEN YOU GET WHAT YOU WANT.
SOME OF US HAVE TO *LIVE* HERE.
CLUNK

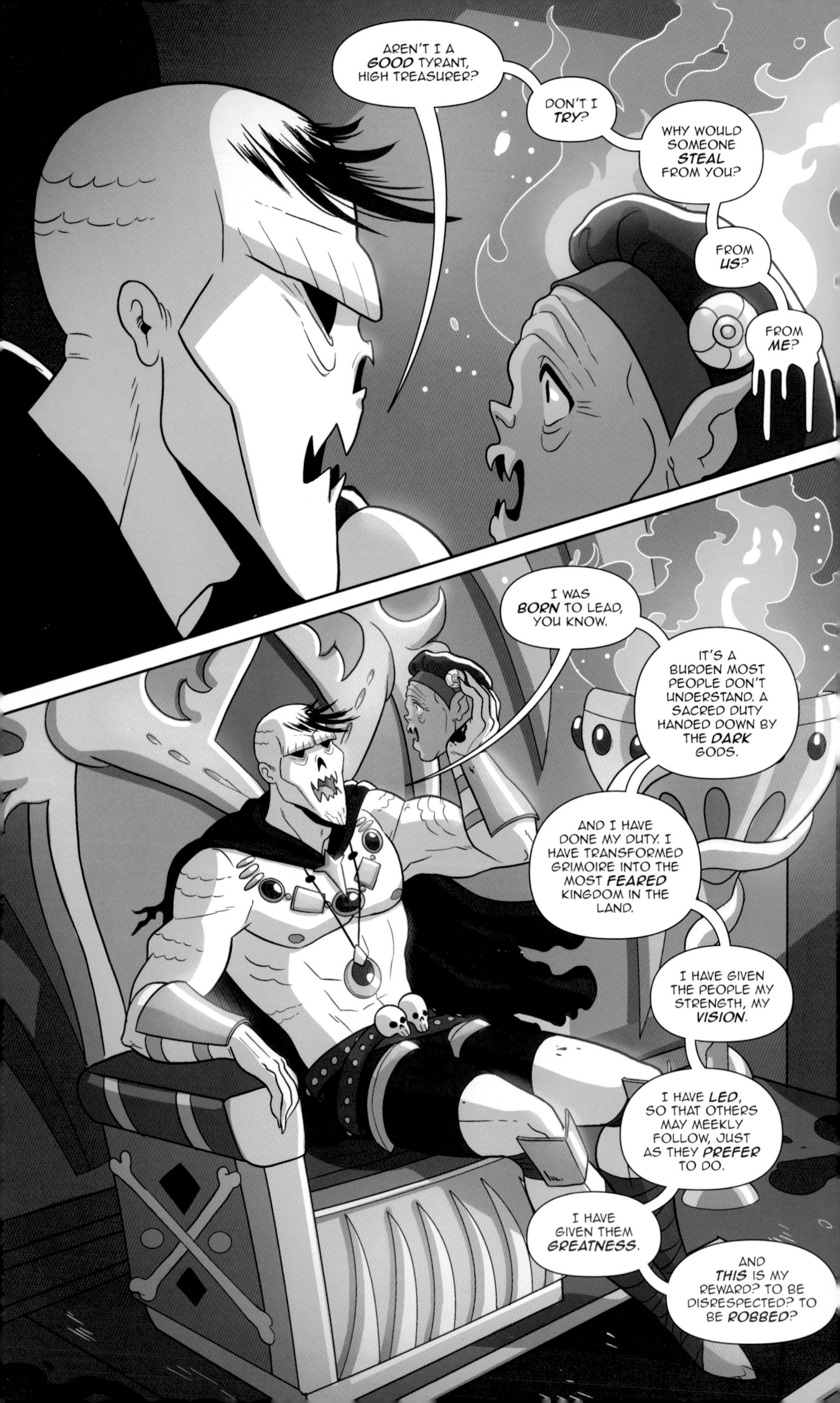
AREN'T I A *GOOD* TYRANT, HIGH TREASURER?
DON'T I *TRY*?
WHY WOULD SOMEONE *STEAL* FROM YOU?
FROM *US*?
FROM *ME*?
I WAS *BORN* TO LEAD, YOU KNOW.
IT'S A BURDEN MOST PEOPLE DON'T UNDERSTAND. A SACRED DUTY HANDED DOWN BY THE *DARK* GODS.
AND I HAVE DONE MY DUTY. I HAVE TRANSFORMED GRIMOIRE INTO THE MOST *FEARED* KINGDOM IN THE LAND.
I HAVE GIVEN THE PEOPLE MY STRENGTH, MY *VISION*.
I HAVE *LED*, SO THAT OTHERS MAY MEEKLY FOLLOW, JUST AS THEY *PREFER* TO DO.
I HAVE GIVEN THEM *GREATNESS*.
AND *THIS* IS MY REWARD? TO BE DISRESPECTED? TO BE *ROBBED*?

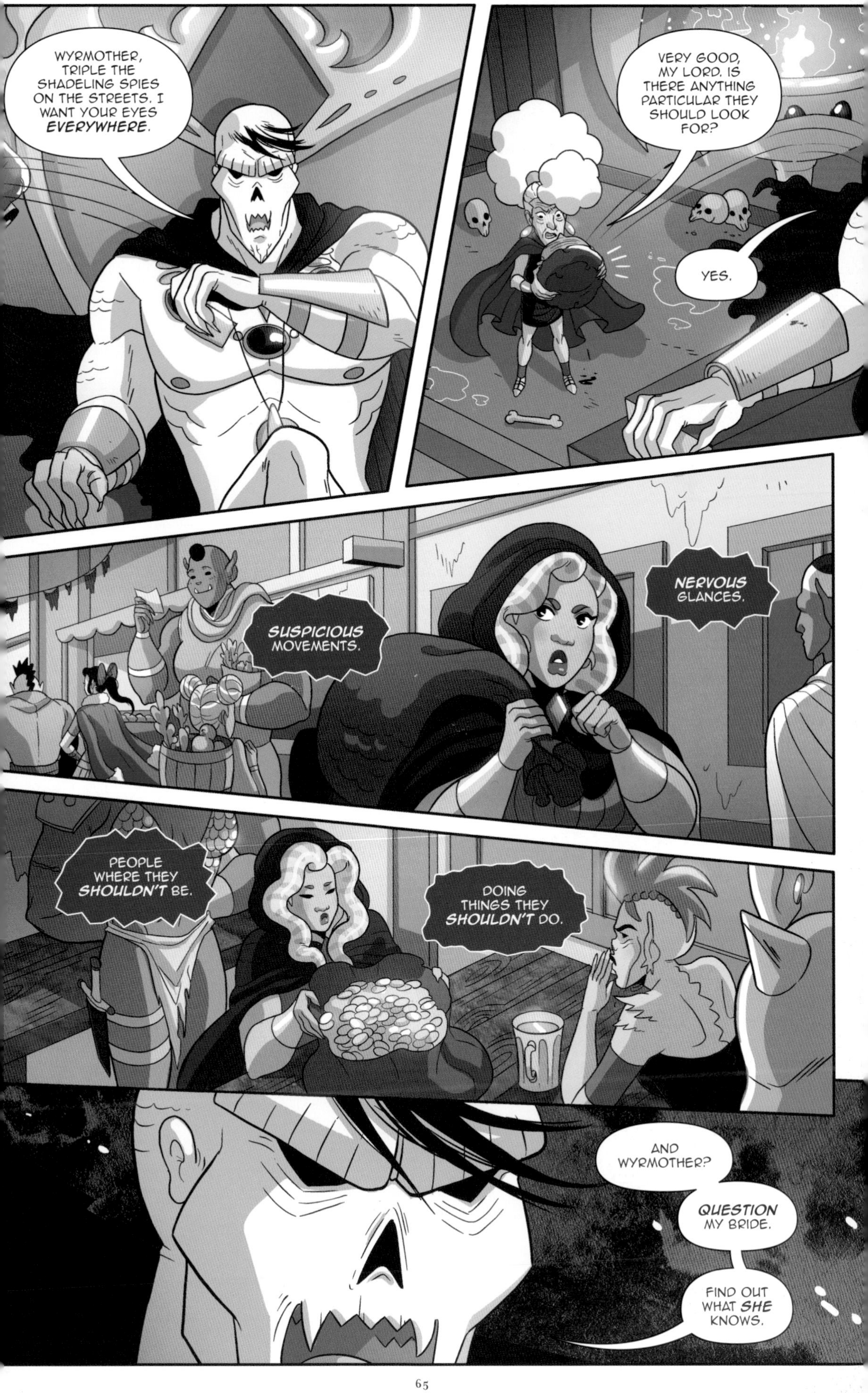
WYRMOTHER, TRIPLE THE SHADELING SPIES ON THE STREETS. I WANT YOUR EYES *EVERYWHERE*.
VERY GOOD, MY LORD. IS THERE ANYTHING PARTICULAR THEY SHOULD LOOK FOR?
YES.
SUSPICIOUS MOVEMENTS.
NERVOUS GLANCES.
PEOPLE WHERE THEY *SHOULDN'T* BE.
DOING THINGS THEY *SHOULDN'T* DO.
AND WYRMOTHER?
QUESTION MY BRIDE.
FIND OUT WHAT *SHE* KNOWS.

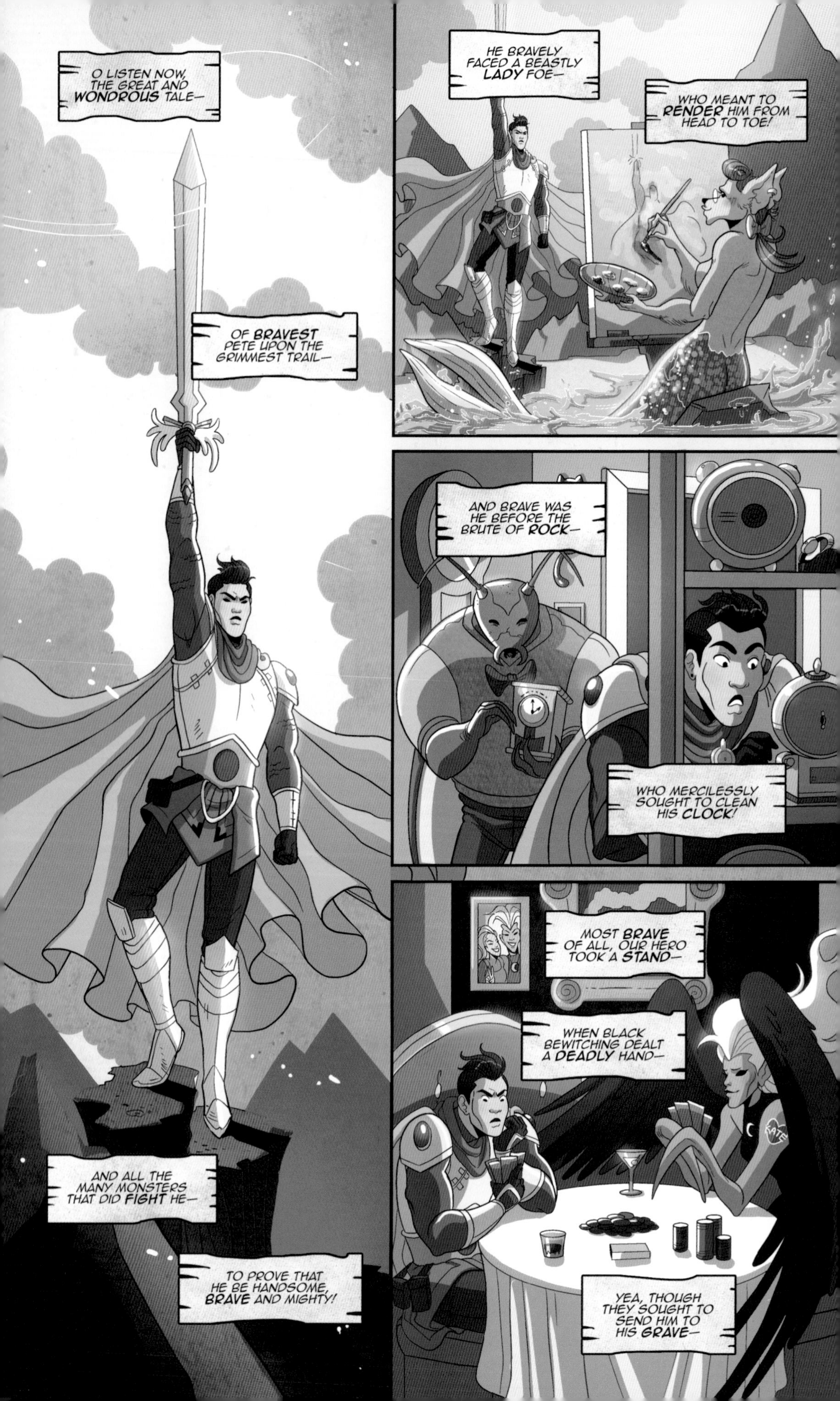
O LISTEN NOW, THE GREAT AND **WONDROUS** TALE—
OF **BRAVEST** PETE UPON THE GRIMMEST TRAIL—
AND ALL THE MANY MONSTERS THAT DID **FIGHT** HE—
TO PROVE THAT HE BE HANDSOME, **BRAVE** AND MIGHTY!
HE BRAVELY FACED A BEASTLY **LADY** FOE—
WHO MEANT TO **RENDER** HIM FROM HEAD TO TOE!
AND BRAVE WAS HE BEFORE THE BRUTE OF **ROCK**—
WHO MERCILESSLY SOUGHT TO CLEAN HIS **CLOCK**!
MOST **BRAVE** OF ALL, OUR HERO TOOK A **STAND**—
WHEN BLACK BEWITCHING DEALT A **DEADLY** HAND—
KATE
YEA, THOUGH THEY SOUGHT TO SEND HIM TO HIS **GRAVE**—

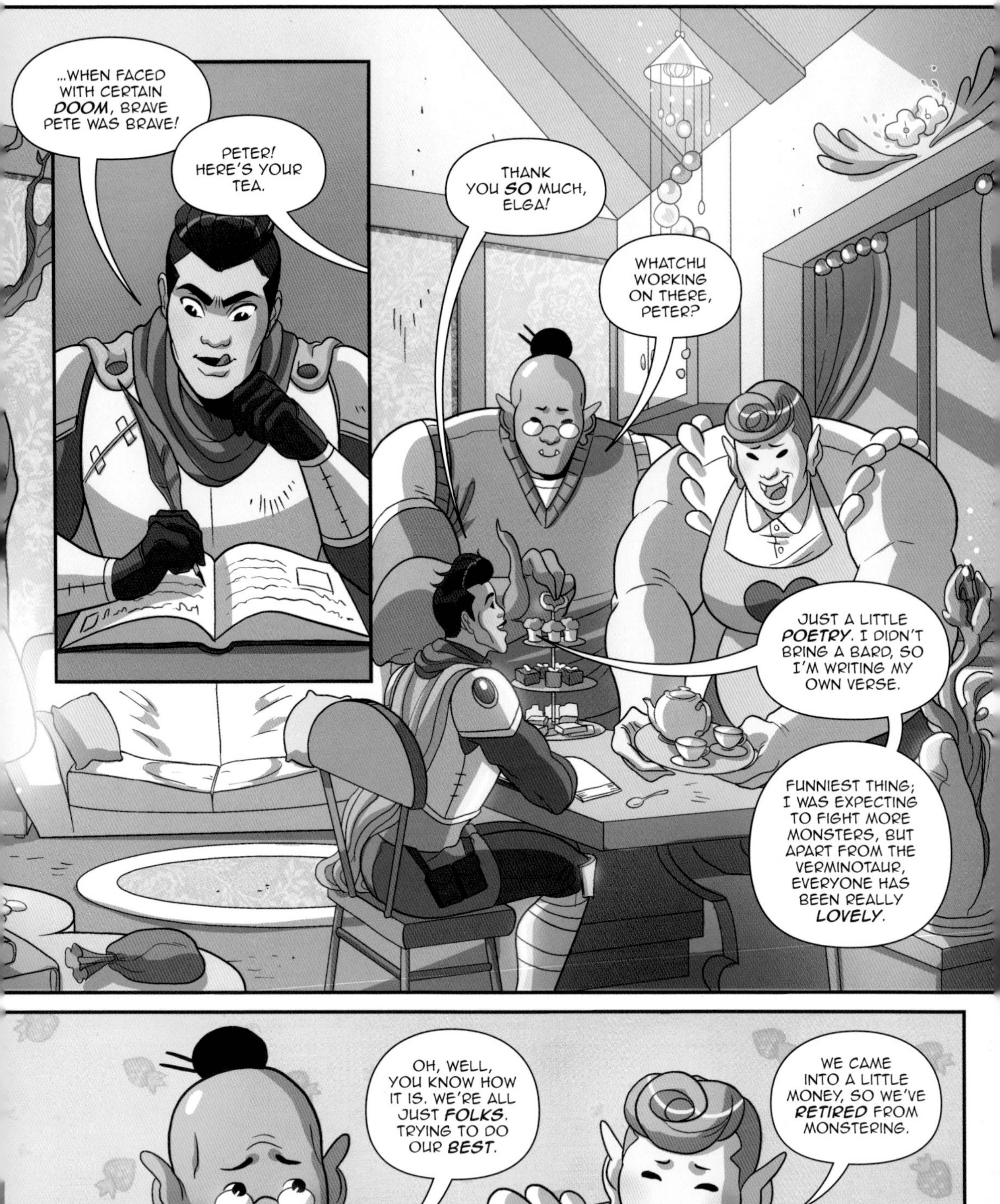
...WHEN FACED WITH CERTAIN DOOM, BRAVE PETE WAS BRAVE!
PETER! HERE'S YOUR TEA.
THANK YOU SO MUCH, ELGA!
WHATCHU WORKING ON THERE, PETER?
JUST A LITTLE POETRY. I DIDN'T BRING A BARD, SO I'M WRITING MY OWN VERSE.
FUNNIEST THING; I WAS EXPECTING TO FIGHT MORE MONSTERS, BUT APART FROM THE VERMINOTAUR, EVERYONE HAS BEEN REALLY LOVELY.

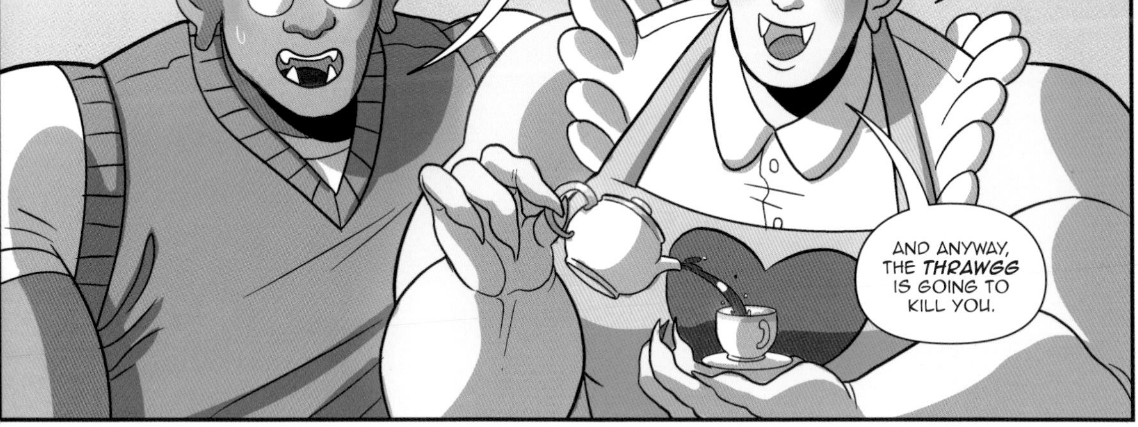
OH, WELL, YOU KNOW HOW IT IS. WE'RE ALL JUST FOLKS. TRYING TO DO OUR BEST.
WE CAME INTO A LITTLE MONEY, SO WE'VE RETIRED FROM MONSTERING.
AND ANYWAY, THE THRAWGG IS GOING TO KILL YOU.

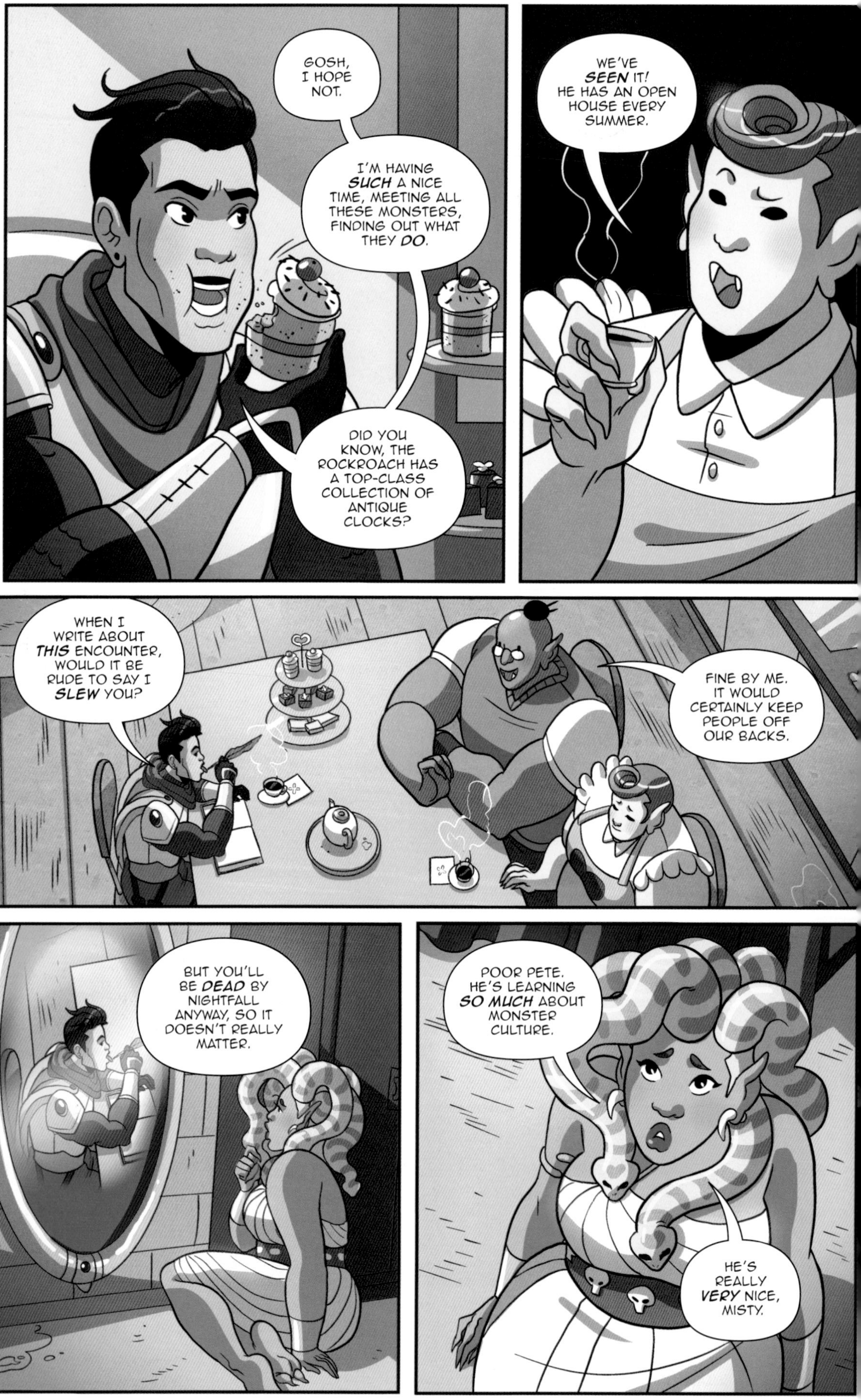
GOSH, I HOPE NOT.
I'M HAVING **SUCH** A NICE TIME, MEETING ALL THESE MONSTERS, FINDING OUT WHAT THEY **DO**.
DID YOU KNOW, THE ROCKROACH HAS A TOP-CLASS COLLECTION OF ANTIQUE CLOCKS?
WE'VE **SEEN** IT! HE HAS AN OPEN HOUSE EVERY SUMMER.
WHEN I WRITE ABOUT **THIS** ENCOUNTER, WOULD IT BE RUDE TO SAY I **SLEW** YOU?
FINE BY ME. IT WOULD CERTAINLY KEEP PEOPLE OFF OUR BACKS.
BUT YOU'LL BE **DEAD** BY NIGHTFALL ANYWAY, SO IT DOESN'T REALLY MATTER.
POOR PETE. HE'S LEARNING **SO MUCH** ABOUT MONSTER CULTURE.
HE'S REALLY **VERY** NICE, MISTY.

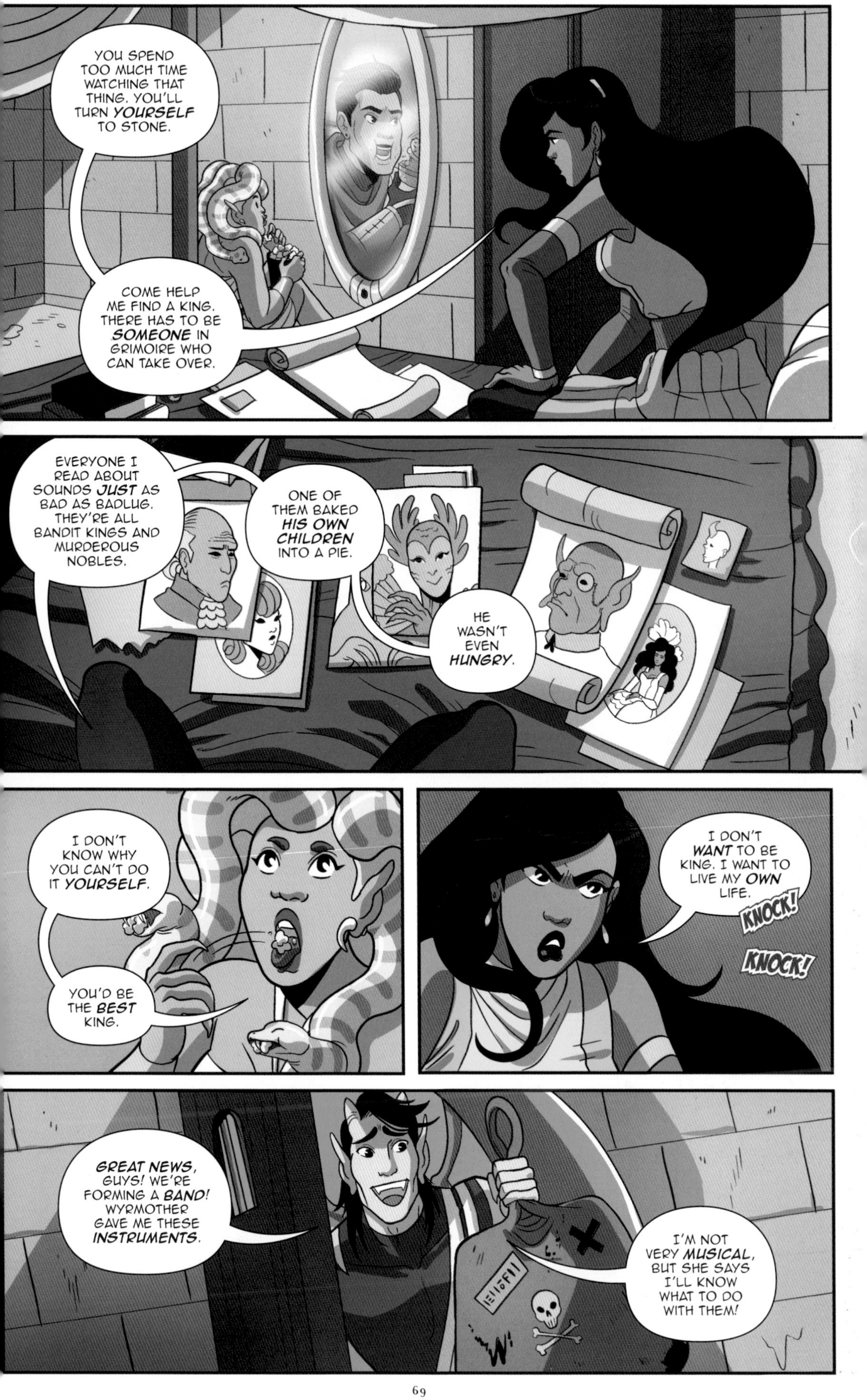

YOU SPEND TOO MUCH TIME WATCHING THAT THING. YOU'LL TURN *YOURSELF* TO STONE.
COME HELP ME FIND A KING. THERE HAS TO BE *SOMEONE* IN GRIMOIRE WHO CAN TAKE OVER.
EVERYONE I READ ABOUT SOUNDS *JUST* AS BAD AS BADLUG. THEY'RE ALL BANDIT KINGS AND MURDEROUS NOBLES.
ONE OF THEM BAKED *HIS OWN CHILDREN* INTO A PIE.
HE WASN'T EVEN *HUNGRY*.
I DON'T KNOW WHY YOU CAN'T DO IT *YOURSELF*.
YOU'D BE THE *BEST* KING.
I DON'T *WANT* TO BE KING. I WANT TO LIVE MY *OWN* LIFE.
KNOCK!
KNOCK!
GREAT NEWS, GUYS! WE'RE FORMING A *BAND*! WYRMOTHER GAVE ME THESE *INSTRUMENTS*.
I'M NOT VERY *MUSICAL*, BUT SHE SAYS I'LL KNOW WHAT TO DO WITH THEM!

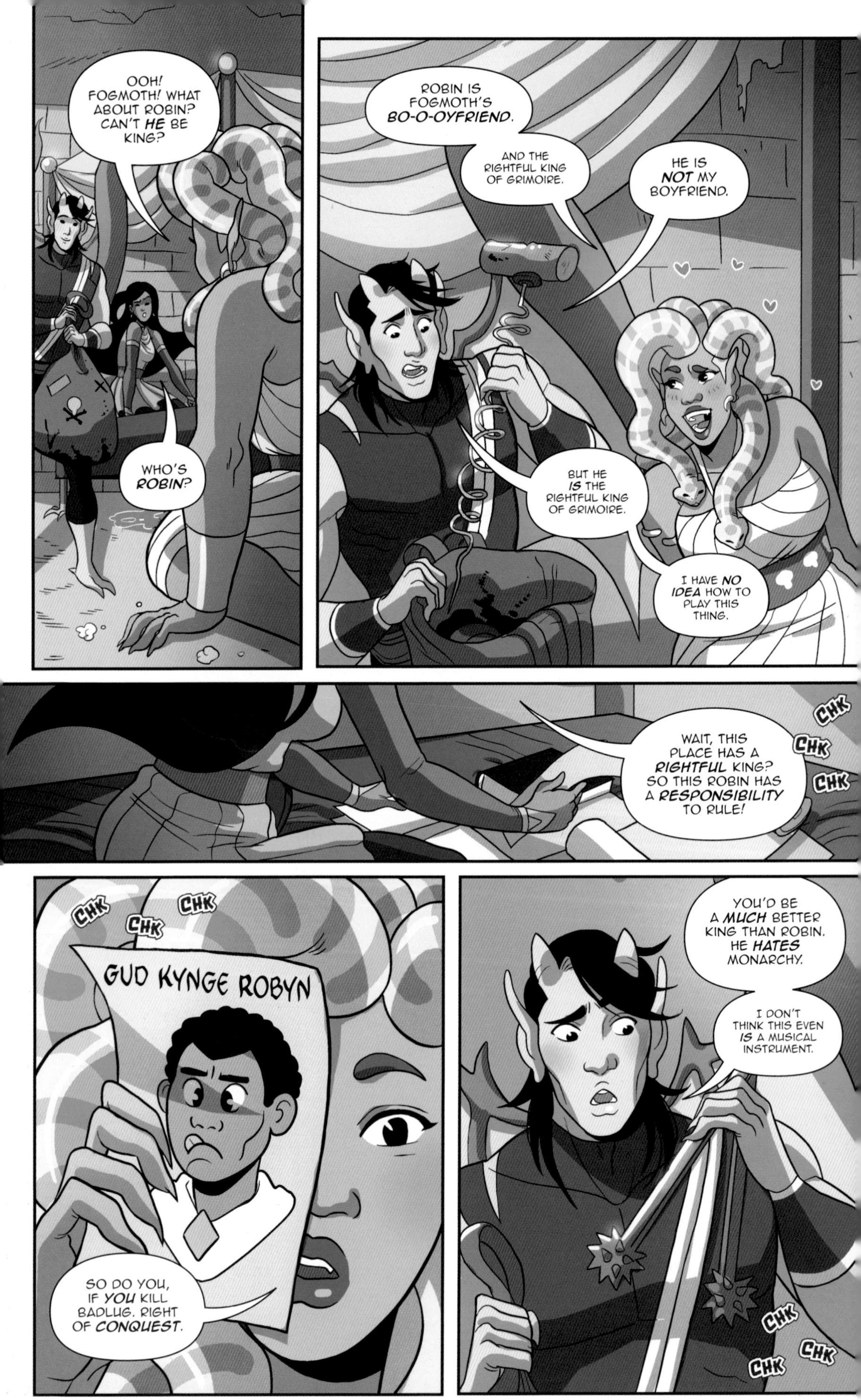

OOH! FOGMOTH! WHAT ABOUT ROBIN? CAN'T HE BE KING?
WHO'S ROBIN?
ROBIN IS FOGMOTH'S BO-O-OYFRIEND.
AND THE RIGHTFUL KING OF GRIMOIRE.
HE IS NOT MY BOYFRIEND.
BUT HE IS THE RIGHTFUL KING OF GRIMOIRE.
I HAVE NO IDEA HOW TO PLAY THIS THING.
WAIT, THIS PLACE HAS A RIGHTFUL KING? SO THIS ROBIN HAS A RESPONSIBILITY TO RULE!
CHK
CHK
CHK
CHK
CHK
CHK
GUD KYNGE ROBYN
SO DO YOU, IF YOU KILL BADLUG. RIGHT OF CONQUEST.
YOU'D BE A MUCH BETTER KING THAN ROBIN. HE HATES MONARCHY.
I DON'T THINK THIS EVEN IS A MUSICAL INSTRUMENT.
CHK
CHK
CHK

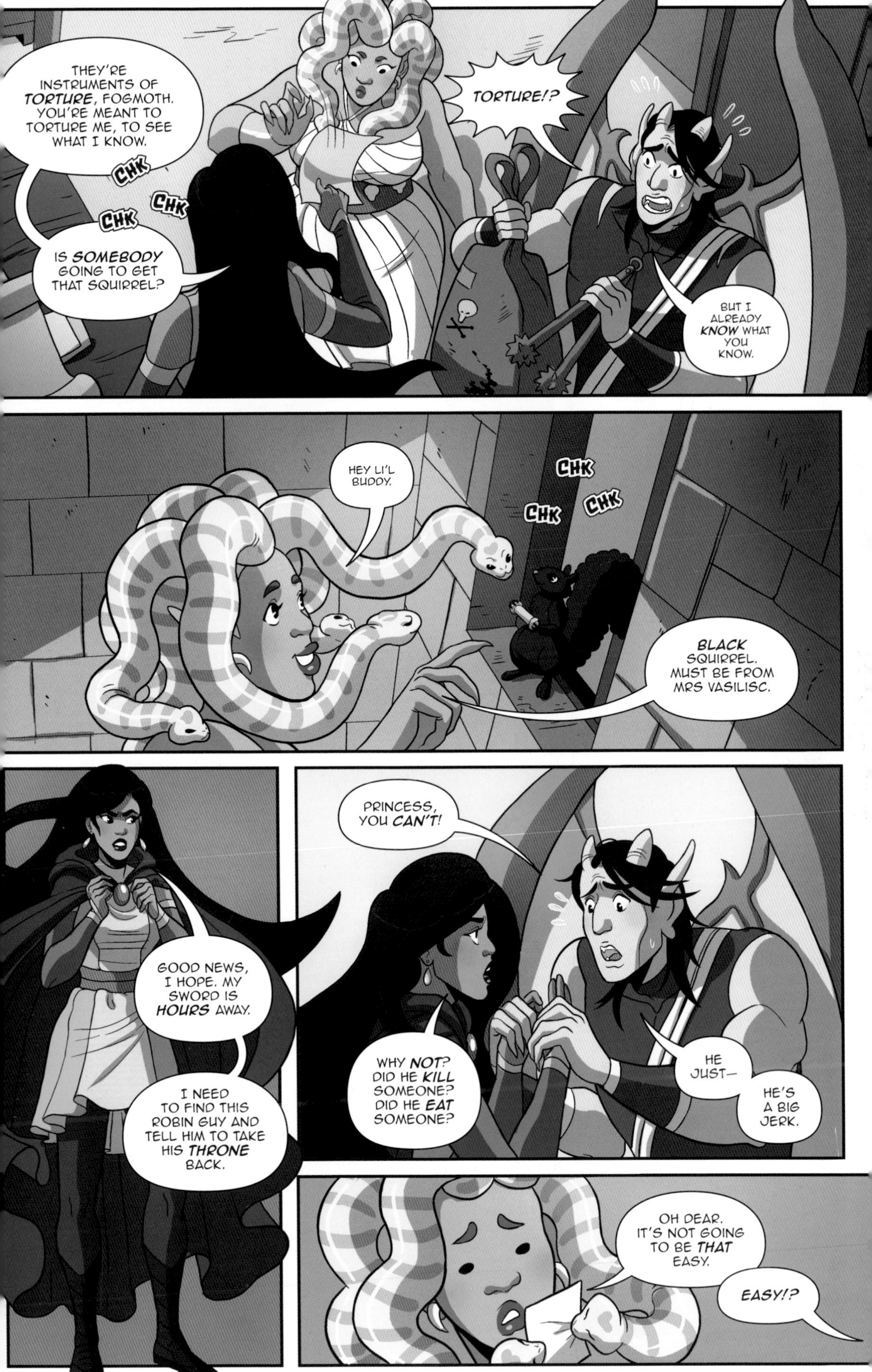
THEY'RE INSTRUMENTS OF TORTURE, FOGMOTH. YOU'RE MEANT TO TORTURE ME, TO SEE WHAT I KNOW.
TORTURE!?
CHK
CHK
CHK
IS SOMEBODY GOING TO GET THAT SQUIRREL?
BUT I ALREADY KNOW WHAT YOU KNOW.
HEY LI'L BUDDY.
CHK
CHK
CHK
BLACK SQUIRREL. MUST BE FROM MRS VASILISC.
GOOD NEWS, I HOPE. MY SWORD IS HOURS AWAY.
I NEED TO FIND THIS ROBIN GUY AND TELL HIM TO TAKE HIS THRONE BACK.
PRINCESS, YOU CAN'T!
WHY NOT? DID HE KILL SOMEONE? DID HE EAT SOMEONE?
HE JUST—
HE'S A BIG JERK.
OH DEAR. IT'S NOT GOING TO BE THAT EASY.
EASY!?

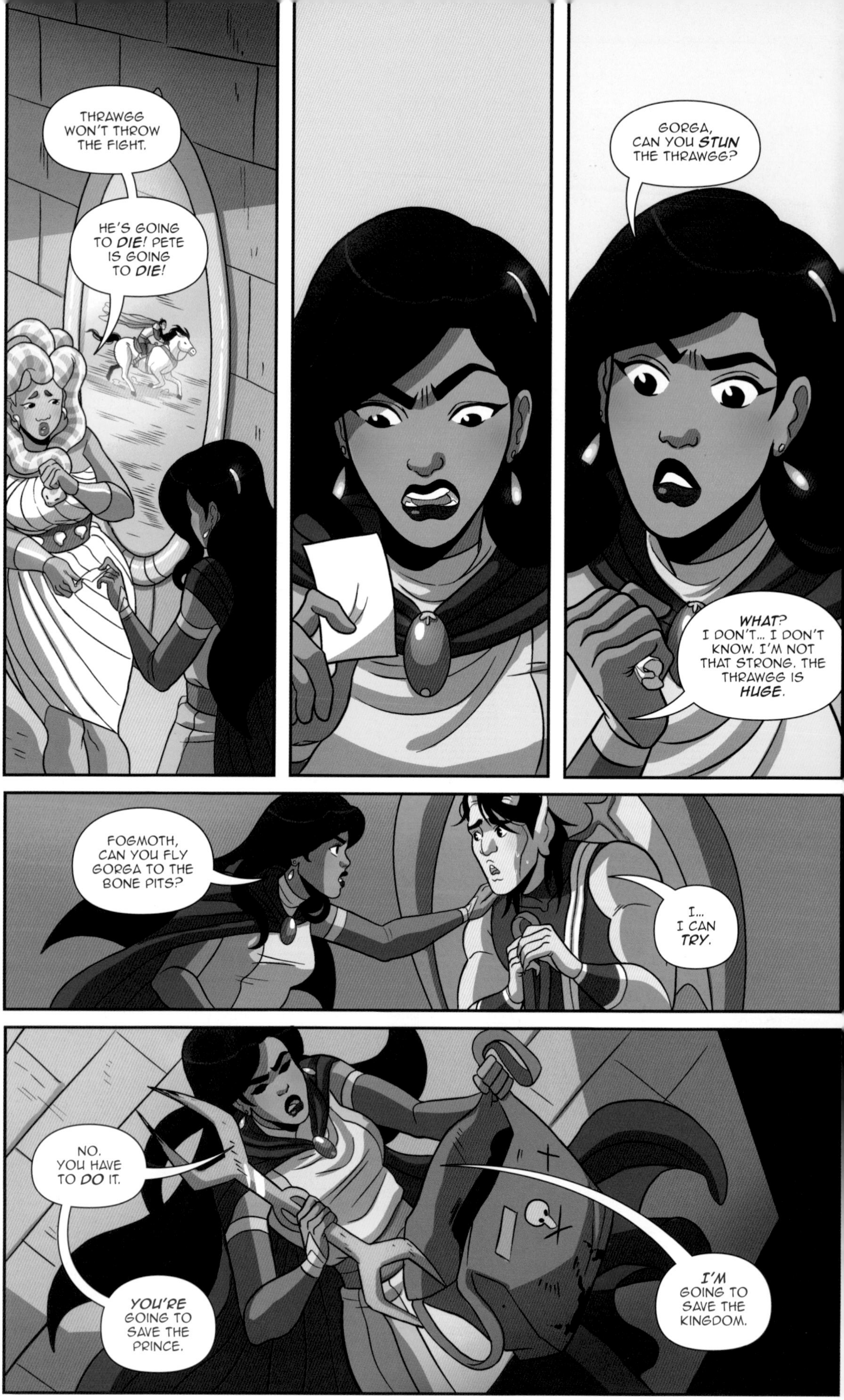
THRAWGG WON'T THROW THE FIGHT.
HE'S GOING TO DIE! PETE IS GOING TO DIE!
GORGA, CAN YOU STUN THE THRAWGG?
WHAT? I DON'T... I DON'T KNOW. I'M NOT THAT STRONG. THE THRAWGG IS HUGE.
FOGMOTH, CAN YOU FLY GORGA TO THE BONE PITS?
I... I CAN TRY.
NO. YOU HAVE TO DO IT.
YOU'RE GOING TO SAVE THE PRINCE.
I'M GOING TO SAVE THE KINGDOM.

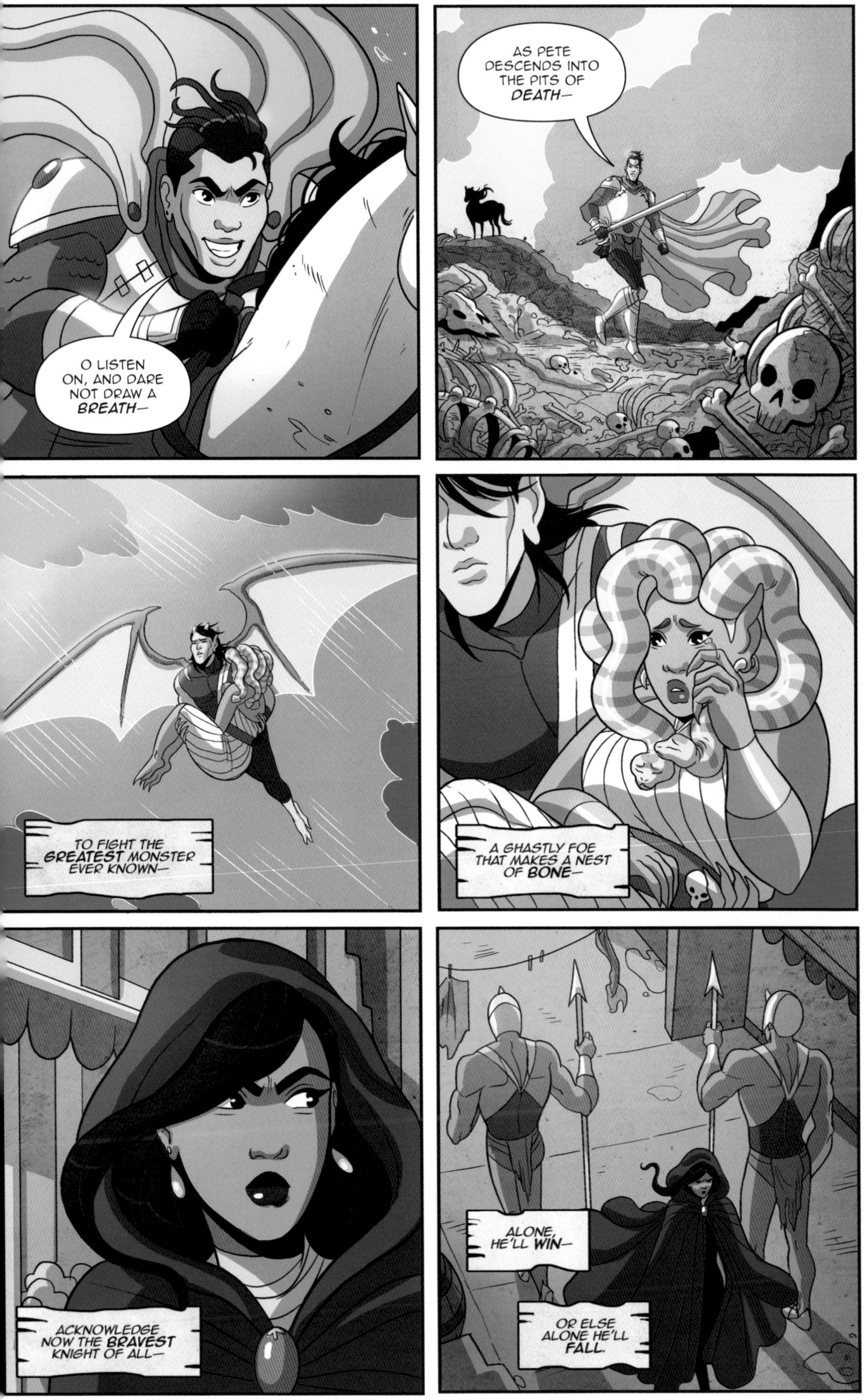
O LISTEN ON, AND DARE NOT DRAW A **BREATH**—
AS PETE DESCENDS INTO THE PITS OF **DEATH**—
TO FIGHT THE **GREATEST** MONSTER EVER KNOWN—
A GHASTLY FOE THAT MAKES A NEST OF **BONE**—
ACKNOWLEDGE NOW THE **BRAVEST** KNIGHT OF ALL—
ALONE, HE'LL **WIN**—
OR ELSE ALONE HE'LL **FALL**.

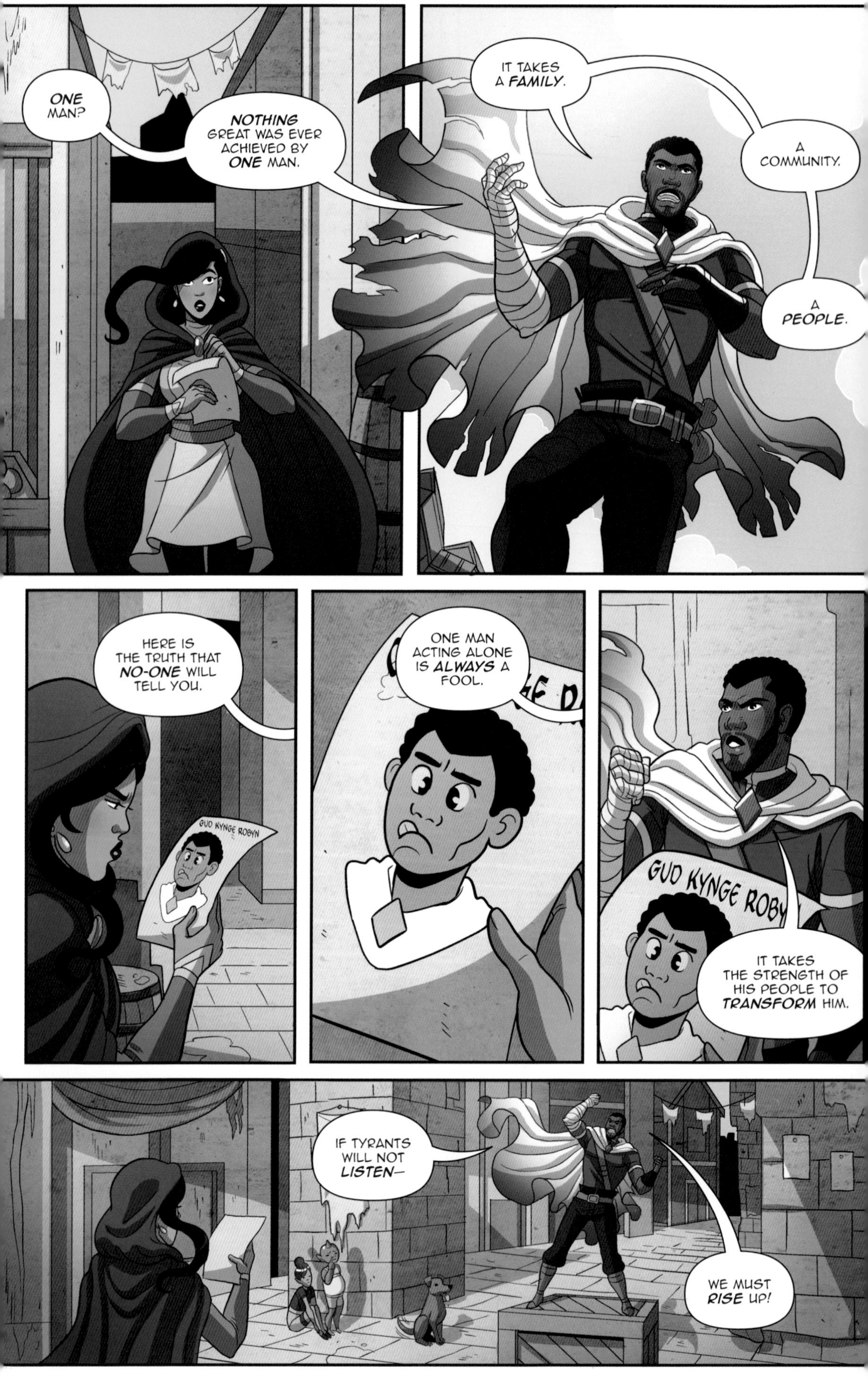
ONE MAN?
NOTHING GREAT WAS EVER ACHIEVED BY ONE MAN.
IT TAKES A FAMILY.
A COMMUNITY.
A PEOPLE.
HERE IS THE TRUTH THAT NO-ONE WILL TELL YOU.
GUD KYNGE ROBYN
ONE MAN ACTING ALONE IS ALWAYS A FOOL.
GUD KYNGE ROBY
IT TAKES THE STRENGTH OF HIS PEOPLE TO TRANSFORM HIM.
IF TYRANTS WILL NOT LISTEN—
WE MUST RISE UP!

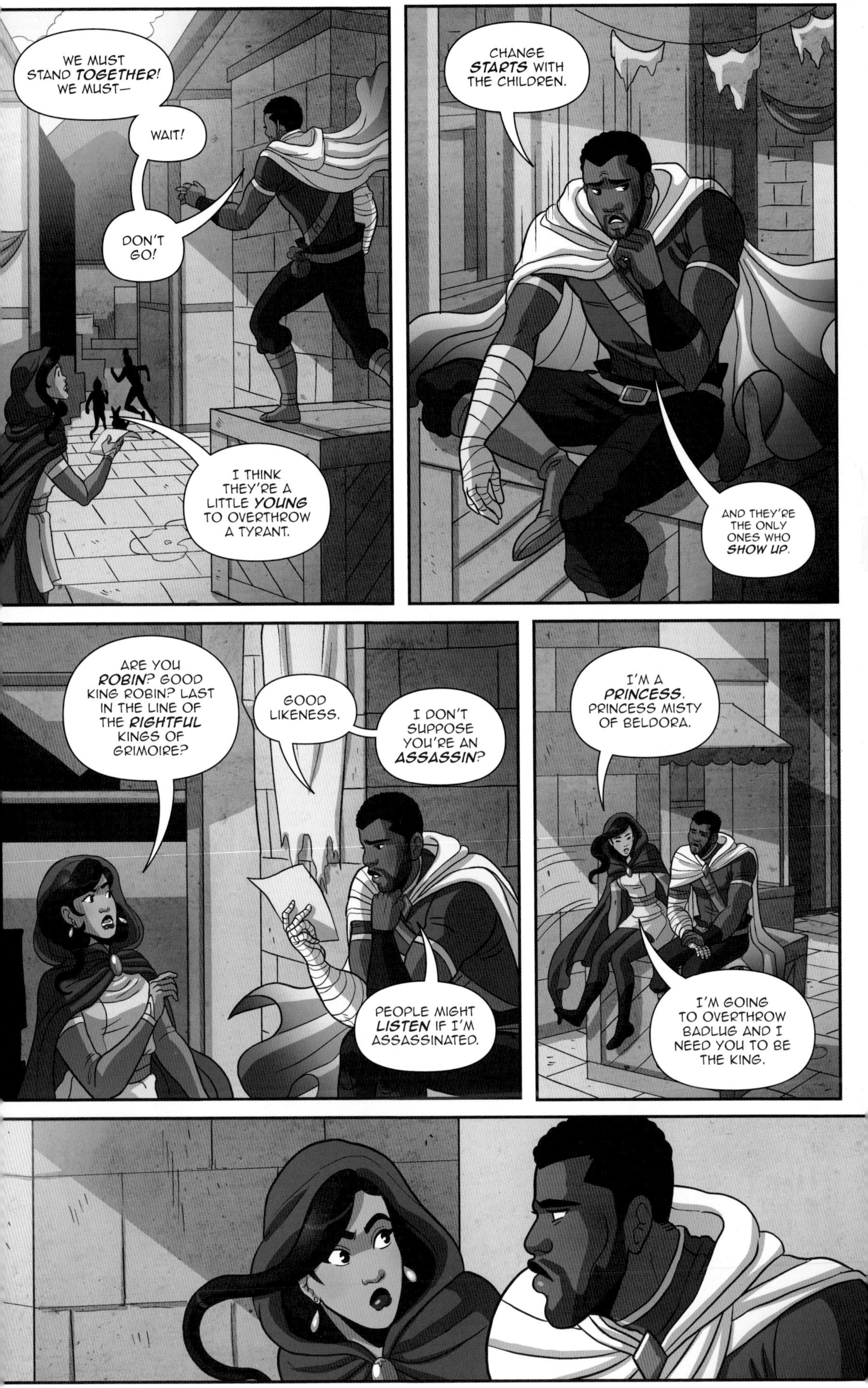
WE MUST STAND TOGETHER! WE MUST—
WAIT!
DON'T GO!
I THINK THEY'RE A LITTLE YOUNG TO OVERTHROW A TYRANT.
CHANGE STARTS WITH THE CHILDREN.
AND THEY'RE THE ONLY ONES WHO SHOW UP.
ARE YOU ROBIN? GOOD KING ROBIN? LAST IN THE LINE OF THE RIGHTFUL KINGS OF GRIMOIRE?
GOOD LIKENESS.
I DON'T SUPPOSE YOU'RE AN ASSASSIN?
PEOPLE MIGHT LISTEN IF I'M ASSASSINATED.
I'M A PRINCESS. PRINCESS MISTY OF BELDORA.
I'M GOING TO OVERTHROW BADLUG AND I NEED YOU TO BE THE KING.

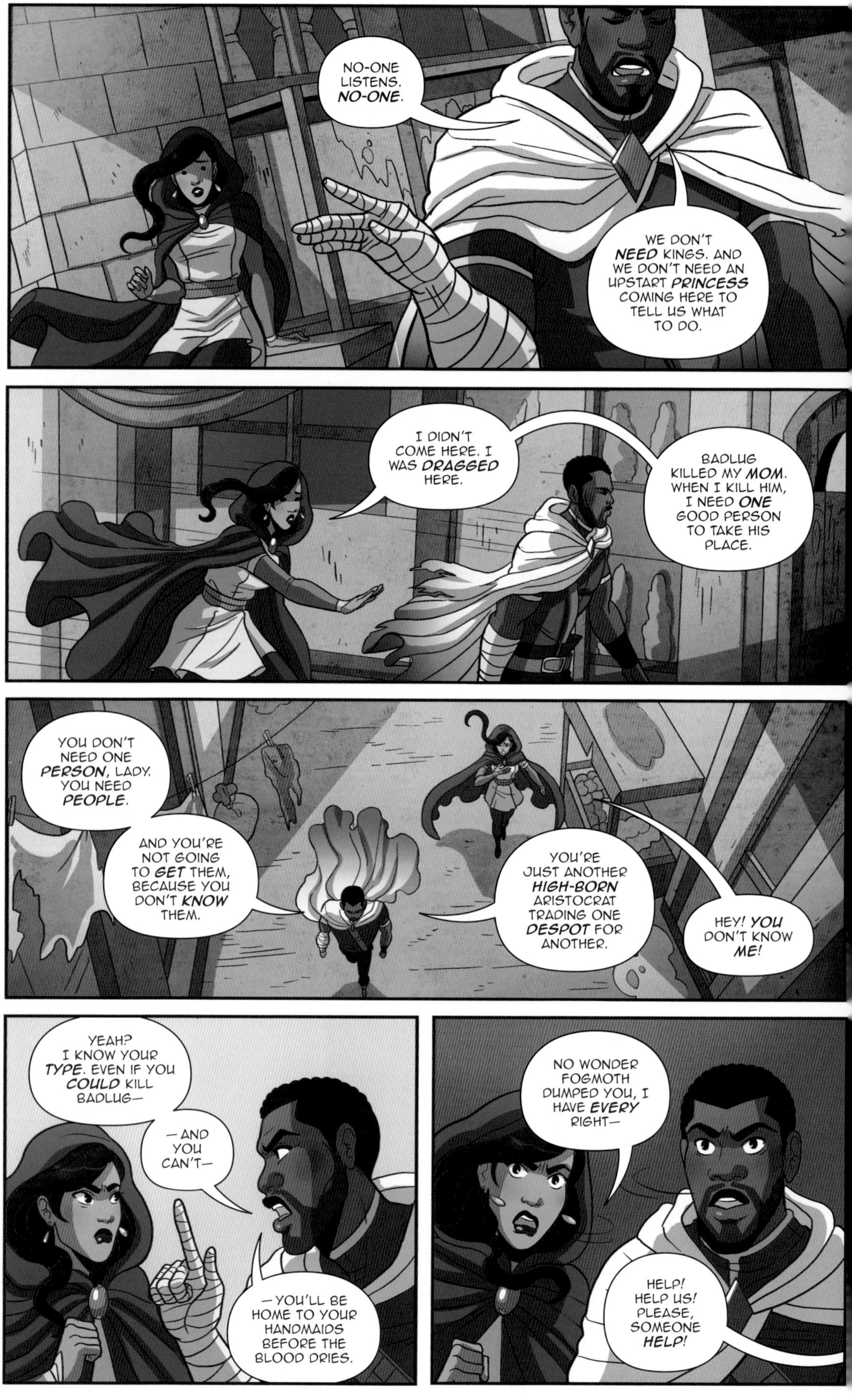
NO-ONE LISTENS. NO-ONE.
WE DON'T NEED KINGS. AND WE DON'T NEED AN UPSTART PRINCESS COMING HERE TO TELL US WHAT TO DO.
I DIDN'T COME HERE. I WAS DRAGGED HERE.
BADLUG KILLED MY MOM. WHEN I KILL HIM, I NEED ONE GOOD PERSON TO TAKE HIS PLACE.
YOU DON'T NEED ONE PERSON, LADY. YOU NEED PEOPLE.
AND YOU'RE NOT GOING TO GET THEM, BECAUSE YOU DON'T KNOW THEM.
YOU'RE JUST ANOTHER HIGH-BORN ARISTOCRAT TRADING ONE DESPOT FOR ANOTHER.
HEY! YOU DON'T KNOW ME!
YEAH? I KNOW YOUR TYPE. EVEN IF YOU COULD KILL BADLUG—
—AND YOU CAN'T—
—YOU'LL BE HOME TO YOUR HANDMAIDS BEFORE THE BLOOD DRIES.
NO WONDER FOGMOTH DUMPED YOU, I HAVE EVERY RIGHT—
HELP! HELP US! PLEASE, SOMEONE HELP!

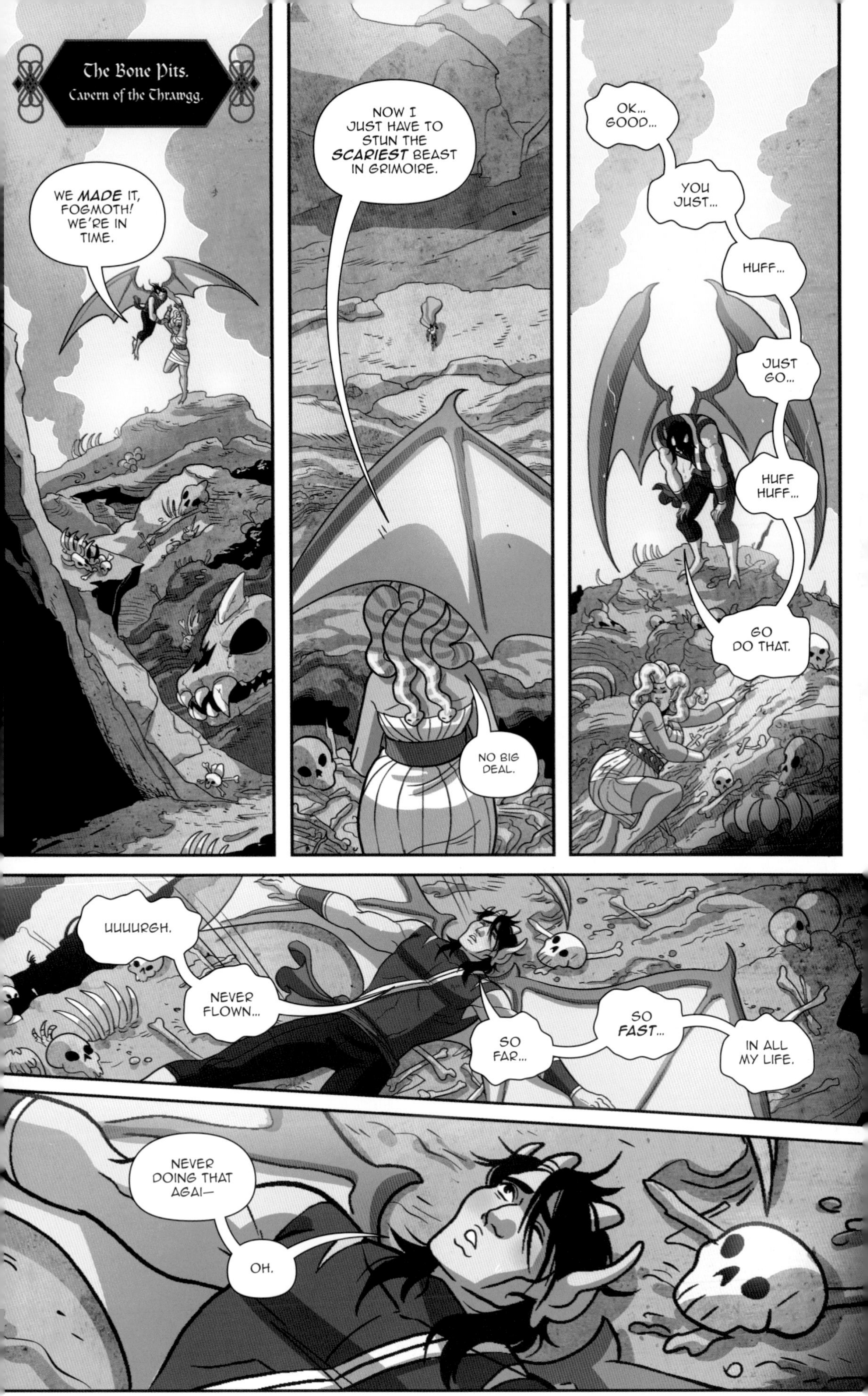
The Bone Pits.
Cavern of the Thrawgg.
WE MADE IT, FOGMOTH! WE'RE IN TIME.
NOW I JUST HAVE TO STUN THE SCARIEST BEAST IN GRIMOIRE.
NO BIG DEAL.
OK... GOOD...
YOU JUST...
HUFF...
JUST GO...
HUFF HUFF...
GO DO THAT.
UUUURGH.
NEVER FLOWN...
SO FAR...
SO FAST...
IN ALL MY LIFE.
NEVER DOING THAT AGAI—
OH.

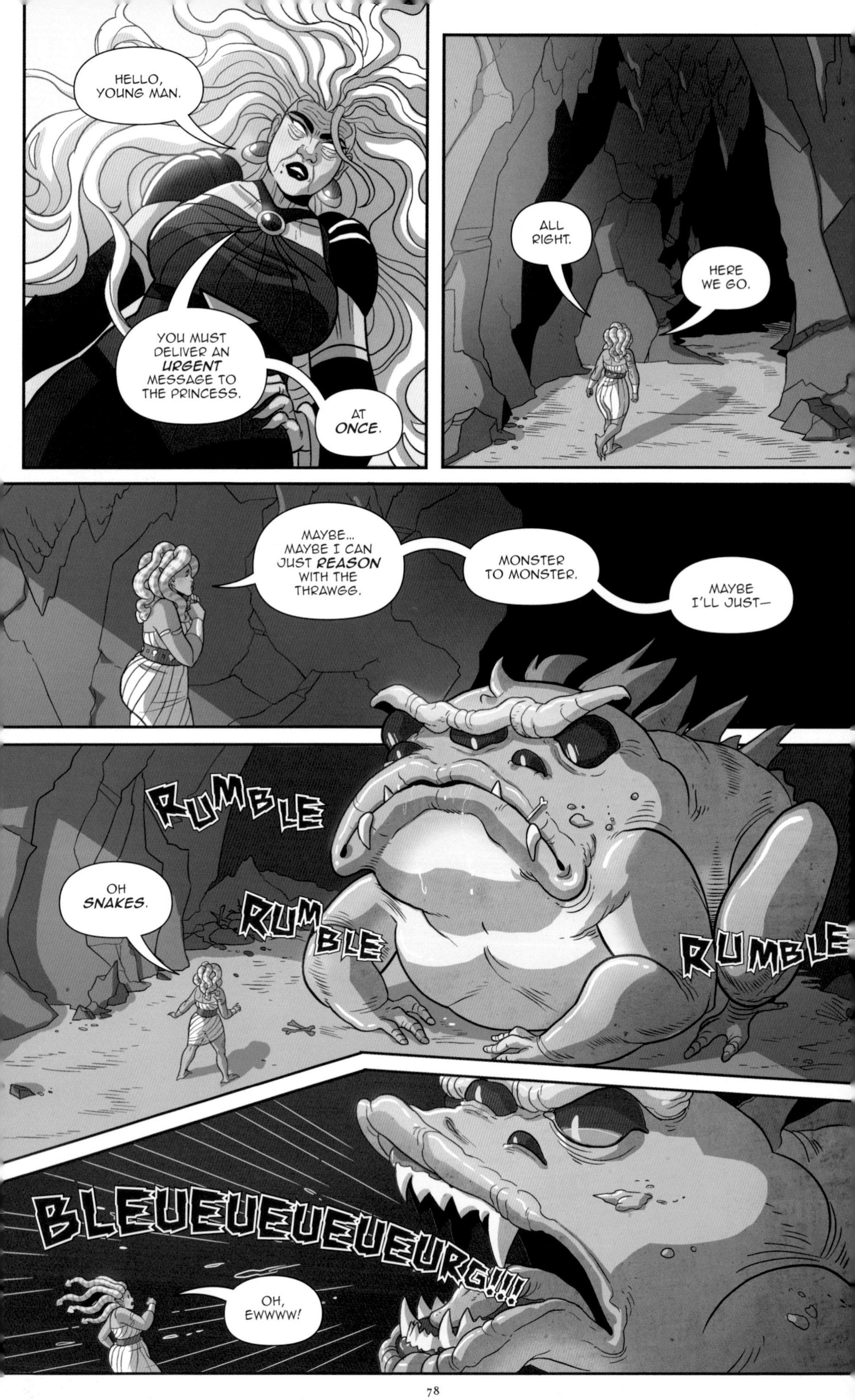
HELLO, YOUNG MAN.
YOU MUST DELIVER AN URGENT MESSAGE TO THE PRINCESS.
AT ONCE.
ALL RIGHT.
HERE WE GO.
MAYBE... MAYBE I CAN JUST REASON WITH THE THRAWGG.
MONSTER TO MONSTER.
MAYBE I'LL JUST—
RUMBLE
OH SNAKES.
RUMBLE
RUMBLE
BLEUEUEUEUEUEURG!!!
OH, EWWWW!

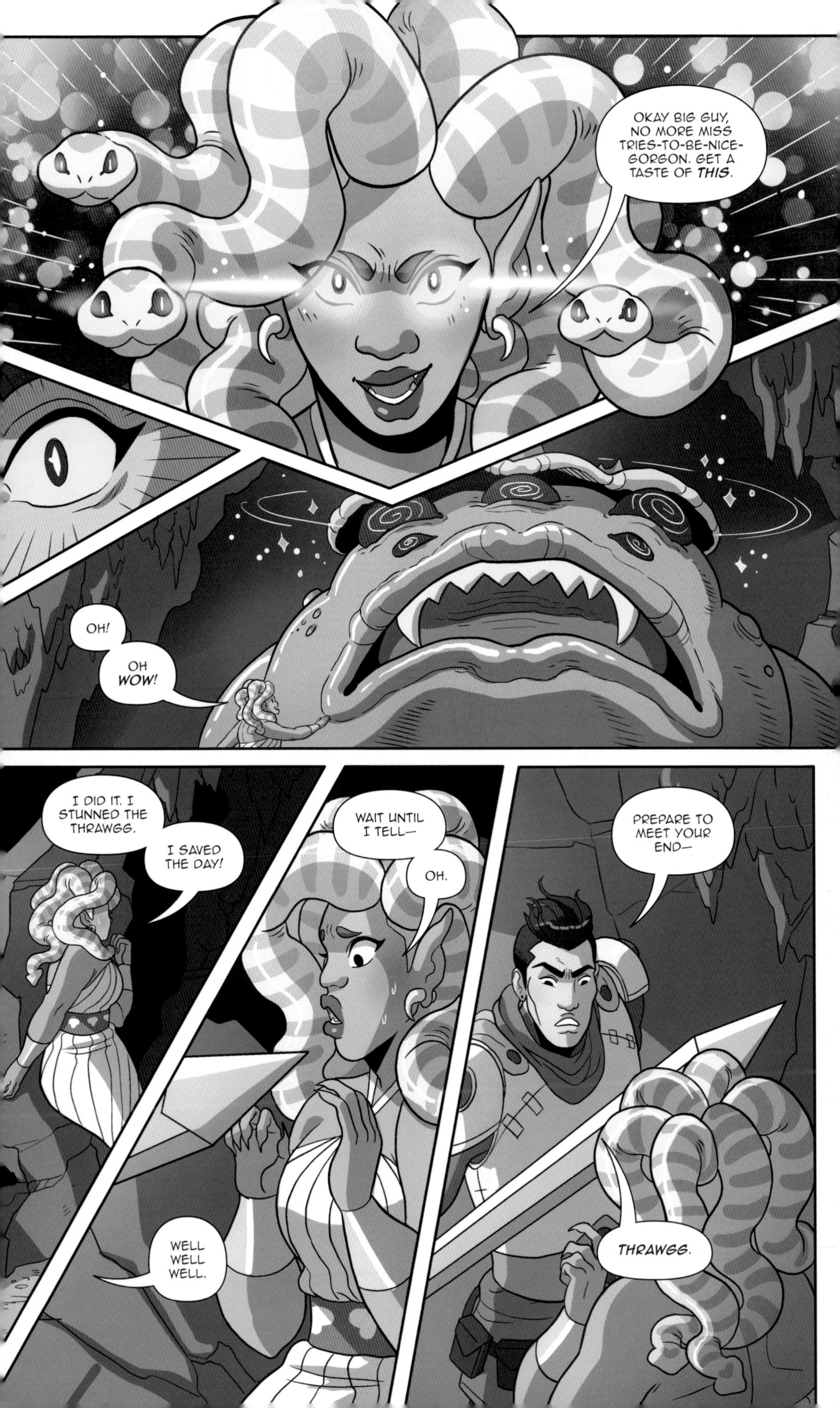
OKAY BIG GUY, NO MORE MISS TRIES-TO-BE-NICE-GORGON. GET A TASTE OF *THIS*.
OH!
OH *WOW!*
I DID IT. I STUNNED THE THRAWGG.
I SAVED THE DAY!
WAIT UNTIL I TELL—
OH.
PREPARE TO MEET YOUR END—
WELL WELL WELL.
THRAWGG.

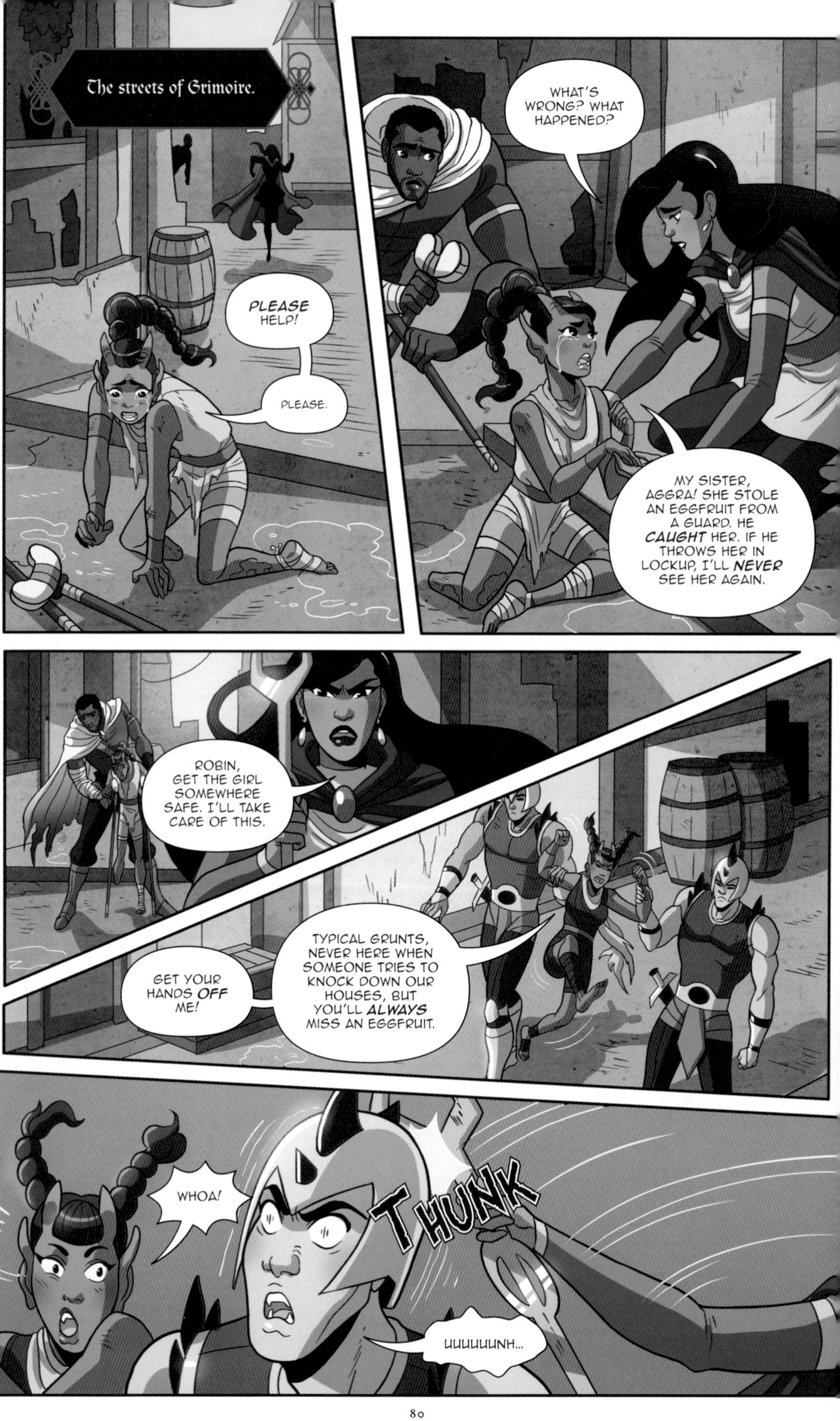
The streets of Grimoire.
PLEASE HELP!
PLEASE.
WHAT'S WRONG? WHAT HAPPENED?
MY SISTER, AGGRA! SHE STOLE AN EGGFRUIT FROM A GUARD. HE CAUGHT HER. IF HE THROWS HER IN LOCKUP, I'LL NEVER SEE HER AGAIN.
ROBIN, GET THE GIRL SOMEWHERE SAFE. I'LL TAKE CARE OF THIS.
GET YOUR HANDS OFF ME!
TYPICAL GRUNTS, NEVER HERE WHEN SOMEONE TRIES TO KNOCK DOWN OUR HOUSES, BUT YOU'LL ALWAYS MISS AN EGGFRUIT.
WHOA!
THUNK
UUUUUUNH...

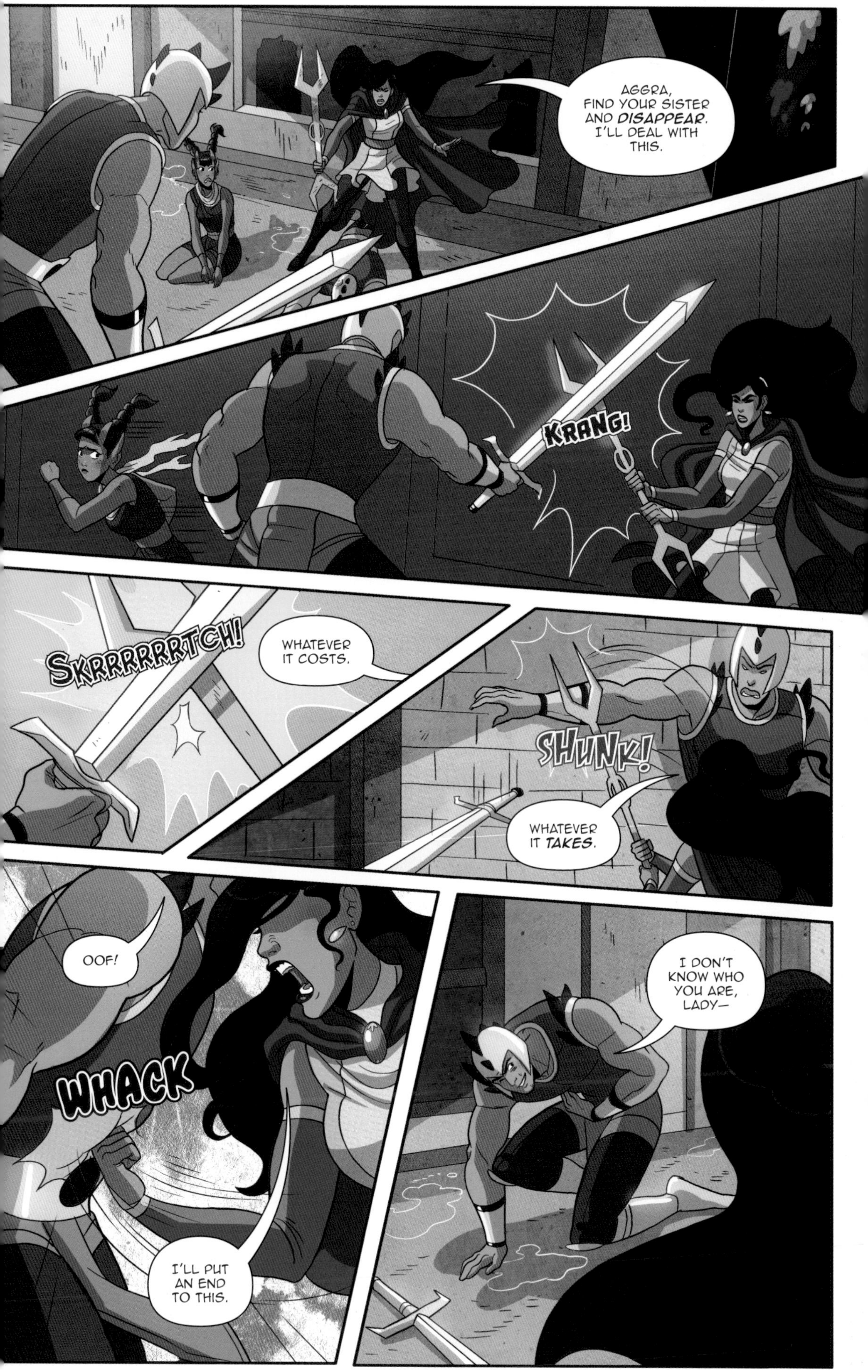
AGGRA, FIND YOUR SISTER AND DISAPPEAR. I'LL DEAL WITH THIS.
KRANG!
SKRRRRRRTCH!
WHATEVER IT COSTS.
SHUNK!
WHATEVER IT TAKES.
OOF!
WHACK
I'LL PUT AN END TO THIS.
I DON'T KNOW WHO YOU ARE, LADY—

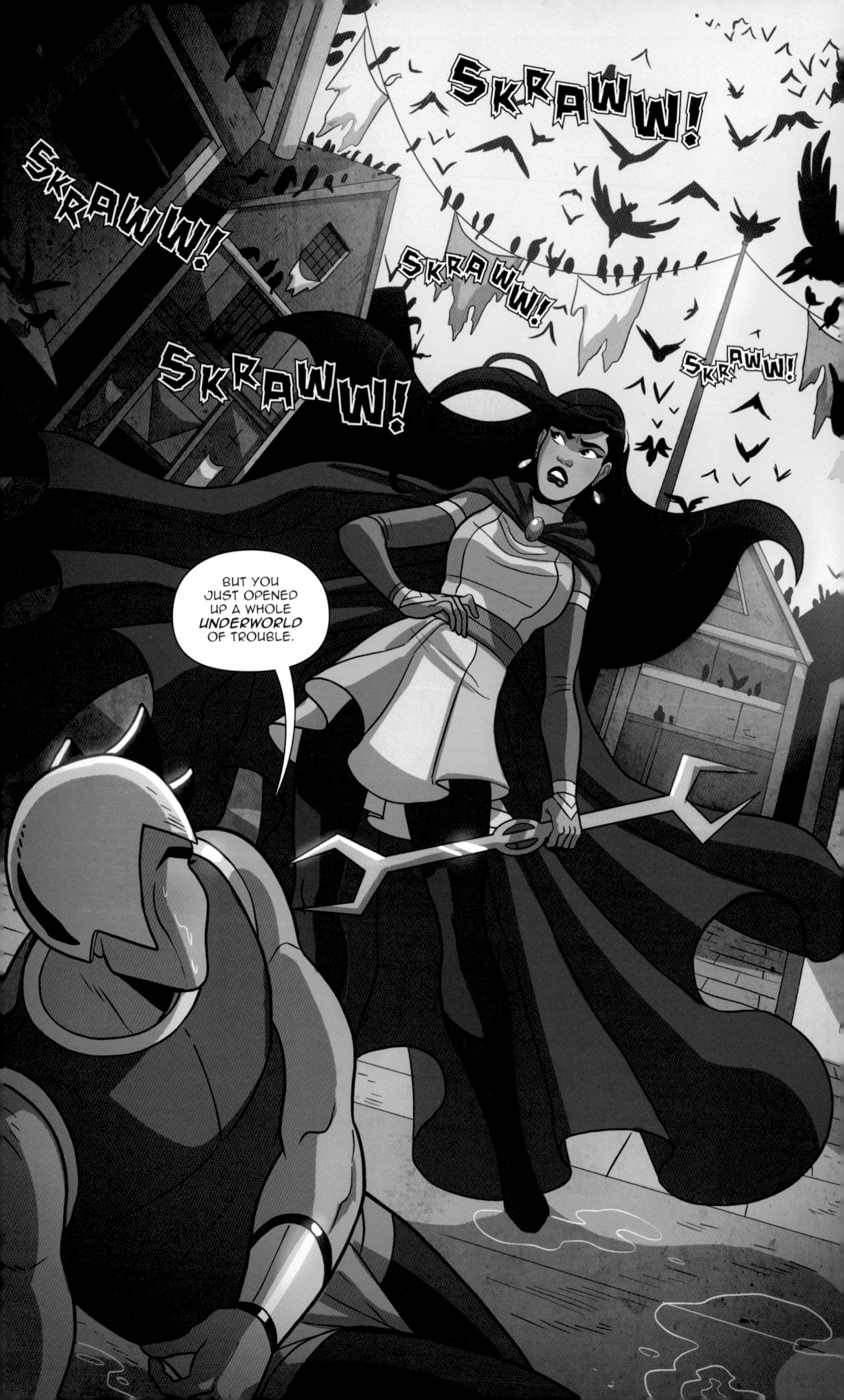
SKRAWW!
SKRAWW!
SKRAWW!
SKRAWW!
SKRAWW!
BUT YOU JUST OPENED UP A WHOLE UNDERWORLD OF TROUBLE.

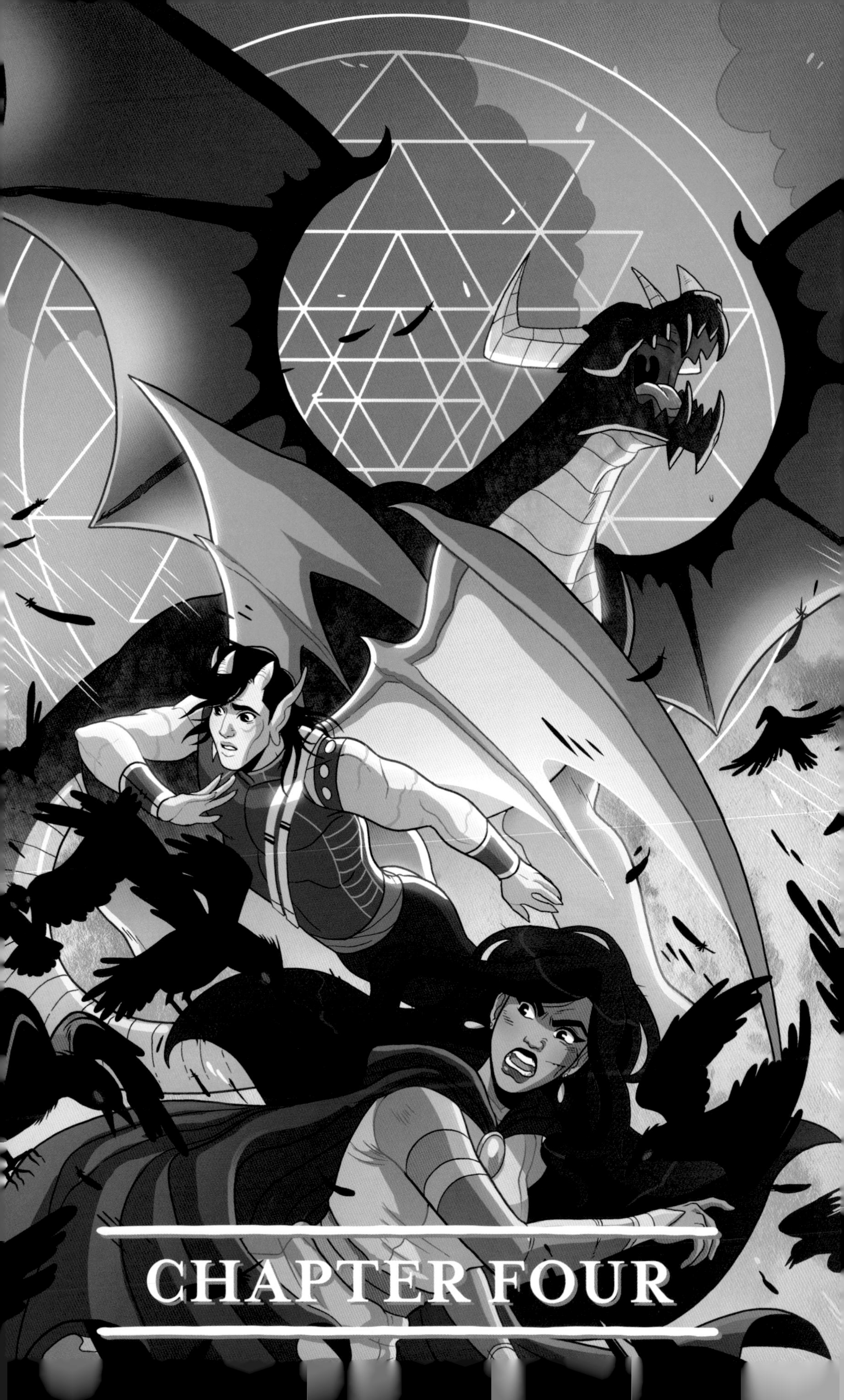

CHAPTER FOUR

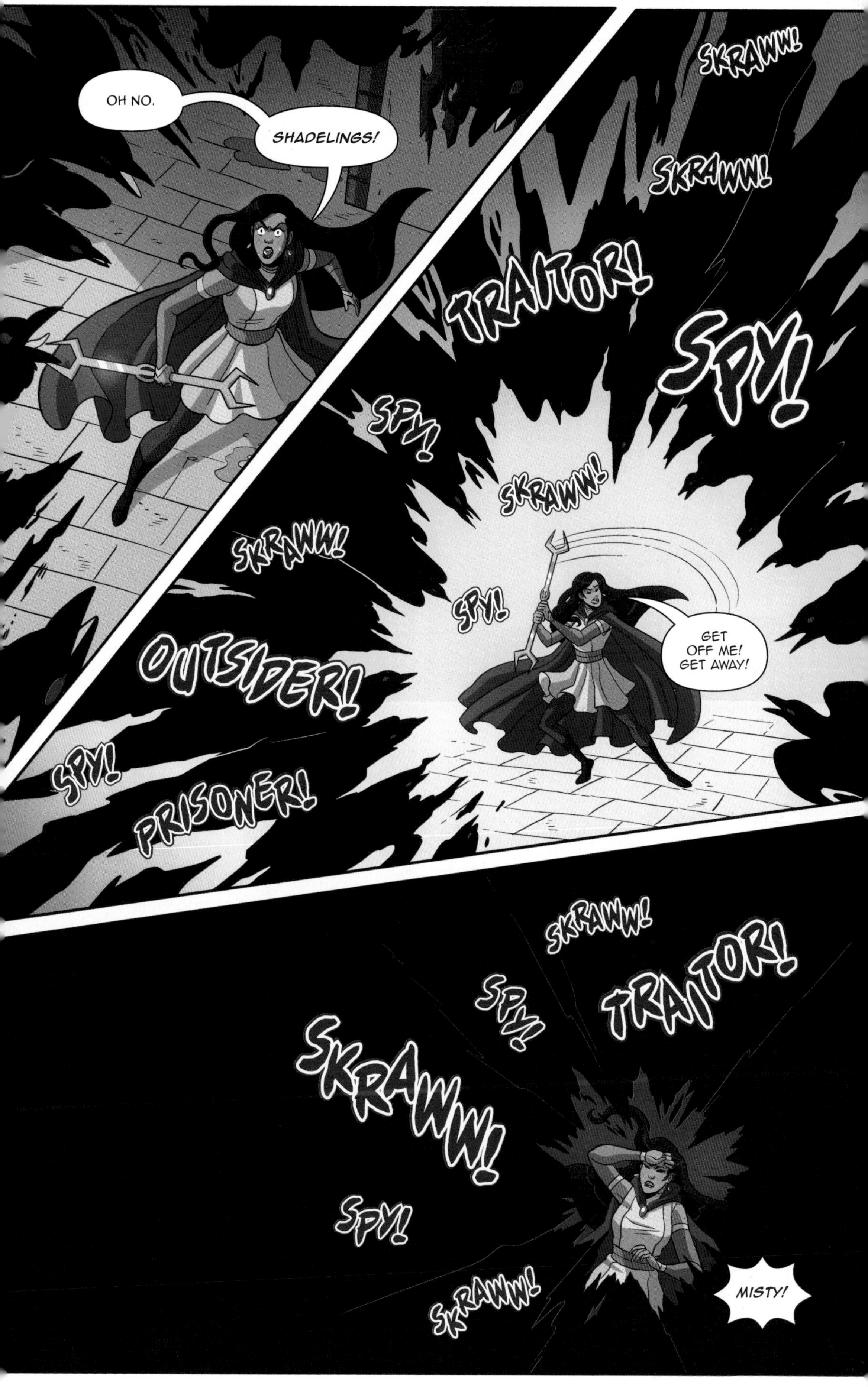
OH NO.
SHADELINGS!
SKRAWW!
SKRAWW!
TRAITOR!
SPY!
SPY!
SKRAWW!
SKRAWW!
SPY!
GET OFF ME! GET AWAY!
OUTSIDER!
SPY!
PRISONER!
SKRAWW!
SPY!
TRAITOR!
SKRAWW!
SPY!
SKRAWW!
MISTY!

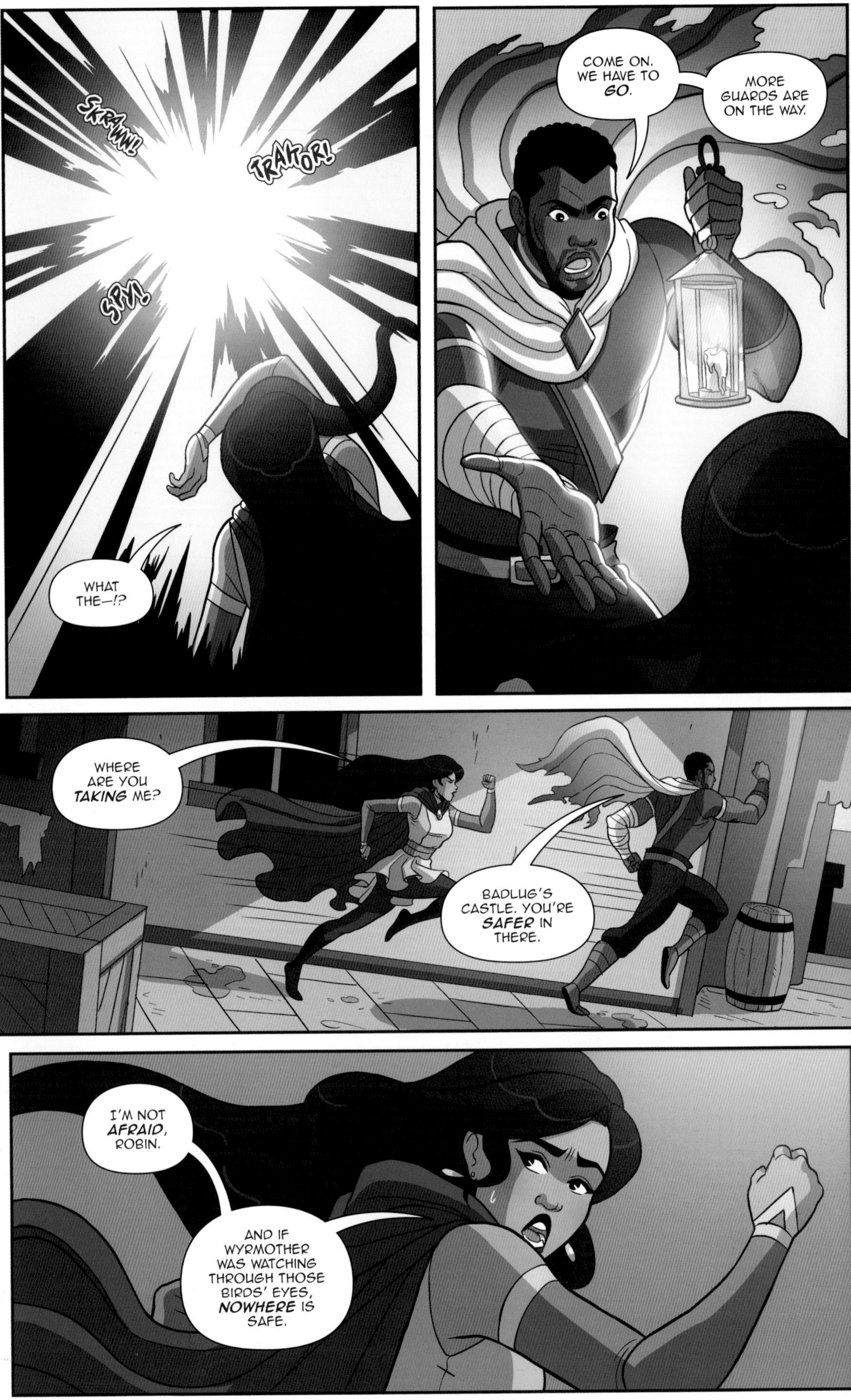
SKRAWW!
TRAKOR!
SPY!
WHAT THE—!?
COME ON. WE HAVE TO GO.
MORE GUARDS ARE ON THE WAY.
WHERE ARE YOU TAKING ME?
BADLUG'S CASTLE. YOU'RE SAFER IN THERE.
I'M NOT AFRAID, ROBIN.
AND IF WYRMOTHER WAS WATCHING THROUGH THOSE BIRDS' EYES, NOWHERE IS SAFE.

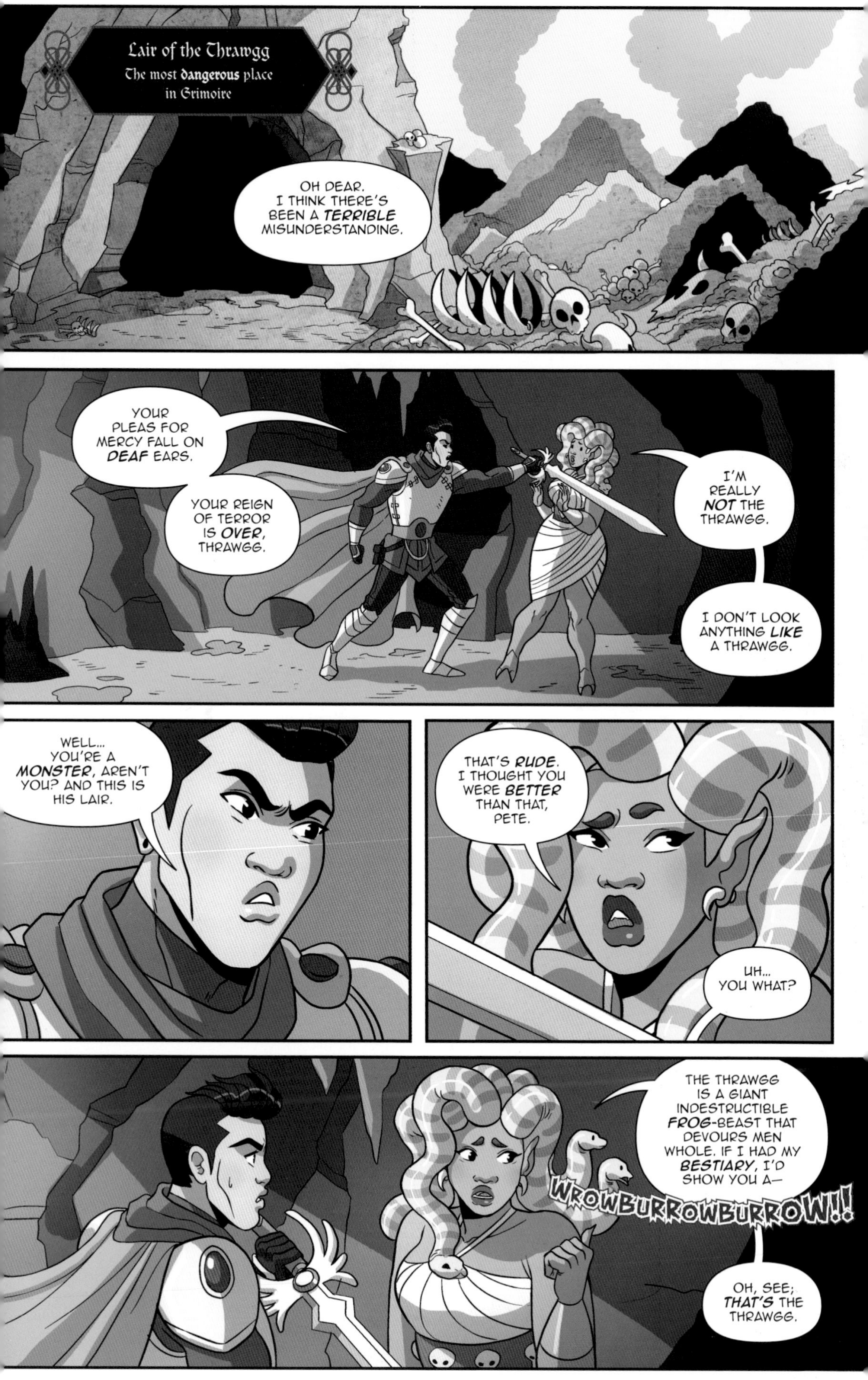

Lair of the Thrawgg
The most **dangerous** place in Grimoire
OH DEAR. I THINK THERE'S BEEN A *TERRIBLE* MISUNDERSTANDING.
YOUR PLEAS FOR MERCY FALL ON *DEAF* EARS.
YOUR REIGN OF TERROR IS *OVER*, THRAWGG.
I'M REALLY *NOT* THE THRAWGG.
I DON'T LOOK ANYTHING *LIKE* A THRAWGG.
WELL... YOU'RE A *MONSTER*, AREN'T YOU? AND THIS IS HIS LAIR.
THAT'S *RUDE*. I THOUGHT YOU WERE *BETTER* THAN THAT, PETE.
UH... YOU WHAT?
THE THRAWGG IS A GIANT INDESTRUCTIBLE *FROG*-BEAST THAT DEVOURS MEN WHOLE. IF I HAD MY *BESTIARY*, I'D SHOW YOU A—
WROWBURROWBURROW!!
OH, SEE; *THAT'S* THE THRAWGG.

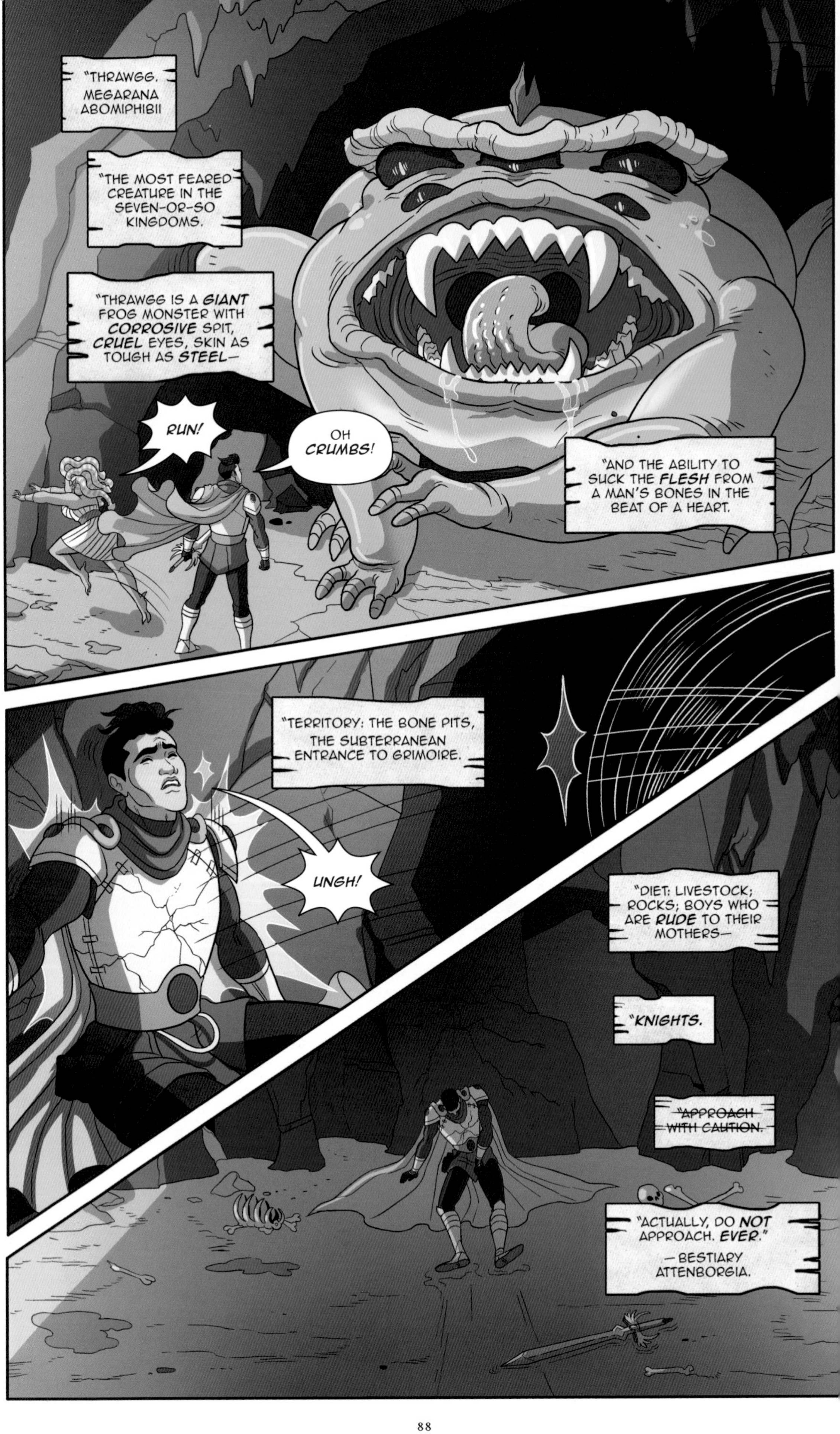
"THRAWGG. MEGARANA ABOMIPHIBII
"THE MOST FEARED CREATURE IN THE SEVEN-OR-SO KINGDOMS.
"THRAWGG IS A GIANT FROG MONSTER WITH CORROSIVE SPIT, CRUEL EYES, SKIN AS TOUGH AS STEEL—
RUN!
OH CRUMBS!
"AND THE ABILITY TO SUCK THE FLESH FROM A MAN'S BONES IN THE BEAT OF A HEART.
"TERRITORY: THE BONE PITS, THE SUBTERRANEAN ENTRANCE TO GRIMOIRE.
UNGH!
"DIET: LIVESTOCK; ROCKS; BOYS WHO ARE RUDE TO THEIR MOTHERS—
"KNIGHTS.
~~"APPROACH WITH CAUTION.~~
"ACTUALLY, DO NOT APPROACH. EVER."
—BESTIARY ATTENBORGIA.

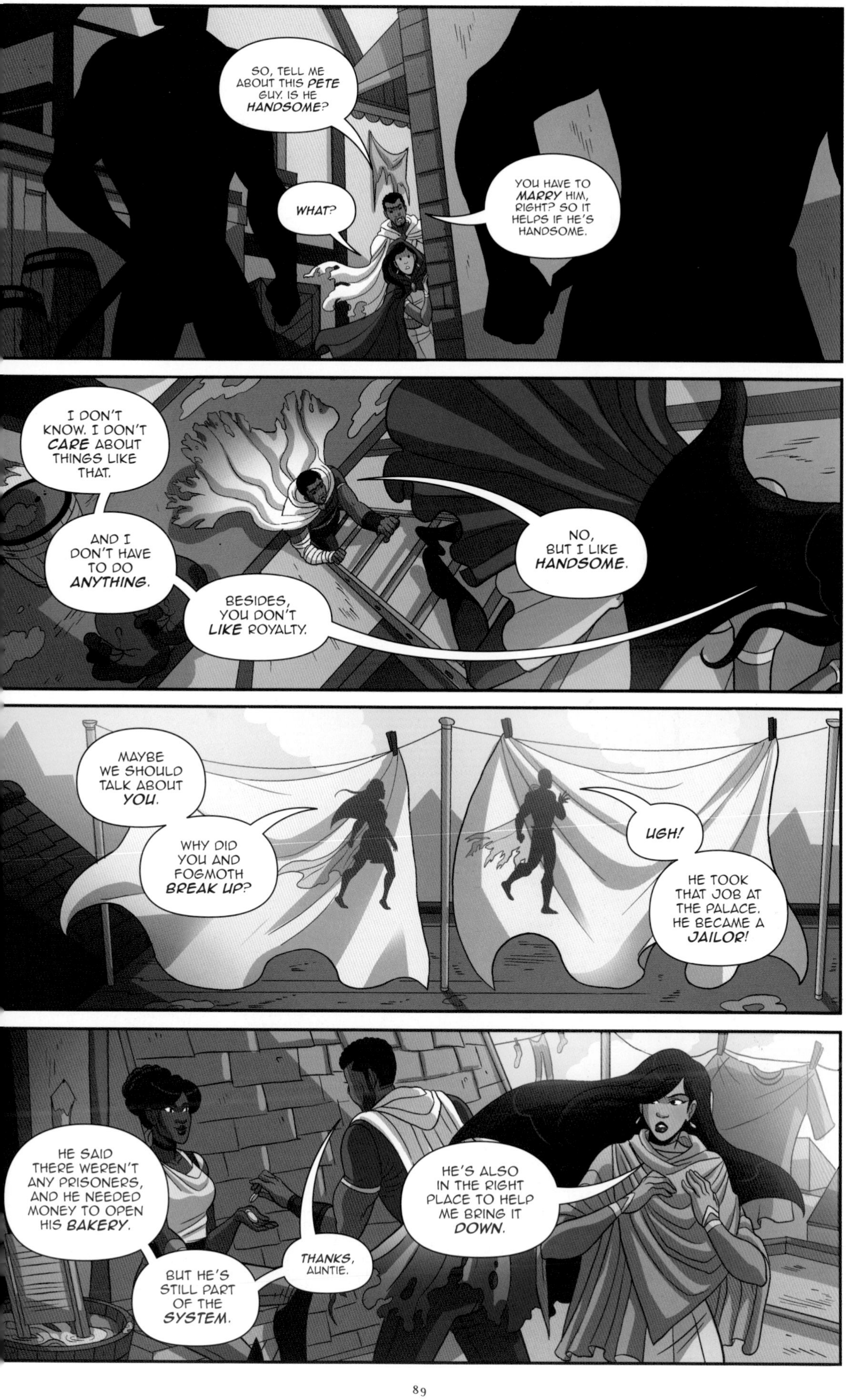

SO, TELL ME ABOUT THIS PETE GUY. IS HE HANDSOME?
WHAT?
YOU HAVE TO MARRY HIM, RIGHT? SO IT HELPS IF HE'S HANDSOME.
I DON'T KNOW. I DON'T CARE ABOUT THINGS LIKE THAT.
AND I DON'T HAVE TO DO ANYTHING.
BESIDES, YOU DON'T LIKE ROYALTY.
NO, BUT I LIKE HANDSOME.
MAYBE WE SHOULD TALK ABOUT YOU.
WHY DID YOU AND FOGMOTH BREAK UP?
UGH!
HE TOOK THAT JOB AT THE PALACE. HE BECAME A JAILOR!
HE SAID THERE WEREN'T ANY PRISONERS, AND HE NEEDED MONEY TO OPEN HIS BAKERY.
BUT HE'S STILL PART OF THE SYSTEM.
THANKS, AUNTIE.
HE'S ALSO IN THE RIGHT PLACE TO HELP ME BRING IT DOWN.

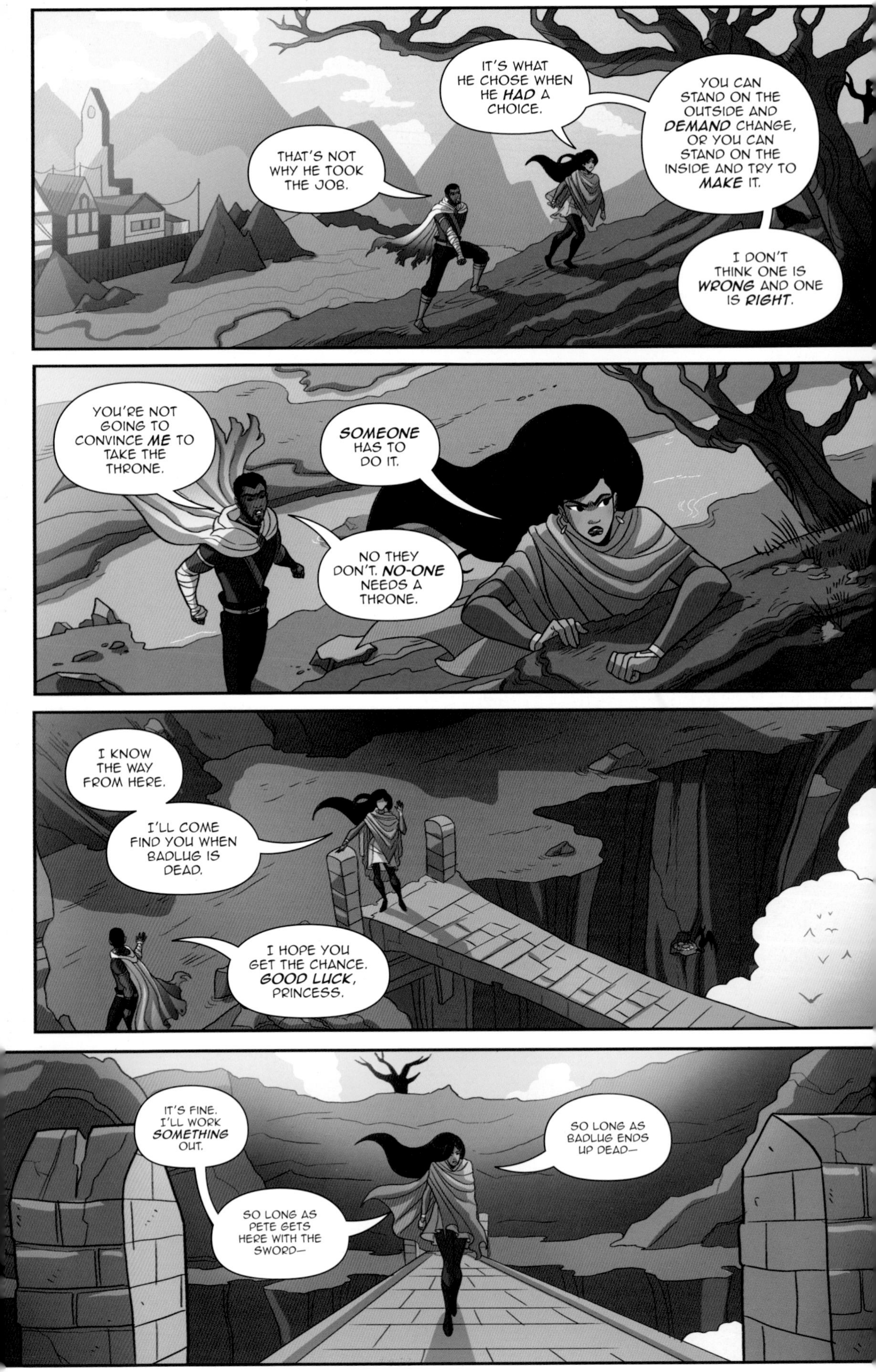

THAT'S NOT WHY HE TOOK THE JOB.
IT'S WHAT HE CHOSE WHEN HE *HAD* A CHOICE.
YOU CAN STAND ON THE OUTSIDE AND *DEMAND* CHANGE, OR YOU CAN STAND ON THE INSIDE AND TRY TO *MAKE* IT.
I DON'T THINK ONE IS *WRONG* AND ONE IS *RIGHT*.
YOU'RE NOT GOING TO CONVINCE *ME* TO TAKE THE THRONE.
SOMEONE HAS TO DO IT.
NO THEY DON'T. *NO-ONE* NEEDS A THRONE.
I KNOW THE WAY FROM HERE.
I'LL COME FIND YOU WHEN BADLUG IS DEAD.
I HOPE YOU GET THE CHANCE. *GOOD LUCK*, PRINCESS.
IT'S FINE. I'LL WORK *SOMETHING* OUT.
SO LONG AS PETE GETS HERE WITH THE SWORD—
SO LONG AS BADLUG ENDS UP DEAD—

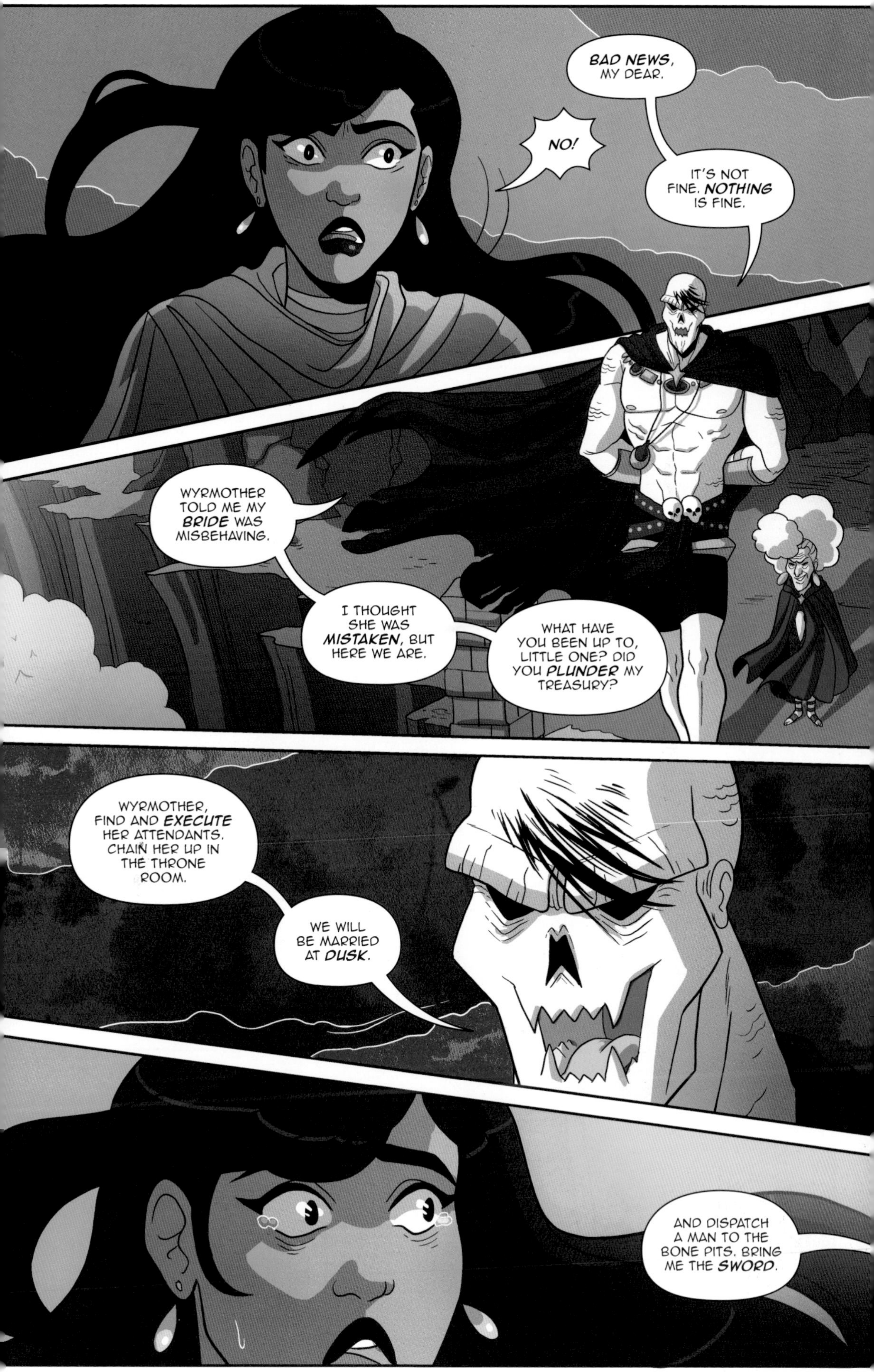
BAD NEWS, MY DEAR.
NO!
IT'S NOT FINE. NOTHING IS FINE.
WYRMOTHER TOLD ME MY BRIDE WAS MISBEHAVING.
I THOUGHT SHE WAS MISTAKEN, BUT HERE WE ARE.
WHAT HAVE YOU BEEN UP TO, LITTLE ONE? DID YOU PLUNDER MY TREASURY?
WYRMOTHER, FIND AND EXECUTE HER ATTENDANTS. CHAIN HER UP IN THE THRONE ROOM.
WE WILL BE MARRIED AT DUSK.
AND DISPATCH A MAN TO THE BONE PITS. BRING ME THE SWORD.

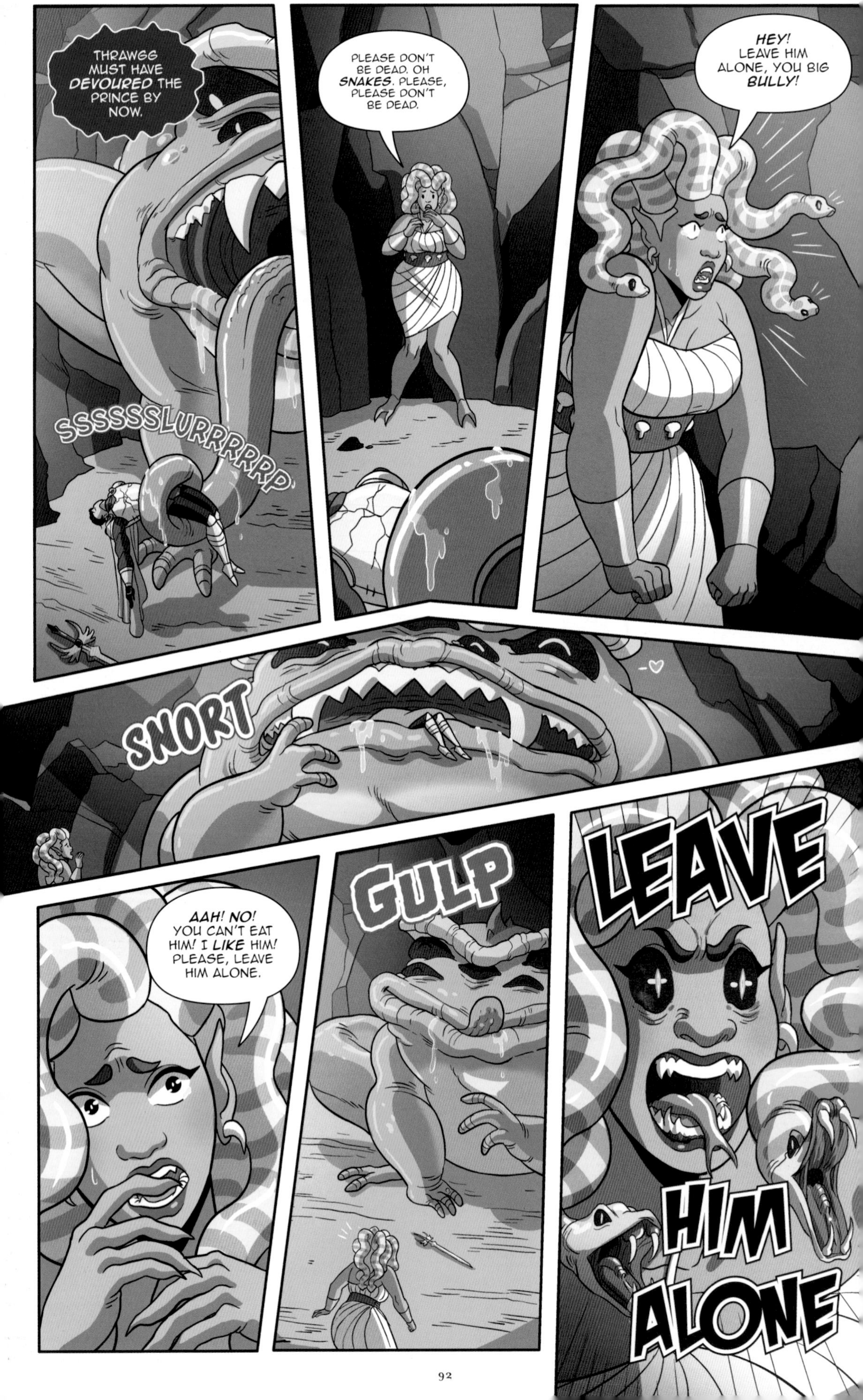
THRAWGG MUST HAVE DEVOURED THE PRINCE BY NOW.
SSSSSSLURRRRRRP
PLEASE DON'T BE DEAD. OH SNAKES. PLEASE, PLEASE DON'T BE DEAD.
HEY! LEAVE HIM ALONE, YOU BIG BULLY!
SNORT
AAH! NO! YOU CAN'T EAT HIM! I LIKE HIM! PLEASE, LEAVE HIM ALONE.
GULP
LEAVE HIM ALONE

OH GOSH.

OH **GOSH!**

I DID IT. I—

KRRRRKKK

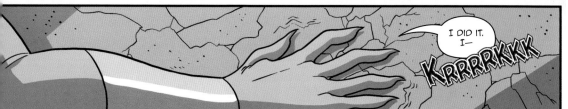

PETE!

FWOOOOMP!!!

PETE, WAKE UP! I DEFEATED THE MIGHTY **THRAWGG.** IT'LL TAKE **FOREVER** TO PUT HIM BACK TOGETHER!

I THOUGHT I'D NEVER GRADUATE PAST STUNNING.

STU— STUNNING?

OH.

STUNNING.

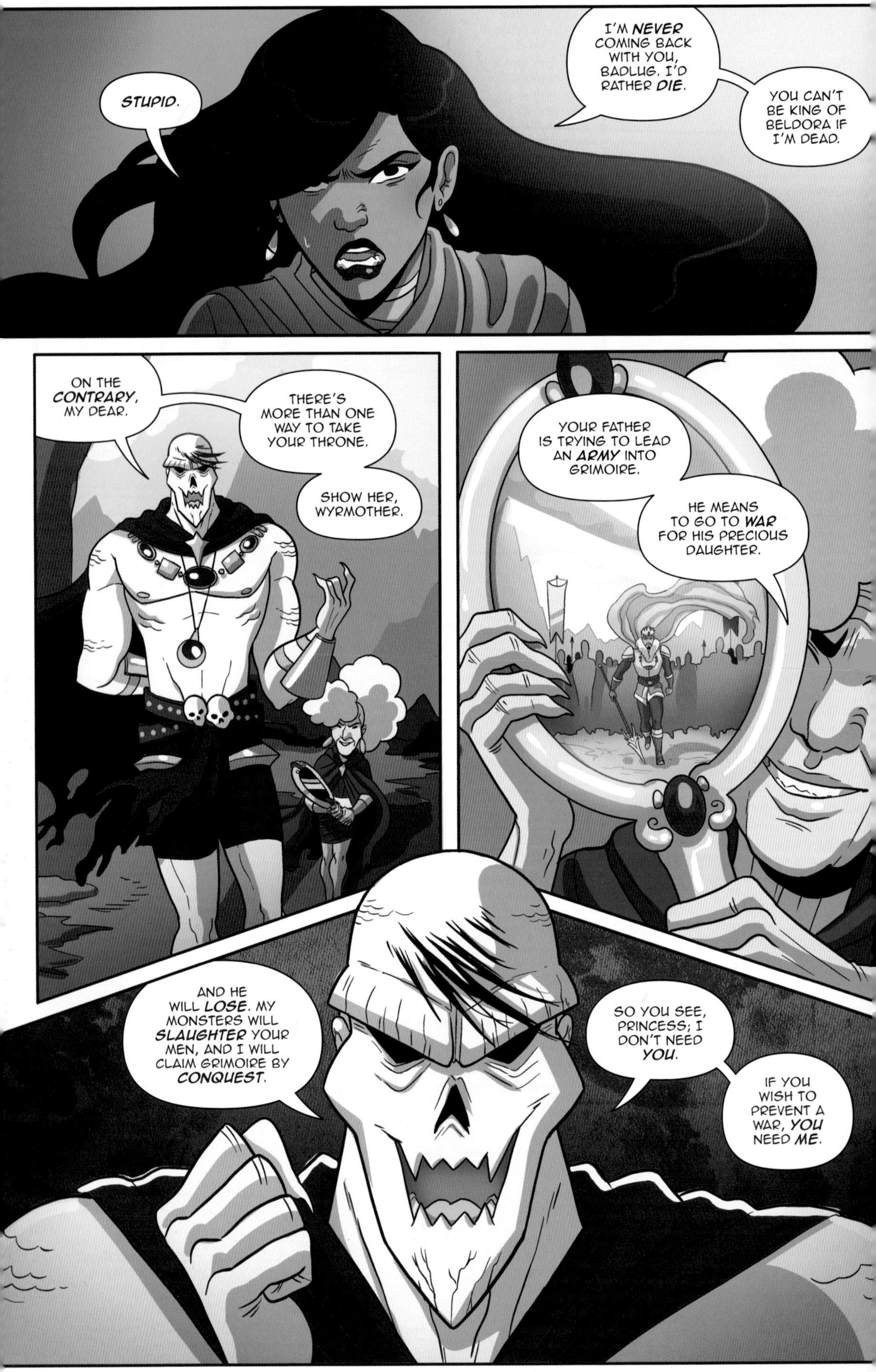
STUPID.
I'M NEVER COMING BACK WITH YOU, BADLUG. I'D RATHER DIE.
YOU CAN'T BE KING OF BELDORA IF I'M DEAD.
ON THE CONTRARY, MY DEAR.
THERE'S MORE THAN ONE WAY TO TAKE YOUR THRONE.
SHOW HER, WYRMOTHER.
YOUR FATHER IS TRYING TO LEAD AN ARMY INTO GRIMOIRE.
HE MEANS TO GO TO WAR FOR HIS PRECIOUS DAUGHTER.
AND HE WILL LOSE. MY MONSTERS WILL SLAUGHTER YOUR MEN, AND I WILL CLAIM GRIMOIRE BY CONQUEST.
SO YOU SEE, PRINCESS; I DON'T NEED YOU.
IF YOU WISH TO PREVENT A WAR, YOU NEED ME.

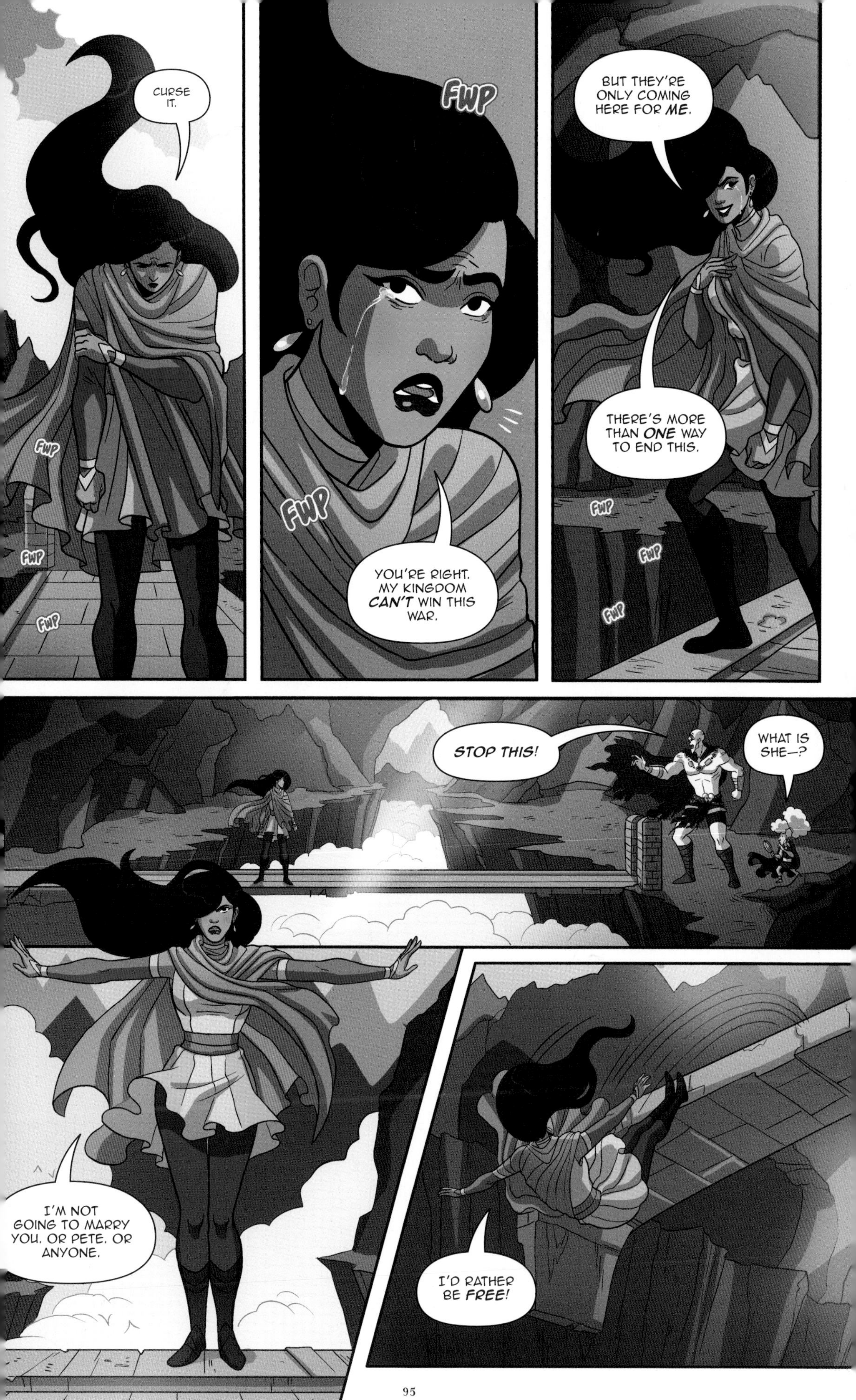
CURSE IT.
FWP
FWP
FWP
FWP
FWP
YOU'RE RIGHT. MY KINGDOM CAN'T WIN THIS WAR.
BUT THEY'RE ONLY COMING HERE FOR ME.
THERE'S MORE THAN ONE WAY TO END THIS.
FWP
FWP
FWP
STOP THIS!
WHAT IS SHE—?
I'M NOT GOING TO MARRY YOU. OR PETE. OR ANYONE.
I'D RATHER BE FREE!

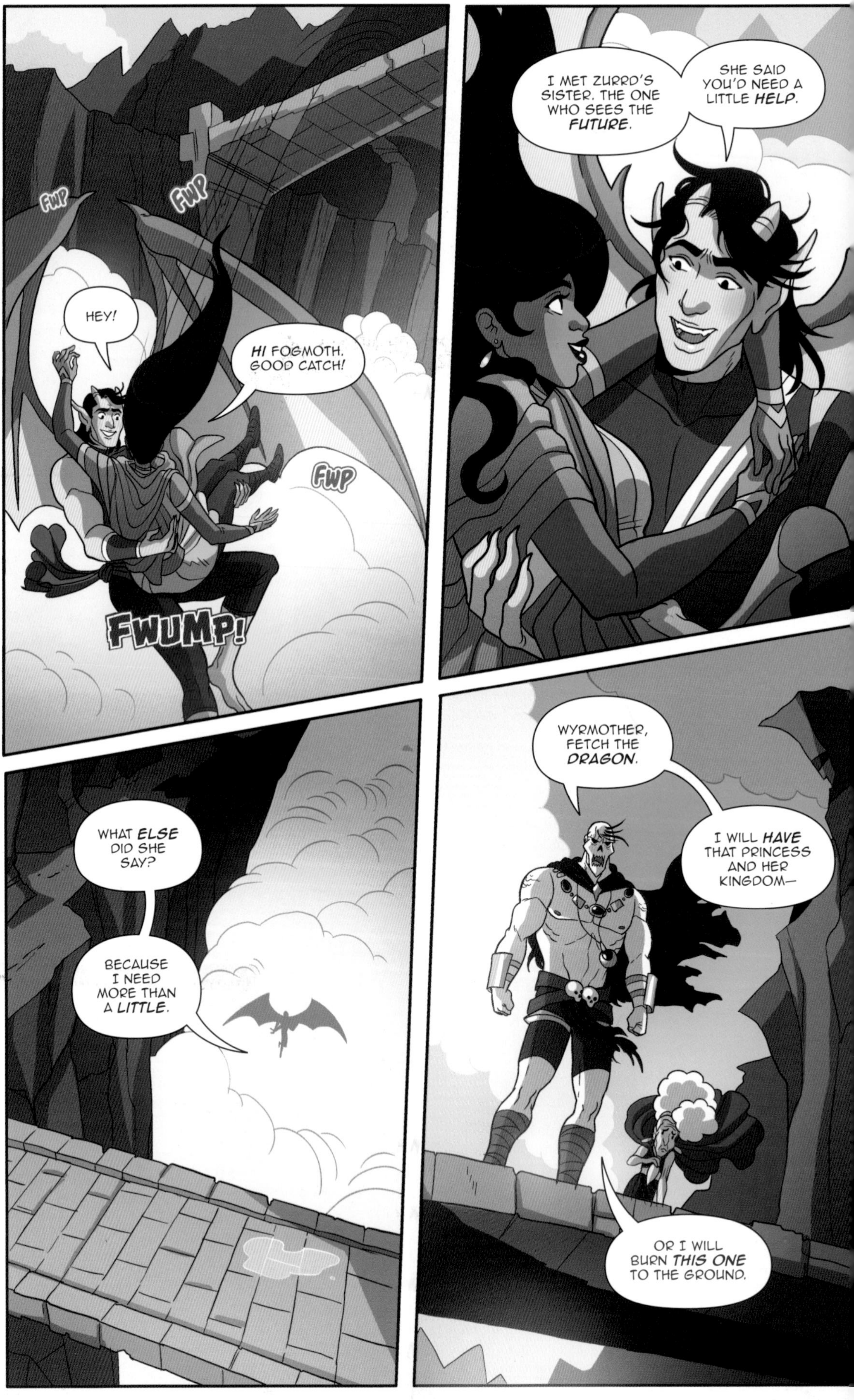
FWP
FWP
HEY!
HI FOGMOTH. GOOD CATCH!
FWP
FWUMP!
I MET ZURRD'S SISTER. THE ONE WHO SEES THE FUTURE.
SHE SAID YOU'D NEED A LITTLE HELP.
WHAT ELSE DID SHE SAY?
BECAUSE I NEED MORE THAN A LITTLE.
WYRMOTHER, FETCH THE DRAGON.
I WILL HAVE THAT PRINCESS AND HER KINGDOM—
OR I WILL BURN THIS ONE TO THE GROUND.

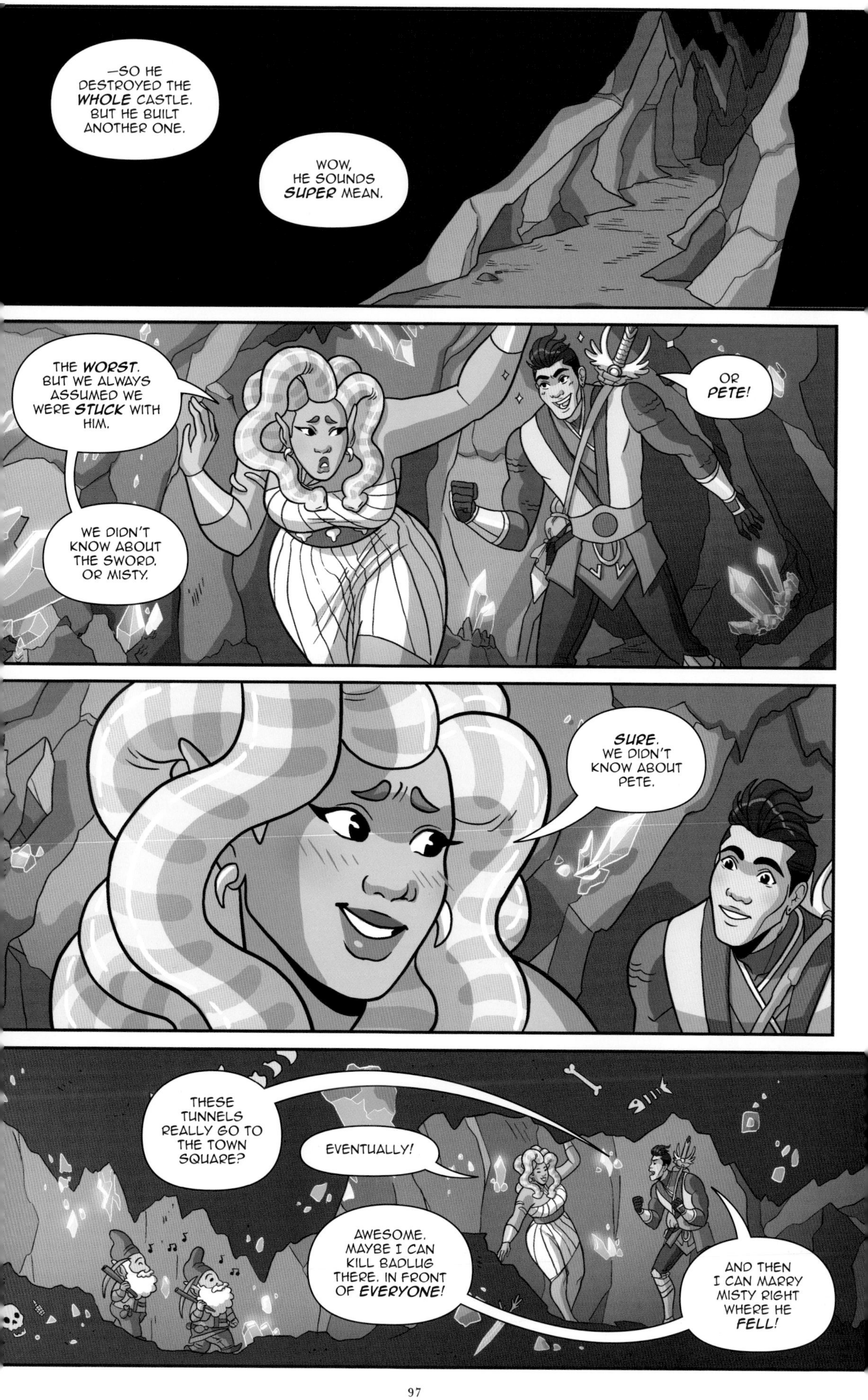
—SO HE DESTROYED THE **WHOLE** CASTLE. BUT HE BUILT ANOTHER ONE.
WOW, HE SOUNDS **SUPER** MEAN.
THE **WORST**. BUT WE ALWAYS ASSUMED WE WERE **STUCK** WITH HIM.
WE DIDN'T KNOW ABOUT THE SWORD. OR MISTY.
OR **PETE**!
SURE. WE DIDN'T KNOW ABOUT PETE.
THESE TUNNELS REALLY GO TO THE TOWN SQUARE?
EVENTUALLY!
AWESOME. MAYBE I CAN KILL BADLUG THERE. IN FRONT OF **EVERYONE**!
AND THEN I CAN MARRY MISTY RIGHT WHERE HE **FELL**!

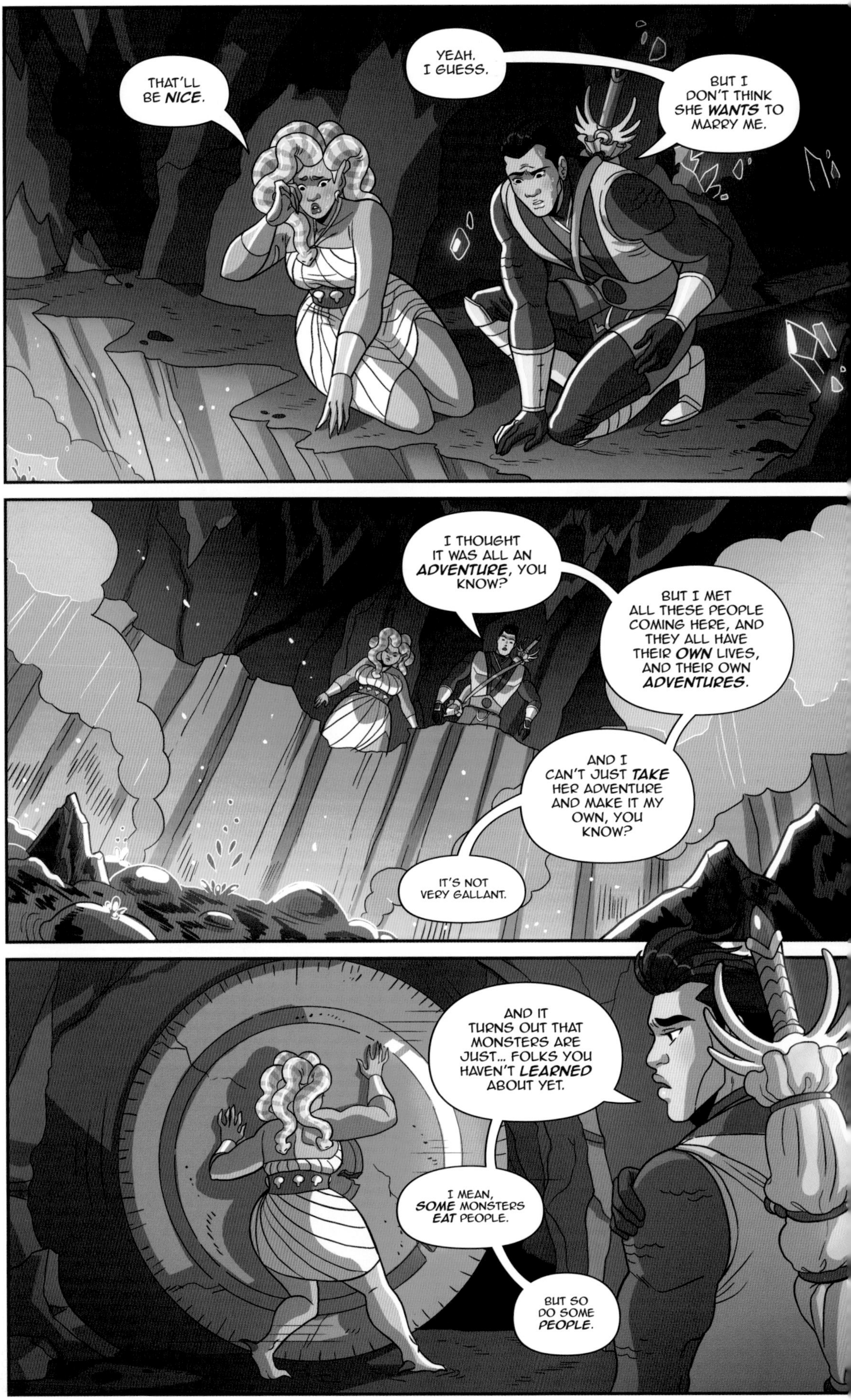
THAT'LL BE NICE.
YEAH. I GUESS.
BUT I DON'T THINK SHE WANTS TO MARRY ME.
I THOUGHT IT WAS ALL AN ADVENTURE, YOU KNOW?
BUT I MET ALL THESE PEOPLE COMING HERE, AND THEY ALL HAVE THEIR OWN LIVES, AND THEIR OWN ADVENTURES.
AND I CAN'T JUST TAKE HER ADVENTURE AND MAKE IT MY OWN, YOU KNOW?
IT'S NOT VERY GALLANT.
AND IT TURNS OUT THAT MONSTERS ARE JUST... FOLKS YOU HAVEN'T LEARNED ABOUT YET.
I MEAN, SOME MONSTERS EAT PEOPLE.
BUT SO DO SOME PEOPLE.

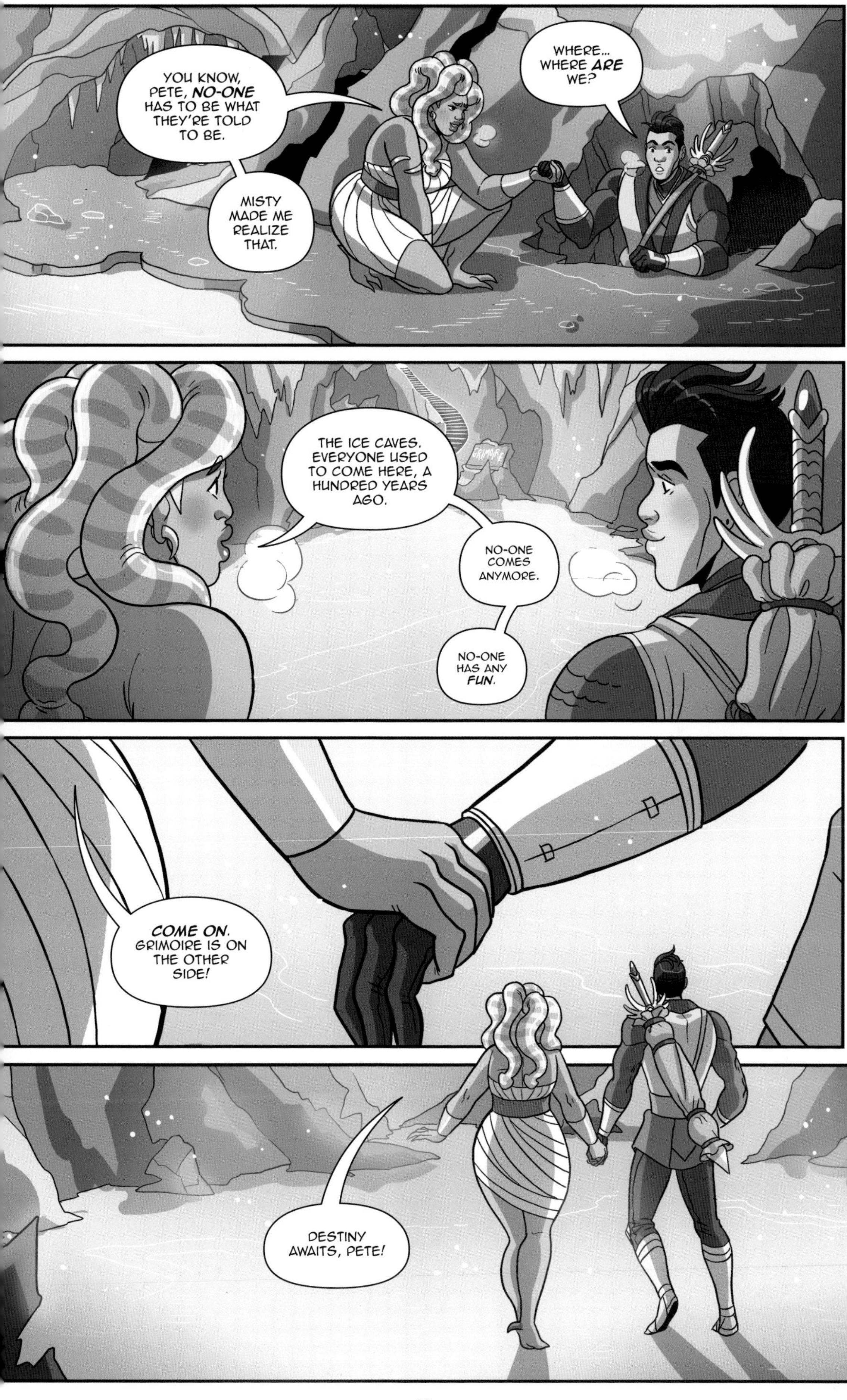
YOU KNOW, PETE, NO-ONE HAS TO BE WHAT THEY'RE TOLD TO BE.
MISTY MADE ME REALIZE THAT.
WHERE... WHERE ARE WE?
THE ICE CAVES. EVERYONE USED TO COME HERE, A HUNDRED YEARS AGO.
NO-ONE COMES ANYMORE.
NO-ONE HAS ANY FUN.
GRIMOIRE
COME ON. GRIMOIRE IS ON THE OTHER SIDE!
DESTINY AWAITS, PETE!

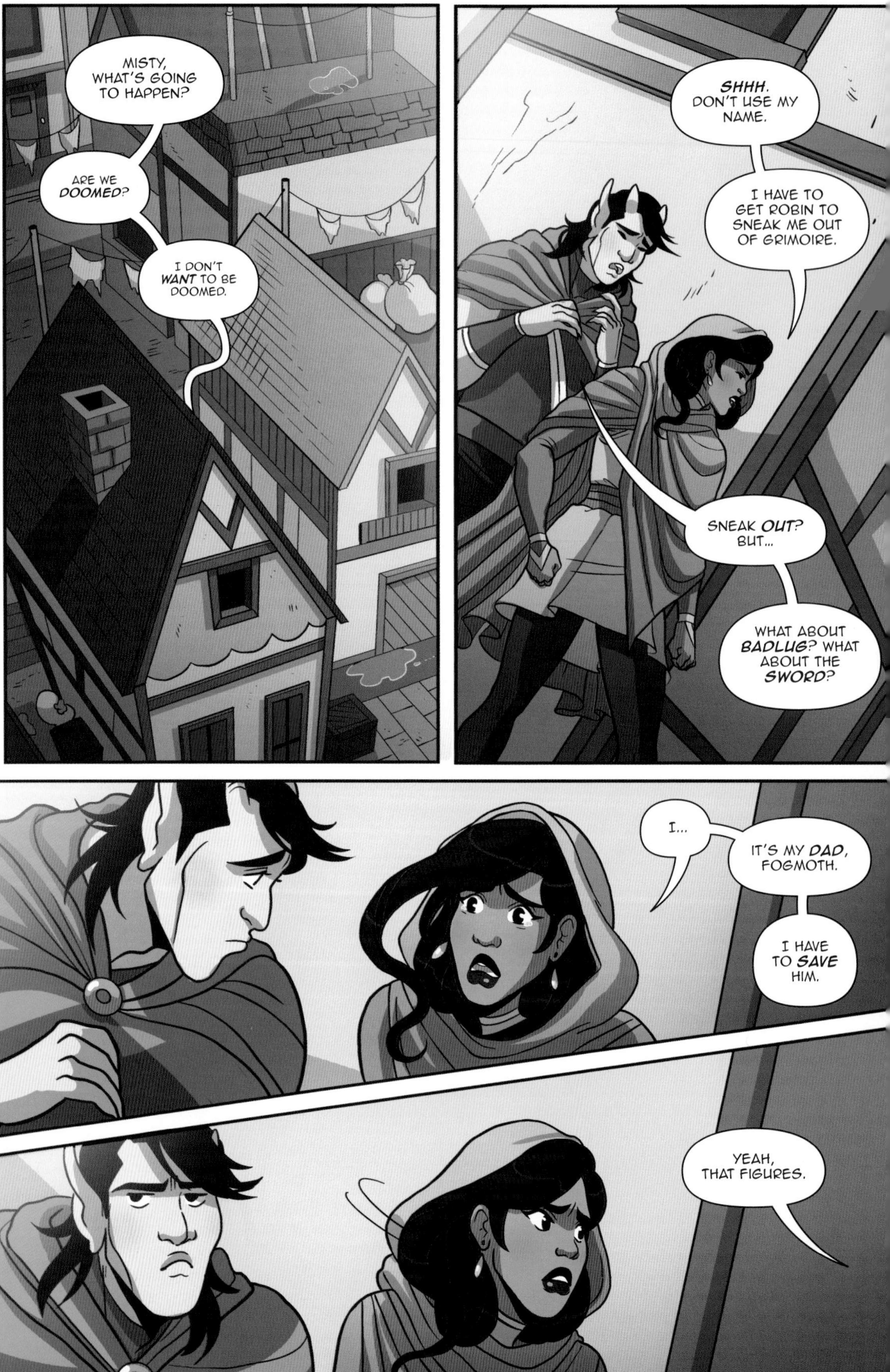
MISTY, WHAT'S GOING TO HAPPEN?
ARE WE *DOOMED*?
I DON'T *WANT* TO BE DOOMED.
SHHH. DON'T USE MY NAME.
I HAVE TO GET ROBIN TO SNEAK ME OUT OF GRIMOIRE.
SNEAK *OUT*? BUT...
WHAT ABOUT *BADLUG*? WHAT ABOUT THE *SWORD*?
I...
IT'S MY *DAD*, FOGMOTH.
I HAVE TO *SAVE* HIM.
YEAH, THAT FIGURES.

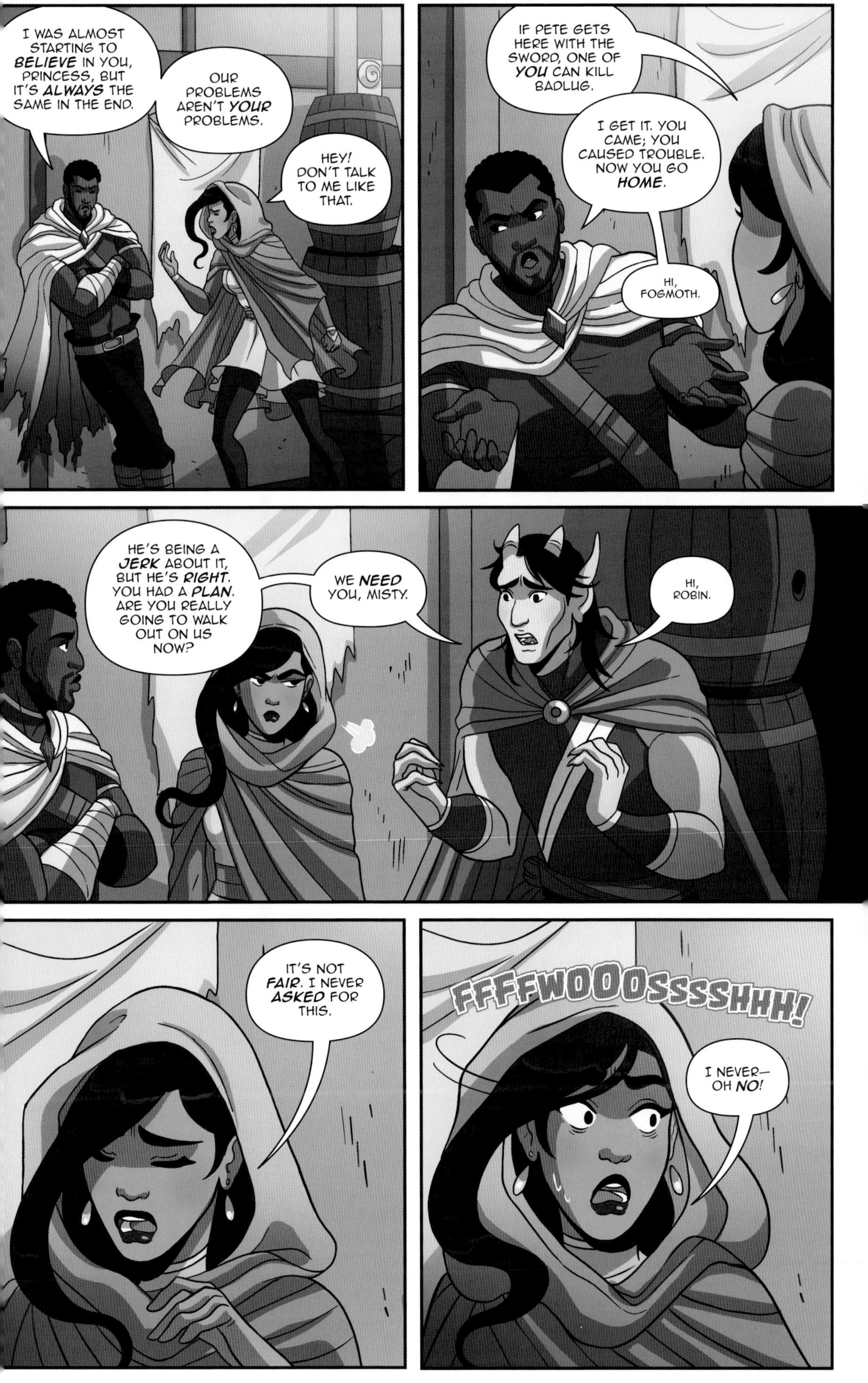
I WAS ALMOST STARTING TO BELIEVE IN YOU, PRINCESS, BUT IT'S ALWAYS THE SAME IN THE END.
OUR PROBLEMS AREN'T YOUR PROBLEMS.
HEY! DON'T TALK TO ME LIKE THAT.
IF PETE GETS HERE WITH THE SWORD, ONE OF YOU CAN KILL BADLUG.
I GET IT. YOU CAME; YOU CAUSED TROUBLE. NOW YOU GO HOME.
HI, FOGMOTH.
HE'S BEING A JERK ABOUT IT, BUT HE'S RIGHT. YOU HAD A PLAN. ARE YOU REALLY GOING TO WALK OUT ON US NOW?
WE NEED YOU, MISTY.
HI, ROBIN.
IT'S NOT FAIR. I NEVER ASKED FOR THIS.
FFFFWOOOOSSSSSHHHH!
I NEVER— OH NO!

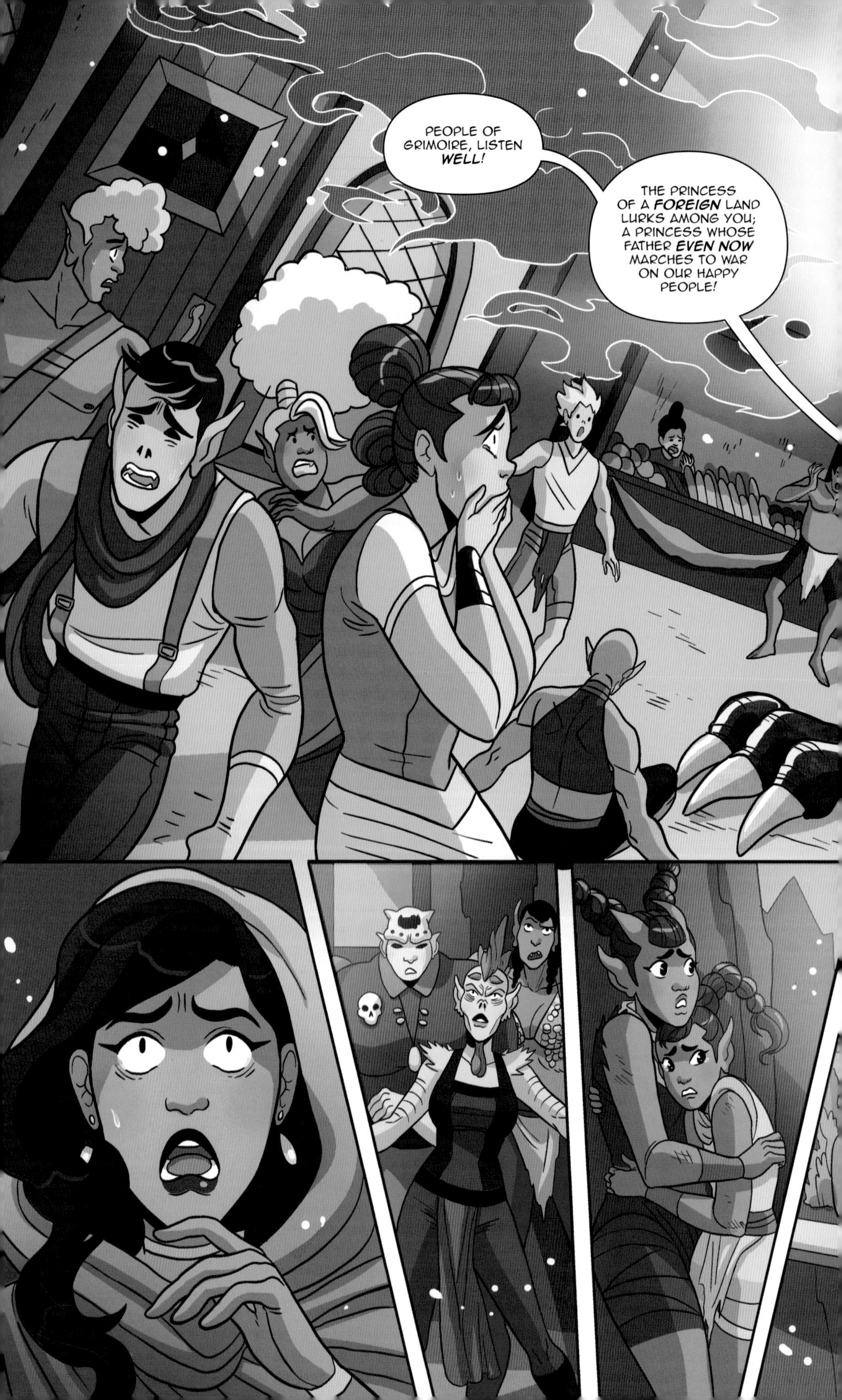
PEOPLE OF GRIMOIRE, LISTEN **WELL**!
THE PRINCESS OF A **FOREIGN** LAND LURKS AMONG YOU; A PRINCESS WHOSE FATHER **EVEN NOW** MARCHES TO WAR ON OUR HAPPY PEOPLE!

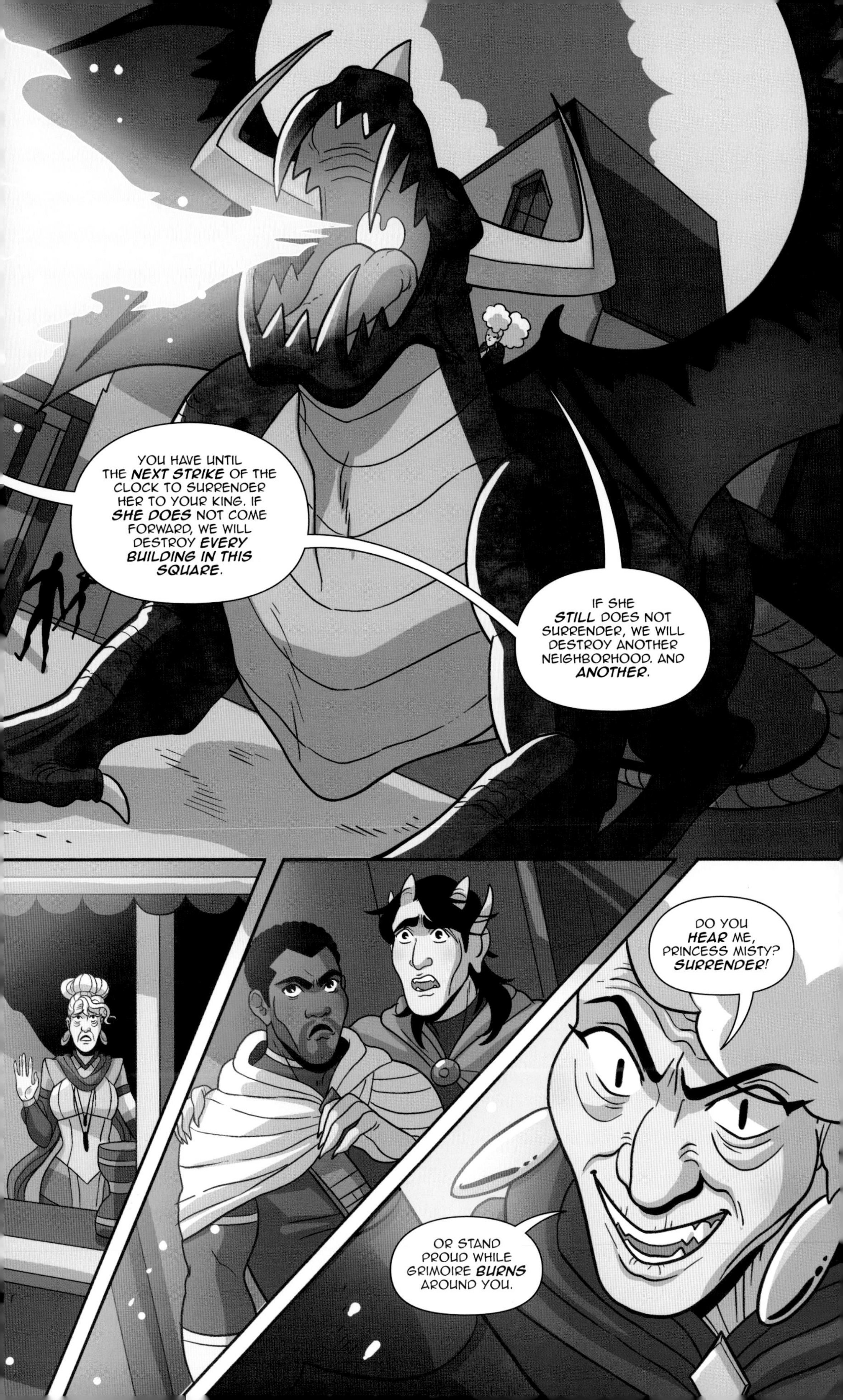
YOU HAVE UNTIL THE NEXT STRIKE OF THE CLOCK TO SURRENDER HER TO YOUR KING. IF SHE DOES NOT COME FORWARD, WE WILL DESTROY EVERY BUILDING IN THIS SQUARE.
IF SHE STILL DOES NOT SURRENDER, WE WILL DESTROY ANOTHER NEIGHBORHOOD. AND ANOTHER.
DO YOU HEAR ME, PRINCESS MISTY? SURRENDER!
OR STAND PROUD WHILE GRIMOIRE BURNS AROUND YOU.

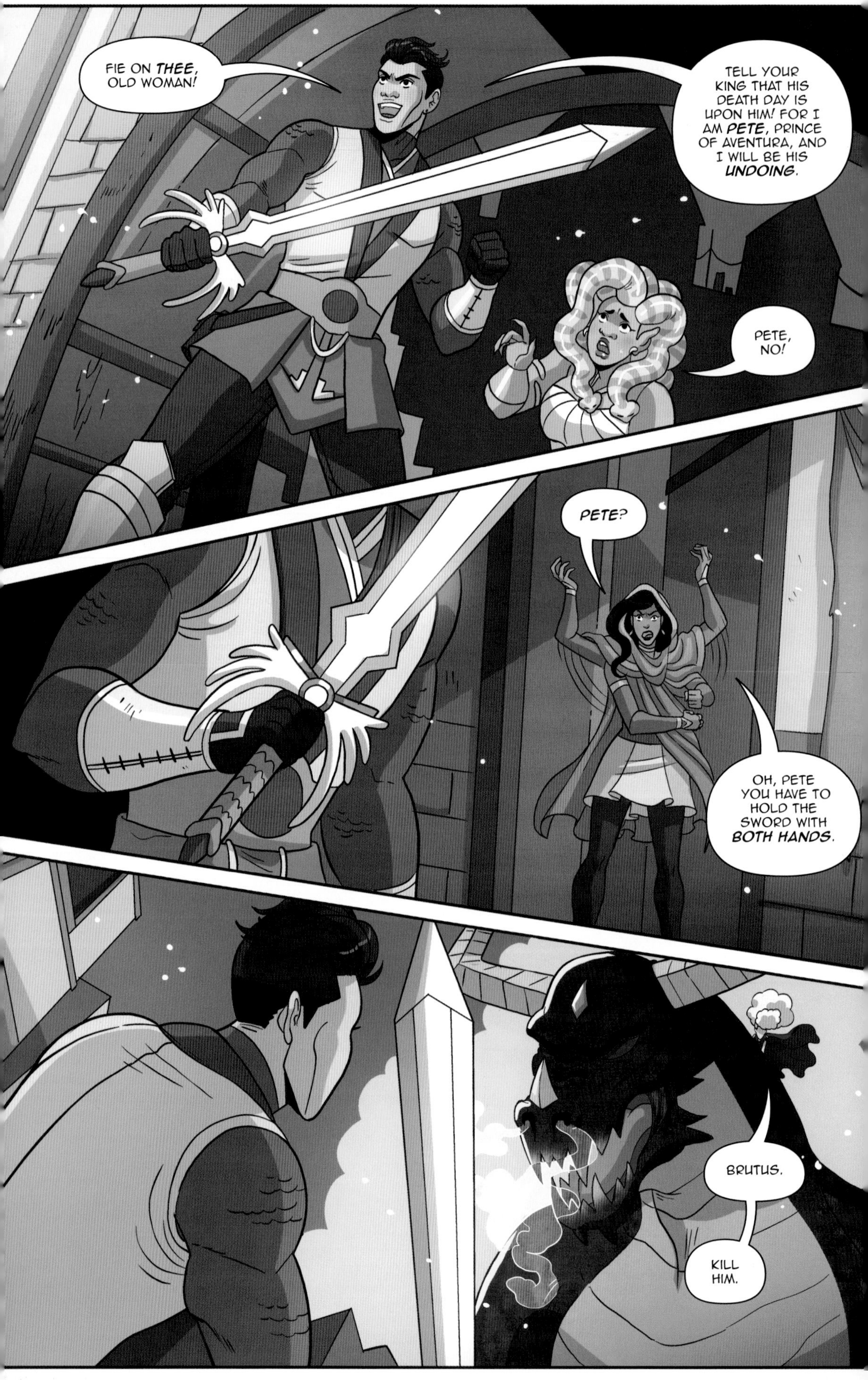
FIE ON *THEE*, OLD WOMAN!
TELL YOUR KING THAT HIS DEATH DAY IS UPON HIM! FOR I AM *PETE*, PRINCE OF AVENTURA, AND I WILL BE HIS ***UNDOING***.
PETE, NO!
PETE?
OH, PETE YOU HAVE TO HOLD THE SWORD WITH ***BOTH HANDS***.
BRUTUS.
KILL HIM.

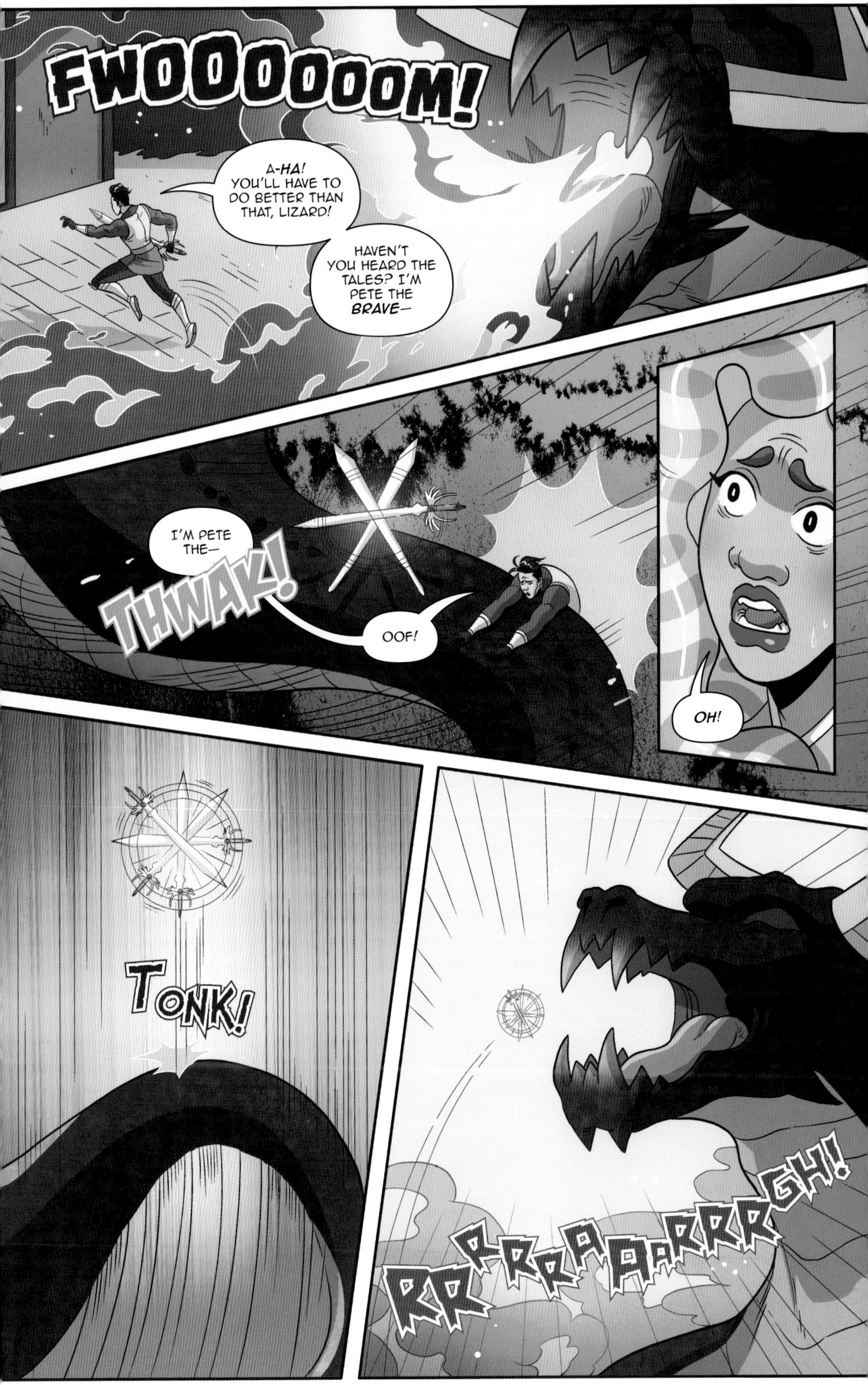

FWOOOOOOOM!
A-HA! YOU'LL HAVE TO DO BETTER THAN THAT, LIZARD!
HAVEN'T YOU HEARD THE TALES? I'M PETE THE BRAVE—
I'M PETE THE—
THWAK!
OOF!
OH!
TONK!
RRRRRAAARRRGH!

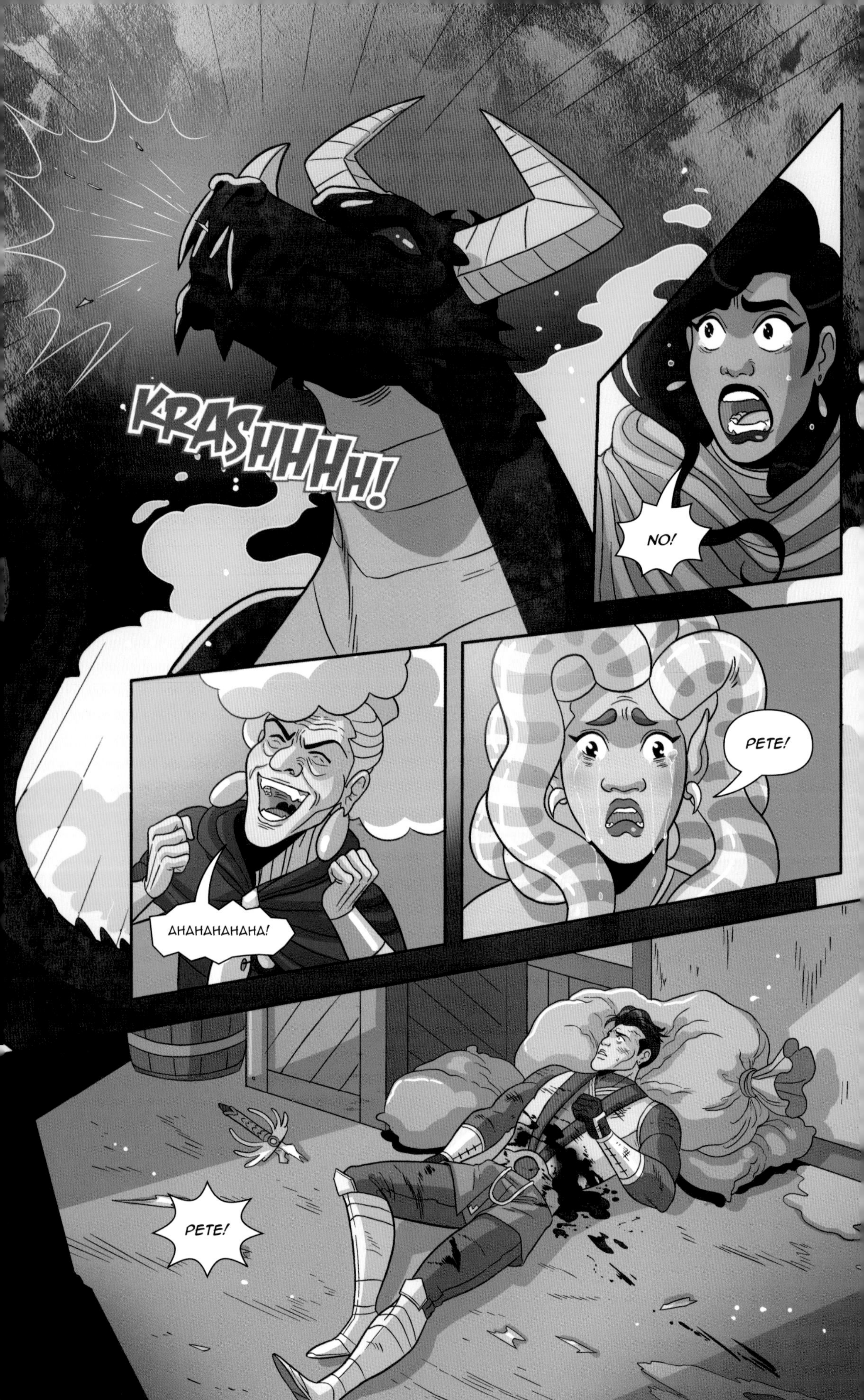
KRASHHHHH!
NO!
AHAHAHAHAHA!
PETE!
PETE!

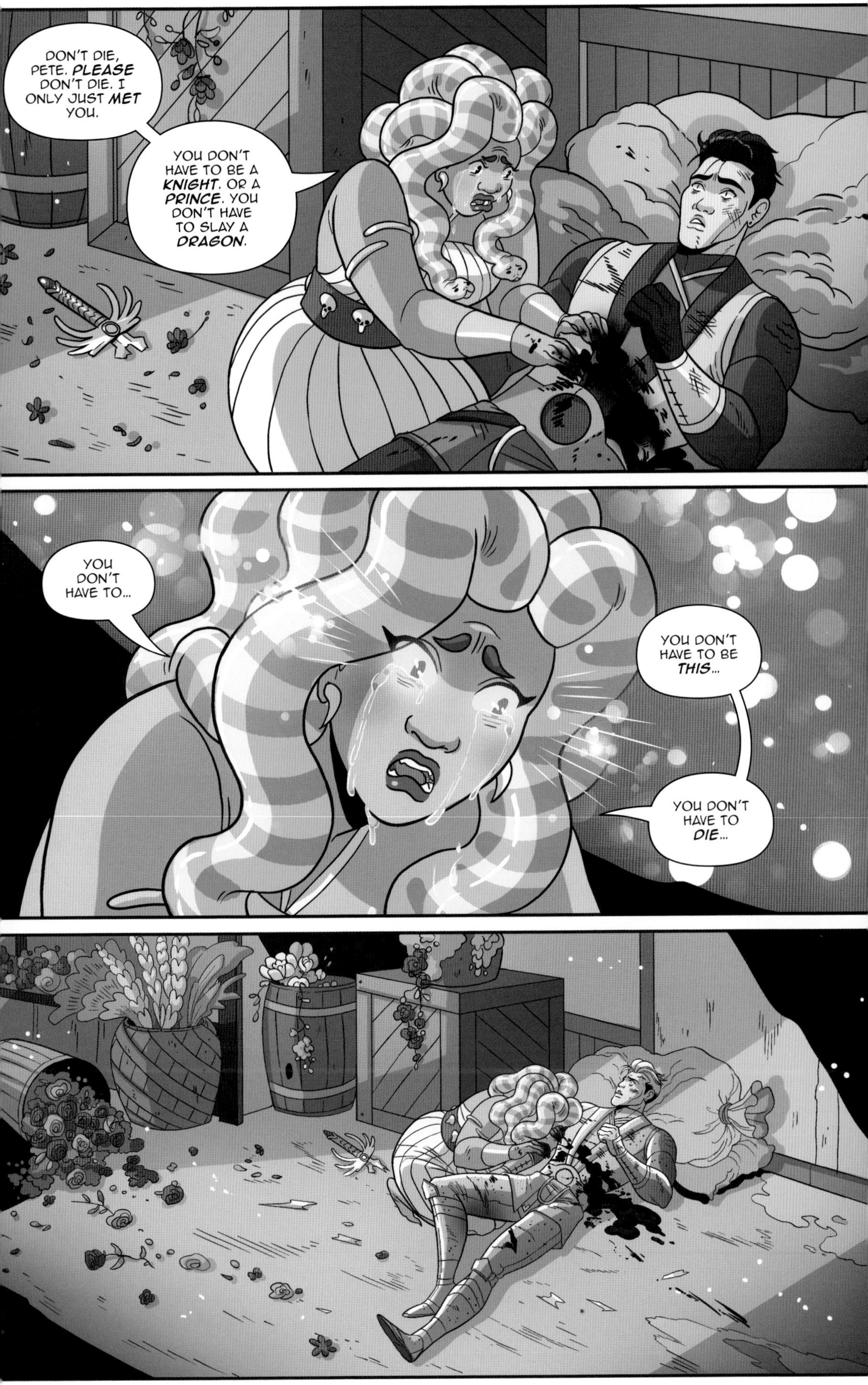
DON'T DIE, PETE. PLEASE DON'T DIE. I ONLY JUST MET YOU.
YOU DON'T HAVE TO BE A KNIGHT. OR A PRINCE. YOU DON'T HAVE TO SLAY A DRAGON.
YOU DON'T HAVE TO...
YOU DON'T HAVE TO BE THIS...
YOU DON'T HAVE TO DIE...

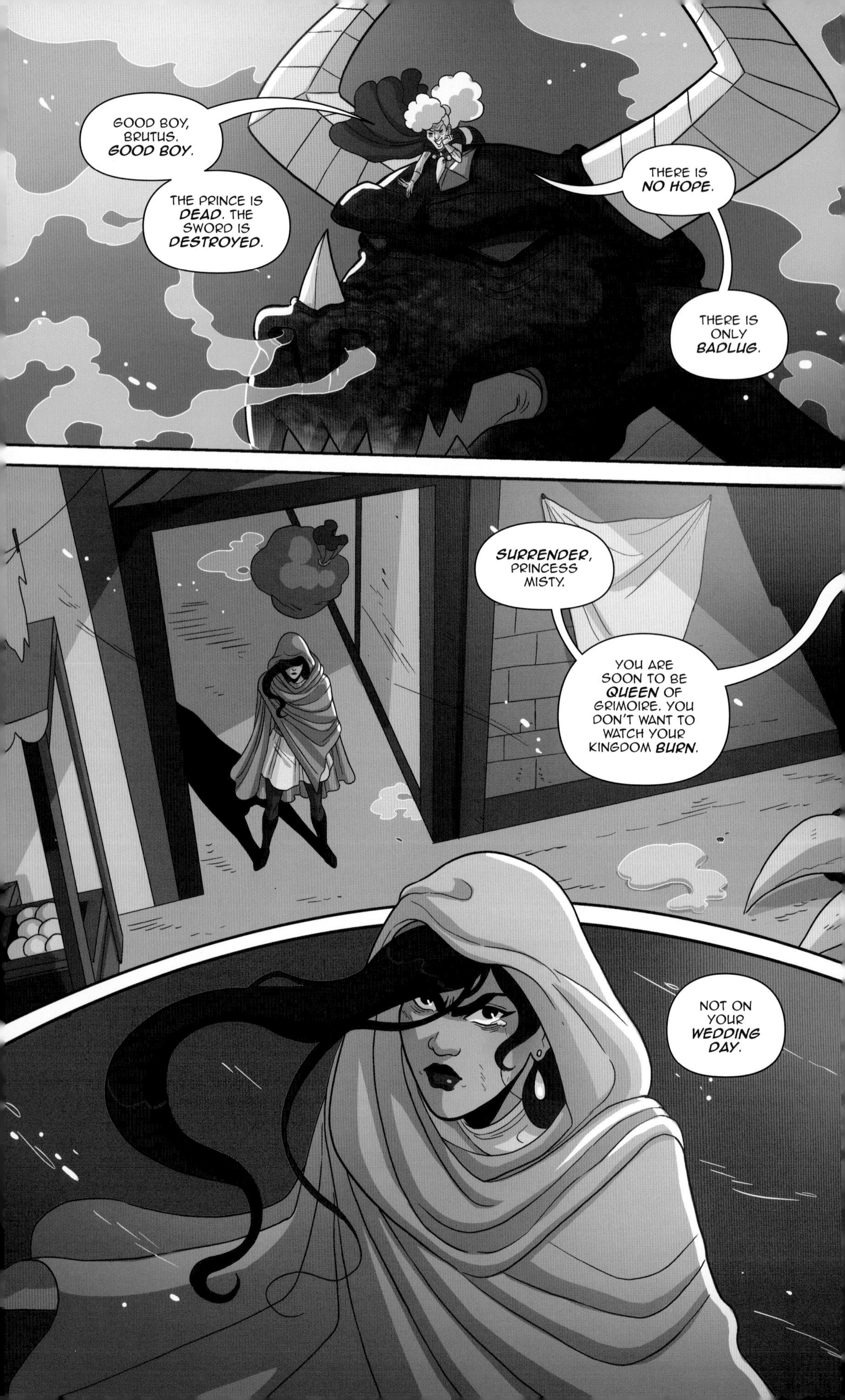
GOOD BOY, BRUTUS. GOOD BOY.
THE PRINCE IS DEAD. THE SWORD IS DESTROYED.
THERE IS NO HOPE.
THERE IS ONLY BADLUG.
SURRENDER, PRINCESS MISTY.
YOU ARE SOON TO BE QUEEN OF GRIMOIRE. YOU DON'T WANT TO WATCH YOUR KINGDOM BURN.
NOT ON YOUR WEDDING DAY.

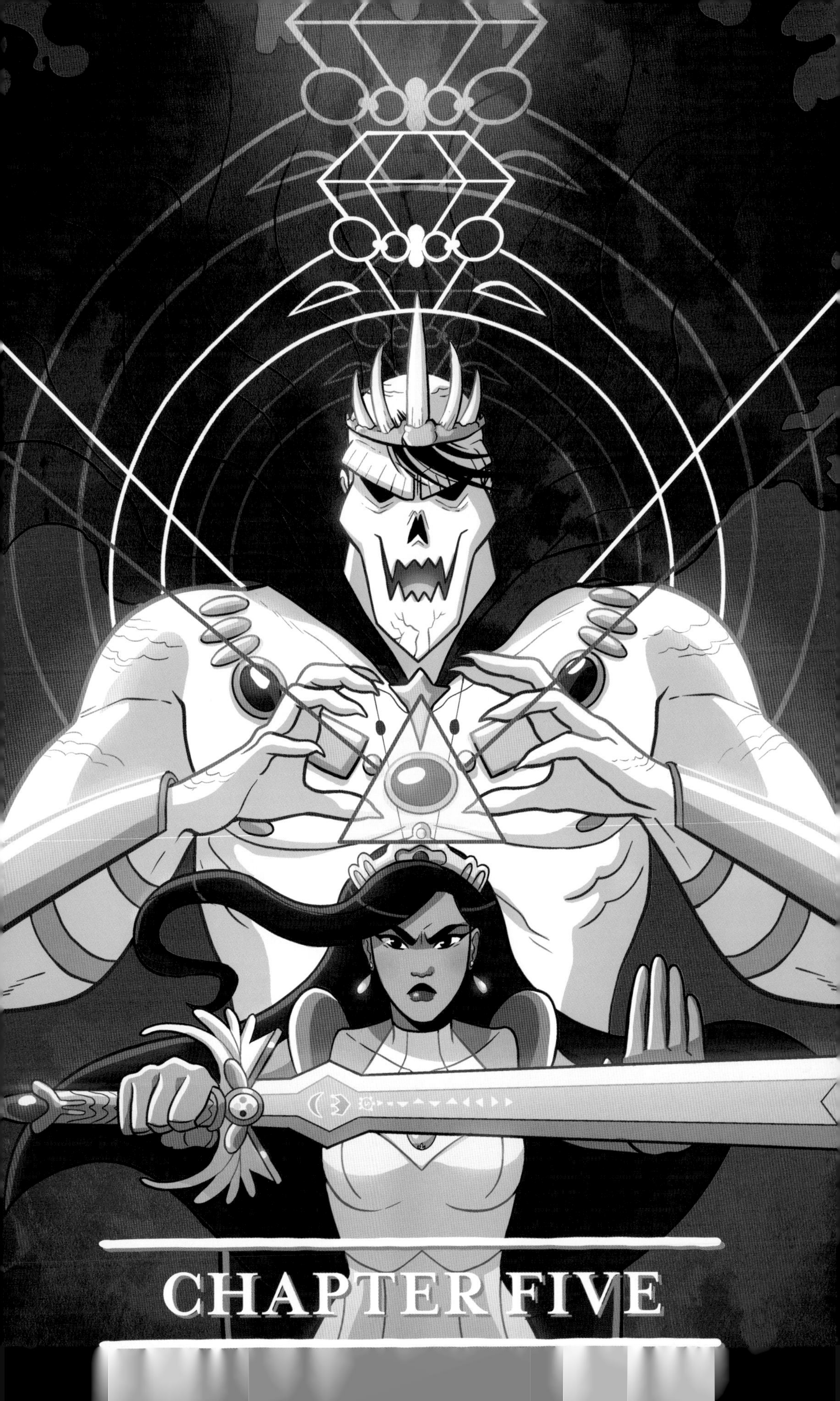

CHAPTER FIVE

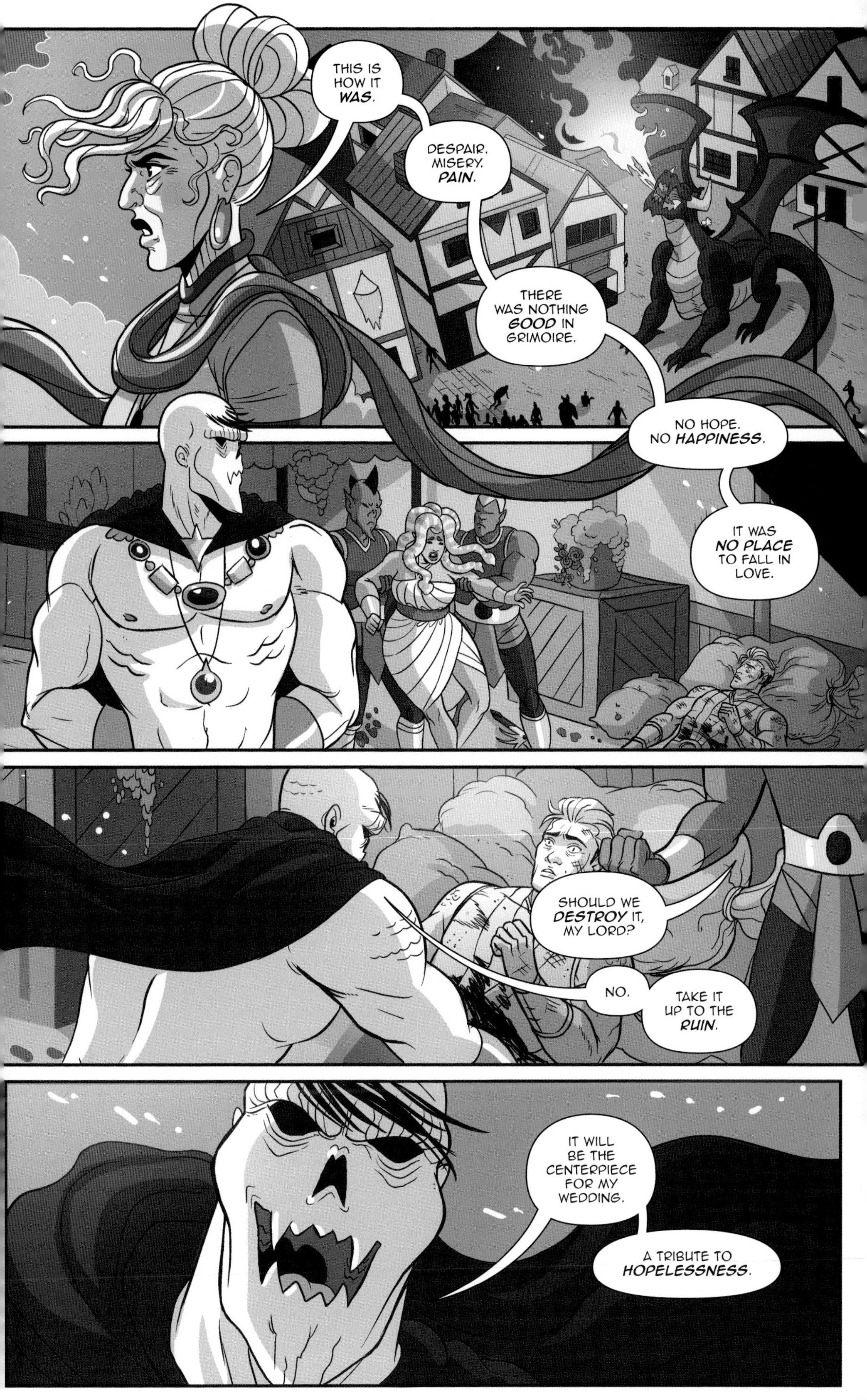
THIS IS HOW IT WAS.
DESPAIR. MISERY. PAIN.
THERE WAS NOTHING GOOD IN GRIMOIRE.
NO HOPE. NO HAPPINESS.
IT WAS NO PLACE TO FALL IN LOVE.
SHOULD WE DESTROY IT, MY LORD?
NO.
TAKE IT UP TO THE RUIN.
IT WILL BE THE CENTERPIECE FOR MY WEDDING.
A TRIBUTE TO HOPELESSNESS.

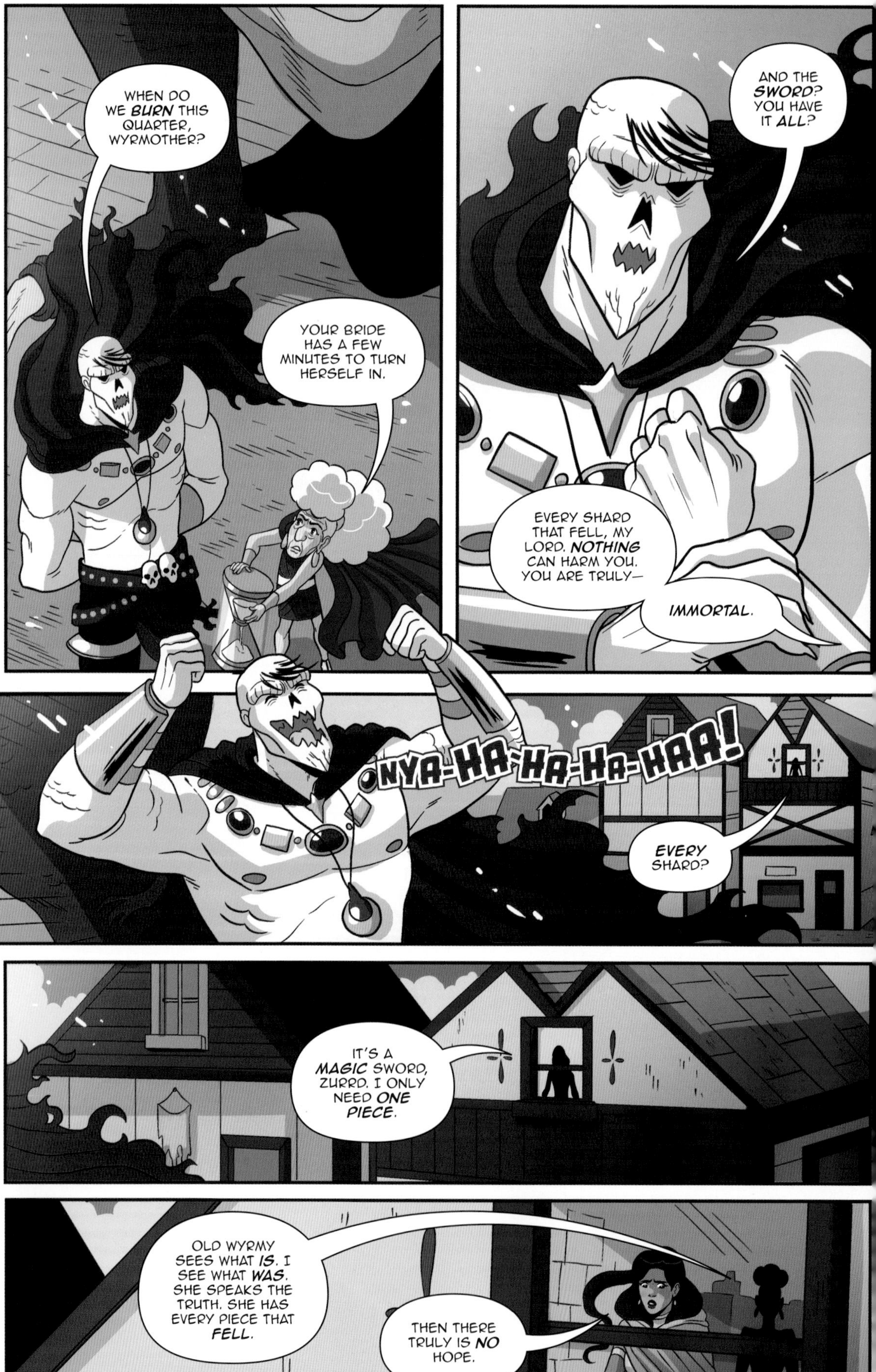
WHEN DO WE BURN THIS QUARTER, WYRMOTHER?
YOUR BRIDE HAS A FEW MINUTES TO TURN HERSELF IN.
AND THE SWORD? YOU HAVE IT ALL?
EVERY SHARD THAT FELL, MY LORD. NOTHING CAN HARM YOU. YOU ARE TRULY—
IMMORTAL.
NYA-HA-HA-HA-HAA!
EVERY SHARD?
IT'S A MAGIC SWORD, ZURRD. I ONLY NEED ONE PIECE.
OLD WYRMY SEES WHAT IS. I SEE WHAT WAS. SHE SPEAKS THE TRUTH. SHE HAS EVERY PIECE THAT FELL.
THEN THERE TRULY IS NO HOPE.

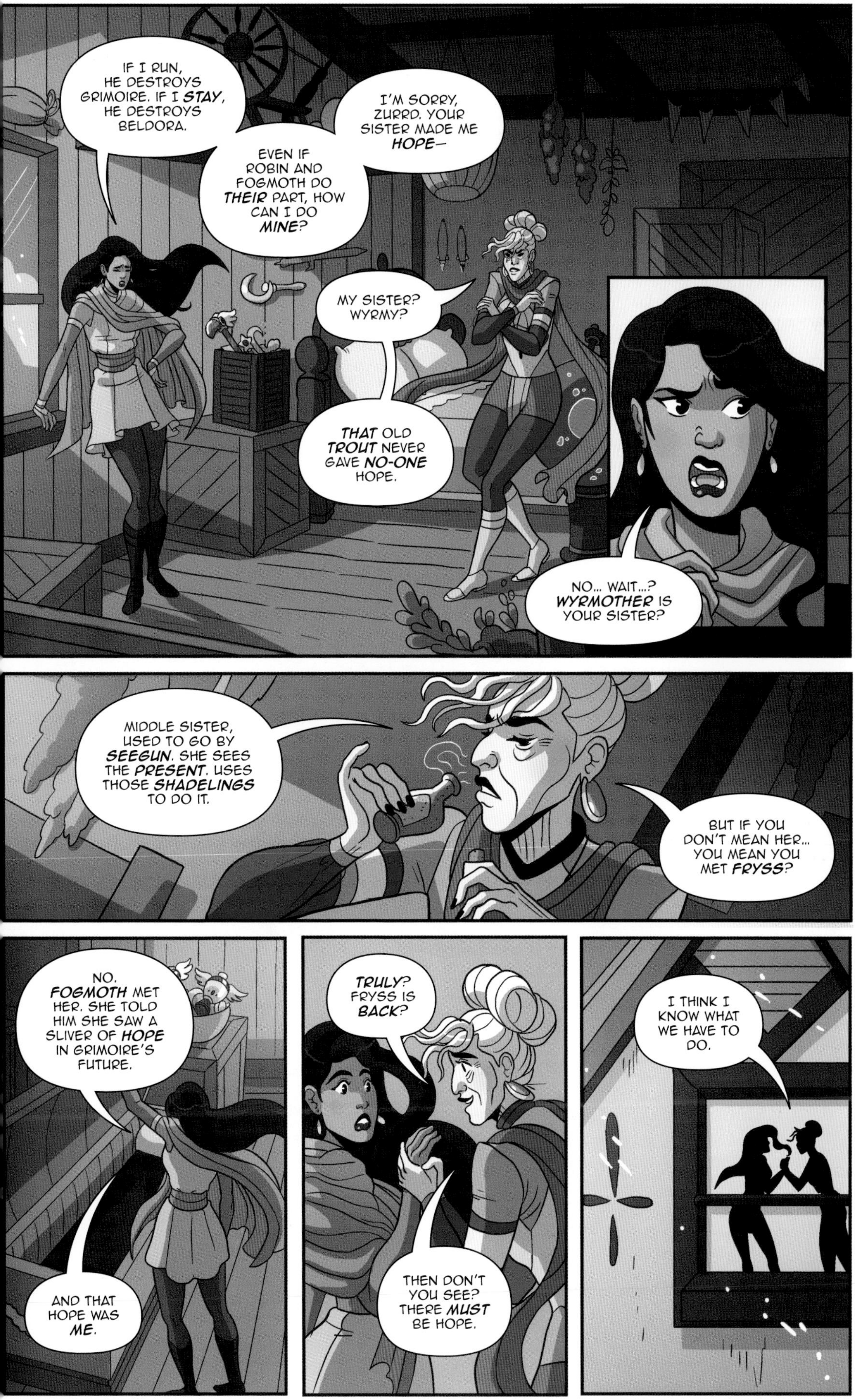
IF I RUN, HE DESTROYS GRIMOIRE. IF I STAY, HE DESTROYS BELDORA.
EVEN IF ROBIN AND FOGMOTH DO THEIR PART, HOW CAN I DO MINE?
I'M SORRY, ZURRD. YOUR SISTER MADE ME HOPE—
MY SISTER? WYRMY?
THAT OLD TROUT NEVER GAVE NO-ONE HOPE.
NO... WAIT...? WYRMOTHER IS YOUR SISTER?
MIDDLE SISTER, USED TO GO BY SEEGUN. SHE SEES THE PRESENT. USES THOSE SHADELINGS TO DO IT.
BUT IF YOU DON'T MEAN HER... YOU MEAN YOU MET FRYSS?
NO. FOGMOTH MET HER. SHE TOLD HIM SHE SAW A SLIVER OF HOPE IN GRIMOIRE'S FUTURE.
AND THAT HOPE WAS ME.
TRULY? FRYSS IS BACK?
THEN DON'T YOU SEE? THERE MUST BE HOPE.
I THINK I KNOW WHAT WE HAVE TO DO.

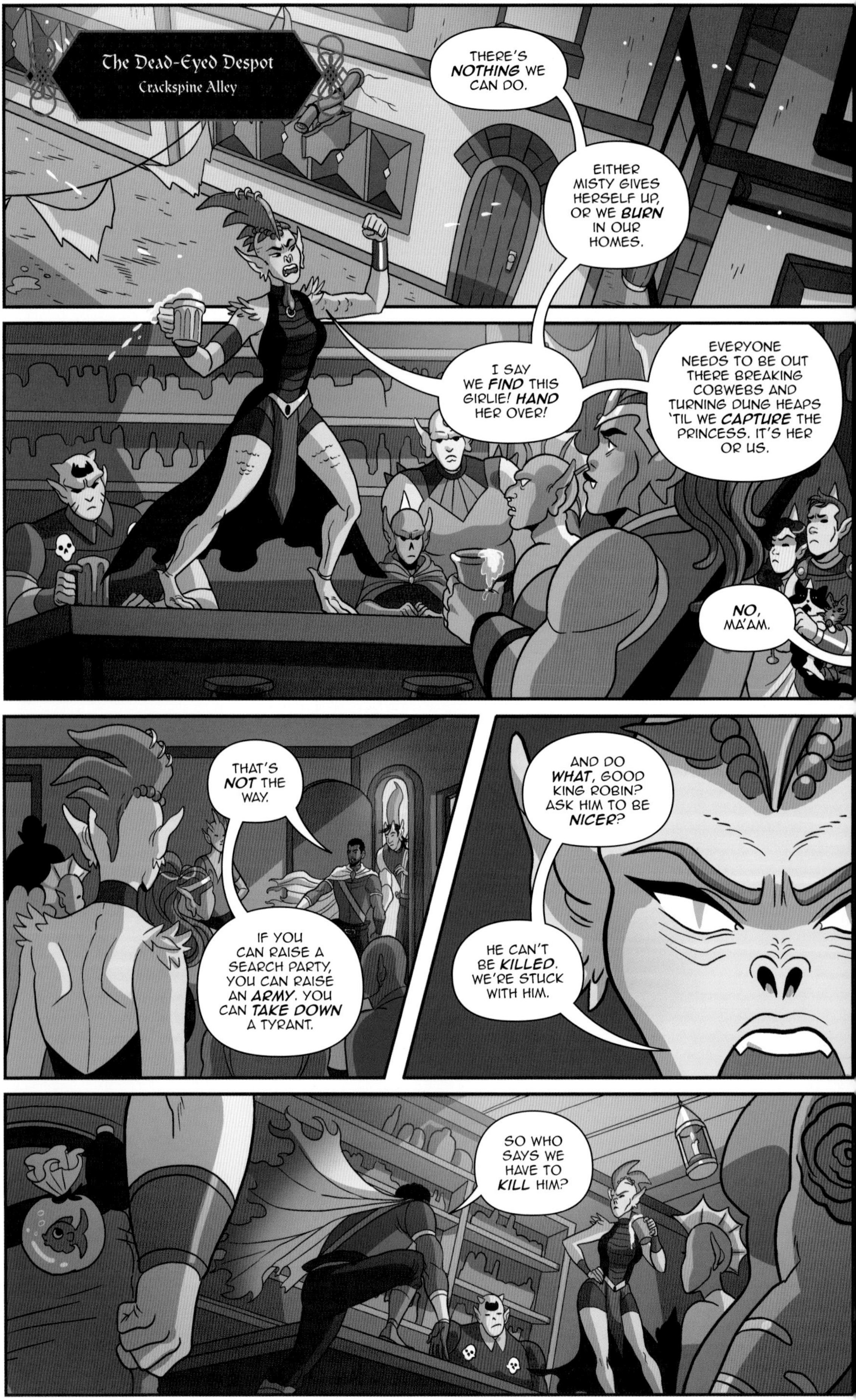
The Dead-Eyed Despot
Crackspine Alley
THERE'S NOTHING WE CAN DO.
EITHER MISTY GIVES HERSELF UP, OR WE BURN IN OUR HOMES.
I SAY WE FIND THIS GIRLIE! HAND HER OVER!
EVERYONE NEEDS TO BE OUT THERE BREAKING COBWEBS AND TURNING DUNG HEAPS 'TIL WE CAPTURE THE PRINCESS. IT'S HER OR US.
NO, MA'AM.
THAT'S NOT THE WAY.
IF YOU CAN RAISE A SEARCH PARTY, YOU CAN RAISE AN ARMY. YOU CAN TAKE DOWN A TYRANT.
AND DO WHAT, GOOD KING ROBIN? ASK HIM TO BE NICER?
HE CAN'T BE KILLED. WE'RE STUCK WITH HIM.
SO WHO SAYS WE HAVE TO KILL HIM?

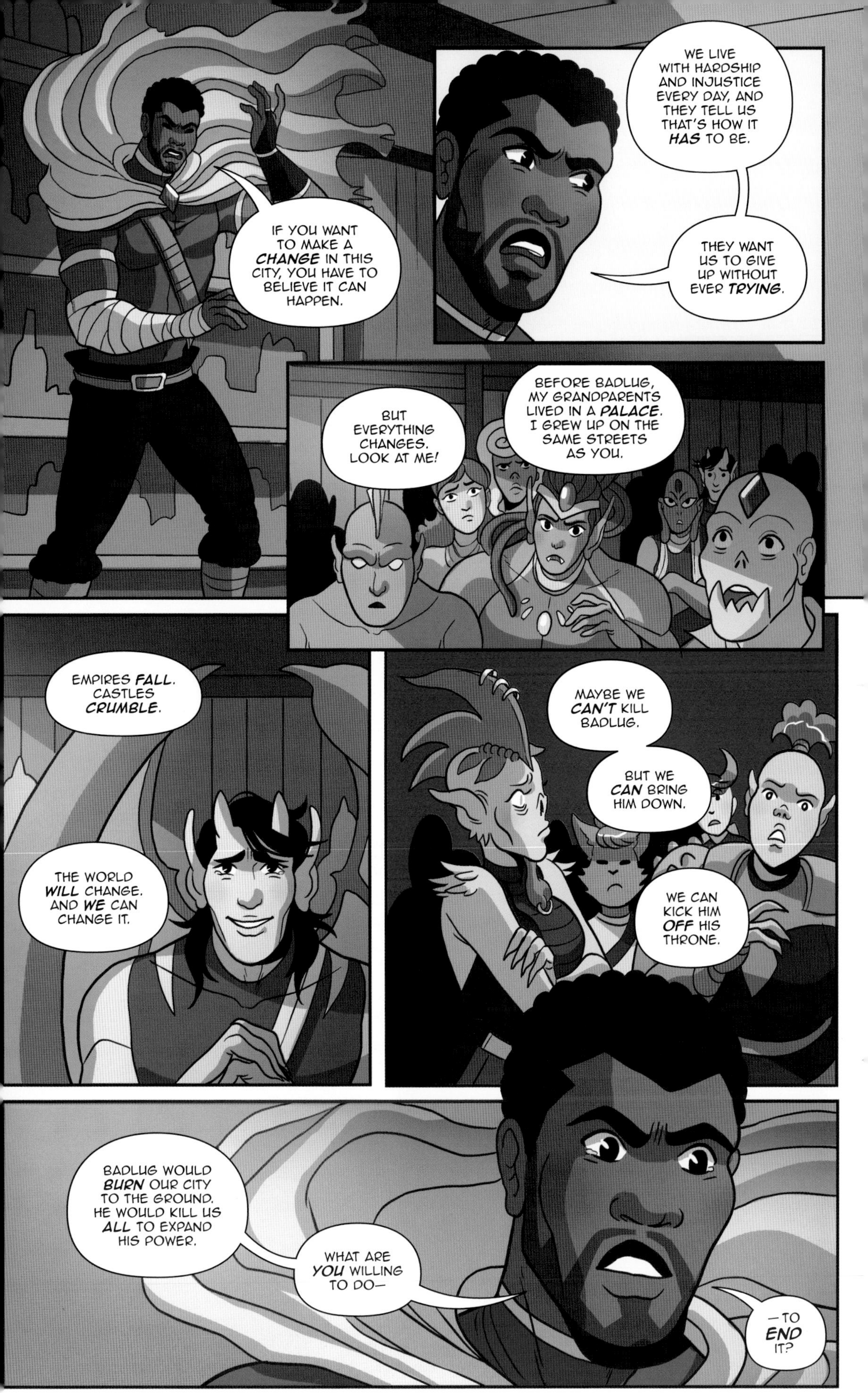
IF YOU WANT TO MAKE A CHANGE IN THIS CITY, YOU HAVE TO BELIEVE IT CAN HAPPEN.
WE LIVE WITH HARDSHIP AND INJUSTICE EVERY DAY, AND THEY TELL US THAT'S HOW IT HAS TO BE.
THEY WANT US TO GIVE UP WITHOUT EVER TRYING.
BUT EVERYTHING CHANGES. LOOK AT ME!
BEFORE BADLUG, MY GRANDPARENTS LIVED IN A PALACE. I GREW UP ON THE SAME STREETS AS YOU.
EMPIRES FALL. CASTLES CRUMBLE.
THE WORLD WILL CHANGE. AND WE CAN CHANGE IT.
MAYBE WE CAN'T KILL BADLUG.
BUT WE CAN BRING HIM DOWN.
WE CAN KICK HIM OFF HIS THRONE.
BADLUG WOULD BURN OUR CITY TO THE GROUND. HE WOULD KILL US ALL TO EXPAND HIS POWER.
WHAT ARE YOU WILLING TO DO—
—TO END IT?

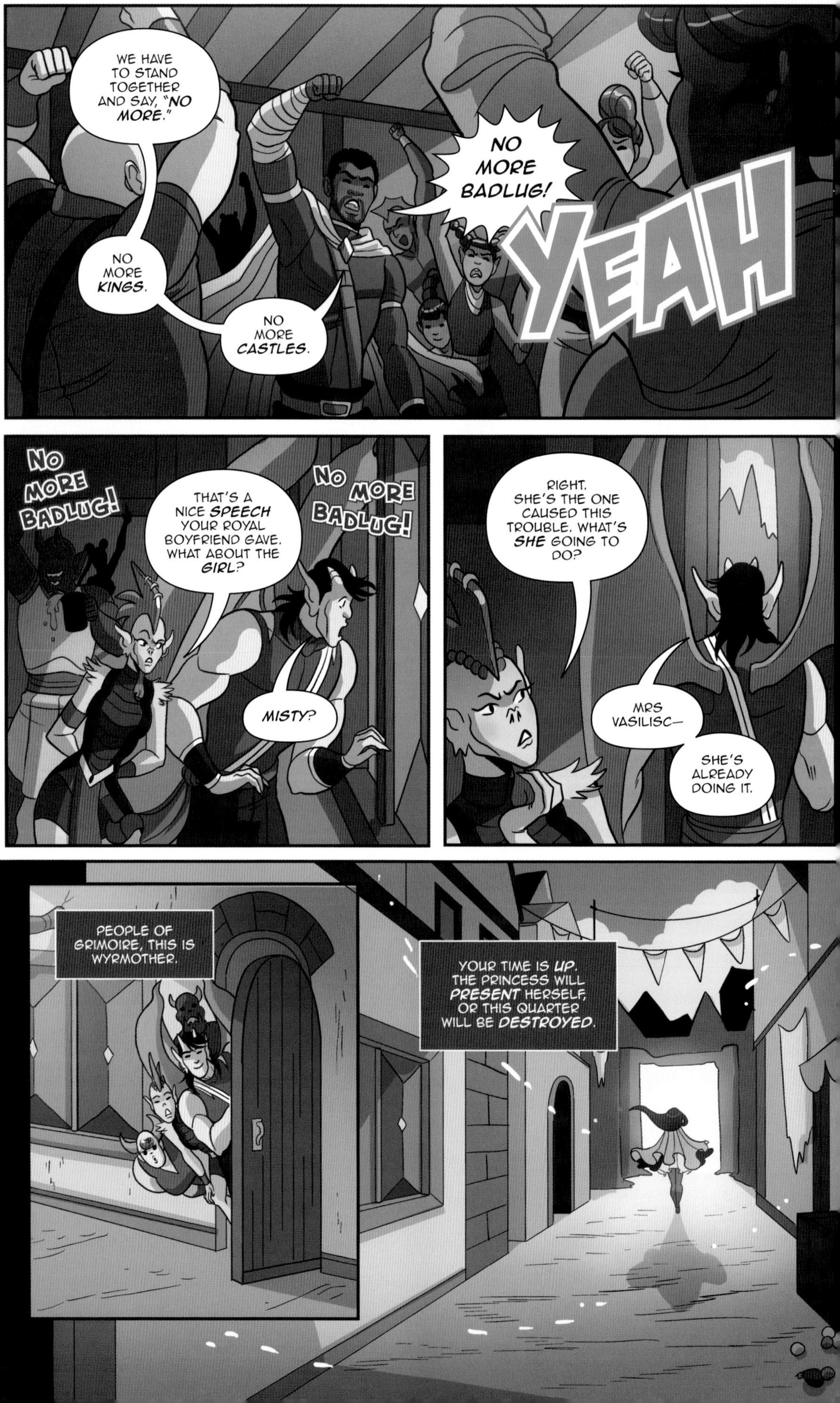

WE HAVE TO STAND TOGETHER AND SAY, "NO MORE."
NO MORE KINGS.
NO MORE CASTLES.
NO MORE BADLUG!
YEAH
NO MORE BADLUG!
THAT'S A NICE SPEECH YOUR ROYAL BOYFRIEND GAVE. WHAT ABOUT THE GIRL?
NO MORE BADLUG!
MISTY?
RIGHT. SHE'S THE ONE CAUSED THIS TROUBLE. WHAT'S SHE GOING TO DO?
MRS VASILISC—
SHE'S ALREADY DOING IT.
PEOPLE OF GRIMOIRE, THIS IS WYRMOTHER.
YOUR TIME IS UP. THE PRINCESS WILL PRESENT HERSELF, OR THIS QUARTER WILL BE DESTROYED.

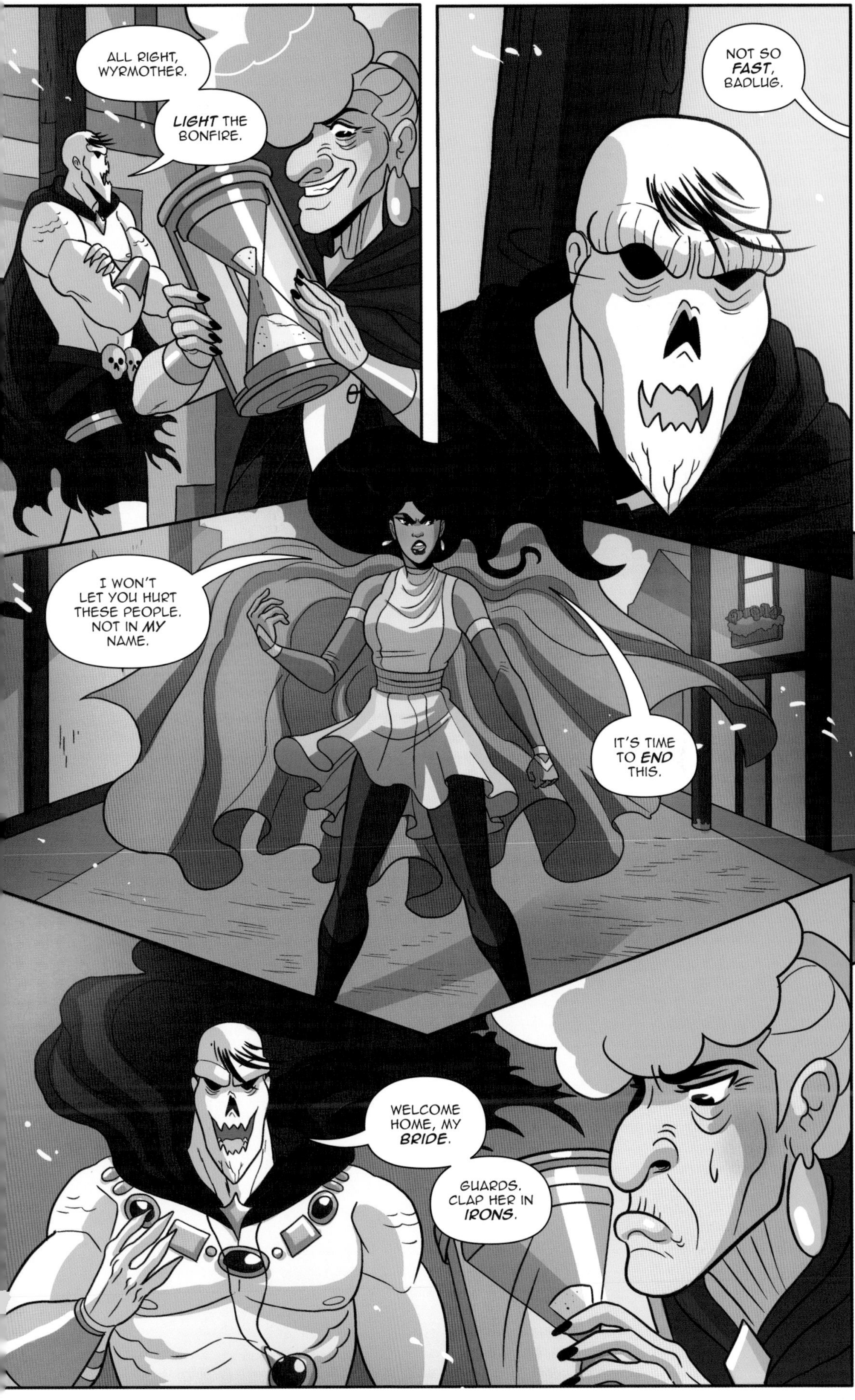
ALL RIGHT, WYRMOTHER.
LIGHT THE BONFIRE.
NOT SO FAST, BADLUG.
I WON'T LET YOU HURT THESE PEOPLE. NOT IN MY NAME.
IT'S TIME TO END THIS.
WELCOME HOME, MY BRIDE.
GUARDS. CLAP HER IN IRONS.

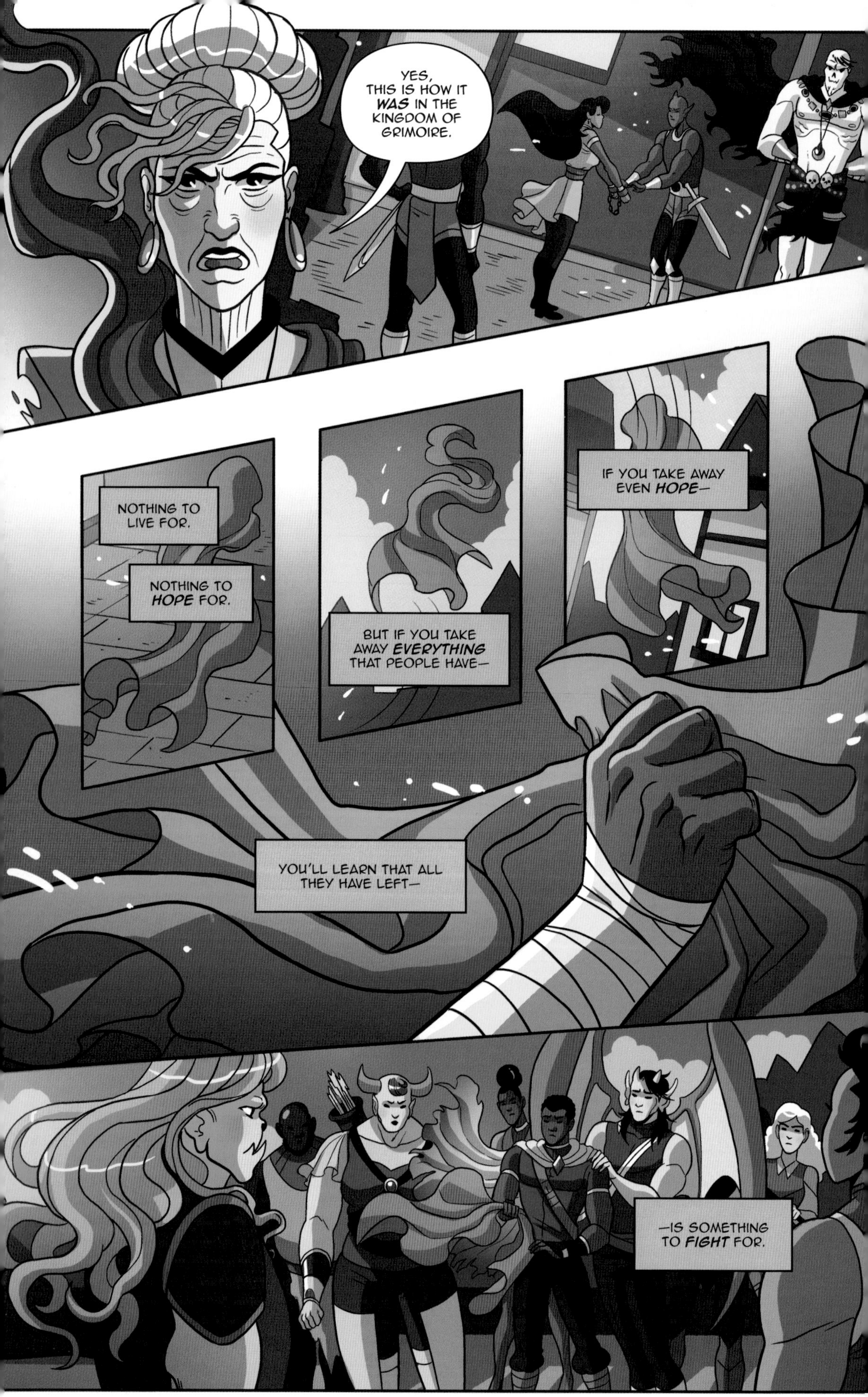

YES, THIS IS HOW IT WAS IN THE KINGDOM OF GRIMOIRE.
NOTHING TO LIVE FOR.
NOTHING TO HOPE FOR.
BUT IF YOU TAKE AWAY EVERYTHING THAT PEOPLE HAVE—
IF YOU TAKE AWAY EVEN HOPE—
YOU'LL LEARN THAT ALL THEY HAVE LEFT—
—IS SOMETHING TO FIGHT FOR.

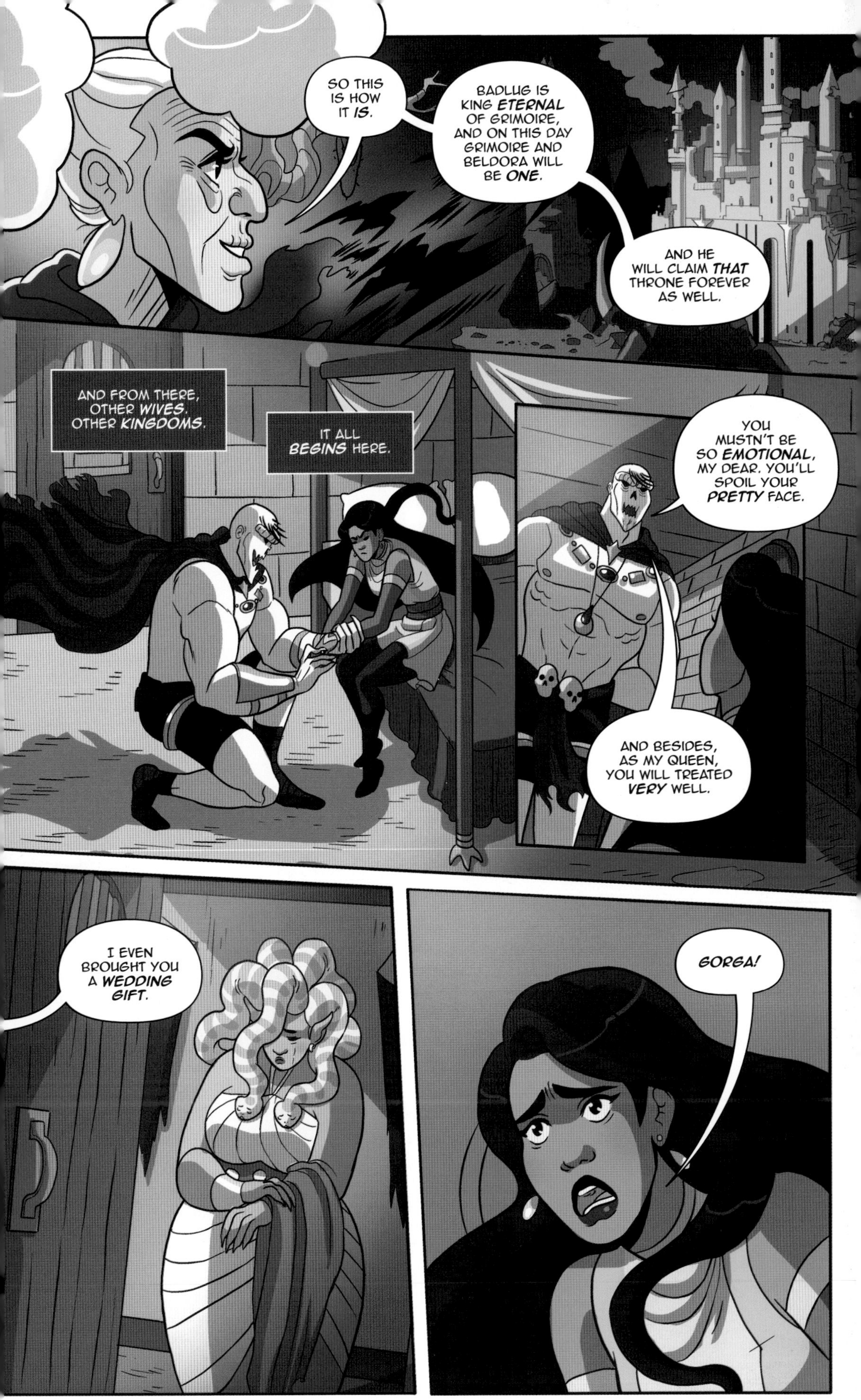
SO THIS IS HOW IT IS.
BADLUG IS KING ETERNAL OF GRIMOIRE, AND ON THIS DAY GRIMOIRE AND BELDORA WILL BE ONE.
AND HE WILL CLAIM THAT THRONE FOREVER AS WELL.
AND FROM THERE, OTHER WIVES. OTHER KINGDOMS.
IT ALL BEGINS HERE.
YOU MUSTN'T BE SO EMOTIONAL, MY DEAR. YOU'LL SPOIL YOUR PRETTY FACE.
AND BESIDES, AS MY QUEEN, YOU WILL TREATED VERY WELL.
I EVEN BROUGHT YOU A WEDDING GIFT.
GORGA!

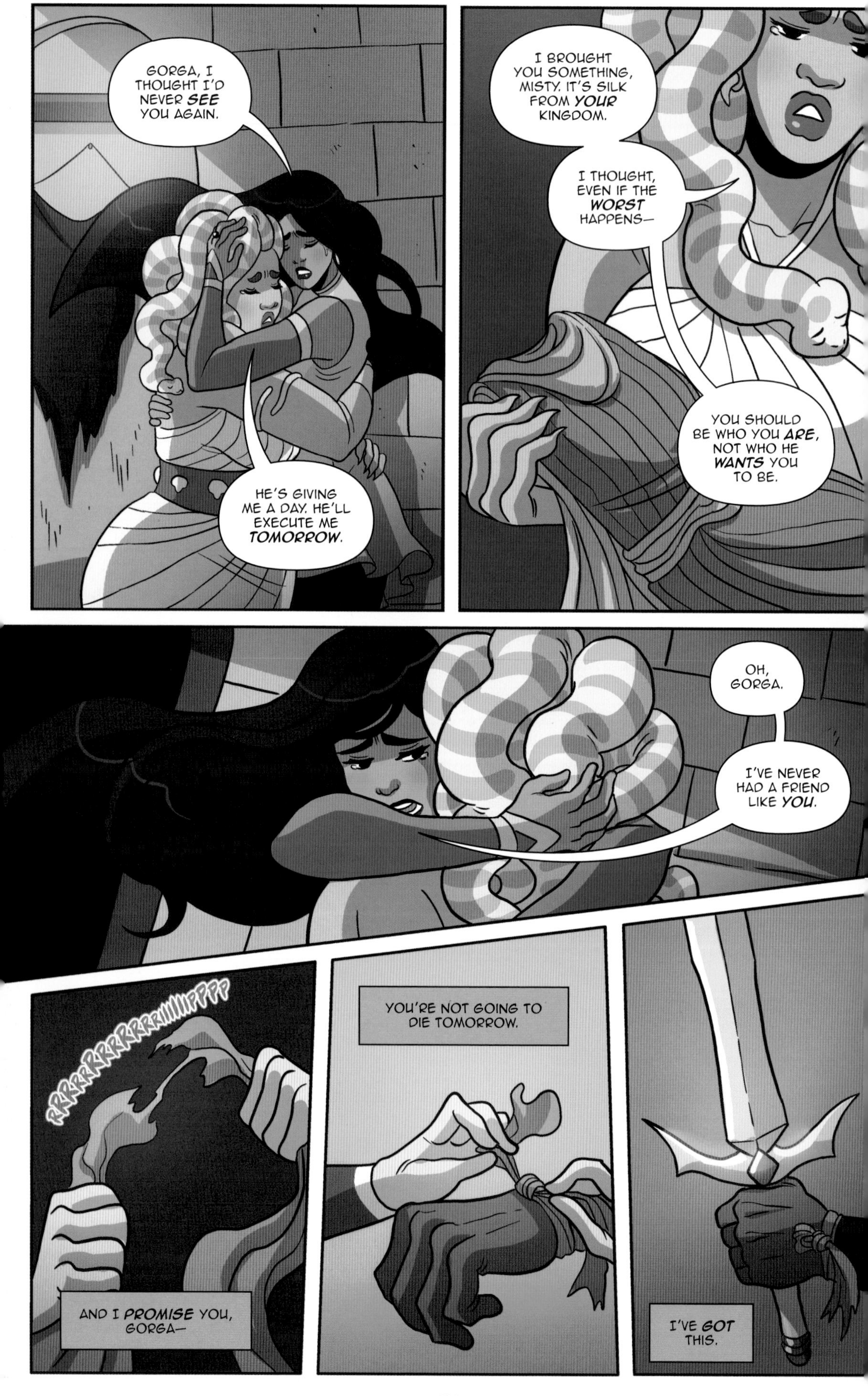
GORGA, I THOUGHT I'D NEVER SEE YOU AGAIN.
HE'S GIVING ME A DAY. HE'LL EXECUTE ME TOMORROW.
I BROUGHT YOU SOMETHING, MISTY. IT'S SILK FROM YOUR KINGDOM.
I THOUGHT, EVEN IF THE WORST HAPPENS—
YOU SHOULD BE WHO YOU ARE, NOT WHO HE WANTS YOU TO BE.
OH, GORGA.
I'VE NEVER HAD A FRIEND LIKE YOU.
RRRRRRRRRRRRIIIIIPPPP
AND I PROMISE YOU, GORGA—
YOU'RE NOT GOING TO DIE TOMORROW.
I'VE GOT THIS.

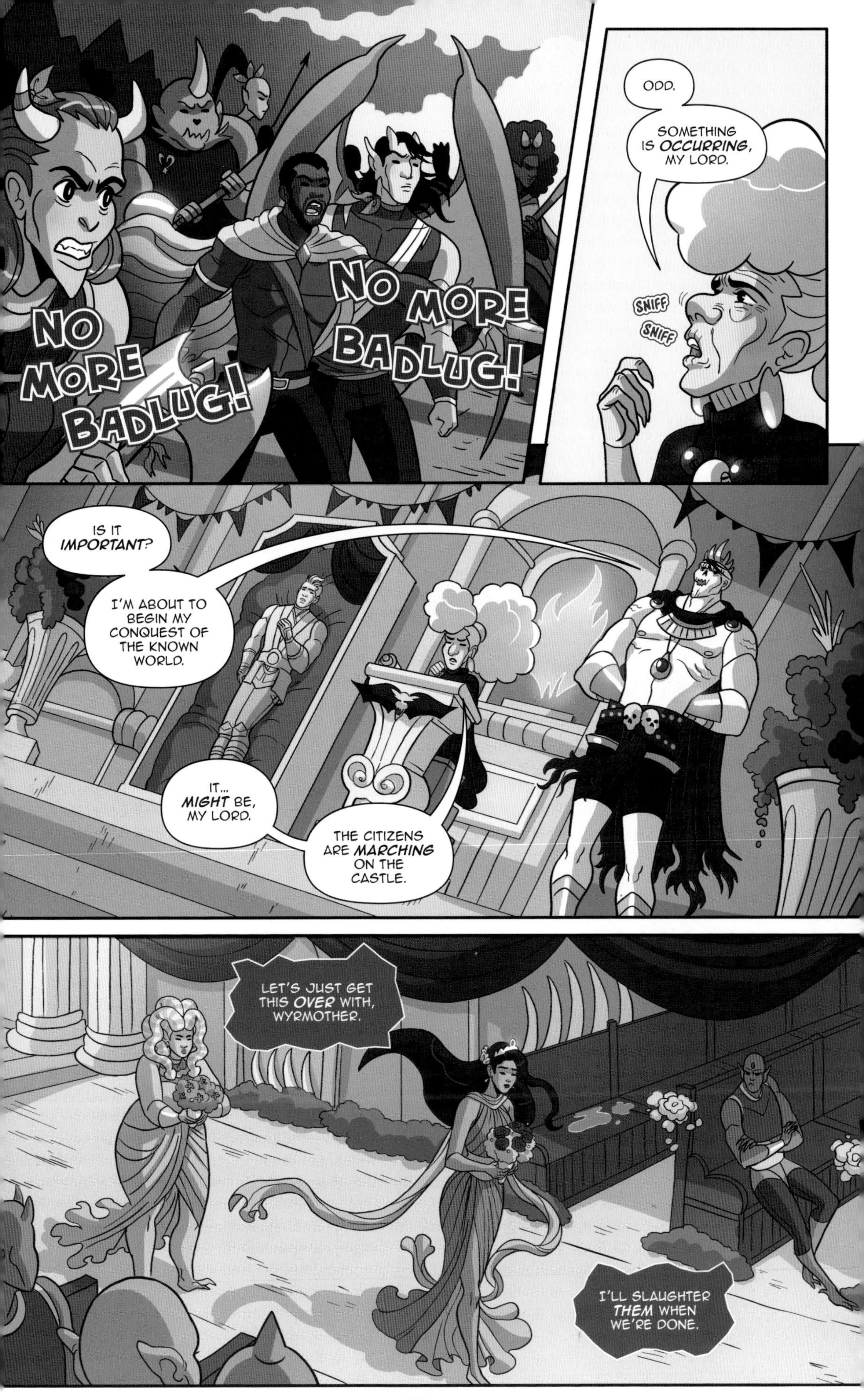

NO MORE BADLUG!
NO MORE BADLUG!
ODD.
SOMETHING IS OCCURRING, MY LORD.
SNIFF
SNIFF
IS IT IMPORTANT?
I'M ABOUT TO BEGIN MY CONQUEST OF THE KNOWN WORLD.
IT... MIGHT BE, MY LORD.
THE CITIZENS ARE MARCHING ON THE CASTLE.
LET'S JUST GET THIS OVER WITH, WYRMOTHER.
I'LL SLAUGHTER THEM WHEN WE'RE DONE.

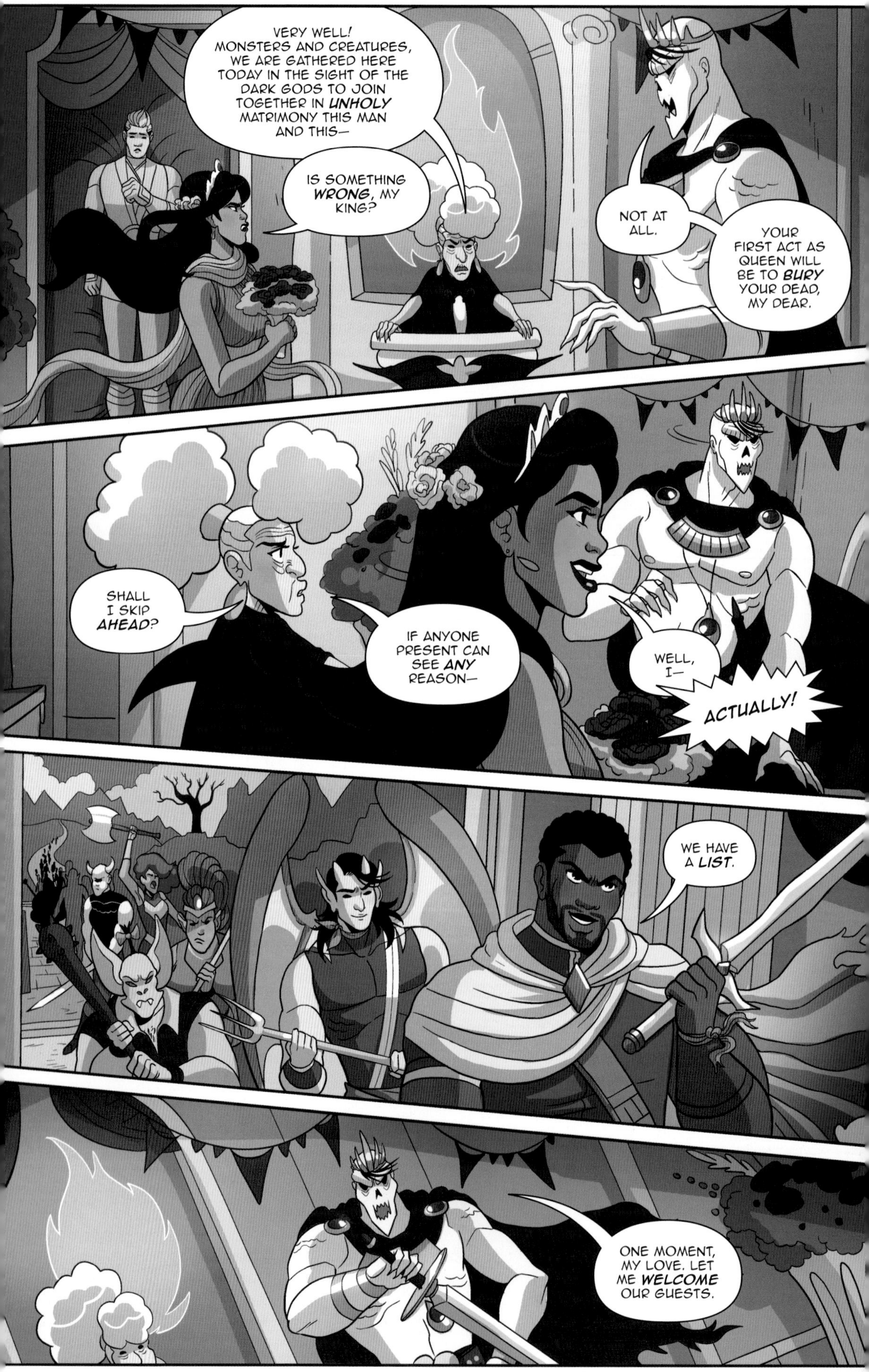
VERY WELL! MONSTERS AND CREATURES, WE ARE GATHERED HERE TODAY IN THE SIGHT OF THE DARK GODS TO JOIN TOGETHER IN UNHOLY MATRIMONY THIS MAN AND THIS—
IS SOMETHING WRONG, MY KING?
NOT AT ALL.
YOUR FIRST ACT AS QUEEN WILL BE TO BURY YOUR DEAD, MY DEAR.
SHALL I SKIP AHEAD?
IF ANYONE PRESENT CAN SEE ANY REASON—
WELL, I—
ACTUALLY!
WE HAVE A LIST.
ONE MOMENT, MY LOVE. LET ME WELCOME OUR GUESTS.

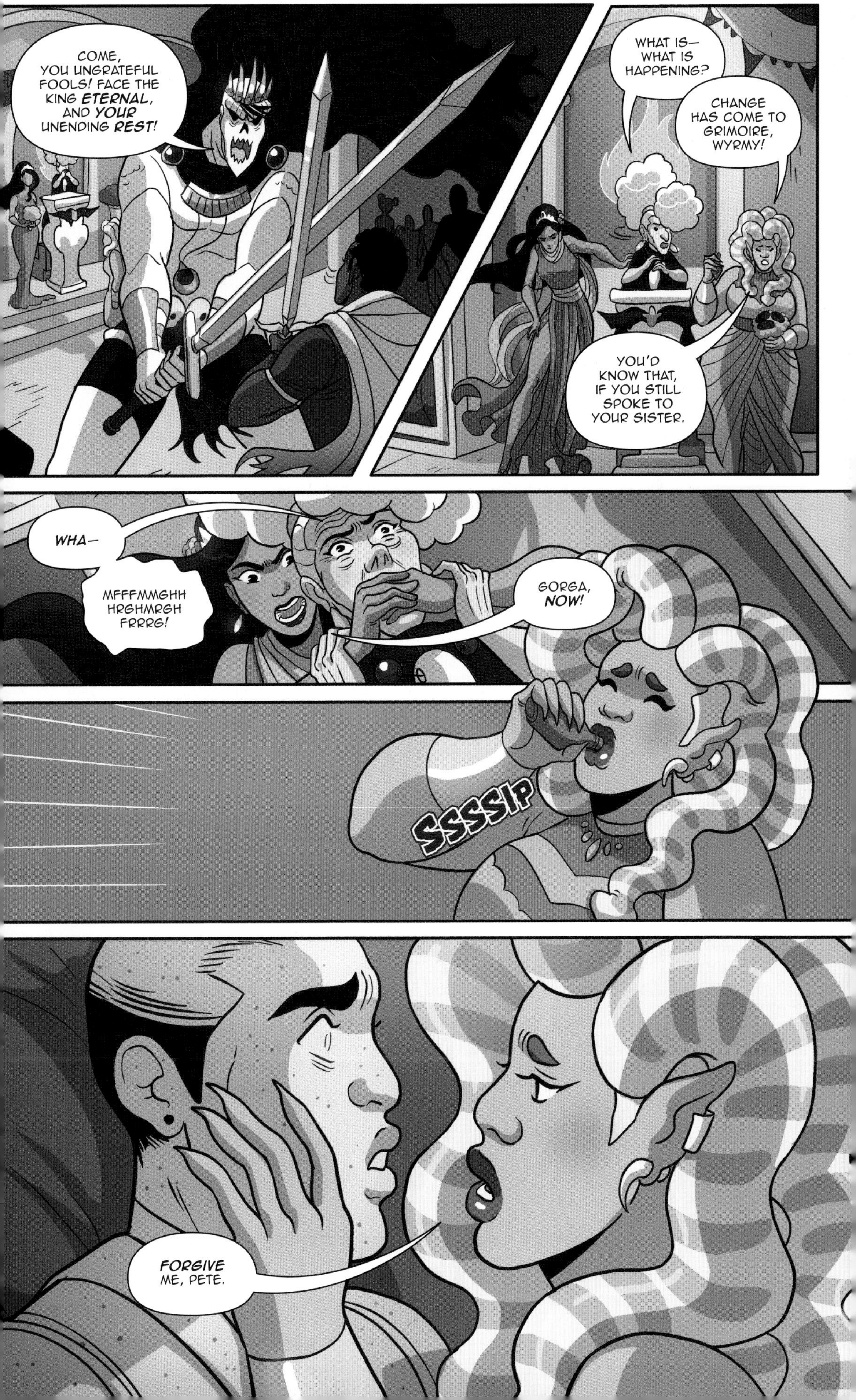
COME, YOU UNGRATEFUL FOOLS! FACE THE KING *ETERNAL*, AND *YOUR* UNENDING *REST*!
WHAT IS— WHAT IS HAPPENING?
CHANGE HAS COME TO GRIMOIRE, WYRMY!
YOU'D KNOW THAT, IF YOU STILL SPOKE TO YOUR SISTER.
WHA—
MFFFMMGHH HRGHMRGH FRRRG!
GORGA, *NOW!*
SSSSIP
FORGIVE ME, PETE.

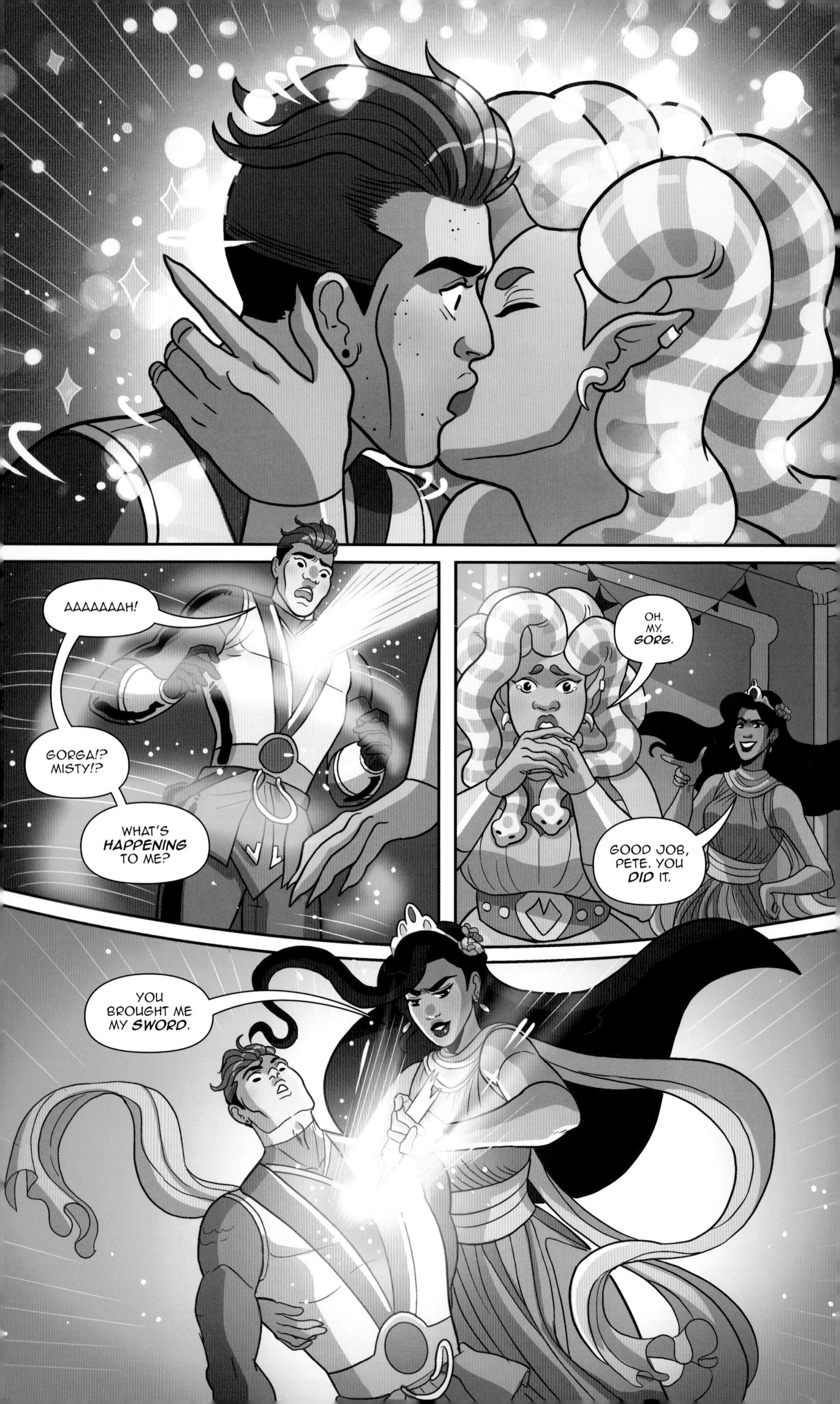
AAAAAAAH!
GORGA!? MISTY!?
WHAT'S **HAPPENING** TO ME?
OH. MY. **GORG.**
GOOD JOB, PETE. YOU **DID** IT.
YOU BROUGHT ME MY **SWORD**.

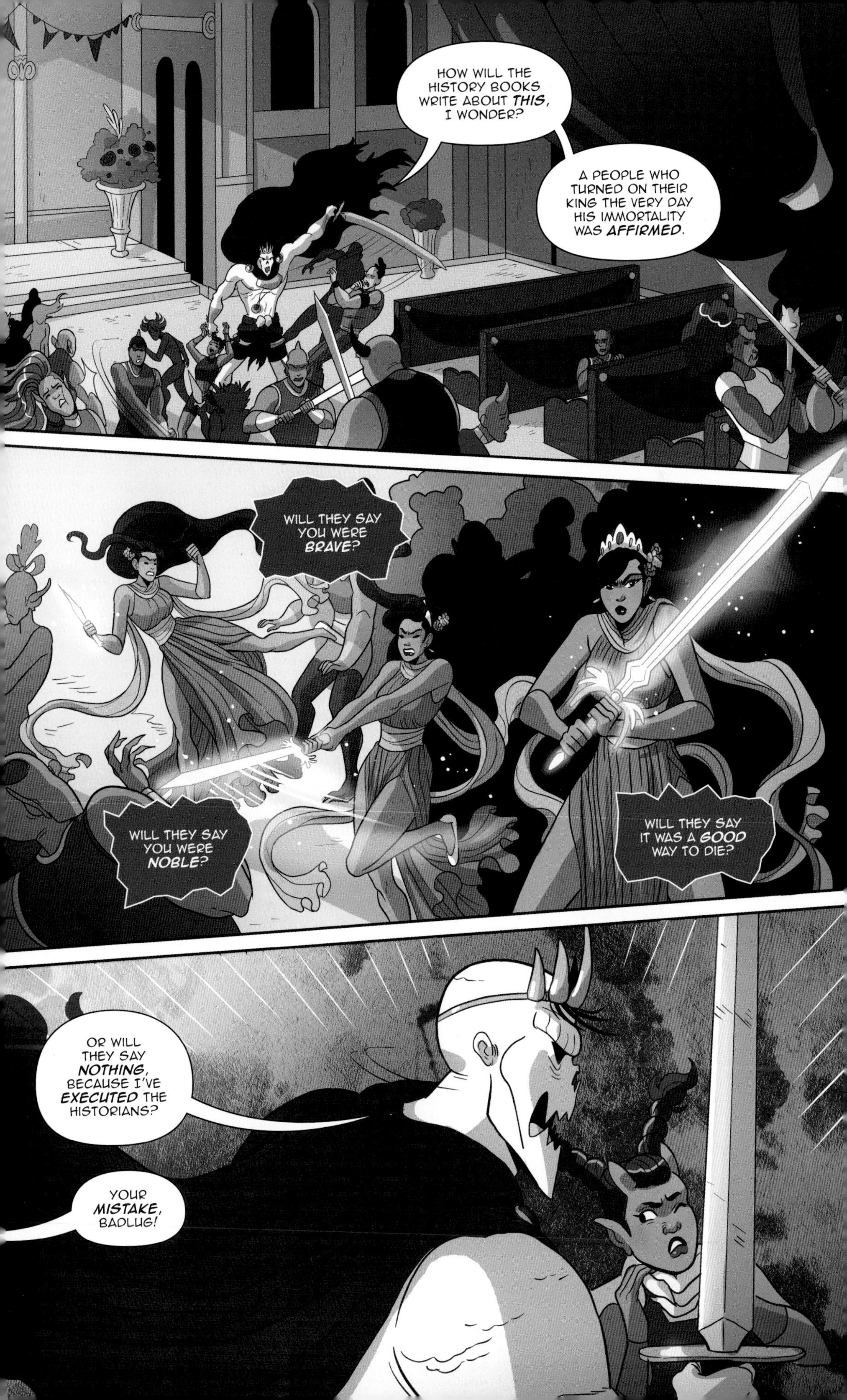
HOW WILL THE HISTORY BOOKS WRITE ABOUT *THIS*, I WONDER?
A PEOPLE WHO TURNED ON THEIR KING THE VERY DAY HIS IMMORTALITY WAS *AFFIRMED*.
WILL THEY SAY YOU WERE *BRAVE*?
WILL THEY SAY YOU WERE *NOBLE*?
WILL THEY SAY IT WAS A *GOOD* WAY TO DIE?
OR WILL THEY SAY *NOTHING*, BECAUSE I'VE *EXECUTED* THE HISTORIANS?
YOUR *MISTAKE*, BADLUG!

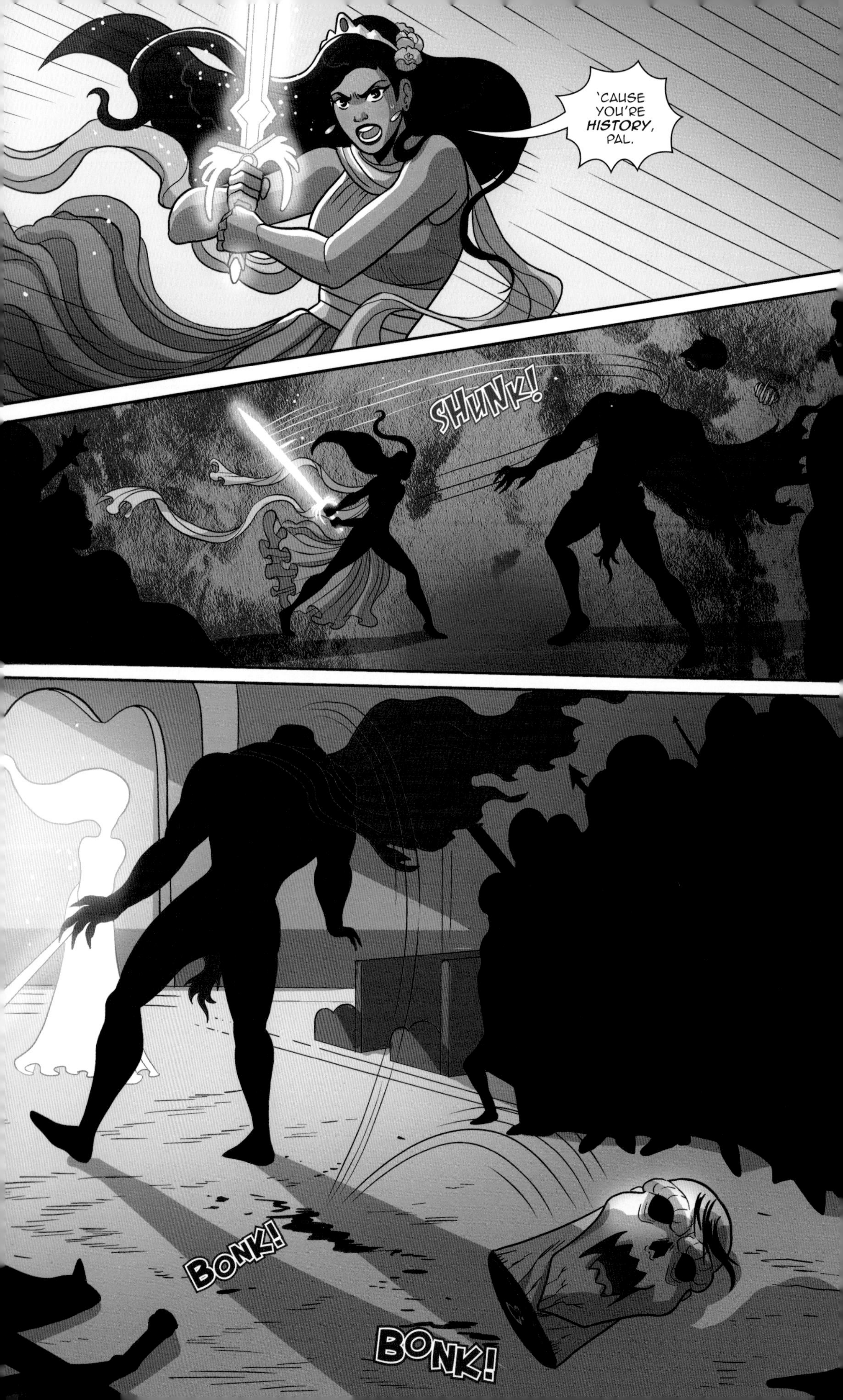
'CAUSE YOU'RE HISTORY, PAL.
SHUNK!
BONK!
BONK!

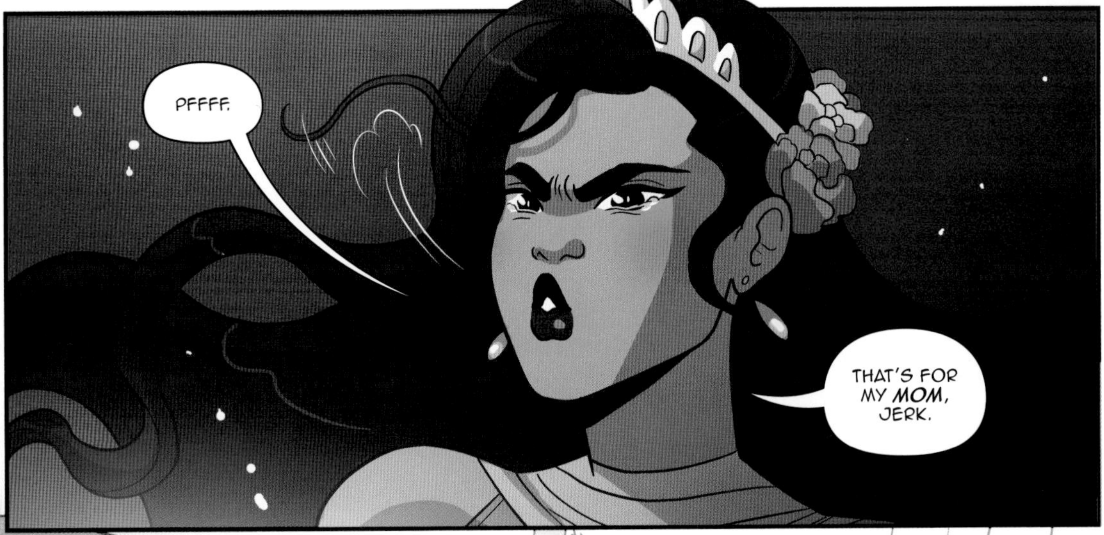
PFFFF.
THAT'S FOR MY **MOM**, JERK.

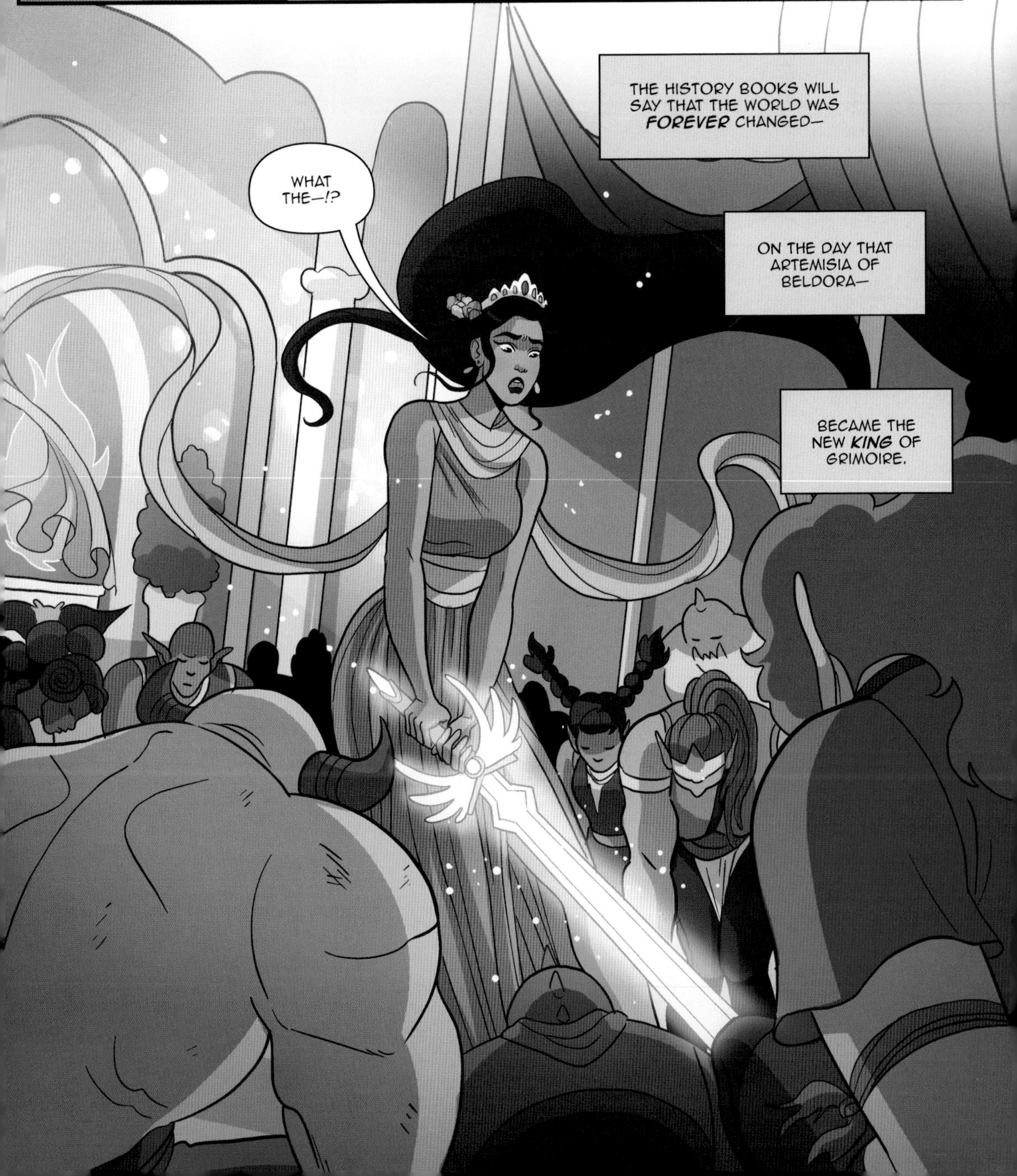
THE HISTORY BOOKS WILL SAY THAT THE WORLD WAS **FOREVER** CHANGED—
WHAT THE—!?
ON THE DAY THAT ARTEMISIA OF BELDORA—
BECAME THE NEW **KING** OF GRIMOIRE.

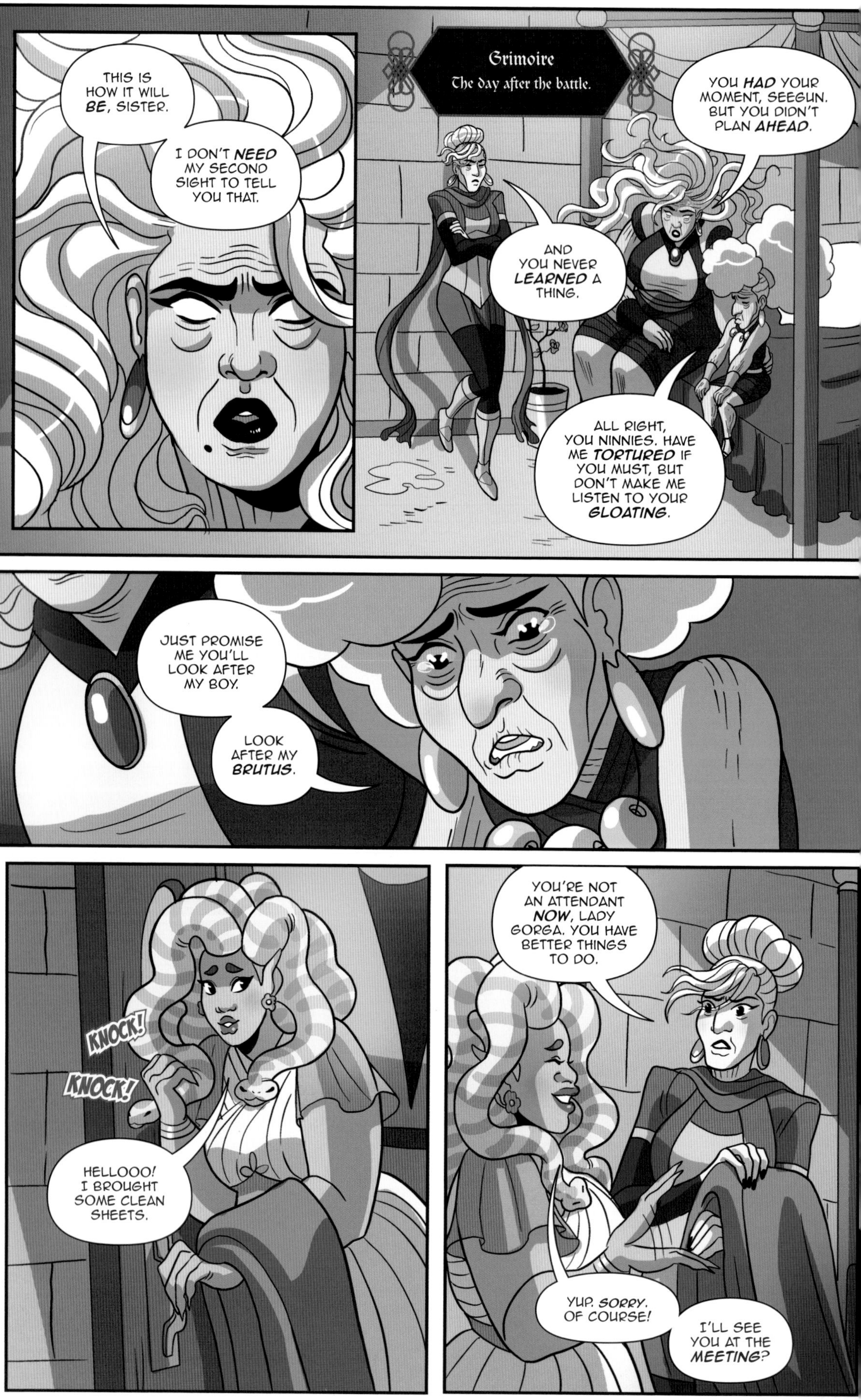
Grimoire
The day after the battle.
THIS IS HOW IT WILL BE, SISTER.
I DON'T NEED MY SECOND SIGHT TO TELL YOU THAT.
YOU HAD YOUR MOMENT, SEEGUN. BUT YOU DIDN'T PLAN AHEAD.
AND YOU NEVER LEARNED A THING.
ALL RIGHT, YOU NINNIES. HAVE ME TORTURED IF YOU MUST, BUT DON'T MAKE ME LISTEN TO YOUR GLOATING.
JUST PROMISE ME YOU'LL LOOK AFTER MY BOY.
LOOK AFTER MY BRUTUS.
KNOCK!
KNOCK!
HELLOOO! I BROUGHT SOME CLEAN SHEETS.
YOU'RE NOT AN ATTENDANT NOW, LADY GORGA. YOU HAVE BETTER THINGS TO DO.
YUP. SORRY. OF COURSE!
I'LL SEE YOU AT THE MEETING?

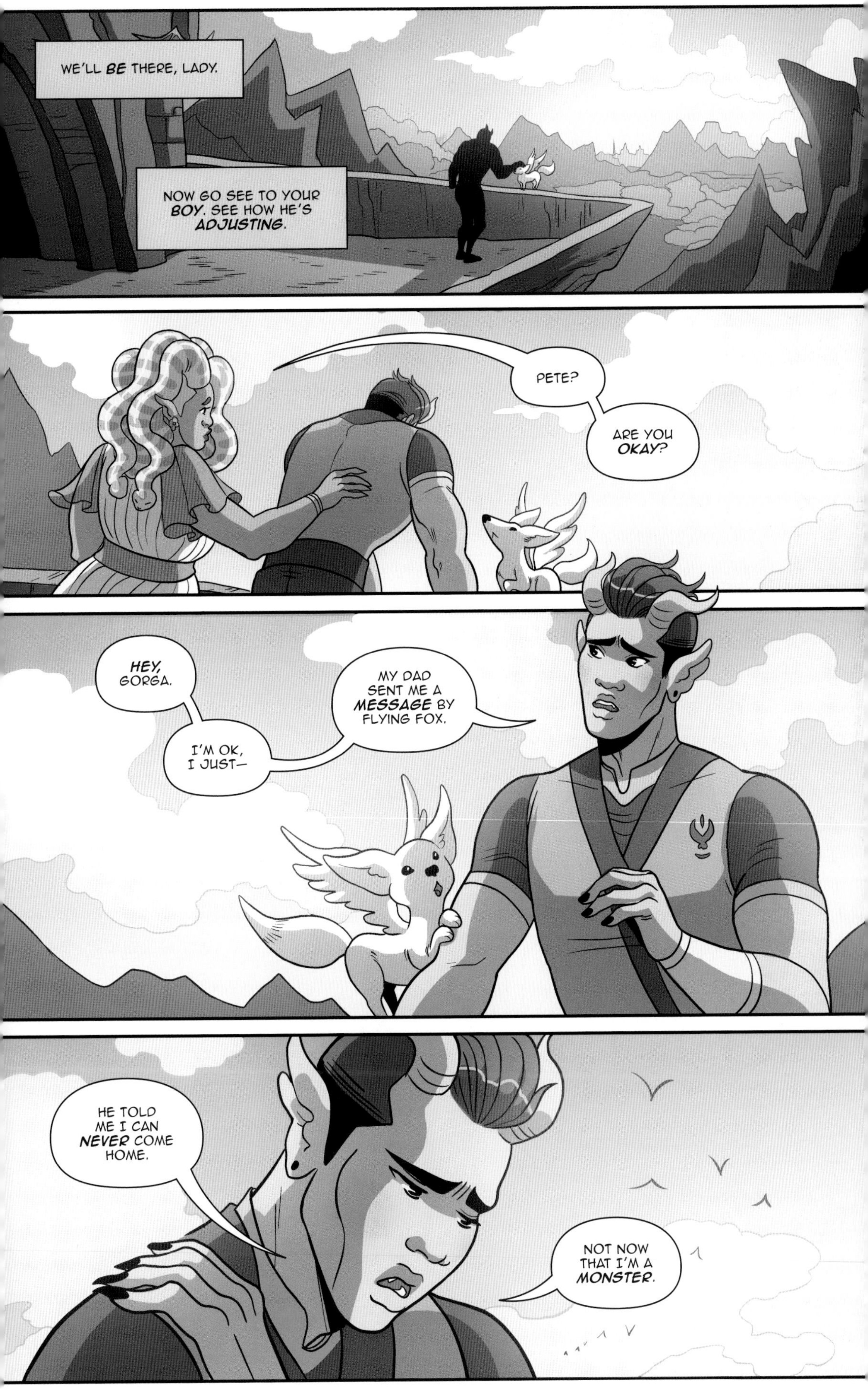
WE'LL BE THERE, LADY.
NOW GO SEE TO YOUR BOY. SEE HOW HE'S ADJUSTING.
PETE?
ARE YOU OKAY?
HEY, GORGA.
I'M OK, I JUST—
MY DAD SENT ME A MESSAGE BY FLYING FOX.
HE TOLD ME I CAN NEVER COME HOME.
NOT NOW THAT I'M A MONSTER.

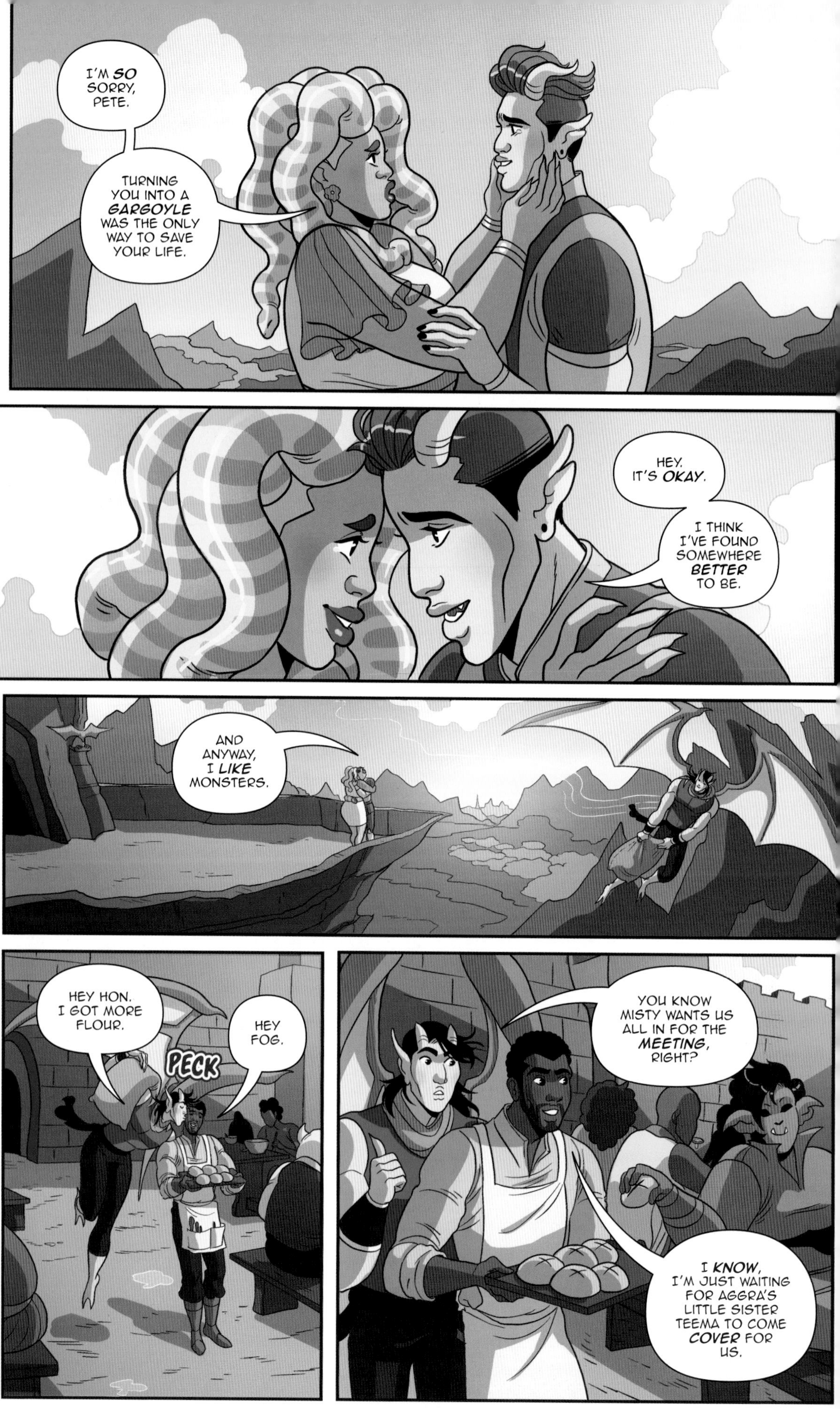
I'M SO SORRY, PETE.
TURNING YOU INTO A GARGOYLE WAS THE ONLY WAY TO SAVE YOUR LIFE.
HEY. IT'S OKAY.
I THINK I'VE FOUND SOMEWHERE BETTER TO BE.
AND ANYWAY, I LIKE MONSTERS.
HEY HON. I GOT MORE FLOUR.
PECK
HEY FOG.
YOU KNOW MISTY WANTS US ALL IN FOR THE MEETING, RIGHT?
I KNOW, I'M JUST WAITING FOR AGGRA'S LITTLE SISTER TEEMA TO COME COVER FOR US.

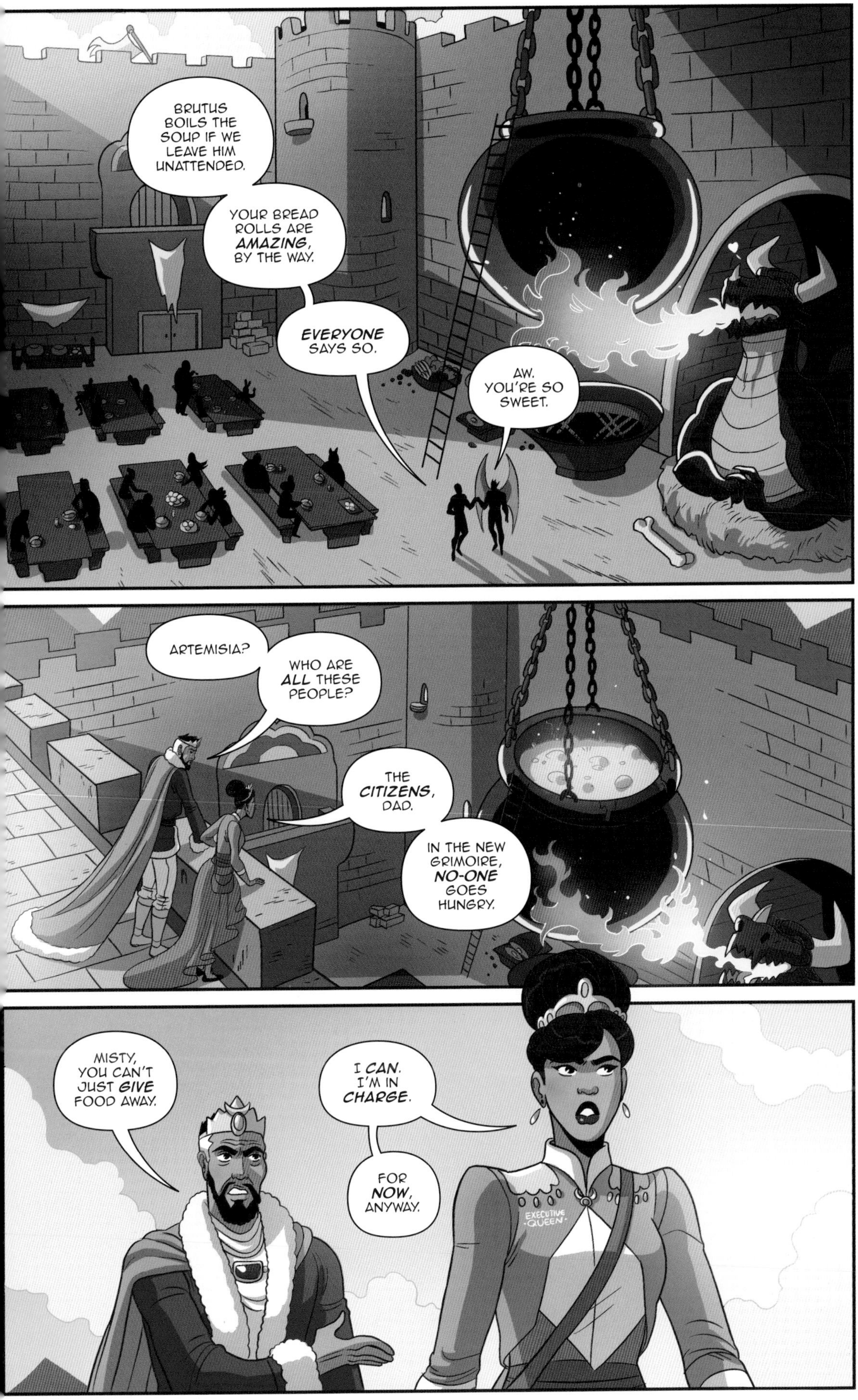
BRUTUS BOILS THE SOUP IF WE LEAVE HIM UNATTENDED.
YOUR BREAD ROLLS ARE AMAZING, BY THE WAY.
EVERYONE SAYS SO.
AW. YOU'RE SO SWEET.
ARTEMISIA?
WHO ARE ALL THESE PEOPLE?
THE CITIZENS, DAD.
IN THE NEW GRIMOIRE, NO-ONE GOES HUNGRY.
MISTY, YOU CAN'T JUST GIVE FOOD AWAY.
I CAN. I'M IN CHARGE.
FOR NOW, ANYWAY.
EXECUTIVE QUEEN

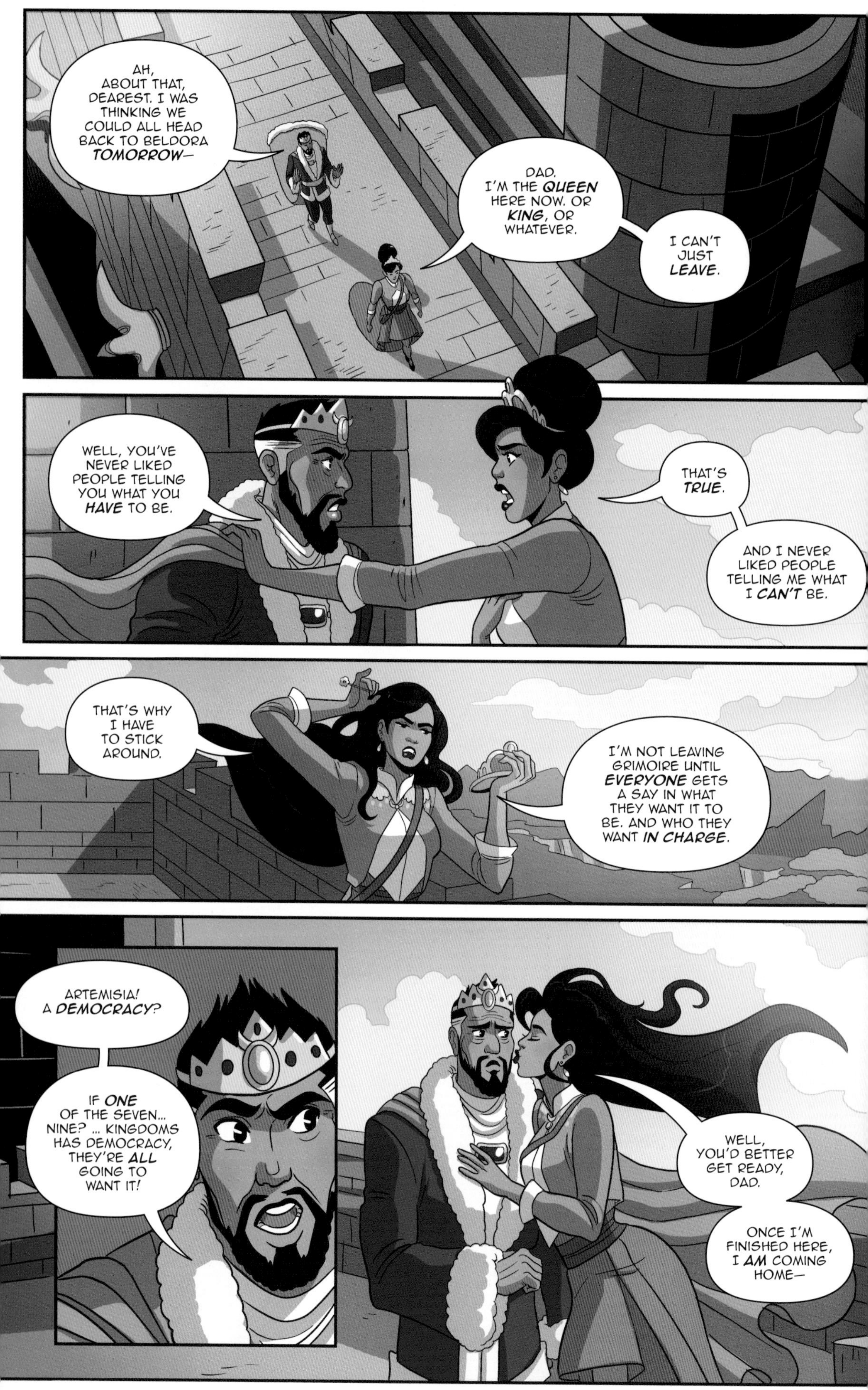
AH, ABOUT THAT, DEAREST. I WAS THINKING WE COULD ALL HEAD BACK TO BELDORA TOMORROW—
DAD. I'M THE QUEEN HERE NOW. OR KING, OR WHATEVER.
I CAN'T JUST LEAVE.
WELL, YOU'VE NEVER LIKED PEOPLE TELLING YOU WHAT YOU HAVE TO BE.
THAT'S TRUE.
AND I NEVER LIKED PEOPLE TELLING ME WHAT I CAN'T BE.
THAT'S WHY I HAVE TO STICK AROUND.
I'M NOT LEAVING GRIMOIRE UNTIL EVERYONE GETS A SAY IN WHAT THEY WANT IT TO BE. AND WHO THEY WANT IN CHARGE.
ARTEMISIA! A DEMOCRACY?
IF ONE OF THE SEVEN... NINE? ... KINGDOMS HAS DEMOCRACY, THEY'RE ALL GOING TO WANT IT!
WELL, YOU'D BETTER GET READY, DAD.
ONCE I'M FINISHED HERE, I AM COMING HOME—

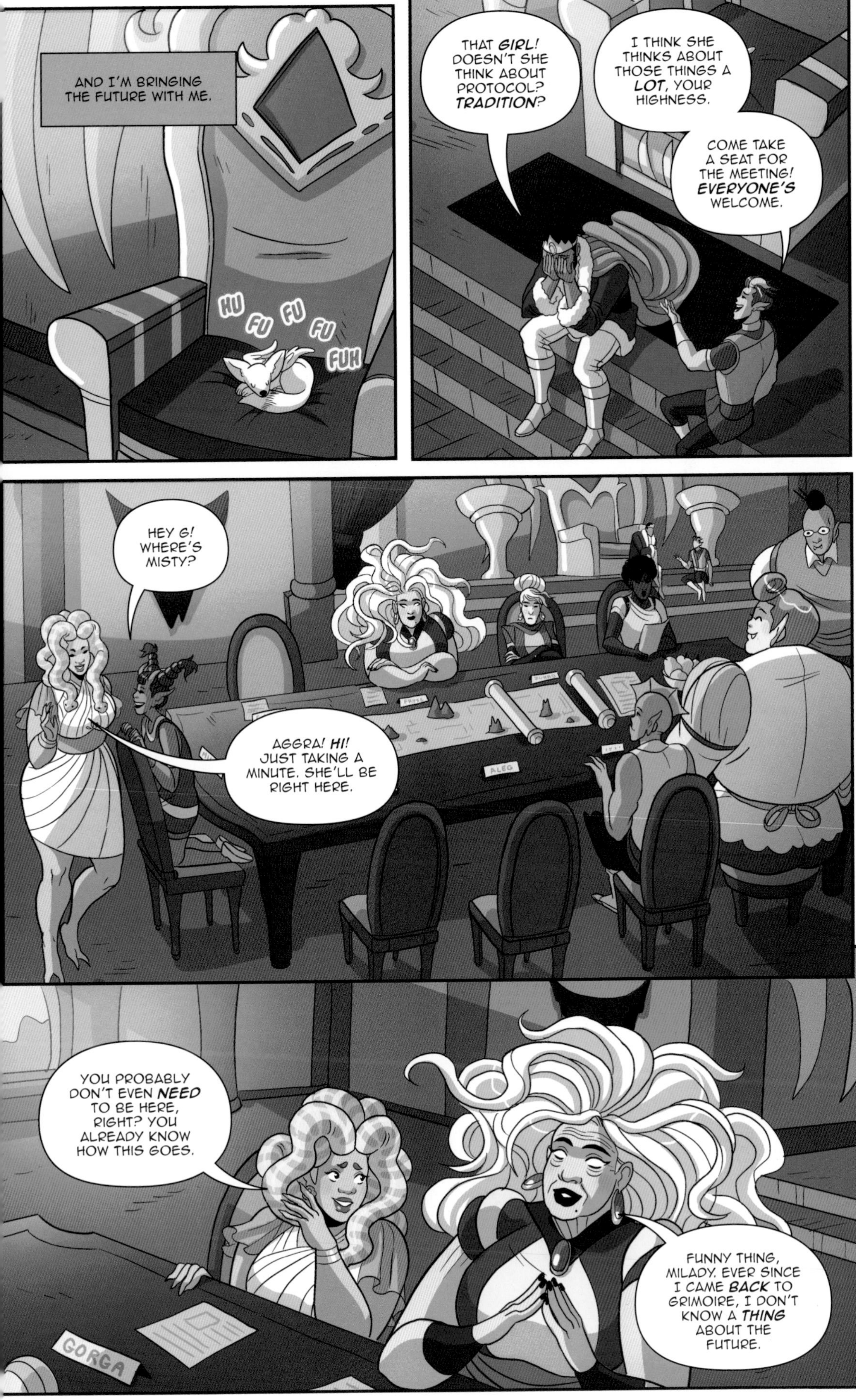
AND I'M BRINGING THE FUTURE WITH ME.
HU FU FU FU FUH
THAT GIRL! DOESN'T SHE THINK ABOUT PROTOCOL? TRADITION?
I THINK SHE THINKS ABOUT THOSE THINGS A LOT, YOUR HIGHNESS.
COME TAKE A SEAT FOR THE MEETING! EVERYONE'S WELCOME.
HEY G! WHERE'S MISTY?
AGGRA! HI! JUST TAKING A MINUTE. SHE'LL BE RIGHT HERE.
ALEG
YOU PROBABLY DON'T EVEN NEED TO BE HERE, RIGHT? YOU ALREADY KNOW HOW THIS GOES.
GORGA
FUNNY THING, MILADY. EVER SINCE I CAME BACK TO GRIMOIRE, I DON'T KNOW A THING ABOUT THE FUTURE.

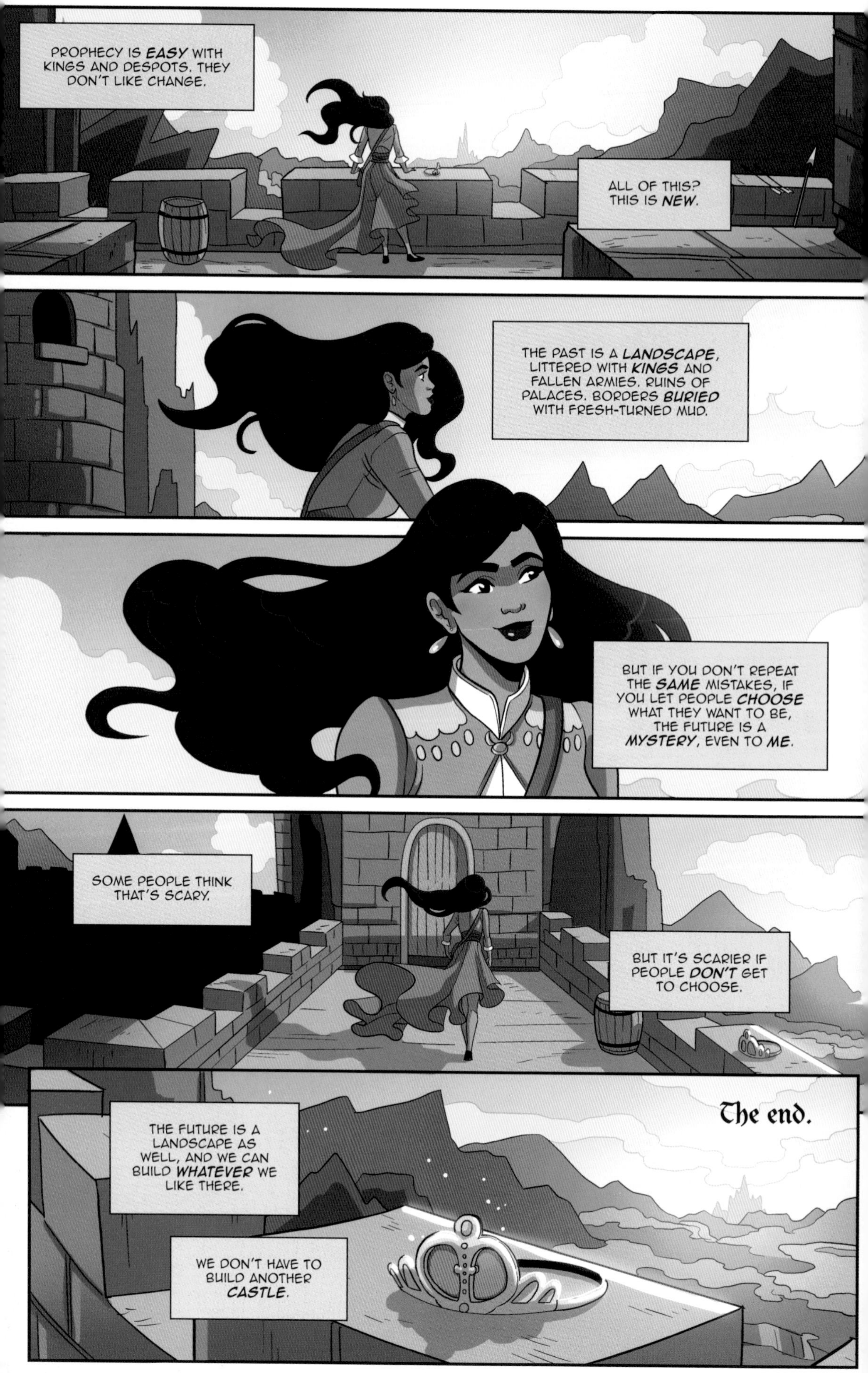
PROPHECY IS EASY WITH KINGS AND DESPOTS. THEY DON'T LIKE CHANGE.
ALL OF THIS? THIS IS NEW.
THE PAST IS A LANDSCAPE, LITTERED WITH KINGS AND FALLEN ARMIES. RUINS OF PALACES. BORDERS BURIED WITH FRESH-TURNED MUD.
BUT IF YOU DON'T REPEAT THE SAME MISTAKES, IF YOU LET PEOPLE CHOOSE WHAT THEY WANT TO BE, THE FUTURE IS A MYSTERY, EVEN TO ME.
SOME PEOPLE THINK THAT'S SCARY.
BUT IT'S SCARIER IF PEOPLE DON'T GET TO CHOOSE.
THE FUTURE IS A LANDSCAPE AS WELL, AND WE CAN BUILD WHATEVER WE LIKE THERE.
The end.
WE DON'T HAVE TO BUILD ANOTHER CASTLE.

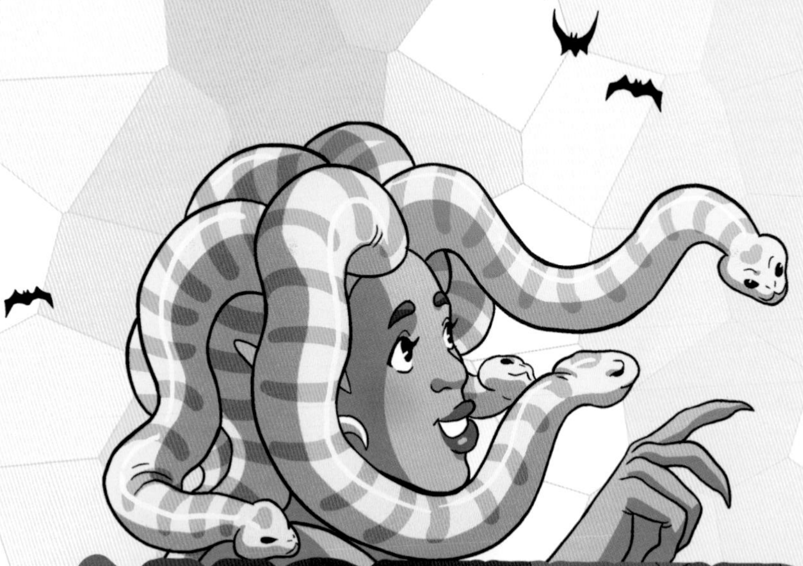

ANOTHER CASTLE

COVER GALLERY

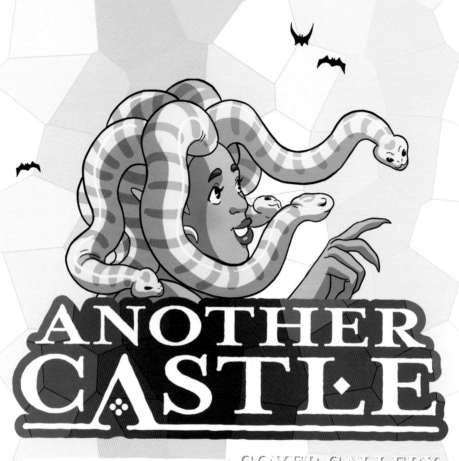

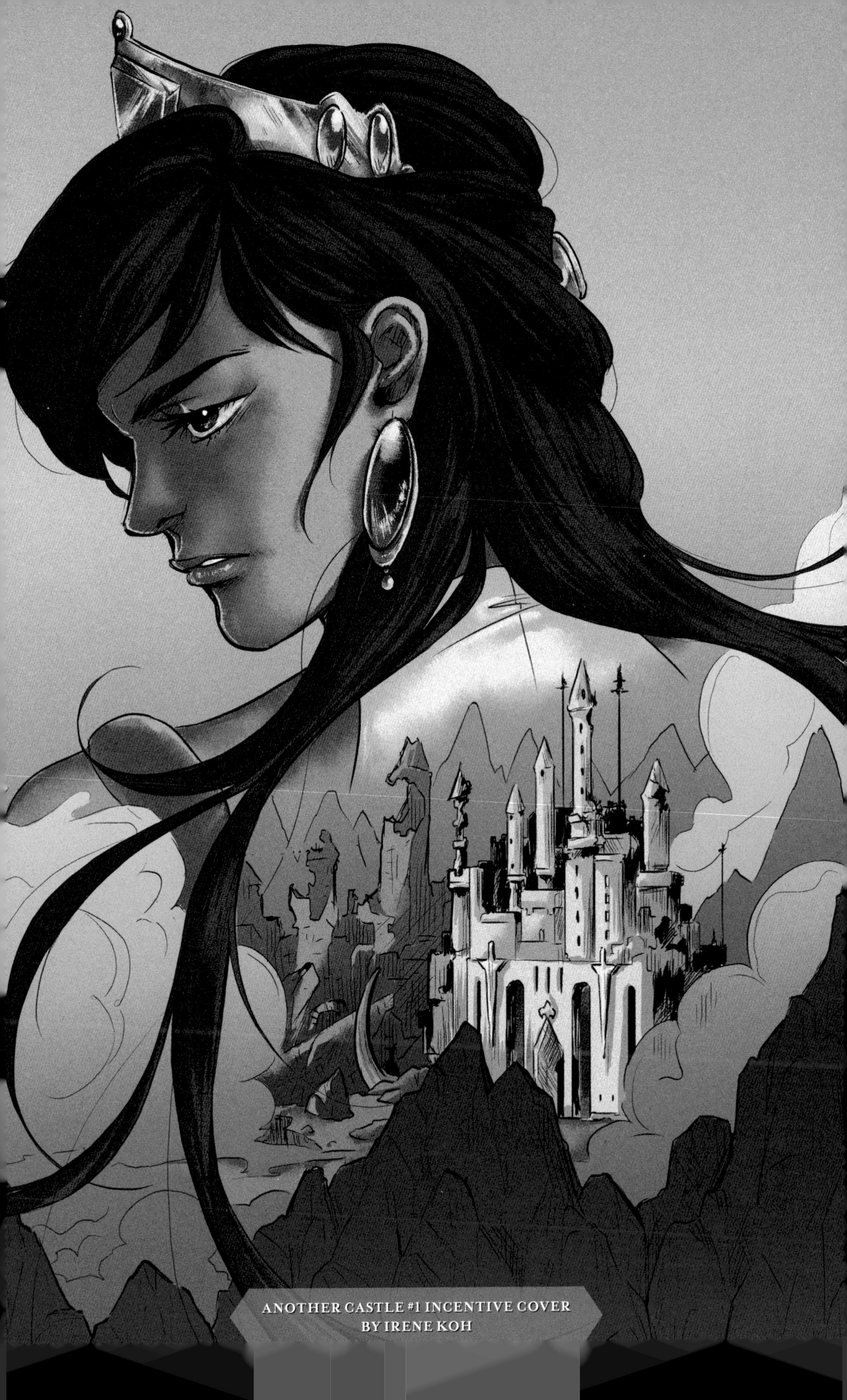

ANOTHER CASTLE #1 INCENTIVE COVER
BY IRENE KOH

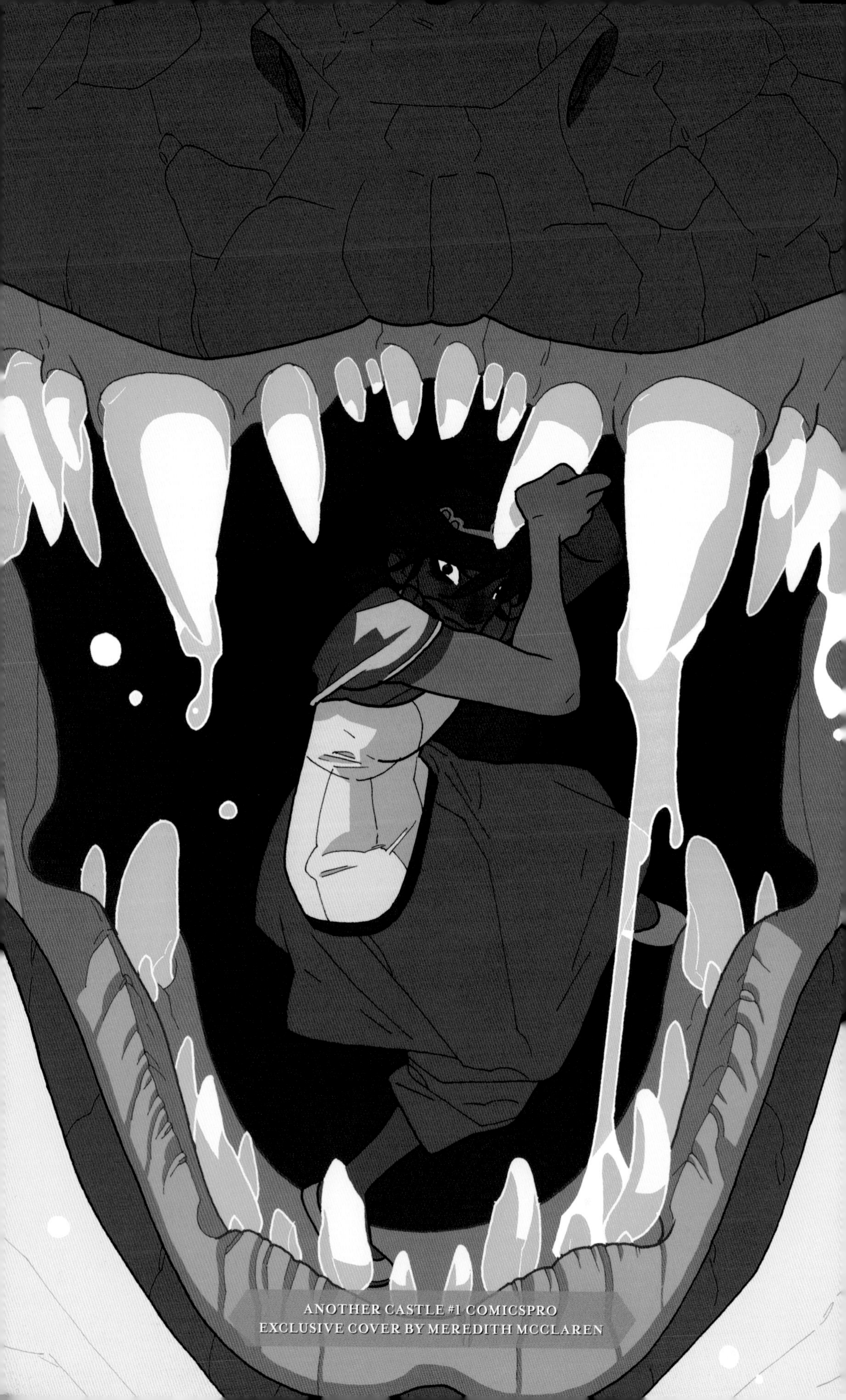

ANOTHER CASTLE #1 COMICSPRO
EXCLUSIVE COVER BY MEREDITH MCCLAREN

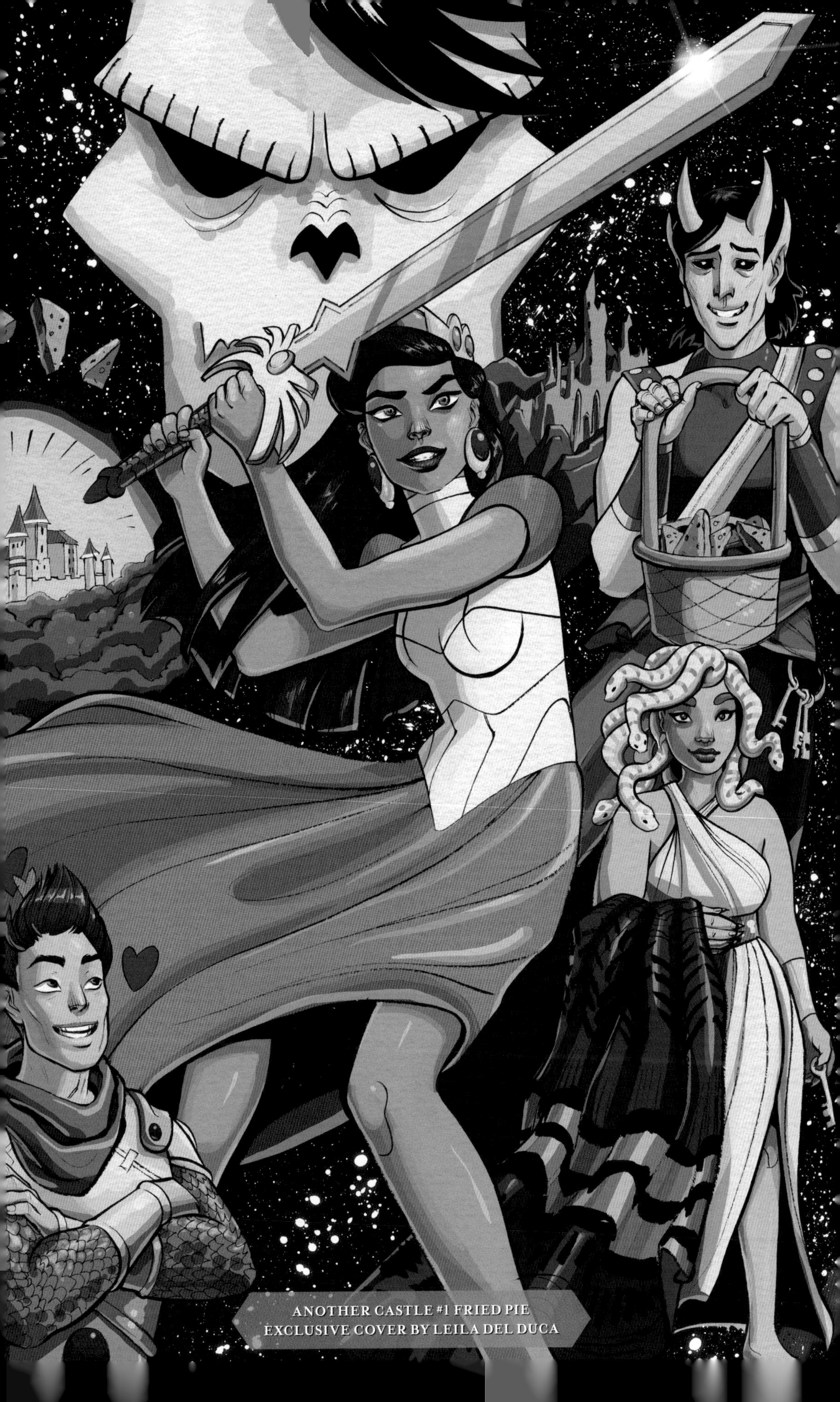

ANOTHER CASTLE #1 FRIED PIE
EXCLUSIVE COVER BY LEILA DEL DUCA

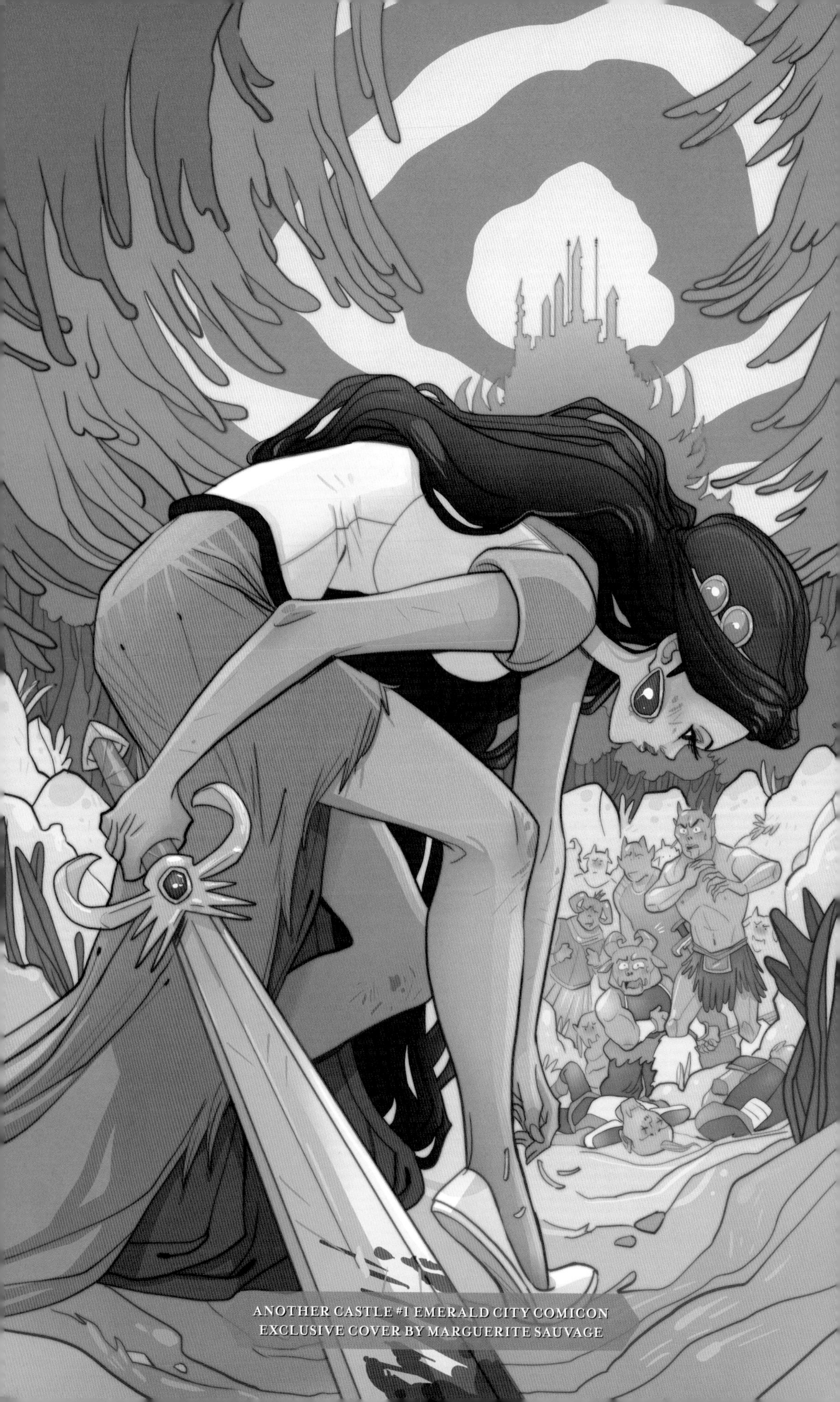

ANOTHER CASTLE #1 EMERALD CITY COMICON
EXCLUSIVE COVER BY MARGUERITE SAUVAGE

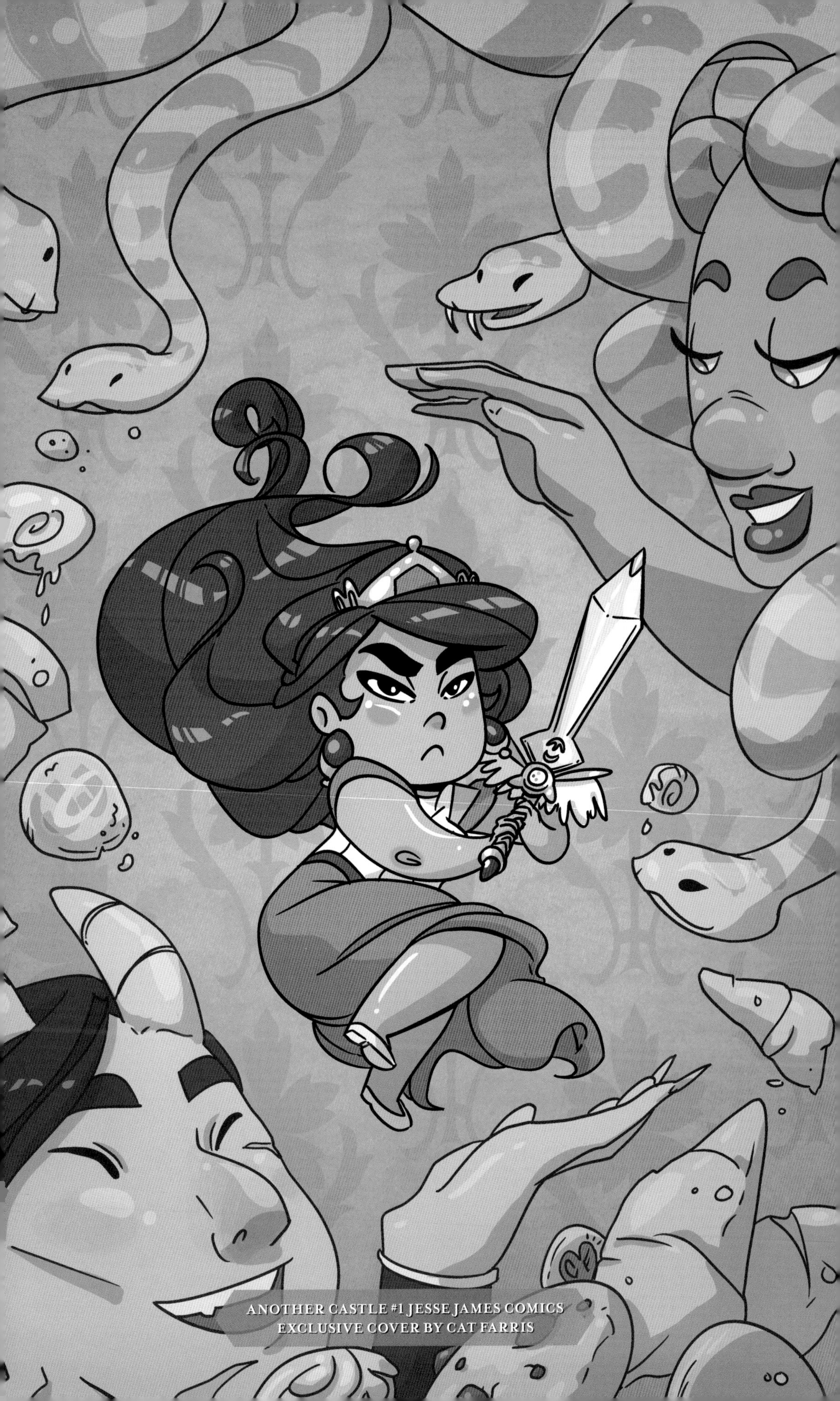

ANOTHER CASTLE #1 JESSE JAMES COMICS
EXCLUSIVE COVER BY CAT FARRIS

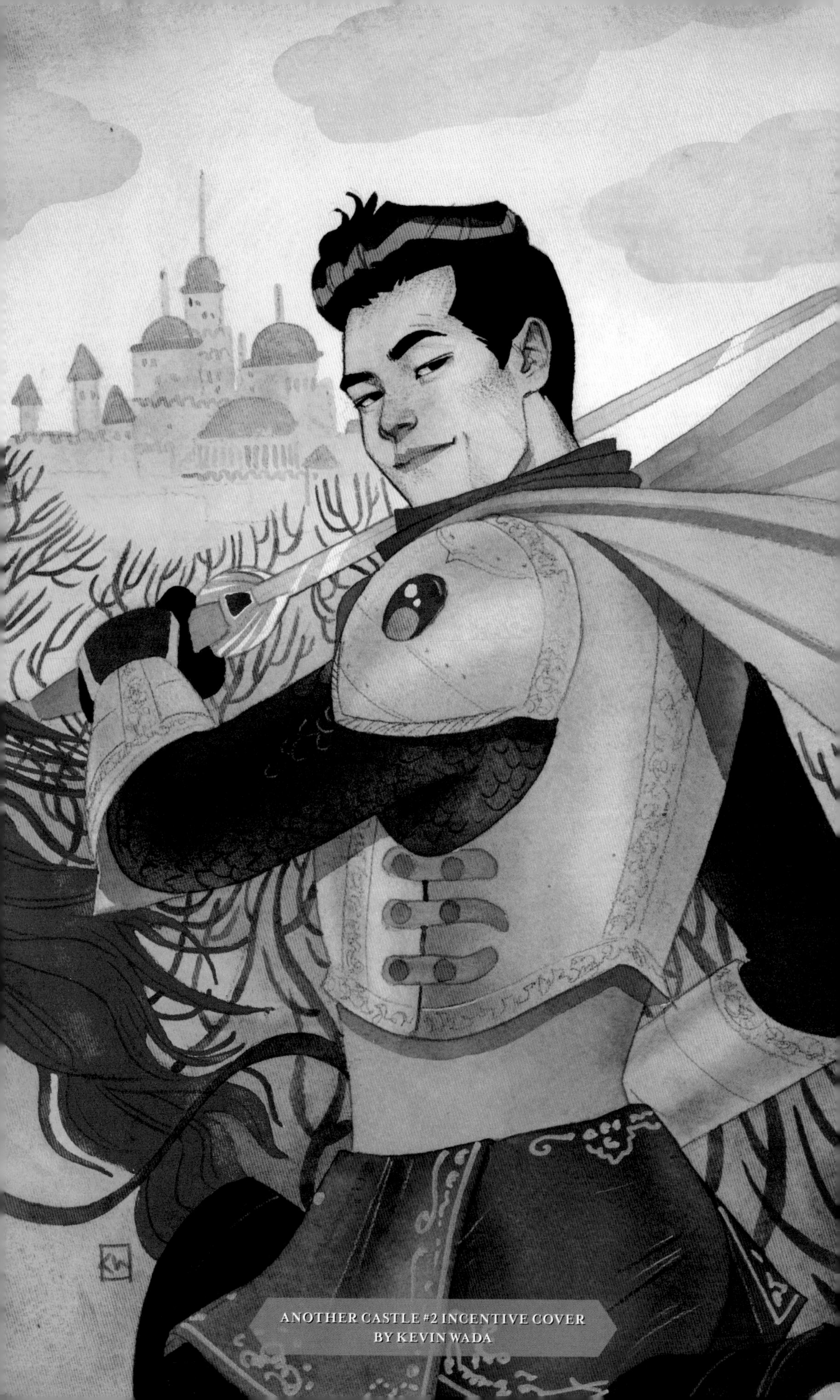

ANOTHER CASTLE #2 INCENTIVE COVER
BY KEVIN WADA

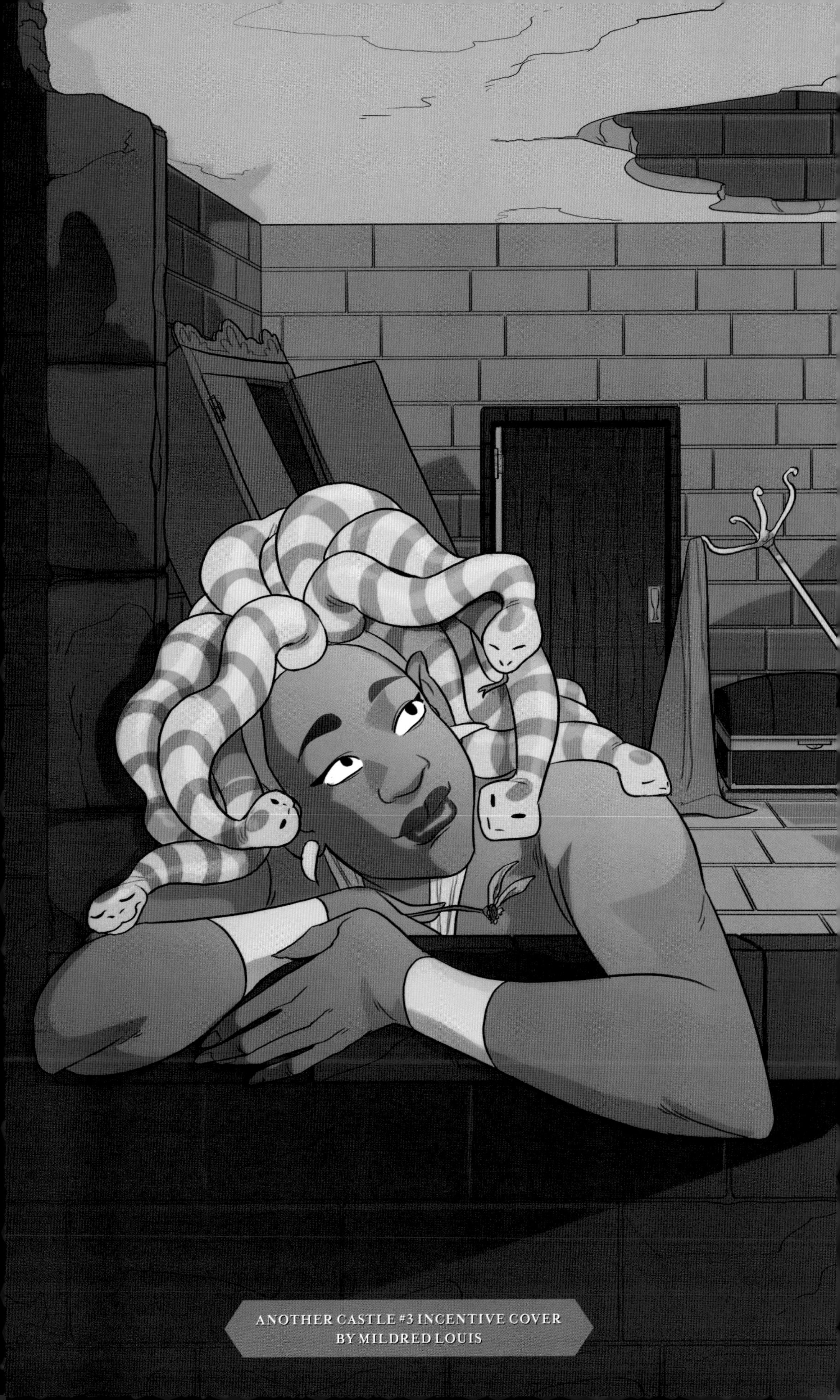

ANOTHER CASTLE #3 INCENTIVE COVER
BY MILDRED LOUIS

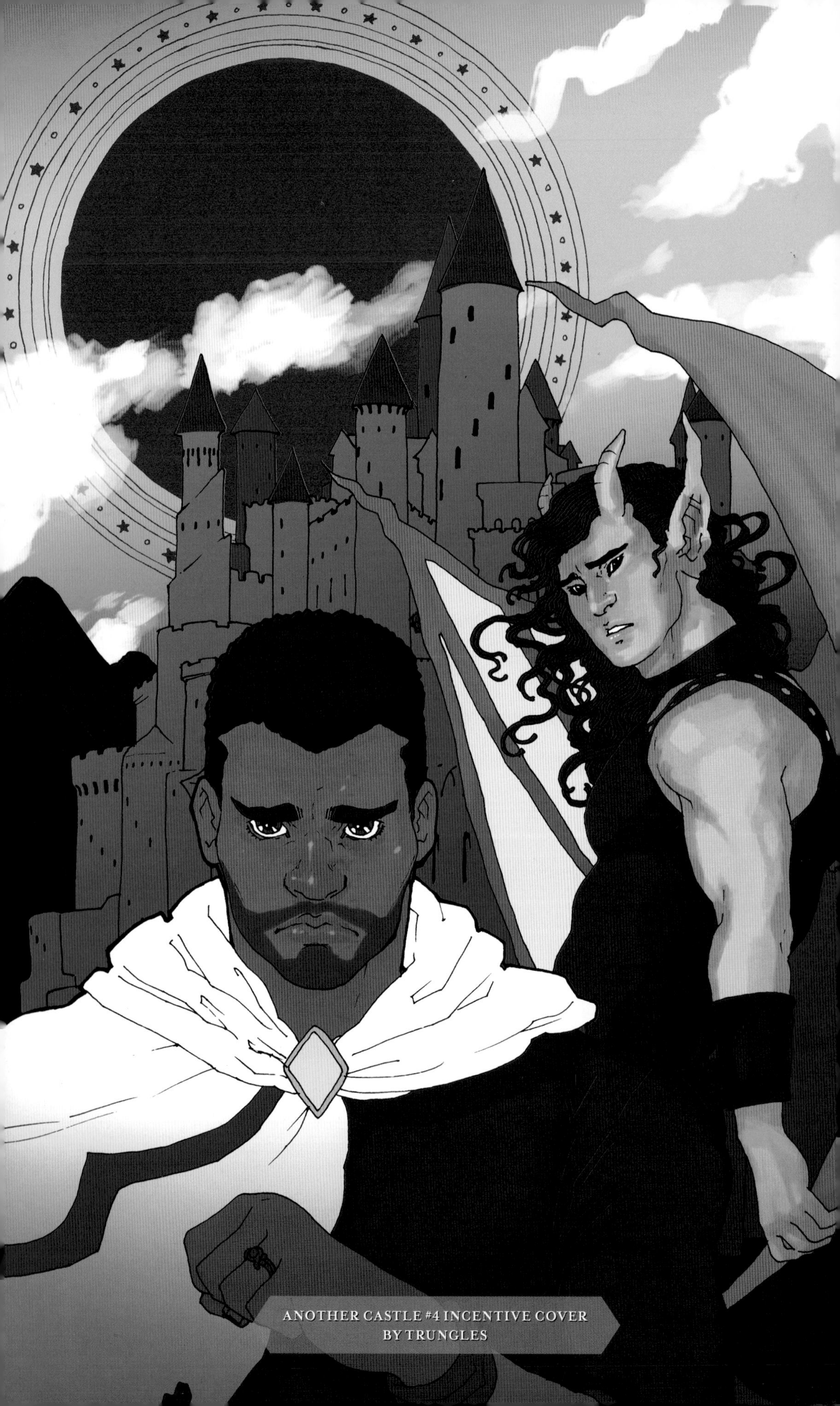

ANOTHER CASTLE #4 INCENTIVE COVER
BY TRUNGLES

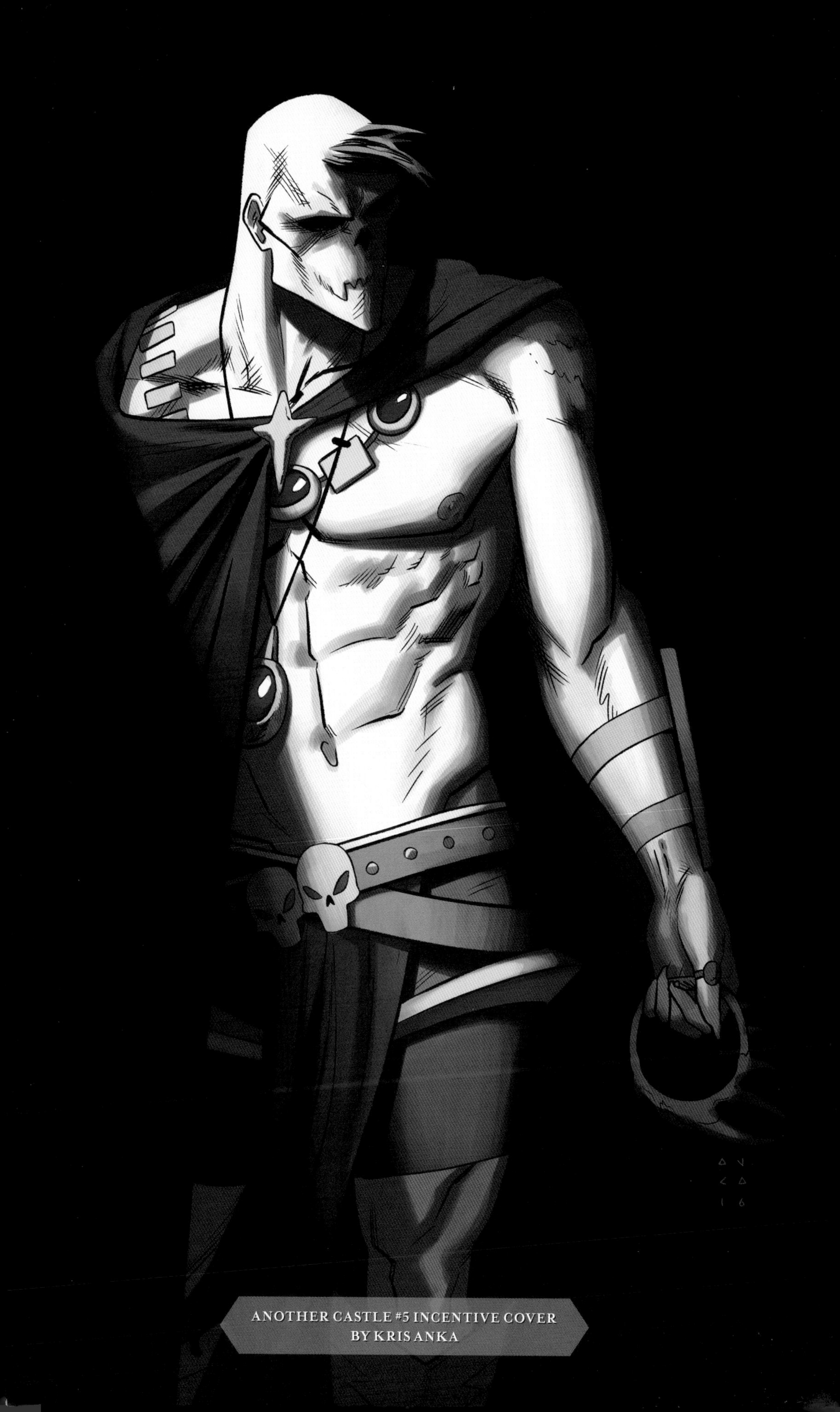

ANOTHER CASTLE #5 INCENTIVE COVER
BY KRIS ANKA

INTERVIEW WITH

Andrew Wheeler & Paulina Ganucheau

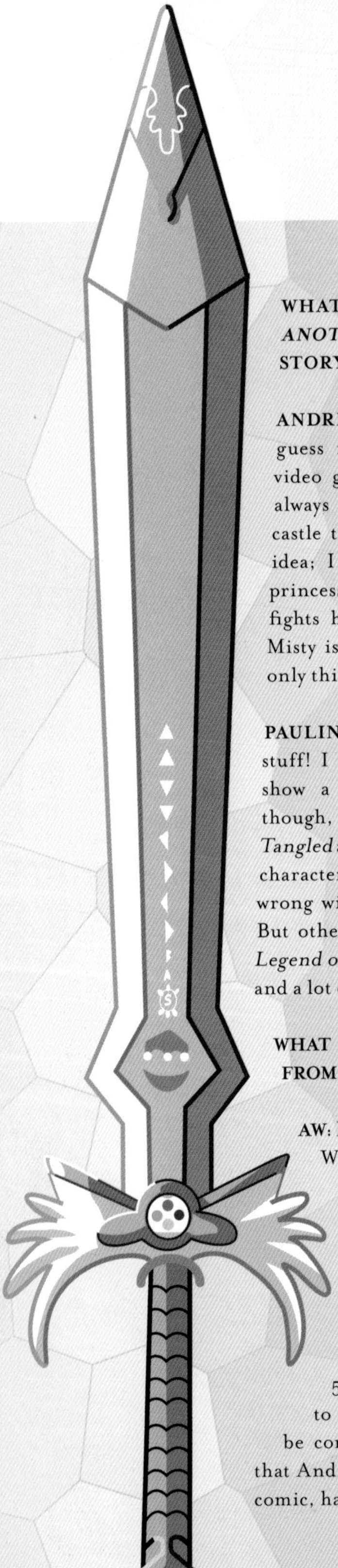

WHAT WAS THE INSPIRATION FOR *ANOTHER CASTLE*, BOTH IN THE STORY AND THE ART?

ANDREW WHEELER: As you might guess from the title, it started with video games, and how the princess is always supposedly just waiting at the castle to be rescued. I didn't like that idea; I wanted to know what else the princess might be up to while the hero fights his way towards the castle. But Misty is the hero of this story, and the only thing she's waiting for is her sword.

PAULINA GANUCHEAU: Jeez, so much stuff! I think most things I love always show a bit in my work. Specifically though, I remember looking at the *Tangled* art book a LOT when I started the character designs. I mean, how can you go wrong with the fluidity of Glen Keane? But other inspirations are *Dragon Age*, *Legend of Zelda*, *Magic Knight Rayearth*, and a lot of historical art, surprisingly.

WHAT IS SOMETHING YOU LEARNED FROM MAKING *ANOTHER CASTLE*?

AW: I learned that this is so much fun. Working with Paulina, working with the Oni crew, and having this idea turn into something I can share with the world, it's incredibly exciting!

PG: That I still love princesses as much as I did when I was a 5-year-old and how amazing it is to draw a feminine pink princess be completely fierce. Also, I learned that Andrew is crazy good at writing this comic, haha.

WHAT'S YOUR FAVORITE ASPECT OF CREATING THE COMIC?

AW: Getting the pages back, definitely. Always so gorgeous! But also, whenever Paulina gets to design another character, I really love that. Her costumes and her designs are phenomenal. I always think I know what these characters look like in my head, and then I get Paulina's version, and I think, "nope, that's what they look like."

PG: Character building is definitely up there for me, but also just showing the relationships between the characters. Acting and emotion is so crazy important for me. I love it.

IF YOU LIVED IN BELDORA OR GRIMOIRE, WHO DO YOU THINK YOU WOULD BE?

AW: Oh boy. Maybe I'd try my hand at being a bard in Beldora? I bet the squires all swoon for a good bard.

PG: I'd be Misty's best friend back in Beldora that you never see 'cause she's too busy drawing tapestries of the kingdom's history.

Misty: "Hey, you want to hang out today?"
Me: "Naw girl, I'm on a deadline. Go save the kingdom tho. Love ya!"

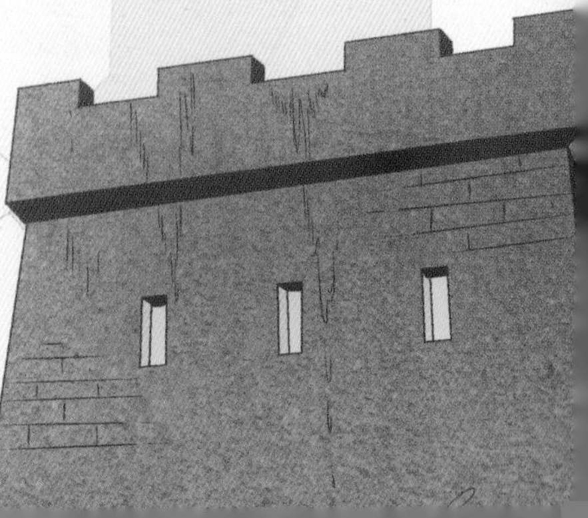

How a Cover is Created

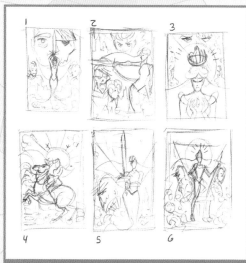

We went through a lot of ideas before deciding on the design for the cover of the first issue, but in the end, we settled on idea #1!

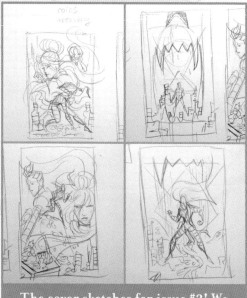

The cover sketches for issue #2! We decided to use sketch #4, since it was very dynamic and also included our three main characters for that issue.

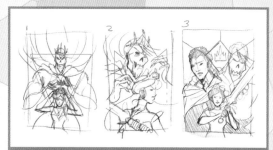

Cover ideas for issue #3. We went with idea #3, but swapped out Badlug for wonderful Prince Pete.

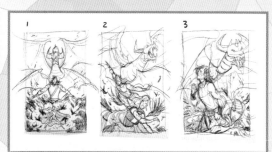

Cover ideas for issue #4. We ended up going with #2, which we thought was the most exciting.

Cover ideas for issue #5. We used the second idea, since it showed Misty in a stronger position.

COVER PROCESS

For This Very Book!

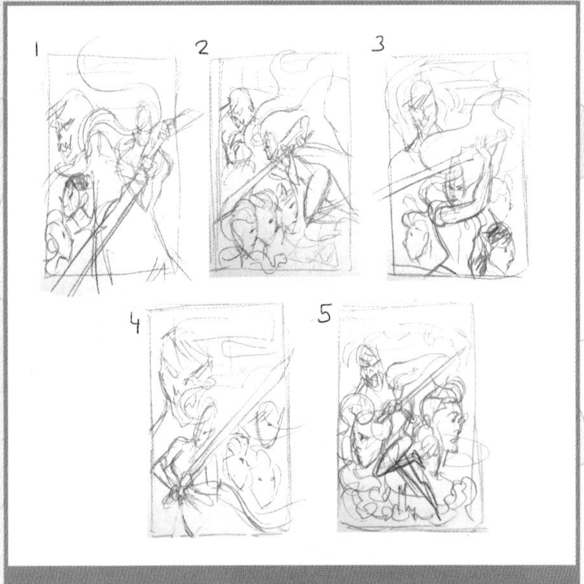
1
2
3
4
5

First, a few sketches of different ideas.

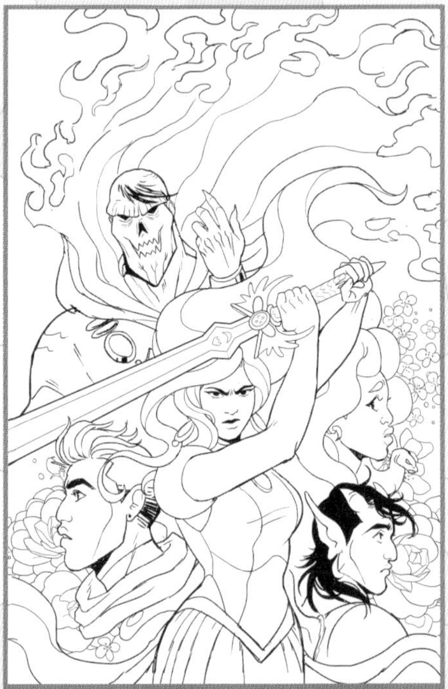

Then pencils!

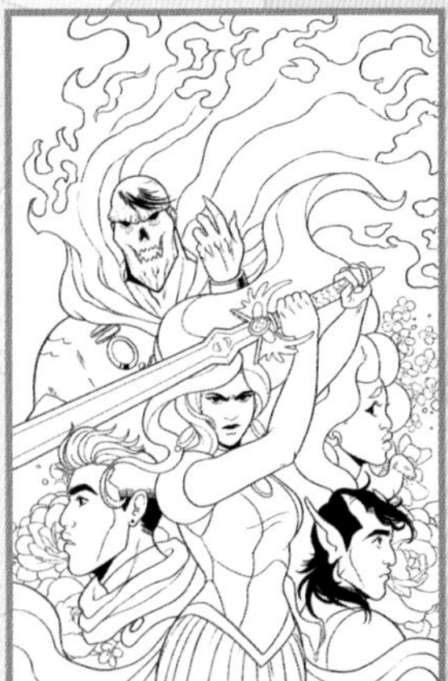

Then inks!

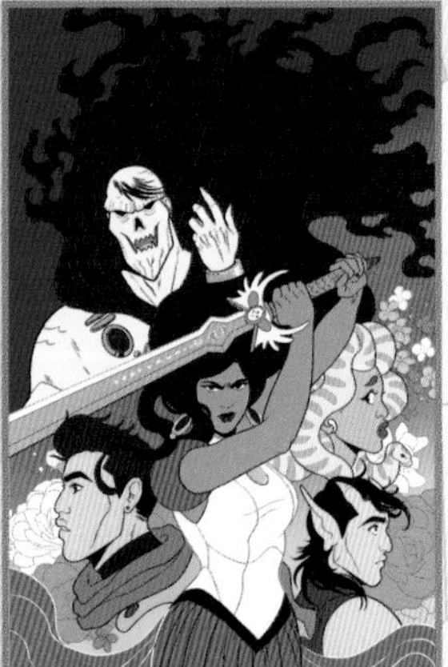

Then flat colors!

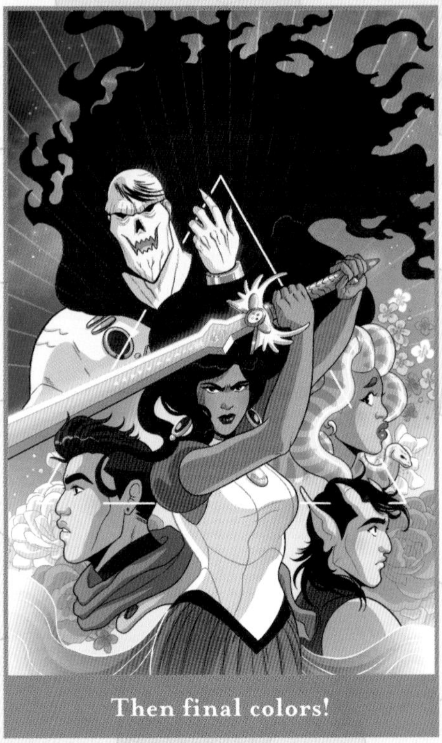

Then final colors!

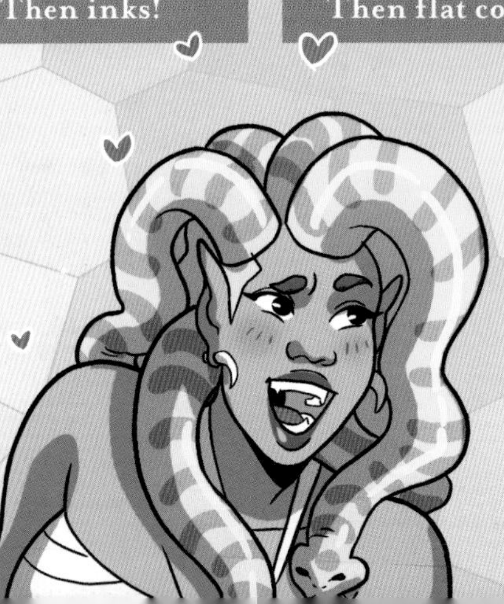

DESIGN PROCESS

Characters & Set

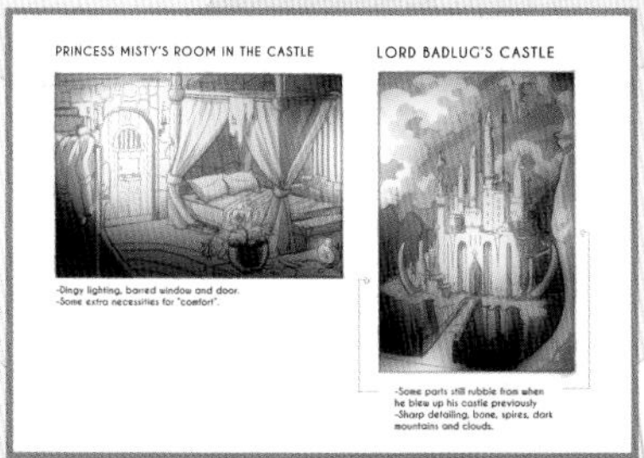
PRINCESS MISTY'S ROOM IN THE CASTLE
LORD BADLUG'S CASTLE
-Dingy lighting, barred window and door.
-Some extra necessities for "comfort".
-Some parts still rubble from when he blew up his castle previously
-Sharp detailing, bone, spires, dark mountains and clouds.

Before we started work on the book, we needed to figure out what the locations were going to look like!

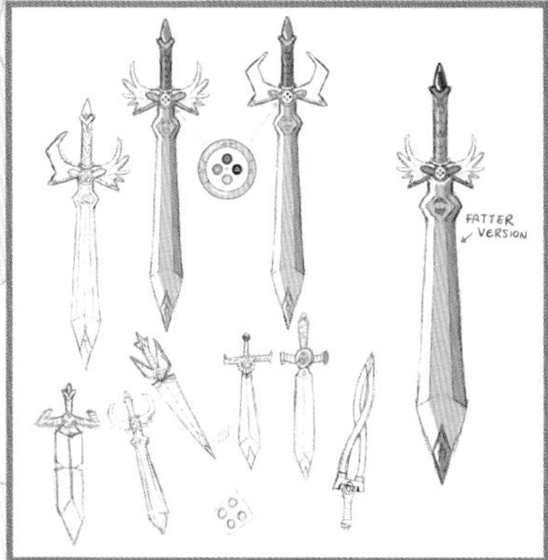
FATTER VERSION

Some ideas for Leveler, inspired by video games. Leveler is a very important part of the book, so we wanted to make sure its design was distinct and significant.

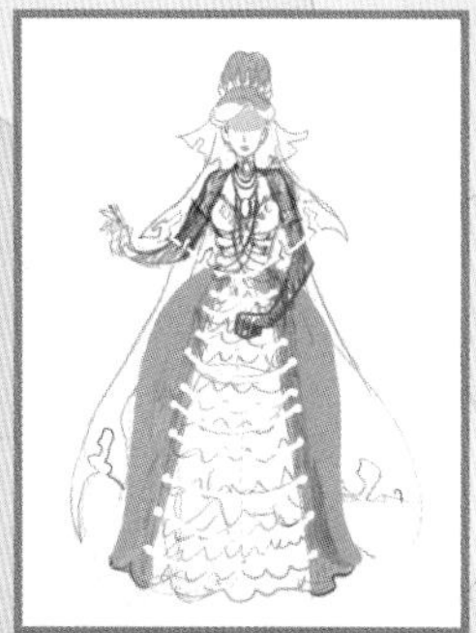

An early design for Misty's wedding dress.

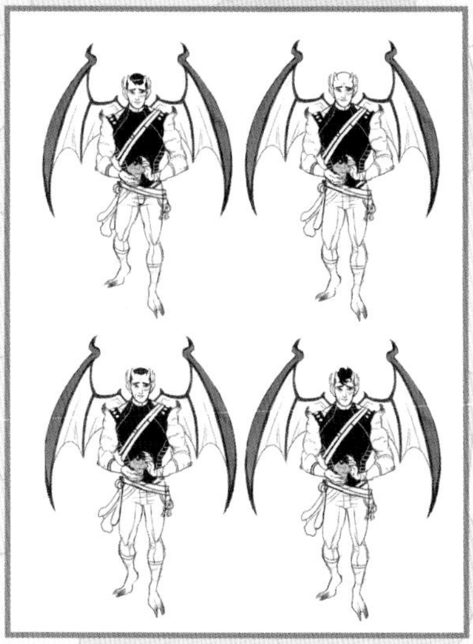

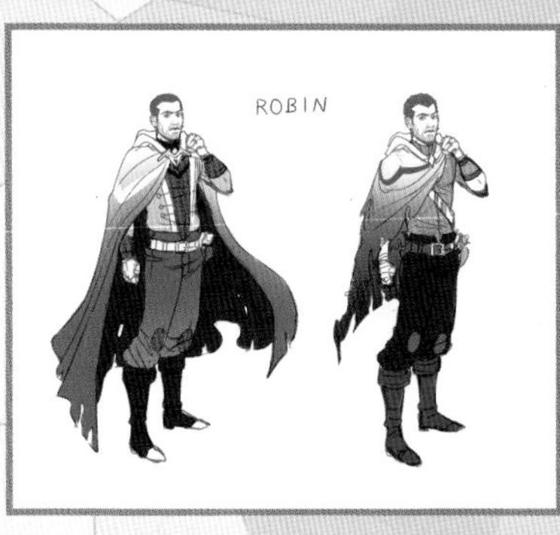
ROBIN

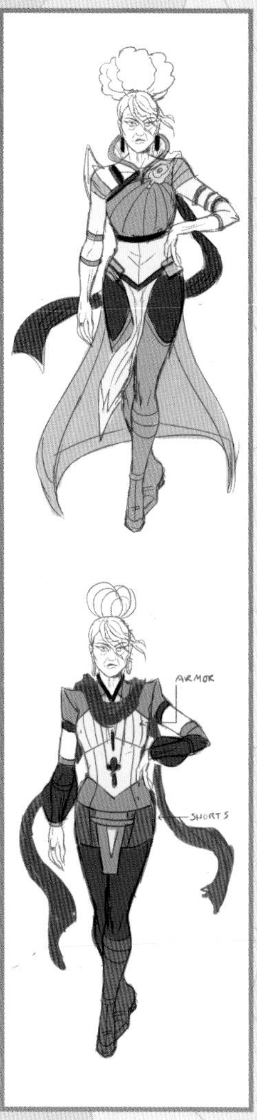
ARMOR
SHORTS

We went through a lot of designs for each character!

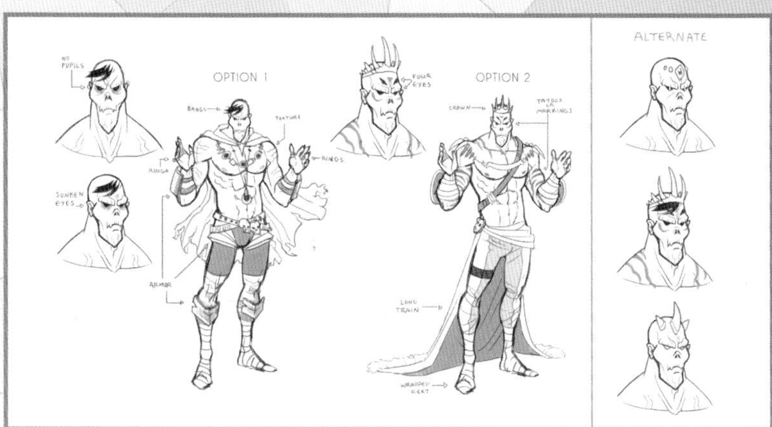
OPTION 1
OPTION 2
ALTERNATE
NO PUPILS
SUNKEN EYES
FOUR EYES
BANGS
TEXTURE
RINGS
ARMOR
CROWN
LONG TRAIN

DESIGN PROCESS

Characters & Set

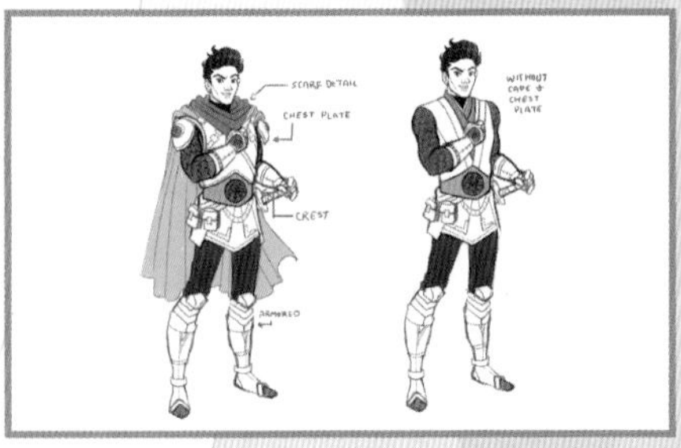
SCARF DETAIL
CHEST PLATE
CREST
WITHOUT CAPE & CHEST PLATE

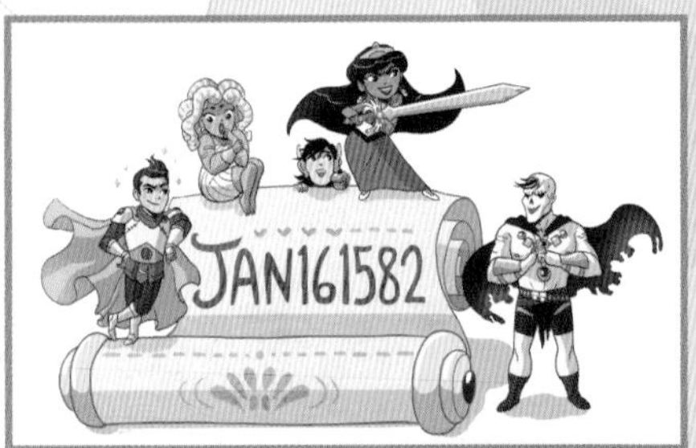
JAN161582

When you publish a comic book, readers can preorder it through their local comic shops by using an unique code. This was the code for Another Castle issue #1!

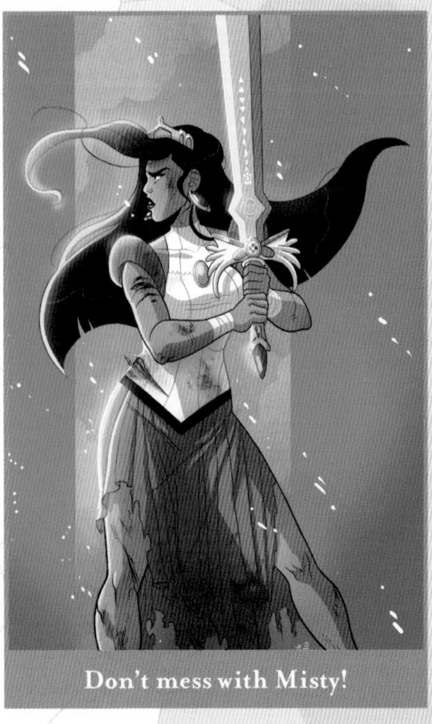

Don't mess with Misty!

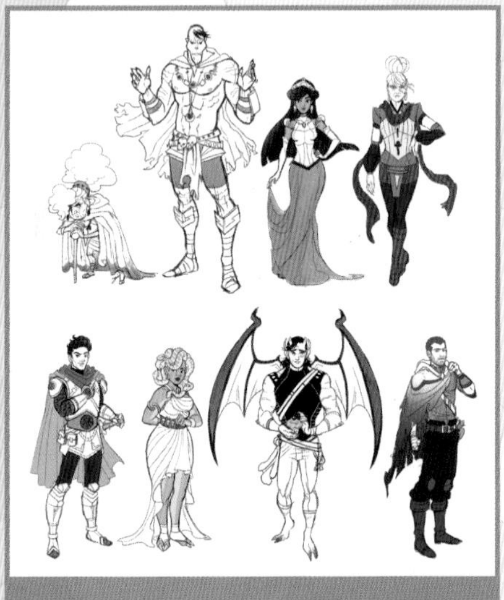

Our final lineup!

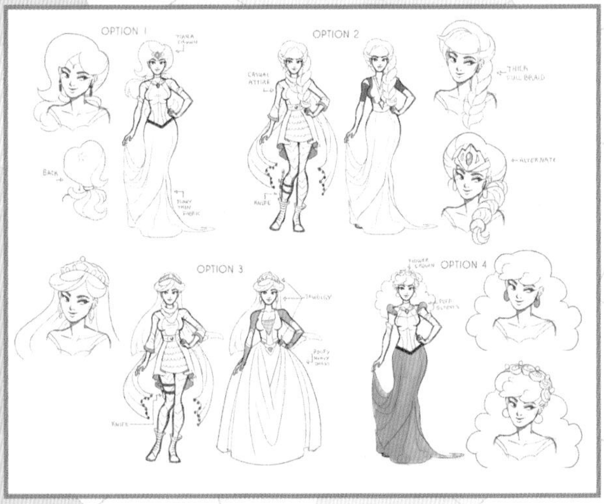
OPTION 1
OPTION 2
OPTION 3
OPTION 4

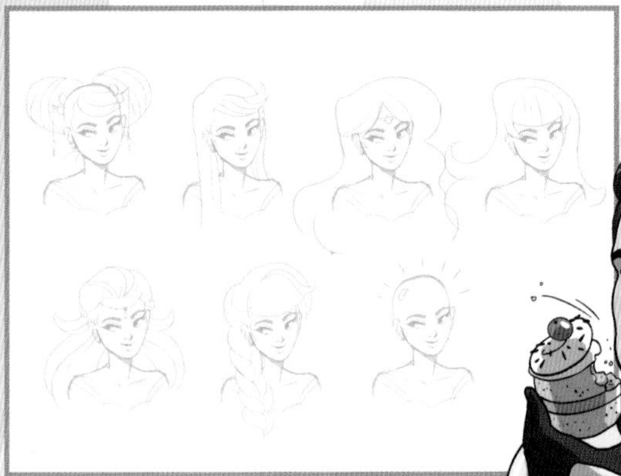

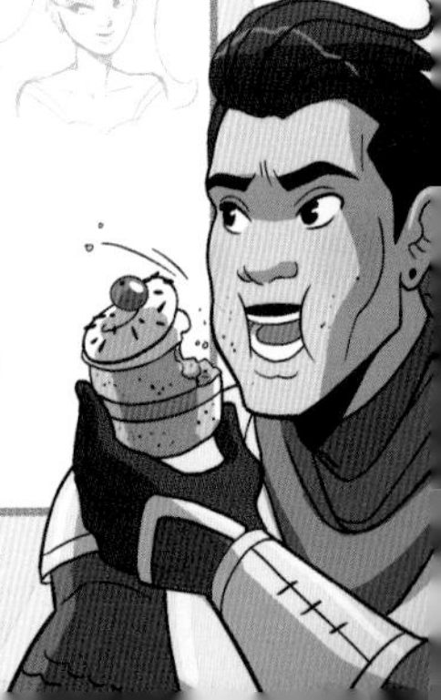

@WHEELER

ANDREW WHEELER is a liberal European gay immigrant who moved to Canada to be nearer the cheese curds. He's the editor of Eisner Award-winning comics and culture site *ComicsAlliance*, a food writer and culture critic, and the author of the Parsec-nominated podcast serial *Valentin & The Widow. Another Castle* is his first major comics work.

@PLINAGANUCHEAU

PAULINA GANUCHEAU is a comic artist and illustrator located in Maryland. She is the co-creator of *Zodiac Starforce*. Her hobbies include watching pro wrestling, cloud photography and following cats on Instagram.

@JENVYJAMS

JENNY VY TRAN is a graphic designer, cookie aficionado, and knows a lot of big words thanks to watching every episode of *Frasier*. She discovered her love for drawing at the age of five, but forgot about it until five years ago. She has worked on other Oni Press books such as *Hopeless Savages Break* and *The Lion Of Rora*.

READ MORE
FROM ONI PRESS!

**SPACE BATTLE LUNCHTIME,
VOLUME 1: LIGHTS, CAMERA,
SNACKTION!**

By Natalie Riess
120 pages, softcover, color interiors
ISBN 978-1-62010-313-5

**PRINCESS PRINCESS
EVER AFTER**

By Katie O'Neill
56 pages, hardcover, color interiors
ISBN 978-1-62010-340-1

**THE MIGHTY ZODIAC:
STARFALL**

By J. Torres, Corin Howell,
and Maarta Laiho
152 pages, softcover, color interiors
ISBN 978-1-62010-315-9

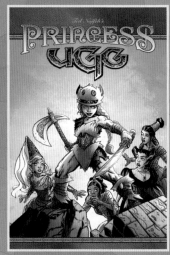

PART-TIME PRINCESSES

By Monica Gallagher
168 pages, softcover, b&w interiors
ISBN 978-1-62010-217-6

**WET MOON, BOOK ONE:
FEEBLE WANDERINGS,
NEW EDITION**

By Sophie Campbell
184 pages, softcover, b&w interiors
ISBN 978-1-62010-304-3

PRINCESS UGG, VOLUME 1

by Ted Naifeh
120 pages, softcover, color interiors
ISBN 978-1-62010-178-0

ONI PRESS
www.onipress.com

For more information on these and other fine Oni Press comic books and graphic novels visit
www.onipress.com. To find a comic specialty store in your area visit www.comicshops.us.